The Waiting Room

Rod Hacking

To Dr Nicholas Bradbury

FÜR ELISE

Ludwig van Beethoven

Whereof one cannot speak, thereof one must be silent
Ludwig Wittgenstein

If he is not enlightened by my silence,
Neither will he enlightened by my words
A Desert Father

But I pray most to those
whose act of suffering
claims no tears or praise
but is voluntary and strong
in a long triumph of peace
Peter Levi

PART ONE: 1959 - 2006

Gail

Elise Rosewarne had a lovely speaking voice. It was smooth and gentle, and in her second year as an undergraduate someone had suggested she consider putting it to good use, perhaps applying to BBC Radio or one of the commercial stations. She decided, however, that she might put it to better use by training to be a Samaritan. Although she was only 21 and originally Canadian with a trace of that accent still present, she completed the training and passed the sensitivity training exercise, allowing her to begin supervised work.

The organisation had begun in the crypt of the Church of St Stephen, Walbrook, in the heart of the city of London where the organisation had been founded in 1953 by Chad Varah, vicar of the church. He had been first alarmed to the realities of despair and suicide as a young priest taking the funeral of 14-year-old girl who had taken her own life when she had her first period in Lincoln in 1935. The work would spread across the world, often called "The Befrienders" though Chad Varah himself disliked the way the service had ceased to be primarily there for the desperate and suicidal.

After her probationary period, she took on a regular Saturday night shift. This interfered less with her studies and allowed her to catch up on sleep on Sunday. Usually, she worked with just one other person, and they were always busy, at least until about 3am when the number of calls began to fall off. It was work she enjoyed and although it meant attending to those who were often unhappy and confused, she found herself enriched by her colleagues and even many of those who called in.

Elise was a student at SOAS, the School of Oriental and African Studies, part of the University of London, studying middle and Near Eastern language and culture. When she had applied two years earlier, she had indicated that she had no religion, and it was true that she did not and never had participated in any religious activities in her life. Something had changed, however, as she studied, with the realisation that almost everything and everyone in the institution had a profound hatred of Israel, even though her department dealt with nations with far worse human rights records. She had chosen to specialise in Hebrew language and opted for her third year abroad to spend it at the Hebrew University in Jerusalem, thereby bringing upon herself considerable opprobrium from most of her fellow students and tutors alike.

When she had arrived at university a year earlier, Elise knew very little about Middle Eastern politics, her great interest being linguistics, but quickly assumed, though to no great degree, the common pro-Palestinian point of view when it came to speaking about Israel. However, during that first year she also realised that a great deal of this concern that led to some of her fellow students protesting outside the Israeli embassy, was founded more upon a deep-rooted anti-Semitism less than a care for Palestinians, an attitude she knew was characteristic of most of the nations surrounding Israel.

Up to the present she had never actually given thought to the fact that though it had barely ever been mentioned as she grew up, Elise recalled that once upon a time she had heard a mention that her mother had been born a Jew in Canada. This had consequences for herself, for if her mother was a Jew, she was herself Jewish, as it is passed through the mother.

To check this out, she wrote to her aunt Nancy, who still lived in the town in southern Ontario in which Elise had spent the first 14 years of her life. Her aunt and her mother had not been in contact for years and Elise could recall that even when they had lived in the same town, there was animosity between them.

Nancy had replied with details of her family history of which Elise had known nothing, but which confirmed that her great-grandparents and others had perished in the Holocaust, that her grandparents had escaped the Nazis to life in Canada where, even there, anti-Semitism was rife, and they had learned to keep their heads down even to the extent of denying to themselves their Jewish heritage. But her aunt confirmed that through the distaff, Elise was Jewish by birth.

She spoke about this to no one, not even her mother who had never shown any even slight religious instincts to Elise in the twenty years of her lifetime, but she gave great thought to it and began to read about anti-Semitism and even more about the Holocaust and the founding of the modern state of Israel in 1948. Gradually, she began to think about the consequences of being a Jew, something she had never thought of before, and what it might mean to belong to a people so hated by so many, including most of her fellow students. She even began to consider the possibility of practising as a Jew, even though she knew so very little about it and what it was that Jews did that characterised their lifestyle. It was this that had led her to a decision to study in Jerusalem and to concentrate on Hebrew language, though her secondary language was Arabic.

One of the reasons she most enjoyed meeting with other Samaritans (the name derived from a sect in Israel in ancient times) was that political chatter and prejudice played no part in their time together. The only aspect of her work with the Samaritans she disliked were the sex calls, mostly men occupying lines that might be needed by people more in need, simply in the hope of hearing a woman's voice speaking about sex, which they were using as a means of masturbation. There were always some calling in on a Saturday night but once she realised what they were doing she ended the calls.

On this particular night she was paired with one of her regular colleagues, a blind man called Henry, accompanied by his guide dog, Bruce. From when they began at 10:00 they were constantly busy, very often too busy to even get themselves a drink. It was at about 11 o'clock that she received a call from a young woman. At first, as often was the case, the voice was hesitant (often in itself a sign that it was serious). Elise did not ask a lot of questions but ascertained her name as Gail, and it was after about half an hour that Gail revealed that she had taken a considerable overdose of tablets with the intent of dying, and that she wanted Elise just to be there talking with her as she did so. Elise asked if she could obtain an ambulance to take Gail to hospital but received a definite refusal.

'I want to do this. It's what I choose. I'm not calling you to help me stop but to be there so I'm not totally alone, as I approach what I choose, which is to die tonight.'

'If that's what you choose, Gail, then I can assure you I will not hang up on you but perhaps as we talk you can tell me why it is you are doing this.'

Slowly, Gail told a story of a sense of complete helplessness and pointlessness in her life. The death of her parents had robbed her of the only people who ever really cared for her. In her teens she had become mixed up with those who took drugs and who had encouraged her to do so, which she did. It was not an easy time to get employment and she had no real qualifications other than meaningless grades in GCSE. For a while she had taken up with various boys but quickly came to the realisation that their supposed concern for her was founded less on her needs than on theirs. At the present time she was living in a council-provided flat consisting of just one room.

This account emerged slowly with long silences between sentences, and Elise began to realise that some of Gail's words were beginning to be slurred and making less sense. Once again, she asked if she could arrange for help to come. The Samaritans always had on standby something called the Flying Squad, a Samaritan who would be willing to attend if alerted by the team on the phone, but when Elise said she could get someone to call and see her, Gail constantly refused.

In theory at least, it might have been possible to get the call traced and an address found and help directed but this would have necessitated another person able to do it and at this time on a Saturday night her colleague was never off the phone even if Gail had agreed, and she did not. The Samaritans maintained that if someone wished to take their own life, they were free to do so and that it was not part of their remit to stop that happening if that is what the client wished, and on this night, and for the only time in her service as a Samaritan, Elise new this was happening. She also knew that her voice was comforting to Gail.

The silences grew longer and Gail's voice fainter, finally failing. Elise remained on the telephone speaking to Gail without any reply for half an hour, and then kept the line open for a further half hour, before deciding that she had to end the call. She felt numb and unable to answer the next call which came through almost immediately. Hearing the noise of the call which Elise did not feel able to answer, Henry realised that there must be something wrong and once he had ended his own call, he too did not attend to the next, but came over to where Elise was sitting. Slowly and deliberately, she told him what had happened, and he was quite brilliant with her, affirming the action she had taken which in this instance was not to engage in any physical activity of calling help, but the far harder action of just being with this woman as she did what was her right.

Elise was strengthened by his words and rose to make them both a drink of coffee, also bringing with her a bowl of water for Bruce. By this time Henry was once again attending to a call and after drinking her coffee, by which time it was almost 2 o'clock in the morning, she eventually picked up the next call to come in.

Before they completed their shift at 9-00 am, Elise and Henry had written up as many of their calls as they could and Elise returned to her own flat in Hackney where, much to her surprise she was able to sleep until mid-afternoon.

When she had dressed and was making herself something to eat, the strangest of thoughts came to her: "As a Jew, how do I feel about this woman's death?" She was completely taken aback by this thought and had no idea how she should respond, but it was the first time in her life that she had taken seriously the fact that she was a Jew.

This was not something she felt she could talk over with her flatmate Ginny, who was training as a singer at the Guildhall and whose whole life was taken up with opera and recitals, which she somehow managed to combine with belonging to some sort of Christian evangelical sect. Mercifully, whilst often talking music, she had never tried to convert her to anything religious, and Elise from the beginning of their sharing the flat had given off effective signals to keep religion away. Nor did she think she could speak of it to her parents. Her dad, in any case, was not Jewish and there was no sign in her mum's existence that she could identify as Jewish other than the fact of her birth to a Jewish mother who had herself died when she was still a baby. Her upbringing was entirely secular.

She rose early on the Monday to prepare to go into college, listening as usual to local radio which would let her know of any problems with the buses or tube, when a news item made her freeze. It was a report that on the previous day the bodies of a young woman and her two-month-old baby had been found in a council flat in Clapton. Her name was given as Gail Bretherton and at this stage the police welcomed anyone who knew Ms Bretherton to make contact but that were not looking for anyone in connection with the deaths. The news then turned to sport.

Gail had never mentioned a baby – she was sure of that. Had she done so, sending someone to her address would have been an absolute priority because the baby's life was at risk if the mother was taking her own, though Elise wondered if the baby were already dead when Gail had called and that this was what caused Gail to wish to die.

She had to sit and steady herself. Two people had died, and she had done nothing other than allow it to happen and was the second death actually a murder which it would be if the mother had even just allowed the baby to die after her own death. Might Gail have given the baby the same tablets she had used to bring about her own death? The thoughts rushed upon her too swiftly for her to feel anything but total confusion and a mounting sense of dread.

Should she call the police? But might she then be held responsible for an assisted suicide because she did not intervene and stop it happening, and also, albeit unknowingly brought about the death of the baby too?

Gail had said nothing about having recently given birth but surely there would have been midwives or health visitors in frequent touch with Gail if her baby had been born so recently.

Also, there must have been a doctor who had prescribed the tablets she had used – if she was suffering from post-natal depression, surely that would have been followed up. But Gail had spoken only of all that had gone wrong in her life, her sense of being unwanted by anyone, of drugs, homelessness and completely vulnerable.

But she hadn't been homeless when she had called, and Elise realised she had missed something vital. Gail had said she had been housed by the council, and that could only have come about if she had been pregnant or with a baby. Elise had made an awful blunder not to have realised this and her mistake could well have cost two lives!

Sitting in the kitchen she burst into tears and began to shake. She knew for certain she needed help with this, and so picked up the phone. The irony, as she made the call, was that she was calling the Samaritans!

Rabbi Samuel

Elise knew that the Centre did not open until 9:00 and that the number to reach the office staff was different to that used by callers seeking help. She allowed fifteen minutes to pass before calling, but when she got through, she was told that the two full-time counsellors who directed the branch were fully booked for the day.

'The thing is I need to speak to someone urgently about the death of one of our callers at the weekend.'

'Ok, just hold for a moment.'

Elise was in a call box outside the SOAS building and it was beginning to rain. Eventually the receptionist spoke.

'Mark says he can meet you here in about half an hour. Can you make that?"

'Thank you. Yes. I'll come at once.'

Elise had booked a spot in a linguistics lab for 10:00 and decided at once to cancel it, before making her way to Goodge St Tube Station, changing onto the Central Line before walking through what was now heavy rain to the entrance of the Samaritans. Instead of going downstairs as she usually did, she went up the short staircase and knocked on the office door.

'Hi Elise,' said Katie, the cheery young woman who opened the door to her and was the administrator. She led her along a corridor to a door which she opened where, waiting for with a mug of tea was Mark Greene, one of those who had trained her. Her first feeling was of relief as he smiled and motioned to her to sit alongside him.

'I asked Katie to get me your notes from Saturday night and I assume you are talking about the caller with the name of Gail?'

'Yes.'

'From our time together during your training I knew you have a lovely soothing voice and I'm sure all who speak to you are appreciative of that, and it will encourage them to open up, but please tell me.'

Elise recounted the details of the call and ensuing silence, but then added all she had heard on the morning news. Mark listened attentively, just occasionally playing with his glasses, but keeping his eyes fixed firmly on Elise.

'So, it's clear,' she concluded, 'that I missed the signs that should have led to the discovery of the baby who also died, which makes me an indirect accessory to murder as well as to an assisted suicide.'

'I assume you don't know that councils have a statutory duty to house the homeless who are vulnerable, especially young women and not just the pregnant, so I think it unlikely you missed an important sign. If there had been the merest hint, I'm sure you would have picked it up. Elise, you did what you were there to do to the very best of your ability and I think you did it as well as anyone within our organisation could possibly have done. You listened with incredible sensitivity to a young woman in great distress without ever imposing your will upon her. It is a fundamental tenet of what we do that we are not here to stop people taking their own lives should they be determined to do so. I think Gail was truly fortunate to have you to accompany her to her end which is what she was hoping for. There is nothing wrong with death, you know, and for some, whether 19 or 90, it may be the right thing for them to choose. You have been a good Samaritan, Elise, and although the context is bleak, you should be proud of your service to this poor woman, the very last act of kindness she could know.'

Elise had tears coursing down her cheeks and could not speak. Mark passed her the box of paper handkerchiefs on his desk.

'Though many people assume we are a religious organisation, we don't supply any kind of spiritual guidance. Are you religious?'

'No, I'm Jewish.'

Mark clapped his hands and laughed.

'What a wonderful answer. But do you belong to a congregation?'

'No. I'm as surprised as you by my answer, as it has been only recently that I have made the discovery and it's too long and complicated a story to explain, but Mark, there is a question I must ask. The police will discover that she made a very long telephone call during the night in which she died and want to know the content of that call to see if it can assist their enquiries into her death. What do I do then?'

'If they trace the call and, sadly, I very much doubt that she will warrant any more attention in death than she did in life, they will recognise our number and know well enough that there are no circumstances in which we would reveal the identity of one of our volunteers nor the content of any call. They have tried in the past and met an insurmountable wall, as they would now.

'But Elise do you think it might help if you went and spoke with another of our volunteers, who doubles as a rabbi not far from where you live. We know him as Sam 1876 and he's what is known as a Reform rabbi. You won't get heavy religion; I can promise you that.'

It was not until late afternoon that she was able to make the call he had suggested.

'You must be Elise 2651. Mark said you might call. Why don't we meet tomorrow?'

As she was to discover, he typically suggested they meet in a coffee shop he knew and said that with lots of people around it was possible to have a private conversation and enjoy not just excellent coffee but wonderful pastries, to which he said he was addicted!

Sam1876, or Rabbi Samuel, as he said he was in "real life" was not remotely like she had expected a rabbi to be, and, as she was to discover, unusually on time! She was, however, immediately struck by his capacity for listening without interruption.

After her account of suddenly realising that she was a Jew when faced with the anti-Semitism at the university and more recently in her inner response to the tragedy of the last days, he picked up his pastry and took a big bite and washed it down with his coffee, before saying anything.

'Do you read Molière?' he finally asked.

'I did some for French A-level.'

'And do you recall Monsieur Jourdain's amazing discovery that he had lived forty years and only just discovered that he had been speaking prose all that time?'

Elise smiled.

'Yes.'

'Well, Elise, Shalom! You've just discovered after twenty years that you've been Jewish all this time. It would perhaps come as something of a shock to those who give voice to anti-Semitism just how effective they are in bringing Jews such as yourself to an awareness of who they are.

'You and I belong to a people who have suffered for three thousand years. A French Christian in the fifth century called Vincent, said his faith was "what has been believed everywhere, always, and by all", but being Jewish means having been hated everywhere, always and by all. So however you might choose to pursue your identity, never lose sight of that.

'But are you willing to tell me about the call you received on Saturday night? It's not against the confidentiality rule because I am Sam 1876, a fellow Sam.'

She did so, becoming aware that against the hubbub of the coffee shop all she was saying was as private as it would have been in the rabbi's study. She did not however mention Gail's name and Sam did not ask.

'This truly is a tragedy but thankfully (albeit for small mercies) the last voice she ever heard was yours. I honestly think you could read the Talmud to me last thing at night and send me safely off to sleep! But perhaps the Almighty moves in a peculiar way, and that this realisation of your Jewishness comes an opportunity to bring a possible redemption, that into the dark world that your poor young woman knew, even there you might bring light.'

Elise felt and obviously looked puzzled.

He continued, 'I would imagine that the language of redemption strikes you as something familiar perhaps from Christianity for which it largely means converting to be saved, but as with many other things, including the man they call Jesus, they stole it from us. For Jews it's something quite different. We are always trying to redeem the circumstances in which we find ourselves, to make the best of them and for people who have had to survive the Holocaust, that is no mean feat, but it is what we are about.'

'To be honest,' said Elise, 'I cannot see any redeeming aspect in the particular circumstance which involved the death of a mother and her baby though at least you're not trying to paint it over with some sort of religious gloss which I suppose I assumed a rabbi would do.'

'And religion today,' said Samuel, 'is assumed by most of the young to be like that, a category they are not interested in because it's presented in the form of unlikely and untestable beliefs. The trouble with some people is that they learn to be religious before they ever learn to be human. Your recent terrible experience is unlikely to allow you ever to do that. For me religion is not about beliefs.'

'Surely religion is all about beliefs.'

'That is certainly what you will always hear from religious people. As Jews, it's not so much what we think, as what we *do*: the various things to be done in the course of the year, in the course of the week, and even in the course of the day, but we are remarkably unreligious. What we *do* as humans is certainly much more than engaging in discussion about unprovable metaphysics, which is what most religious people go on about and which people, and especially the young, understandably reject together with all the accoutrements of it which they occasionally see on television.'

'I'm feeling very confused,' said Elise. 'All that happened was that hearing the anti-Semitic rants in college made me unexpectedly realise that they were of course anti-me, and in response to what happened the other night, for reasons I just don't understand, I found myself asking what this meant to me as a Jew? It's bizarre I know, though no more bizarre than meeting a rabbi to discuss these things in a coffee shop!'

'Don't you like coffee? Or is it that you imagine holiness can only be found in special places and approached with hushed voices? Is HaShem present less here than in churches or even synagogues. For me, Elise, our conversation is likely to be the most holy and important I am likely to have this month, not just this week. I suppose we could have met in my study, but my coffee is not as good as here and my partner doesn't allow me pastries at home.'

'She's worried about your waistline, is she?'

'My partner's called Solly.'

'Oh, I'm sorry.'

'I'm not, as we are very happy together and have been for quite some time. I belong to what is sometimes called Reform Judaism, the unwanted liberal family member of the strict Orthodox, who regard us as somewhat beyond the pale but that's perfectly fine by me. But my point is simply that there is no place on the earth holier than any other and I prefer to be here than stuck in my study with all those books and letters and phone calls I wish to avoid.'

'But don't you have services in synagogues?'

'They word synagogue originally in the 5th century BCE meant a council put together by Ezra to consider various matters, and later became simply to mean a "meeting house" where Jews gather to listen, discuss, argue and occasionally pray. They're not like churches, not least because they're very noisy places and yes, we do gather on the morning of Shabbat, but that's just a tiny part of my work as a rabbi and the work of all the members who are actively living out what being a Jew means to them in their work and in their homes. But truly, Elise, if I were you, I would forget all about it. Living as a Jew will only bring you hatred and misunderstanding and nobody in their right mind would want that, especially if you ever mention it to your fellow students.'

For the first time in their conversation, Elise was feeling irritated rather than entranced.

'Rabbi, I'm not a potential convert, I *am* a Jew, and if people don't like me simply because of that, that's something I will have to live with.'

'But how will you cope with the privileges, which other people regard as burdens, that we live with? The regulations about kosher food – surely you will miss bacon butties – and keeping Shabbat, for you're a young woman and almost certainly want to go out clubbing on Friday nights or shopping on Saturdays.'

'Rabbi,' she said with a sigh, 'nice try! For the first time in my life, I have been brought face-to-face, albeit indirectly on a telephone with death, depression and misery, and for the first time in my life I have also been brought face-to-face with my own identity. Perhaps it will sound strange to you. This is not a conversion, it's a realisation, and there is the world of difference between the two. I can fully understand why you are trying to put me off but in fact it has simply served to strengthen my determination to be who I am: Elise, a young Jewish woman, a student of Oriental languages at SOAS.'

'You read Hebrew?'

'And Aramaic, Greek and Latin. And our conversation has strengthened my desire for my year abroad, as I have arranged to go and study in Jerusalem, for isn't it my homeland?'

'In which case,' said Samuel, 'we should celebrate with another cup of coffee and a delicious pastry each.'

' I agree,' said Elise, 'but first I must pay a visit. Tell me Rabbi, as a Jew is there a special way of going to the loo?'

'How I would love to tease you and tell you that there is, but you must do what you must do as you know how to do it. And you have that from the Rabbi's mouth!'

Elise's first lesson in rabbinic Judaism kept a smile on her face as she made her way back to the flat. Before she had left, she had asked Samuel to recommend some reading but instead he said she would learn very much more from a family. He would be in touch with her and suggest a particular family he had in mind, whom he was sure would invite her for the traditional Friday evening meal in their home and allow her to stay with them until Saturday evening, not doing all the things that they didn't do either! It would be much better than any number of books and provide the opportunity to come to the synagogue and meet others. Elise thought this was a brilliant idea and eagerly awaited his call.

Elise was sure she would never forget the conversation with

Gail and that awful moment when she heard the news on the radio, but the conversations with Mark and Samuel had enabled her to come to terms with what, gently using her voice, she had achieved for Gail. Death is inevitable for each one of us. Elise now knew that there are worse things than death and that what matters is how we live and learn to give love to others that Samuel had given her in the most oblique fashion imaginable. Perhaps that was the start of what he meant by redemption, though she suspected her flatmate Ginny would not agree!

The Jacobs

Elise's teachers were the Jacobs family: Jerry, Leah, and their children, Ruth and Sarah. Jerry (short for Jeremiah) was an Ear, Nose and Throat Consultant at the nearby Whipps Cross Hospital, Leah taught mathematics at a local Jewish School, and herself a volunteer with the Samaritans, Ruth and Sarah were seven-year-old identical twins who frequently gave her the run around pretending to be the other! And within a short while Elise became one of the family. She had moved out of her flat at the end of term and spent the next seven months living with the Jacobs rent-free in return for babysitting and sharing in the life of the home, which meant acquiring the skills of Jewish cooking.

The contrast between her new family and that of her parents could hardly have been greater. Ironically, given that Jewish identity is passed through the female line, the greatest hostility she received came from her mother who was appalled by Elise's refusal to eat pork when she came to stay with them at Christmas after the celebrations of Hanukkah had been completed.

'To think, my own daughter could do such a thing!' she had protested when Elise had first told her mum and dad.

'Oh mum, you never sounded more Jewish than when you said that!', which did not go down well.

'You know that your grandparents repudiated their Jewish background and now you choose to spit on all that they did.'

'I can only honour their achievements, but they had to suppress their Judaism to achieve what they did, because even in Canada there was considerable anti-Semitism, accusing us of conspiracy and getting filthy rich at the expense of the workers.'

'Don't you dare include me in your "us". The very idea that being Jewish is passed on from one generation to another is simply a ludicrous form of racism, and now, here is my own daughter claiming that I am responsible for her extreme silliness. There are reasons why the Labour movement is suspicious of Jews and their links to international commerce. Your grandparents knew this, as I do, and you've now allied yourself to the enemies of the working people of all lands. I think it's quite horrible.'

Her dad was not quite so vociferous but equally opposed to her decision to become a Jew.'

'I didn't decide, dad. I am a Jew and always have been.'

A truce broke out over the Christmas celebrations and Elise sadly avoided the pigs-in-blankets with which her mother deliberately sought to tempt her, and which she had always loved. They even laughed together and played games on Christmas night. The highlight for Elise was a conversation she overheard whilst she was doing the washing up in the kitchen.

'I can't comment on what you've passed on to Elise of a religious nature,' said her dad to her mum, 'but you can take great pride from having passed on your ability to engage in an argument and hold her line. It's like listening to two of you at once. She truly is your daughter.'

'I hope she will use it well and not get her first-class brain ruined by involvement with the indefensible.'

By the time she had to register at The Hebrew University of Jerusalem in its *Givat Ram* campus at the beginning of September, the university founded in 1918 by none other than Albert Einstein and Chaim Weizmann, Elise had discovered that her considerable skills in Hebrew had produced smiles and laughter when she arrived, because when she spoke it apparently sounded as it might had a visitor to England known only Shakespearean English, so her first task was to update her Biblical linguistics into the modern Hebrew that everyone around her spoke. As she later remembered with great embarrassment, she had approached the welcoming committee with the equivalent of "Hast thou chambers prepared for myself?", but she quickly adapted, not least by listening hard and speaking hardly at all. She did, however, continue to speak English to the two American women she studied alongside, Rachel and Shira.

Jerusalem cannot be described as anything other than a crazy place for crazy people. In her year, Elise visited the Old City and the Western Wall on only three occasions and always returned vowing each would be the last! The place was awash with Hasidic Jews in their outfits derived from 18th century Poland, most of whom lived in the *Mea Shearim* area of the city, a ghetto of strict religious lunacy where cars were stoned if they dared to drive through on Shabbat, and where women were mostly invisible. Elise had been accustomed to the sight of Hasid in her part of London, but this was on a scale she had never even imagined, though Rachel assured here that there were more Hasid in New York even than here!

And then there were the Christians clogging up the narrow streets with processions and hymns. The police stopped them holding public services anywhere near the Western Wall, but they would if they had been able to do so. And above them all was the Dome of the Rock, the golden-roofed mosque, third holiest site in Islam, ironically often used on photographs as the embodiment of Jerusalem, but which was on the site of the Temple destroyed by the Romans in 70 CE, now forbidden to Jews as they might unknowingly enter the Holy of Holies.

There is no escaping politics in Israel even if you can escape the religion though Elise and her friends tried their best. Their greatest joy was to go north, through Samaria (which had given its name to the Samaritans) to the Galilee and its beautiful rolling countryside even though too often it was polluted with Christians who felt that up here they were more in touch with the Jesus of their imaginings.

All three women were studying Talmud and soon found themselves in the very Jewish activity of dispute where meanings and interpretations were concerned. It was a great pity, thought Elise, that Christians didn't know that when in their scriptures there were accounts of disputes between Jesus and the Pharisees or Sadducees (two groups that had grown up in the period of Second-Temple Judaism long before the time of Jesus but equally long after the Hebrew Bible had been completed), this was typical of Jewish life: they argue. Two Jews meant three opinions, and when women argued, sometimes two Jews meant at least six opinions! That is an essential part of being Jewish.

It emerged as they got to know one another that both Rachel and Shira wished to be rabbis. This thought had never crossed Elise's mind for herself, and she had been imagining an academic career back in the UK, completing her final year and then go on to a doctorate. She knew she had the ability and application to make a success of research, and even in a short time she developed a passionate love affair for the library housed in her own campus, and widely regarded as the finest Jewish library in the world, to which great scholars, most from the United States, often came to study. But meeting Rachel and Shira triggered the hitherto wholly unanticipated thought that maybe she too should consider the rabbinate.

It was on one evening having a meal in Tel Aviv, where they were visiting to escape some of the religious lunacy of Jerusalem, that Elise felt emboldened to approach the subject with her new friends.

'How did you two first decide you wanted to be rabbis?' she asked. Rachel and Shira looked at one another, and Shira began first.

'Well, it didn't come as a voice in the night as it did to Shmu'el. I wouldn't trust anyone who claimed anything like that. We're Jews and we just get on with it, getting the best people to do the work, and besides which I'm wanting to strengthen the place of women in the rabbinate. I shall be well prepared in terms of study – better than many of the men whose study ended decades ago – but preferably equipped as counsellors and supporters of families. If I'm wanting to be openly Jewish then I want to be doing a good job as a Jewish woman, and so serve as a rabbi.'

'But this surely had to be tested?' said Elise.

Rachel laughed.

'For me as I guess for you, Shira, it was a case of first prove yourself in the study and training, and then we'll see.'

'It was, and that's why as women we probably have to work at least twice as hard as the men to be equal.'

'Why are asking?' said Shira.

'You're my friends and I'm keen to know more about how you got to be here and why? I'm engaged in a year-long part of my degree course and then returning to complete the course in London and assuming an academic career lies before me, but I was just interested to know about you. We usually spend our relaxing times either watching tv or arguing about this or that aspect of the Talmud, so here in the secular city I thought I would ask.'

Almost as soon as she had finished her sentence there was a colossal explosion nearby. They shot up from their table and ran to the door. Less than a hundred metres away there was carnage: bodies lying in the street and cars and shops destroyed or on fire. Sirens and alarms were sounding and people running away or tending the wounded before the arrival of ambulances and other help.

'It must have been a bomb of some sort,' said Shira, 'either in a car or even planted within what used to be that restaurant by a suicide bomber. It could have been in here and those bodies could have been ours.'

The three women ran towards the site but even in such a short time there were police officers turning them back, shouting at them that there might be a second explosion, a booby trap aimed at people trying to help. They stopped, stared and reluctantly turned back. Elise was aware that she was shaking. Nothing in her life had prepared her for this experience of brutal hatred. Within a little while as they stood and watched, ambulances and police arrived in great numbers. Eventually they were moved right away from the scene, having first collected their bags and coats from the restaurant which was already shutting down and erecting barriers across the windows.

'There is often a second bomb,' said the waiter, 'hurry away for your own sake.'

They decided at once to return to their hotel, collect their belongings and drive back up to Jerusalem. Rachel was driving and headed north out of the city centre before turning inland and joining the 6 in order to bypass inevitable traffic hold-ups at Ben Gurion Airport which would have automatically gone into a complete lockdown following the explosion in the city, and eventually joining motorway 1 near Afar Shmu'el and the hordes of other heading away from the coast to the greater security of the city.

Back in their room the news was not good. Already six people had been killed and others were receiving urgent attention in hospital. No one had any doubts who lay behind the killings and the Prime Minister was already promising that these deaths would bring retribution. The women watched in silence, but when eventually they went to bed, Elise could not sleep, her mind going over and over her proximity to hatred and murder. It could have been her lying dead in the street.

In the course of her time at the University and in the city, Elise had met many who had come to Israel fleeing oppression. As Jews, it was their homeland. It is a small country with a land mass equivalent to Wales, insignificant alongside the huge Arab countries surrounding it. For four thousand years the land was coveted by others not least because the immediate coastal area is extremely rich for arable and fruit farming, part of what was known as the Fertile Crescent. But more especially it was not so much the land they wanted as to be rid of the Jews. People in the West, she had come to see, were being conveniently directed to the cause of the "poor Palestinians", being used by the enemies of Israel to set in motion another Holocaust. This was the narrative of so many of the anti-Semites she had encountered in London, and she began to consider whether she did indeed want to go back to complete the final year of her course, or whether to remain in Israel and study here.

She said little of this to Rachel or Shira, but it seemed to double her determination not just to be a proud Jew, but to give real thought to a future serving other Jews as a rabbi. But was this a realistic possibility in the still very male world of Israeli Judaism in which the Orthodox still predominated? There were many liberal synagogues, and even more secular Jews who are glad to live without others hating them, but don't want to bother too much with religion or its demands. It was ironic, she thought, that some of the most rigorous Orthodox, the Hasidim, refused to condemn the bombing in Tel Aviv because they thought of it as a den of vice. They maintained the dead were reaping what they had sown in iniquity.

These were not easy decisions to make and how she would have welcomed the wisdom of Rabbi Samuel to help her decide the direction in which she should now move. It was Rachel who broached the subject of Elise's plans, as they sat together in the café in their college.

'The year is moving on. I was just wondering whether you were giving thought as to what you might do next. I know you are meant to be going back to London to complete your degree but, and forgive me if I'm mistaken, I sense that you are uneasy about that.'

'Yes, I am. In life I know that we have to take one step at a time, and I do not in any way regret the step that brought me here, but when I made that move it was at the time when I was discovering who I was in terms of being a Jew. So, I took the step that was obvious in terms of my university course to come here. I did so without any thought as to what the next step would be other than returning to complete my degree course, but you're quite right, I'm not at all sure about that now.

'I have no doubts that I could pursue an academic career. I have a flair for languages and as you know I'm working hard at various ancient tongues, and I could devote the rest of my days to this form of study. But something happened a while ago, about which I don't speak but has played a very important part in my thinking and, hopefully, my growing. I've become increasingly convinced that life immersed in books with smelly old Jewish scholars is not the right way for me, and that I might just have something to offer as a rabbi, assisting in the task of discovering how to be Jews living with our trials and joys.'

Rachel took hold of Elise's hand.

'Knowing you, Elise, you've been keeping this to yourself for some time so I don't feel rejected that you haven't said anything until now, even though both Shira and myself have suspected it for quite some time, and we haven't said anything either but we are of one mind, that you would make an outstanding rabbi and be able to offer people a great deal. But we also think, you should abandon your course in London and come to Rabbinic School in the States. You will be able to continue your study as we have some fine Jewish scholars, take a degree, even take two, but get yourself ready for Semikhah in the life of a community. It's just a thought of course.'

She gave Elise an impish grin.

'"Just a thought". A likely story, Rachel! And what's most annoying about most of your thoughts, is that you're right.'

The Jewish Daughter

Things never go exactly to plan. Just two weeks after this conversation, Elise received a phone call to say that following a sudden heart attack her dad had died. There was no question in her mind that she must return to be with her mum. As she had not yet completed her studies she negotiated with the Hebrew University, allowing her to come home early and complete the Talmudic studies in which was engaged from home. Typically, SOAS were far more difficult about than this her teachers in Jerusalem who had been greatly impressed by her and knew she would complete the course quite easily with occasional contact with them. Elise was sad to be leaving Rachel and Shira but felt confident that they would be meeting again soon, possibly in New York at the Rabbinate College they would soon be attending.

Her mum met her at Heathrow where they shed tears and, on the journey, Elise learned all the details of her dad's sudden death. There was much to tell of her time away, including the terrible bomb they had been near, but at this stage she felt it better not to mention anything about the possibility of training to be a rabbi and of perhaps doing that in New York. Instead, she listened patiently as her mum described all the arrangement for the funeral, which was to be conducted by a non-religious "funeral celebrant" she had unearthed from the Humanists. Elise was intrigued.

The celebrant, Jason, called to meet Elise on the eve of the funeral (when her mum was out at the flower shop checking for the following day), saying he wanted her to be clear about the content of the "ceremony", as he called it.

'Have you done many funerals?' Jason, Elise asked.

'This will be my fifth.'

'Oh!' replied Elise, allowing Jason to make of it what he would. 'I imagine mum told you she and I are both Jews.'

'Er, no, she didn't mention that.'

'Nor that I have just returned from a year-long study of Talmud in Jerusalem?'

'No.'

'Well, I imagine she thought there was no reason to do so but I will be most interested to see what you do for a secular event such as this.'

'I've never been to a Jewish funeral,' he said, somewhat limply.

Nor had Elise but didn't want to lose such advantage as she might have!

'Is there any particular thing you would want included?' he asked.

'I didn't know humanist funerals made scope for such a possibility.'

'Humanist funerals offer a personal and fitting way to support families in saying goodbye to those who have lived without religion. They honour the person who has died, focusing on the life they led, the relationships they forged, and the legacy they have left.'

'Yes, I read those exact words on the leaflet you gave mum. But as she is paying for the funeral, she who pays the piper calls the tune, as they say in places where there are pipers.'

It was clear Elise was making Jason feel uneasy and when he said he had to go, she tried her best to assure him of how impressed she was that he had come to meet her, and that was she was sure he would do his very best on the next day, and she meant both.

On the following day Jason did his bit satisfactorily, though by the end she felt that it meant no more to most of those present than something like the occasional Church of England funeral service she had attended in the past – such things had to be endured for the sake of the get-together that followed. She could not suppress a laugh, however, when she heard one of the neighbours shaking Jason's hand as they piled out of the crem, with the words "Nice service, vicar"!'

With the funeral behind them, Elise needed to talk to her mum about her future hopes and plans, though not looking forward to the conversation. However, her mum informed her over lunch that Mr Reynolds, the family solicitor who had attended the funeral had requested a meeting with them at 3-00 at home.

Mr Reynolds was in his mid-forties and clearly knew her mum sufficiently well to call her by his first name although Elise had not met him before.

'Hannah, Miss Rosewarne, thank you for agreeing to see me on the day of the funeral but I shall be away from tomorrow for a fortnight and I thought it best to meet with you both before then.

'I want to reveal to you the full details of Eddie's will.'

'I know the contents of his will,' said Hannah.

'That may be the case and Eddie may have told you all about the changes he made some months ago, but as it has consequences for Elise, I thought it best that I come to share it face-to-face.'

'What changes? I didn't know he had made changes!' said Hannah, her Canadian suddenly accent more pronounced than ever, something Elise had always known as a sign that her mother was getting upset.

'Eddie, as I'm sure you know, had shares in a Canadian mining company, and just before last Christmas he sold them for almost 5 million Canadian dollars, which is just over 3 million pounds sterling. This he has reserved in an account which interest daily increases but denies access until January 14th next year. In the new will he has made no substantial changes in terms of the house, contents and all other bank and saving accounts, which now become yours, Hannah. The change in the will is that he is bequeathing the entire contents of the new account to you, Miss Rosewarne.'

'Me? You're kidding surely?'

'No, and furthermore there are no conditions attached to the bequest. From 14th January next you will have free access to over 3 million pounds entirely for your own use.'

Elise was stunned. Hannah was stunned. Mr Reynolds continued.

'Eddie was clear that he did not wish you, Hannah, to be deprived of anything you were already expecting to receive from his will, but wanted Elise to have the freedom to use this money for whatsoever she chose.'

Elise did not know what to say, either before or after the solicitor left having asked mother and daughter to sign various documents completing the process.

'I take it you knew all about this?' she said angrily to Elise.

'Mum, honestly, I knew nothing and I am as shocked as you, but my first thought must be for you. Do you need the money? If so, I will give it all to you. Does what dad has left you provide you with what you need or will you be facing financial difficulties?'

'I suppose I ought first to make sure there are no further surprises waiting for me, though the last time I looked, I shall be more than comfortable, but I knew nothing about the selling of these shares, and it is clear he didn't want me to know because he had other things in mind.'

'I'm overwhelmed and what am I going to do with 3 million pounds? At the moment my bank accounts are just teetering over the edge.'

'As you can't touch the money until January, I can help you, so don't worry about that. I'm just reeling with the realisation that your dad was a millionaire three times over and said nothing.'

'Not so much a dark horse than completely black,' said Elise.

'And whilst we are having a serious discussion, you mentioned on the way back in the car earlier that you wanted to talk with me about your own plans for the future.'

'We can have that talk on another occasion.'

'No, let's have an afternoon of discussion and watch television without interruptions tonight, and do you fancy a takeaway this evening, or aren't you allowed?'

'A takeaway sounds like a very good idea, mum. But it is about my Judaism that I want to speak with you, though this afternoon's news might have to change everything, together with dad's death, which I hadn't reckoned with in my thinking.

'My months in Israel spent in study, living with Rachel and Shira who have become great friends, and the experience of the bomb which might easily have been planted in the restaurant in which we were eating, have strengthened my Jewish identity and our life as a people. I never had to become a Jew because like you, I am a Jew from the moment of my birth from a Jewish mother, herself born of a Jewish mother and so on.'

'That is a remarkably feminist, but why?'

'We mostly all know who gave us birth even if our patrimony is not quite so reliable. I met a woman once with a baby who told me she couldn't be sure who the father was because on a certain night at a party when she knows she conceived there were several possibles.'

'Ye Gods!'

'No, there is but one,' said Elise with a grin. 'First commandment!'

'That makes a great deal of sense but odd that a religion which I have always associated with the worst aspects of masculine control should accord such a high place to women.'

'Well, to those who are mothers.'

'And a Jewish woman doesn't lose that if she marries a non-Jew?'

'No. It was also a defence against rape. The child that was born of a Jewish mother was a Jew whoever the perpetrator was.'

'I grew up knowing nothing of this. My grandmother wanted to forget all of it, including, possibly, her guilt that she escaped to Canada. She never spoke of the Holocaust and said nothing about being born Jewish.'

'That guilt has been a feature of a whole generation of those who escaped the Nazis.'

'But tell me more of your thinking even if now it might be more provisional that it was this morning!'

'The bottom line is simple though the route might now have to be rethought. I want to train to be a rabbi.'

'But how can you be a rabbi? They're old men with beards!'

'I've tried to grow a beard, but it just won't come and in fact, mum, there have been women rabbis for quite some time. Not many in this country, it's true, but when I am a rabbi there will be one more.'

'Darling, this is all too much for me. This morning I attended the funeral of my husband and survived a gathering of people I mostly didn't know; and then I learn that he had squirrelled away a huge amount of money; that my daughter is a millionaire and now wants to be a rabbi. This is too much to take in on one day.'

'Of course it is, mum, and that is why we both need to change our clothes, perhaps have a shower and then do nothing for the rest of the day either than eat and possibly watch one of your videos.'

'Are you thinking of *Fiddler On The Roof* by any chance? You could sing "If I were a rich man".'

'No need. It turns out I'm a rich woman, which I didn't know two hours ago, and as we do nothing, I will begin to face the question of what I am to do now, because my original plans have collapsed about me. I was thinking of going to train as a rabbi with my friends in New York before hearing that dad had died, but now I shall have to do it here because I want to continue to be near you enough to see you regularly.'

'Living with me?'

'No chance, mum. One or other of us would soon commit murder. Commandment number 6. Besides which I choose to live kosher as far as is possible, to have the Friday night meal and keep all the feasts and fasts including Shabbat. I cannot inflict those things on you.'

'It's Friday tomorrow.'

'Yes, and I shall be spending the weekend with the Jacobs, the family I was living with. It will be wonderful to see them, and especially the two girls.'

'And will you go the synagogue on Saturday morning.'

'For certain.'

'Jews are odd,' said Hannah.

'Yes, you are,' came the reply, together with a grin.

Leah, Jerry, Sarah and Ruth were overjoyed to see Elise and to welcome her back into the life of their family and the wider community. They were also anxious to hear about her time in Israel, and not least her near miss with the bombing in Tel Aviv.

'It was very scary, I can tell you, less at the time than afterwards when I lay in bed thinking how close I might have come to being killed. But in a strange way it proved to be a turning point in my thinking about what I want to do with the rest of my life, well ok, at least for the foreseeable future because increasingly making long-term plans hasn't exactly worked out for me.'

'I guess you might say that from earliest times what has changed things for the Jews has not been ideologies or philosophies so much as events and how we have responded to them,' said Jerry. 'I can well imagine being that close to death has caused you to think deeply about the future.'

'I will come straight out with it. I want to train to be a rabbi.'

All four gave shouts of joy.

'That couldn't be better, Elise,' said Leah, 'always provided you maintain your academic study. We need minds like yours, not least because your mind has already been handling experiences of various kinds, shaping it for the better of us all.'

'We hoped this might happen,' said Jerry. 'And I know Rabbi Samuel. But you still have your degree to complete.'

'I had been thinking of giving it up and going to train as a rabbi in New York, where I could complete my Talmudic studies, and my Hebrew is about as good as it can get, but my dad's death means that I can't leave my mum behind in another country. So, I will hope to find sponsorship from our synagogue and rabbi to apply to *Leo Baeck College* here in London. It's a long course but with my degree I may be exempt from some of the course requirements.'

'And you must stay living with us,' said Sarah, 'mustn't she, mummy?'

'Elise must decide, but we want you to know, Elise, that at least for the rest of your course at SOAS, we would be overjoyed to have you with us.'

'I would love that too, but there's another thing I have to tell you.'

'Let me guess,' said Jerry, 'you've met a man, or a woman, and you're wanting to get married.'

'Jerry, whatever you do this weekend, please don't buy a lottery ticket because your guessing is hopelessly inadequate.'

Elise now told them of the details of her father's will.

'I cannot know the will of HaShem for you, Elise, but this is what I mean about events. You will make an excellent rabbi and now you must begin to consider how best to use this new development.'

Siân

Elise remained living with the Jacobs until she began her rabbinic training in the autumn of the following year. Sponsored by her synagogue and with good references, Leo Baeck were glad to welcome her, especially her Talmudic knowledge which was already exhibited in various articles she had published and which they made use of for teaching some of her fellow students. The five-year course was reduced to three given her previous degree and experience of life in Israel.

Over the year before she began, Jerry and Leah noticed changes in Elise. She was much confident than before her time away, which was not surprising, but she also seemed stricter about her practice of Jewish life. This hadn't caused tension, but they did wonder if Rabbi Samuel might chat informally with Elise about this.

It was noticed too by Rachel and Shira when Elise went over to New York, travelling business class! They were both clearly part of a much more liberal tradition than even Elise recognised, and Shira in particular, was now heading the movement for lesbian rabbinic recognition. This was not a problem for Elise, for after all her own rabbi was gay, but it did make her wonder about the overall direction of American Jewish life and practice even within the rabbinic college in which Rachel and Shira were being trained.

She had not told her friends about her new-found wealth and, other than her mum and the Jacobs, had spoken of it to no one, though she had made significant anonymous contributions to the synagogue and the Samaritans. At some stage she knew she would have to seek help with her investments, but it had meant that the fees for her training were secure, and she could easily afford the ludicrously high rent for her flat near the college in Barnet.

It was during the time of her internship with a rabbi in Manchester, that Elise and the rabbi's wife, Sally, decided to have a few days holiday together in North Wales. The rabbi himself was away taking part in some event or other in the United States, leaving Elise to take responsibility for one of the Shabbat services in his absence. On the Sunday, Sally and Elise set off for Rhyll where they would be staying. Sally was older than Elise, but they got on well, sharing a zany sense of humour.

It was on the penultimate day of their brief holiday on their way towards Denbigh to see the castle, as they entered the village of Trefnant, that the car in front made what was clearly an emergency stop. Elise sensed that there must be something amiss, jumped out from the passenger seat and ran forwards. The driver of the car in front was sitting as if paralysed, and in front of the car, Elise saw the reason why. There lay the body of a small child and a bicycle lying alongside. Elise quickly went to the child, a girl perhaps aged 8 or 9, and knelt. Instinctively she knew that the little girl was dead. It was clear that the car, which had been observing the speed limit, had hit her head. Elise could detect no signs of life, no breathing, no pulse. She was a beautiful little girl and Elise sat down on the road and took the child into her arms and held her. It took 45 minutes for an ambulance to arrive, and Elise held the little girl in her arms throughout.

Within a short while there were others gathering, the road blocked in both directions. When a police car arrived and suggested Elise move to allow the traffic to flow, she took no notice and just held on to the beautiful child in her arms. One of the other children told Elise that the girl was called Siân, and that her parents would be out at work, and a neighbour was already trying to reach them.

Elise told Sally later that throughout she had felt nothing other than the desire to hold the child safely, looking constantly at the lovely face that would now never grow to be kissed by a lover or her own children that might have been. She didn't pray as she knew doing that would be only for her own need's sake and not that of the child.

It was only when an ambulance finally arrived that Siân was surrendered to the care of others, and the police were finally able to re-open the road. Elise returned to the car with Sally, and they decided to turn round and make their way back to their hotel. Elise said little on the short journey and once there, they decided to get some lunch. Only as they ate did Elise acknowledge the numbness she was feeling, reminiscent of the evening in Tel Aviv and even more of the death of Gail and her baby. After lunch they decided to cut short their stay and return to Manchester.

But something had happened within Elise, something she couldn't quite put her finger on but which she knew was important. She had no children of her own and felt no particular draw to the idea of marriage, but holding that poor dead child made her wonder whether she would want a child to love closely, not to allow die as Gail had done, but to be cherished and allowed to grow into its full potential as Siân now never could.

This was now the third time she had encountered death so closely. Reflecting back on her dad's funeral she recalled that the reality of death was being wholly avoided in the appalling secular ceremony she had endured in which the man from the Humanists kept talking about her dad having "passed". What? she had wondered, his driving test or a kidney stone? They were being offered a celebration of his life intended simply as an easy way of avoiding the reality of death and what it means?

But there was more. Her first experience of a funeral in England had been following the death of her father's father. She was in her teens and religion meant nothing to her, but as she recalled the service she was not surprised that it meant nothing because the vicar taking the service avoided the reality of her grandpa's death both by talking about the life of the deceased and then offering some simplistic talk of resurrection, of his not really being dead at all. There was nothing in that service that could hold her attention other than sentimentality as the means of avoiding the reality of death: "Nice service, vicar" which meant thank you for not disturbing me in any way that might hint that I too must die!

She recalled from her A-level English reading of George Eliot's masterpiece *Middlemarch* the author's observation once Mr Casaubon learns of his imminent death: "When the commonplace 'We must all die' transforms itself suddenly into the acute consciousness, I must die – and soon". But she knew that Jewish funerals often were the same and that this was not what she wanted to spend the rest of her life doing. If she was simply to be a pedlar of soft soap, there could no possible point to her training. She would need to talk about this once her internship was over and she was back in college.

Death and bereavement were on the agenda for the coming semester, and she listened to her tutors and other students she grasped that few of them had undergone close encounters with death, or at least in the ways she had. Death was spoken of as something "out there", the main emphasis being upon the comfort and support of the bereaved, which of course she approved, but without a better grasp of what she thought of as the ruthless "facticity" of death, how could any of them really minister to their communities?

She knew, however, though spoke of it only to Leah, that she had an added advantage. She had spent the year between school and university working as an auxiliary nurse in St Christopher's Hospice in Sydenham, South London. There she saw death and handled both the dying and the dead almost daily and had become closely familiar with it. It had been an important year and probably helped account for the natural way she had been able to handle Siân's body on the road in Wales. One evening in that year there had occurred something that would later come to play an important part in her life.

Bravely she advanced the idea to the college authorities that each of the students should spend a week with a local Jewish funeral director, sharing in the work of attending a death and seeing all that was involved in the preparation of a body for the funeral.

To this, she added, 'I think too we all of us need to go and see for ourselves what happens behind the scenes in a crematorium.'

'What on earth for?' objected one of the colleagues. 'That is the work of others. We don't expect a reciprocity whereby those workers have to come and learn Hebrew and eat chopped liver.'

'Have you ever been to the business end of a crem?' she replied. 'For that matter how many of us have ever seen a dead person?'

Two students said they had seen their grandparents in a funeral home, but others admitted they had never seen a dead body and saw no reason why they should have to do so.

'We're not Catholic priests anointing the dead, we are concerned with the living. The dead we leave to HaShem,' said another.

'No, you don't. You leave it to funeral directors and those who place a coffin into a cremator and then clean it out at the end and place the remaining bones into a former washing machine containing huge ball bearings to grind them to ashes.'

'How do you know this, Elise?' asked the tutor.

'When my father died, I paid a visit to the crematorium before the secular ceremony – I won't flatter it with the word "service", and asked to be shown what would happen to my dad after the event. They were more than happy to show me. I admired the men who worked there. I even looked through the tiny spy hole into one of the cremators as it did its business. And all of us were present when none other than our Principal read "male and female he cremated them" without noticing his mistake which he wouldn't have made if he had read it in Hebrew.'

This note of levity was welcome in the context of the talk of death, and the tutor was able to continue, albeit making a note to speak to Elise about what she had said, and even more, to address what might underlie it.

When they met on the following afternoon, her tutor adopted a direct approach.

'Elise, I think you need to tell me what it is that lies behind not just all you said yesterday but the passion with which you spoke. Such passion comes from somewhere.'

For the next half hour Elise told him about her close encounters with death, but withholding any mention of the death of the baby on the grounds that she was still bound by confidentiality as a Samaritan. The tutor sat in silence for a while after she concluded the recent experience with little Siân in North Wales, but alone with her on following morning felt able to respond.

'I've had no such experiences, Elise and so anything I might say will perhaps strike you as trite, so forgive me if I am left offering only words, but I wonder if you don't need an opportunity to work closely with a therapist to enable you to express what I feel are powerful energies within you which may express themselves in ways that are sometimes inappropriate.'

'Was what I said yesterday inappropriate?'

'By no means, and already I have been thinking over your suggestions for what out rabbis in training should know and experience, but my concern was the passion with which you spoke, and now after all you have told me, and I'm not so foolish to imagine you have told me everything, but it is enough to make me think that attending to this is an absolute if you are to continue preparing for the rabbinate.'

'You mean you would stop me continuing?'

'No. You will continue the course, and we appreciate how much you are offering us as a teacher, but it would concern me that I might allow you to go forward without having insisted upon some therapy.'

'Insist means no option.'

'It does, but I want also to say that I think you have the makings of a great ministry as a rabbi, and that you should look upon what I am saying as an opportunity to enhance your future work.'

'But where can I get that help?'

'I think I may be able to be of assistance. Have you ever heard of Susie Goldstein? She is a well-known psychotherapist who has been welcomed referrals from the college and is in practice here in North London. I would like you to consider this and in fact, Elise, when you have considered, I want you to go ahead with it. Susie never reports back to us anything she hears so you can tell her what a horrible man I am or anything else, and it will stay with her.'

'I don't think considering before deciding is an option, so what do I do now?'

'I will give you her address and phone number. Her answerphone message she updates each day and will let you know when the best time is to call. The college can help with fees because she's not cheap.'

'And I'm not poor. I'd prefer to do this for myself.'

The tutor let the comment pass.

'Ok. Let me write these things down. One question however is whether you would like me to provide an official referral from the college. It might help with the waiting list if I let her know at what stage you find yourself in the course.'

'That would be a good idea, but I wish you to say nothing about what I have told you today. That is confidential between you and me, please.'

Susie Goldstein

Susie Goldstein was in her mid-fifties and expensively dressed –
even Elise who was much more casual about clothes could see
that, and she led her into a room in which there was a couch but
offered her a comfortable armchair set at a slight angle to her own.
Elise expected her to have a clipboard on which to make notes, but
she held nothing in her hands, and gave her a warm smile.

'I might begin by saying that you must be mad to want to be a
rabbi, but that form of madness we are not here to deal with!'

Elise smiled.

'Instead, I've been told only that in the recent past you've
experienced a number of traumatic events which it might be
helpful to talk through with someone. So why don't you begin by
giving me a straightforward account of those events and we can
deal with practicalities of various kinds later. Important things
first.'

Those were her last words for a considerable amount of time.
She had told Elise that she would allow 90 minutes for their first
meeting, and 60 thereafter, allowing Elise to feel there was no
rush. Elise had earlier spoken to Leah about whether she could tell
Mrs Goldstein the detail of her Samaritan experience. Leah had
said that Susie Goldstein was utterly reliable and that
confidentiality in this instance would be fully protected if she told
her the full story, adding, "And what would be the point of seeing
her if you didn't tell all?" Although no longer living with the family
as she needed to be nearer college, Elise usually spent Friday
evenings and the whole of Shabbat with the Jacobs, and she and

Leah had become very close friends. So, out it all came and with the passion that her tutor had noticed and which had led her there.

'That's a huge amount to have been bearing, Elise, and interestingly, you say you have largely not opened up about any of it to anyone other than your close friend Leah, not even your American friends who were present with you when the bomb went off. We might think about why you have not done so, but I want to hear all about how this journey towards becoming a rabbi began, and of course, something about your background.'

Elise tried to tell the story of her coming from Canada to live in England and unexpectedly burst into tears as she did so.

'Sorry. I can't think why I should be crying about that. It has never been something I've thought about much.'

'It doesn't mean that somewhere inside yourself there hasn't been a voice waiting to be heard and given the chance, has now got something to say. Though you used the word "that" to describe it, I think from your reaction, it is very much still present as a "this".'

And so, for Elise a great deal of unexpressed pain, much of which she hadn't even been aware of, began to come out: the profound loss she felt leaving her friends and her sporting life in Bracebridge, Ontario, the centre of what is known as the Canadian Lake District, where she skied and skated in winter, and canoed, swam and barbecued in summer; the awkwardness she felt trying to fit in at a school where her supposed American accent was often mocked; the animosity she engendered by her academic success into which she had thrown herself as a way of coping without friends. All these things she assumed she had left behind, but with the help of Susie was able to begin to name and attend to, long before the issues she had assumed she would be talking about were faced.

They agreed a contract of twice-weekly sessions which also included a promise that neither would end the pattern without a minimum of two weeks' notice.

'When we do complete the work we are doing,' asked Elise, 'if completion is possible, are you expected to provide some form of certification that I'm now safe to proceed.'

'I will be reporting nothing to the college. Any reporting back will come from you. What goes on here stays here, Elise. It has to, and it will. You of course are free to tell anyone you choose about our sessions. The only person I will speak to is my supervisor who will never know your identity, and, in any case, his main concern will be with me.'

'Might he not guess if he knows that you are handling people from the college?'

'I have clients from lots of different places and institutions. You have to trust me, if you can, that not even he could discover your identity.'

Over the days, weeks and months that followed Elise knew she was learning a great deal, not just about herself but acquiring insights that she hoped she would be able to utilise. Her greatest surprise was that Susie focussed her attention less on the three later events, than on the experiences of her earlier life which had largely been not allowed into the processes of her conscious mind, often because they were too painful. For a few weeks the focus was on her life as a girl growing up in Canada dealing with things she assumed were no part of her life now but which Susie showed her might underlie how she was in her almost strict independence of mind, emotion and reserve.

Psychotherapy from its origins is very much a Jewish discipline and though it had moved on a long way from Freud, the abiding influence of Jews could not be denied. Elise became fascinated by the process and underlying rationale and, typically, read widely, constantly checking out theory and relating it to her own practice. She also went through the typical pattern of falling in love with her therapist, then with feelings of hatred towards her and eventually settling with the knowledge that the two had to live side by side.

Leah remained her closest friend and following a conversation with her, Elise decided that the time had come to stop her regular night at the Samaritans.

'I thought Susie might have advised stopping when you began work with her,' said Leah three months into Elise's therapy.

'She did, but I have found myself playing one of the therapeutic games I have read about, where you become like a child and stubbornly need to fight the parent. She was right, as you are, and besides which I am finding it so exhausting even though I only do it fortnightly, what with all the study I am doing and preparing the teaching I do for the college.'

'Does your mum know about your therapy even though I would imagine she is many ways present with you in your sessions with Susie.'

'That's very insightful of you, Leah.'

'No, it's not. I was in therapy a long time back. I haven't said so before because I didn't want that information to get in the way of your own, but I learned back then that the number of invisible presences that accompanied me into the therapy room was legion.'

Elise laughed.

'You're not kidding, but please don't tell me it was with Susie.'

'No. It was with a man called Gerd Gussman, a German Jew who had fled the Nazis. He was quite old when I began to see him, but his mind was remarkable, and he taught me so much and enabled me to survive what was at that time holding me back from any sort of commitment to anything and anyone. I wouldn't be the me you know if I had not been able to go through that process with Gerd. He's dead now, of course, but our Rabbi Samuel said he respected him greatly.'

'That is praise indeed.'

'But tell me, have you reached a stage in your work with Susie when it has occurred to you what a good therapist you would make?'

'Did that happen with you?'

'I asked first. But, having, like you, been a Samaritan, it did occur to me that I might begin training as a counsellor, but with a full-time job and small children, I realised I could not find the time, let alone the energy to do what would be required.'

'And what sort of time and commitment is involved?'

'As I understand it, to be recognised as a properly trained counsellor, it is a course of three years involving at least one full day a week, having your own therapy, plus in the second year engaging in supervised counselling. I'm sure you would sail through the study, but the time for counselling practice, supervision and your own on-going therapy makes great demands. If you were interested, you might be able to do it as a rabbi but not until.'

'I have thought about it, but the practicalities as you outline them are quite impossible now, but perhaps I can store it at the back of my brain. Besides which, my work with Susie is already making considerable demands upon my emotional energy and I have little to spare.'

'Are you dealing with those recent events I know about, the deaths, I mean.'

'No, and that's most odd because I had assumed that's what I would be talking about most of the time, but Susie says my reactions and responses to such traumatic events are fashioned less by the events themselves but by all that went before, right back to the beginning. She compares it to numbers. Before you can speak of 9, 10 and 11, you need to grasp 1 to 8.'

'What number are you at?' said Leah with a grin.

'Oh, I'm still at minus 5 but ever hopeful!'

'Well, we've come to do some clothes shopping. Much more important than any of this and Elise, it's about time you splashed out on something new and exciting.'

'Leah, I'm training to be a rabbi. Exciting clothes don't come into it?'

'I disagree. There's no reason why you shouldn't look good, and however are you going to find a husband if you always wear a dark skirt and a dark sweatshirt?'

'Leah! You sound like a Jewish mother.'

'I am a Jewish mother.'

'And even worse, my mother's always going on about my need to find a husband.'

'That proves she's Jewish.'

'Perhaps I'll shock her by saying I'm looking for a wife.'

'Are you?'

'No, though lesbian rabbis are all the thing in America now. My friend Shira has come out since going back home.'

'Were you aware of that in Israel when you shared with her and Rachel?'

'There was no real opportunity to mix with anyone outside the confines of the course, but she never spoke of it.'

'She didn't try it on with you or Rachel?'

'Not that I was aware of, though I'm not troubled by it. After all, we're Reform and our rabbi is gay. No doubt Susie will soon be uprooting all sorts of reasons why I don't seem especially sexually aware, but at least for now I'm not. I get on better with women than men but that's not to mean I'm lesbian, just sensible!'

'I know exactly what you mean. I love Jerry but sometimes he drives me completely crazy.'

'He's wonderful, Leah. He does great job of work, he's a smashing dad and supports Tottenham Hotspur. What more can you ask of a Jewish husband?'

'I'll take your word for it!'

Semikhah

As the final year of her training began, her tutor talked through some of what would be involved in seeking an internship and beyond it a synagogue where she would begin to practice as an assistant rabbi. He accepted her suggestion that she should work as an intern with a rabbi chaplain in a general hospital.

'I've never asked, and Mrs Goldstein would never inform me, but are you still seeing her regularly?'

'Twice a week.'

'And are you finding it a positive experience?'

'It can be painful but I'm feeling confident that I'm moving in the right direction, and I think she is too. Even after my semikhah I might continue to see her; she's so very wise about all things Jewish and the psychological implications of how Jewish life affects people. I'm learning a great deal even as I'm working on myself.'

The final year went by quickly with the necessity of finding someone and somewhere to work, and the need to find somewhere to live and all the practicalities that come with ceasing to be a student.

Rabbi Janice Samuels served a Reform congregation in Cambridge, both residents and students. One of her colleagues was leaving and the place required rabbis with good academic ability to work there. Janice was American and delighted to meet and discover that Elise would be ideal to serve in the university city. The committee on meeting and interviewing Elise agreed, and she was duly appointed.

Semikhah, Elise's ordination, a Hebrew word meaning the formal transmission of authority from Moses to the present time, took place in college. Four Cantors and three other students were to be given their authority at the gathering. Elise was presented to the Head of the College and two other rabbis by Samuel, announced as being called Rabbi Elise Rosewarne and then Samuel pronounced a great blessing upon her. Rabbi Elise was greeted with cheers from all those present.

All four Jacobs had come for the ceremony as had Susie Goldstein, and Rachel and Shira had flown over especially to be with her on the great day and even her mum, which was a great surprise to Elise.

She was not entirely finished with college life as she had been invited to have a role as a part-time teacher of Talmud and would be returning regularly, and also still seeing Susie. Elise knew semikhah was not an end, but the beginning and she had no idea what might lie ahead of her.

Not having studied at the University, it took a little while for the new rabbi to come to terms with how the university functioned through its many colleges. She knew that most of the colleges had an Anglican ethos, with a chaplain and a dean who was usually an Anglican priest and that the really big events usually were set in the context of that religious tradition. One of her first tasks was visit the Jewish Chaplaincy where a husband and wife, both rabbis operated.

'Is there any sort of tension between what you're doing and our synagogue?' she asked Rabbi Ellen, who hailed from San Francisco.

'I suspect we get more hostility than you as we're around the multiplicity of students all the time. Israel is the problem and although Baruch and I are not Israelis, and don't defend the actions of the government of Israel, it is widely assumed that all Jews are the oppressors of Palestinians.'

'Yes, I came across it at SOAS too. Not that the constant pro-Palestinian press bias helps.'

'What do you mean?' asked Baruch a little more aggressively

than Elise might have expected.

'I mean that I was about a hundred metres from a bomb planted by a Palestinian suicide bomber, a woman, in a restaurant in Tel Aviv which killed six of our fellow Jews simply because they are Jews and badly injured many more. When I saw how it was being reported on television in the west, it gave the impression that it was a legitimate act, and the concerns were more for the family of the killer than those who died and who injured. I was amazed to see it, and it is typical of all other reports.'

'But you're not justifying what the Israeli government is doing on the West Bank?'

Elise was sensing a wholly unexpected tension in the conversation.

'I assume you have a map of the Middle East. Iran wishes the destruction of Israel and the Palestinians are a wonderful means as their proxy of making the Western nations increasingly sympathetic to their overall cause. I spent a year in Israel and I totally support anything that will prevent a second Holocaust. Don't you?'

'If you say things like that to students, you will bring down on your head aggression and contempt. We are here to care for Jewish students, many of whom have a difficult time as it is without the student body being fed a pro-Israeli line. We are engaged in a balancing act. To support Jews does not, at least to Ellen and myself, mean we support Israel.'

'In which case,' said Elise, 'I am glad to know how you are operating. I have no role in the university, and I don't argue with anyone other than my fellow Jews. But I care passionately about the fate of the millions of my people under constant threat, and I think you should too.'

'I take it Janice knows of your views.'

'Of course she does, but she also knows that my primary concern is not actively politicking but caring for our community and encouraging them not to abandon that handed down to us from generation to generation just because not everybody likes us. That, I'm sure, is the basis of your own work.'

'Yes it is,' replied Baruch, now getting cross, 'but I hope it will not be put at risk by the Reform synagogue in the city.'

'As I'm sure the Reform synagogue will not welcome hearing that Jews ministering in a university do not care about the fate of their homeland,' responded Elise, with a broad smile. 'I must be going and I'm grateful to you for being so open. Trust me, I will do all I can, at all times, to provide support for your important work, and I would hate you to think otherwise.'

As she walked back to her flat, Elise was uneasy that the two chaplains were clearly compromised by the impact of what she understood was unquestionable anti-Semitism behind the mask of pro-Palestinian publicity. Although in her own teaching and preaching she was above all concerned with how people live as Jews in their daily life, which for her included the joys of prayer and the feasts and fasts, she could not be unconcerned with what was happening to her fellow Jews in Israel, as well as the daily hostility many experience within this country.

She decided to talk it over with Janice who had been in the University city of the synagogue for three years.

'It's true that we get quite a few students in synagogue because it's safer for them to be here than the chaplaincy, but I can fully understand the reticence of the chaplains as this is a very difficult time for all sorts of people whose views are supposedly controversial.'

'I'm certainly not wanting to stir up difficulties,' said Elise, 'and in universities ideas are presumably flying around all the time, stirring up this group or that, but neither am I prepared to wholly abandon any mention of the hatred manifested towards us wherever it might be, and it's my understanding that as a rabbi I am there to provide comfort and support for those who might be on the receiving end.'

'Yes, but don't forget that you're out of college now, out of the safe environment you have been able to take for granted. Out here you also will be hated by many, but changing the subject slightly,' said Janice, 'our greatest opponent telephoned me this morning and said how much he would like to meet you.'

'By our which I take it you mean Rabbi Isaac from the Orthodox?'

'I do, but as opponents go, he's a good guy, and even better is Rebecca, his American wife. I have a feeling she was the only Jew in New Mexico and quite how she and Isaac met I have no idea. Anyway, he said you should give him a ring and perhaps meet for a cup of coffee.'

'I would like to do that. He might even be interested to know that I'm a scholar and teacher of Talmud.'

'Yes, but remember that we, and by which I mean you, are Reform and there remains a considerable gulf between the Orthodox and ourselves, mostly maintained by them, though, of course they say the opposite. And he's most likely not even able to acknowledge you as a rabbi.'

Rabbi Isaac would have been much happier had Elise been a good Orthodox wife, but when she called on him and Rebecca, she received a warm Jewish welcome. It didn't take long for the subject of Israel to come up.

'I spent a year in Israel as part of my degree and was almost killed in Tel Aviv by a bomb, so I'm pretty hot on the cause of defending Jews everywhere but especially in Israel.'

'What were you studying?' asked Rabbi Isaac.

'Talmud. I have an ease with languages, so my Hebrew just needed bringing into the 20th century.'

'That amazes me. I didn't think liberal Jewish training involved as much as that – a whole year.'

'You're right. It usually doesn't as I did mine under the auspices of my university course, but at rabbinic college I was able to continue my study (as I was doing first thing this morning) and also to do teaching Talmud within the college, of which I still do a little.'

'Then it is good that you have come to work in the setting of a university. They have a department for Asian and Middle Eastern Studies, of which Hebrew is a small part, but they might welcome a Talmud scholar.'

'Are you really recommending a female Reform rabbi for such work?'

'I have no doubts that the more you immerse yourself into your study, the more you will gradually become Orthodox in your thinking. As for women rabbis, I do not believe such a thing is possible within Orthodoxy. You will recall Dr Johnson on first hearing of a woman preacher at the Quakers saying to Boswell: "Sir, a woman's preaching is like a dog's walking on his hind legs. It is not done well; but you are surprised to find it done at all."!'

'Thank you for that, rabbi. I will bear it in mind when I preach next and when I take my metaphorical dog out for a walk on its hind legs!'

They laughed.

Rebecca

In the months that followed, Elise settled into life as a rabbi and especially enjoyed the pastoral aspect of the work. She still travelled to London each week to meet with Leah and for a session with Susie but was appreciating the ethos of the university city and the sheer delight of nearby bookshops. She enjoyed too the buildings within and amongst which lucky young people were able to expand their minds or supposed to.

One day she bumped into Rebecca, Rabbi Isaac's wife, having a soup and a roll in a café in Trinity St, in what was a former church, and mentioned intended to go to an Israeli rally she had seen advertised to take part in a debate with pro-Palestinian students.

'Isaac would be impressed but I'm sure, and I'm sure would advise you, as I do, not to do it.'

'In the same way he would advise you not to eat non-Kosher in a café,' she said with a grin.

'No one will attack me for doing so,' replied Rebecca, 'but you should be careful in speaking at that meeting. David needed only his slingshot against Goliath, but something tells me you may need more.'

'Well, I'm certain most of them there will be philistines though without a capital P, as Goliath was. The memory of Tel Aviv is alive in me still and if no one else is willing to stand up for Jews, no one from the Orthodox, then it will have to be a woman from Reform."

'I don't know whether you are brave or foolish, and perhaps a little of both, but I have no doubt my husband will think highly of you and may even come to visit you in hospital afterwards.'

The two women ate their soup for a little while before Rebecca looked up at Elise.

'Tell me, Rabbi, what do you think about Moslem women being made to wear the veil.'

'I think it is a sign of the sort of male oppression not unknown in other religions.'

'You mean even in Judaism? Hasidic and Orthodox for example?'

'I'm not sure what you are saying, Rebecca, but perhaps you mean to say more.'

Rebecca looked straight into the eyes of Elise.

'I wear a Sheitel. Underneath I am shorn.'

'I suppose I had assumed that.'

'It's meant to be an assurance that if it were removed, I would no longer be attractive to other men who might otherwise be interested.'

'Yes. I read Talmud, remember.'

'And do you approve?'

'I'm a scholar, Rebecca. I read and put together insights into the origin of its writings. I don't live by it, but that's not to say that I don't find many of its contents helpful to my own thinking about Judaism.'

'A Sheitel can be quite useful, you know. Ironically it can serve to attract.'

'Yes, I can understand that yours might well do that, though I don't think that will have occurred to the Talmudic writers!'

'It can also serve to cover other things, Elise.'

'Go on,' replied Elise, sensing she was about to hear something she wished she wasn't.'

'Bruises when they go black and blue, for example, the result of my walking backwards into cupboards or wardrobe doors where they conveniently do not show. A facial slap does not leave bruises but a cupboard door when walking backwards into it obviously does, and bruises elsewhere on the body of a Jewish woman are never seen by anyone other than those who clearly stand idly by as they extend the range of their obvious clumsiness.'

'Oh Rebecca, I am devastated to hear what you're saying. How long ...'

'Has this been taking place? I would say for at least three thousand years, wouldn't you? It's one of the reasons why I think you should not speak at that meeting. You would in effect as a woman be defending, no doubt on grounds to do with your own experience, the ways of Jewish men, who whilst claiming only to defend their land and its ways, simultaneously continue to keep wives in a state of concealed terror, concubines in effect whom they can beat at will, and needless to say, rape as often as they wish, though always provided the wife visits the mikveh at the end of her uncleanness so he can begin again.'

Elise was feeling numbed by Rebecca's words.

'Please, Elise, I beg you say nothing of this conversation to anyone and I urge you not to attend that meeting. Nothing will be gained by it, and you will meet only that stupid wall of hostility and hatred so familiar to us.'

'Rebecca,' said Elise, placing her hand on Rebecca's, 'all you have told me I couldn't and wouldn't mention to another soul. I'm shocked but thank you for trusting me and telling me the truth about things I need to know about.'

'What was your gut reaction to what Rebecca told you – your deepest feeling,' asked Susie, after Elise had reluctantly poured out the account of her conversation.

'I wanted to be sick and yes, my insides felt as if they were about to release themselves.'

'Yes, that's what in an extreme form such as this we call a gut reaction, because our guts react and and express things so powerfully, the action of what is known as the vegus nerve.'

'I'm not sure knowing that that would have helped the staff in the café, nor Rebecca, nor for myself for that matter.'

'And since then?'

'I struggled to sleep and when I did, I woke up really sweaty and clammy.'

'Look, Elise, let's come back to Rebecca in a moment. I want to hear about your wish to place yourself at huge risk, wishing to challenge a mob who will not let you speak a word. And you might be in physical danger.'

'But Cambridge is a university city – surely the very place where it should be possible to express ideas and thoughts.'

'I don't want to discuss logistics so much as to puzzle out why you think, and it would be you alone, you should do this. Did you not think to do a risk assessment and decide against.'

'I saw it as a matter of principle.'

'Oh dear, I thought you might think that.'

'But isn't it?'

'It is a matter of principle for them to be holding the meeting in the first place. But I'm more interested to know why you are drawn to being Elise *contra mundum*, and how this relates to your initial Jewish bursting forth when you were at university.'

'What do you mean?'

Susie said nothing.

'Are you implying that I go looking for trouble?'

'Good heavens, no. I'm simply considering the possibility that the deeply repressed feelings of the girl dragged from her homeland, who took refuge from alienation because she was different in academic brilliance, perhaps inevitably identified herself with the Jews, because their pattern was also yours.'

It was now the turn of Elise to remain silent, a silence unbroken for more than two minutes. Eventually Elise spoke.

'I'm far from sure about the implications of what you've just said, Susie.'

'Perhaps one implication would be that you don't expose yourself to hatred you don't deserve and which in any case will not aid Jewish people in any direct or even indirect way. It might also ruin your work as a rabbi because you will acquire a reputation and possibly there will be protests at the synagogue. But of course, it's up to you!'

They both laughed.

'I'm glad you made that clear,' said Elise, still laughing. 'But there are other implications of what you have said that I shall need to give a lot of thought to, but I have often wondered why it is in therapy we have never spent much time on the very issues I thought I was coming here to deal with. I'm just beginning to understand why now.'

'The issues we face, whether in our day-to-day encounters with people, or your responses to the extremely demanding events of your life, are not necessarily wholly determined by our early experiences, but certainly shaped by them'.

'And, I assume, that would also be the case of those who protest and hate.'

'There can be no doubt that many, especially young people, who have never been to any of the Middle Eastern countries, would never realise that in most of them there is considerable constraint on freedom to protest, on being gay, being women, and much more, and that the only country where they could be themselves is the one to which their ears have been systematically poisoned, the way in which if you recall, Hamlet's father was killed – just my little joke! But the resonance of their own early life experiences draws them to this way of self-expression, which is why your attempts to reason with them would be pointless because the damage has already been done.'

'You will recall how often I have been in tears in our sessions together, and I suppose that when I began, I had imagined that might well be the case. I wasn't entirely prepared, however, that what is really a shaking of the foundations of my being.'

'Do you think I should have a warning notice on my front door?' Elise smiled.

'But I would be interested to know if it is a problem. Are there clients who are so affected by what they bring up from their past that they get angry with you. They want to shoot the messenger?'

'Therapists can function only by having engaged thoroughly in the process themselves, and most of us continue to do that, as well as supervision which is compulsory. So, we know that the client can get angry because we've also been clients and when it emerges, we can at least understand where it comes from and why.'

'It is with hesitation that I ask this, Susie but ...'

'You can stop there, Elise, and save your breath, for the answer is that undoubtedly you would make an excellent counsellor and possibly thereafter a psychotherapist. It is not an easy process and the processes of testing and discernment continue throughout the training. You would sail through the academic side of the work though the skills required would be very different from your linguistic and Talmudic studies.

'Were you to give this consideration, I would prefer it if you do not apply for anything without involving me. Not every course is to be recommended.'

'I will mention this to Leah. After all she is a fellow Samaritan, and sensible about everything. As you know, I would have no financial worries about the cost and I would need to discuss the practicalities with my rabbi colleague, but I feel this has been around somewhere inside for a while.'

'I'm sure some clients have the fantasy of changing seats with me, but I know most should not even attempt it, but perhaps, you should consider an exploration.'

Meeting later, Elise told Leah of the direction of the session with Susie.

'The thing is, Elise, you are so very slow. Jerry and I have known that from almost the first time we met you, so I'm glad you've finally caught up.'

'The counselling course lasts three years, and only after considerable practice could I apply for accreditation, and to become a psychotherapist, such as Susie, would take a further three years.'

'Elise, as yet you are not tied down by any family commitments, though they may well come. You have financial security and, for the moment, a worthwhile occupation in a good place. What's not to like?'

'I think we should celebrate with a cake and coffee. So let's do that. Something with lots of cream.'

'Kosher?'

'You a rabbi are asking me, a poor maths teacher?'

'Let's take the risk.'

'As the Hebrews said when Moses offered to part the waters of the Red Sea to let them escape from Egypt.'

Bevan

Elise spent the train journey back to Cambridge deep in thought. Susie's words about the shape of her future, together with her observations that she might be allowing aspects of her past to control her present were extremely unsettling. For the moment, of course, she was fully settled in her role as a rabbi and greatly enjoying the work, but it was regarded as essentially an assistant role from which she ought to consider moving after three to four years, though that was actually in the contract.

She was now settled in her mind that whatever else the future might contain, she wanted to enter counselling training with guidance from Susie. If that worked out, then who knows what possibilities lay before her. She would need to balance being a rabbi with a role that had to be non-religious. Susie was Jewish, or at least she had a Jewish surname and clearly familiar with Jewish life, yet this never intruded into the work they did together, as for most of her early life to which in the main they devoted their attention, Judaism never intruded in any whatsoever. But could she realistically be a counsellor and a rabbi?

As the train pulled into the station, she was aware mostly of questions, but passing a poster for the forthcoming anti-Israel meeting, she knew that she would not be attending; that at least had become clear. Greater clarity came once she arrived home and checked her emails. There was one from Susie supplying her with the details of a part-time but very demanding, course due to begin in September. It was properly accredited by the British Association of Counselling ad Psychotherapy. Susie said that she had spoken to the course director whom she knew and reserved a place for her in case she decided to go ahead. There would be interviews and Susie had ascertained that she could continue to be recognised by the course as her on-going therapist. Elise did not hesitate to make a call and arrange to meet the two tutors for an interview in the following week. Their website did, however, mention that they often had events on a Saturday, and at least one residential weekend every year! Elise decided she would cross that bridge when it came. For now, there was working waiting for her in her day job.

They met in the home of one of the tutors in the village of Wilburton.

'We've never had a rabbi on the course before,' said Helen one of the two tutors.

'That's ok, I've never been on a counselling course before,' which made them both laugh.

'Did your training as a rabbi not include counselling,' asked the other tutor, Kim.

'I've been in therapy for some time with Susie Goldstein, and although in college there was teaching about what was called counselling, it was nothing like this. It has made me realise that all those in training to be rabbis or priests or whatever should first enter into therapy as a necessary part of their training, not least because without that you are not really equipped to counsel others.'

'I would agree with that,' said Helen. 'It might, though only might, help so many of those clergy of various sorts who get into difficulties later, but would being a rabbi place constraint on who you might be willing to counsel. Would it only be Jews, for example?'

'As a rabbi, I am often in a caring role for members of the congregation, but that is not counselling and if I thought someone needed counselling, I would encourage them to find the best counsellor they could find, religion or no religion. If I was to become a counsellor, I would not do so as a rabbi but as a human first and foremost.'

'Might that include those with views inimical to your own?

Someone with anti-Semitic views for example?'

'Of course. As I understand it, and I have an enormous amount to learn, as a counsellor I would not be there to tell my story. I know next to nothing about Susie, and I think that is how it should be, and I don't know how much you know about Judaism, but we never proselytise – we leave that to the evangelicals. Nor would I feel it was appropriate to pick and choose. I'm Elise, a woman; isn't that enough for a client to know?'

'Yes, though some clients try to discover more about the counsellor and the training process tries to root out those likely to provide it by talking about themselves. That's what our own personal therapy is for.'

'The course is not cheap,' said Kim, 'and grants from various bodies mostly unavailable.'

'That's not a worry.'

'And are you able to make the time commitment? In term-time it is one full day a week of teaching and group work. Later there will be counselling practice and supervision, for which you have to pay for yourself. I would imagine being a rabbi is a full-time job.'

'I have some teaching commitments at my old college in London. I would happily shed them which would free up a whole day, and besides I don't work by myself. I have a colleague and we share the work. Nor are we like vicars, doing baptisms, weddings and funerals for all-comers. I can largely decide my time commitment and could even afford to work part-time if need be, which our treasurer would not complain about.'

'What about Saturdays? We have regular weekend workshops. They are not optional.'

'I may of course risk being struck by a thunderbolt from above, but I'll take the risk.'

The women smiled.

'It's not a problem. I'm Reform Judaism not Orthodox and besides which it would get me out of preaching. This is good news.'

'I think that just about covers everything', said Helen. 'What questions do you have for us?'

Elise asked about the predominant models of counselling they taught and could see straight away why Susie might have recommended this course, as it focussed on developmental material.

'I've been reading some Winnicott and Bowlby, so I'm especially pleased to hear what you what have said. I have no more questions,' said Elise, 'and even fewer answers.'

Helen and Elspeth smiled.

'I think we're glad to hear it,' said Elspeth.

'I'll give you an application form, so we have your details,' added Helen, passing Elise some papers. 'You can scan it and send it to me. There's no need for two referees as Susie vouches for you and that will do for us, and I'm delighted to be able to offer you a place on the course.'

'I shall need a little time to think about it.'

'Of course,' replied Helen.

'Ok,' said Elise, 'I've had the time, and the answer is that I thank you for your offer and I accept.'

They laughed and Elise prepared to leave.

'Oh, I forgot,' said Helen. 'Do you have family commitments?'

'Oh, yes. A mother who is looking for a nice Jewish husband for me! It's less of a commitment; more of a misfortune!'

Elise made her way to where her car was parked, Kim waiting by the open door of her house to see her away. Elise could see some children playing 50 metres or so ahead. It was as she was opening the car door that she heard the noise of car brakes screeching. She turned to look and could see at once that something had taken place and ran to where the children had been playing and saw a small child lying in the road. Instinctively she sat down and picked the child up, desperately trying to find a pulse or breathing or anything else that indicated that there was still life in this child, but immediately she knew there was nothing. She called out for someone to dial 999 but gave her full attention to the little boy she was holding. Unlike the first occasion on which this awful thing had happened, there was blood coming from the nose of the little boy which she feared originated in the brain. Close to

her was the football they had been playing with and which he had
sought not hearing the oncoming car so engrossed was he in their
game. She was told by one of the other children that he was called
Bevan, and she spoke to him using his name without any response.
A crowd was gathering, and the parents were being sought but she
was told that they would be at work, leaving their older child to
look after the younger. Although her attention was mostly given to
this beautiful little boy she held, she could also see that Kim had
come, asking if she could do anything. Elise smiled and shook her
head.

On this occasion, being nearer the big city, the ambulance took
only half-an-hour to arrive but that would mean what doctors
sometimes called the golden hour would have passed by the time
Bevan reached hospital, and in any case, Elise was sure that life
had already drained from him. Reluctantly she handed him over to
the paramedics, urging them to take great care with him, though in
seconds they entered the protocol they had to follow, opening his
airway with a device and the other things they did. When they
were finally ready to take him away, his big sister finally emerged
and said she would accompany him and had already notified her
mother who would meet them at the hospital.

Elise's clothes were dirty, and she had some blood on her skirt,
and Kim insisted that she come back to the house to clean herself
up and just stop, which she was glad to be able to do.

Helen had just been about to leave and saw something of what
had happened, and the two women took Elise into the house,
helped her to remove her bloodstained clothing and to wash her
hands and face. Kim brought a clean jumper and a skirt for her to
wear but more importantly encouraged her to sit down and drink
a cup of tea. They said very little.

'It's quite terrible. This is the second time this has happened to
me,' she said quietly. 'The first time was when I was on holiday
with a friend in North Wales. On that occasion it took forty-five
minutes for the ambulance to come and all I could do was hold the
little girl in my arms knowing she was dead but not wanting to let
go of her. And now it's happened again. It's almost unbelievable. I
know it's utterly pointless asking why – but why?'

Kim shrugged.

'You're right about it being a pointless question but there's something inside of us that instinctively asks why.'

'I've sometimes wondered if our make-up demands it of us, that we seek out meaning, just as we long for happy endings when we read a story or even an explanation', added Helen.

'For now, you must stay here and rest, Elise. Is there anyone I can tell if there's something you've got to do?' said Elspeth.

'Thank you, I will stay a little if I may, and I desperately need the loo. Let me do that before anything else.'

Elspeth showed her where to go. On her return Helen said she had to go as she had a client.

'What you did was amazing, Elise. You clearly didn't hesitate for one moment. I will take that example of courage with me. Thank you so much, and I very much hope look forward to working with you from September.

'Thank you, Helen.'

When she had left, Elise said, 'I hadn't realised she was there.'

'We heard the noise and went out to look and Helen saw you running up the road. She followed and then came back to call for the ambulance when you asked her to.'

'I just called out to anyone. I didn't see her. All I could see was the face of the little boy.'

'And again, I need to ask if there's anyone I should call.'

'No. A slug of whisky would be nice, but as I've sort to drive home, it would perhaps be best if I just had another cup of tea.'

Throughout this time, they had heard various sirens, and as Kim rose to make the tea, the doorbell rang and there was a policeman standing outside.'

'Hello,' he began. 'I was told you were the lady who attended the accident. May I come in.'

'Yes, come in, please, but it wasn't me, it was Elise here. I'm making her a cup of tea; would you like one?'

'Thanks, yes please. Milk, no sugar.'

He sat down opposite Elise.

'Can you tell me your name?'

'Oh, I think so.'

He smiled.
'And it is'
'Elise Rosewarne,'
'Is that Miss, Ms or Mrs.'
'It's Rabbi.'
'Oh!'
'Am I your first?'
'You are.'
'Well, I'm assistant rabbi at the Reform Synagogue in Cambridge and I was just leaving my friend's house when I heard the brakes of a car screeching. I could see there were children there on the pavement and I ran forward. When I got there, I saw a little boy lying in the road. I went and picked him up into my arms and sat with him until the ambulance arrived.'
'You didn't try First Aid?'
'I cleared his airway as best I could and felt his pulse. Neither was showing me any signs of life. I was not intending to hit him on the chest because I knew he was already dead.'
'Did anyone there want to try First Aid?'
'Do you mean did I stop someone from doing so? No. The car driver was in no state to do anything and I was not aware of anyone but children in the first few minutes.'
'How did you know the little boy was no longer alive?'
'Because he was not breathing and there was no indication of a heartbeat.'
'Did anyone try to take the boy away from you?'
'No one. Someone mentioned that his parents would be at work, and they were looking for his elder sister who was meant to be looking after him.'
'I have to ask you this, Rabbi. Do you think that not doing anything other than holding the boy in your arms, though in itself that was a kind thing to do, you may contributed to him not receiving emergency help which might have saved him?'
'The paramedics attempted various things when they arrived, but it seemed to be ages before they got there. In the meantime, no one present suggested or offered to attend to him, including your colleagues who seemed more concerned with the driver of the car

involved and keeping traffic moving. As I have said, it was my understanding that he was killed outright, and I just felt holding him rather than letting him lie on the road was the least I could do as a fellow human being.'

'You didn't do it as a rabbi as such.'

'Last rites are for Catholic priests, not rabbis. Why, were you thinking I might consider circumcising him?' said Elise crossly.

Kim, who had heard all this, now intervened.

'Officer, I know you are only doing your duty, but that is quite enough questioning. Elise has had a terrible shock, acted with great courage and did the very best she could do for a little boy. I know there will be an inquest and I'm sure Elise will be asked to give an account then, but I think you should leave her now.'

He stood.

'I agree completely. I'm sorry, Rabbi, if I've been somewhat brusque and insensitive, I apologise.'

'Thank you for coming.'

Kim returned from showing him out.

'I hope this doesn't cause you any difficulties.'

'It would be an irony if it was to do so, but such things happen. I did everything I could.'

Henry Bloom QC

"According to Mrs Fleur Diamond of Wilburton, the Jewish Rabbi of the Cambridge Reformed Synagogue simply sat by and allowed her son to die without any attempt at resuscitation. 'In effect she killed him,' said Mrs Diamond, 36, after her only son, Bevan, had been hit by a car as he played on Tuesday afternoon. Mrs Diamond maintains that Rabbi Alice Rosewall allowed her Jewish religion to prevent anyone present attempting First Aid so that when the ambulance arrived, it was too late. Addenbrookes confirmed that a boy aged 9, had been dead on arrival following a road traffic accident. Rabbi Rosewall was not available for comment."

It was the day after and in any case, Elise didn't listen to BBC Radio Cambridgeshire and so would anyway have missed the item on the News Headlines at 5-30, and was in London having supper with Leah before heading back later. It was a member of the Reform community who having heard the news item made immediate contact with Janice who, in turn immediately telephoned the solicitor who looked after their affairs. His immediate intervention ensured it was not repeated in the 6:30 headlines, though Janice knew that already great damage had been done.

Janice telephoned Elise her as she was just about to end her meal with Leah.

"'A Jewish rabbi" – whatever next!' was Elise's immediate response until the serious nature of Janice's tone made her realise that this was something she needed to attend to.

'Are you able to stay with your friends for Shabbat? It might be a good idea to be away from home until Sunday at the earliest. I foresee a possible protest gathering outside. Our solicitor has already spoken to a QC in London who wishes to meet with you in the morning to offer advice, though we both know that you have no reason whatsoever to be anxious. By the way, Alice is quite a nice name, Rabbi Rosewall!'

'Gee thanks, Janice, as I often hear you say. Leah, my best friend is here with me and I'm sure they might just be able to squeeze me in over Shabbat. Can you message the information about the QC and I'll be sure to be there? And I was due to preach the sermon this week. Oh well, I'm sure, boss, you can more than fill the breach.'

'Gee thanks.'

'There you are. You have just proved my point!'

Putting her phone down, Leah said, 'You know you are always welcome to stay, but what's happened?'

Elise had already told Leah about the death of the little boy, much to the shock of Leah who knew that this was the second occasion this had happened to her friend. Now she told her about the news report, though still she did so, almost with humour. But this was not shared by her friend.

'Elise, this is a very serious matter, and you are going to need a lot of skilled help to get through it.'

'Surely not. I acted in the best interests of the child. I tried to do the most loving thing I could.'

'Who is the QC you are due to see in the morning?'

'He's called Henry Bloom and I have to meet him in his Chambers.'

'Then please listen to me and take note. You are so loving and always think the best of others far too often, but trust me, your solicitor in Cambridge knows that this is a much more serious matter than you, and that's why he needs you to see Henry Bloom. I know, and I'm pretty sure your counsellor colleagues will be able to confirm, that you acted properly and did what was best for the little boy, which in this instance was to hold him. But you are a Jew, and you are a rabbi, and therefore in the eyes of those who wish to see, you are a killer because you did not rescue and save a child. I think you might have to expect quite a bit of hassle after this, and I'm also sure that you should take every advantage of your friends the Jacobs family for as long as you need to do so. Now, let's get you home.'

It was these words from her closest friend that suddenly brought home to Elise the reality of what she might have to face. She had already accepted that she would have to give evidence at an inquest but had assumed it would be straightforward and that the boy's parents might even be grateful to her. But, as Leah had reminded her, she was a Jew, and perhaps still at the back of people's minds was the idea that Jews were, if not actually baby killers, those who might well allow a Gentile child to die.

On the following morning, Jerry accompanied Elise to meet Mr Bloom. They knew each other of old for every Jewish doctor relied upon potential legal backing. Equally, the courts also knew Mr Bloom's reputation for defending Jewish men and women.

'Rabbi, I need you to go through every aspect of what happened.'

Elise told the story as she had done to Janice, as she had done to Leah and Jerry, and as she had done to herself during a night in which sleep was at a premium. She also added that there had been a previous occasion in which she had held a child who was already dead as they waited for an ambulance in North Wales, near Denbigh. This came as news to Mr Bloom.

'When this happened back then in Wales, were you required to give evidence at an inquest?'

'No. I didn't even have to give my name or address to a police officer. Once the ambulance had taken the little girl away, I rejoined my friend and we returned to our hotel.'

'I need you to give me full information about the date and time of that incident as we will need to read the inquest report to see if your part was recorded.'

Elise remembered it well and was able to give him that information immediately. He was surprised.

'It's not something I'm ever likely to forget and now, it has happened again, and it appears that this too is something I'm not going to forget.'

'Returning to what happened on Tuesday afternoon, can you recall how many children were playing when you approached your car?'

'There were four of them, all about the same age, perhaps eight or nine.'

'This is the summer holiday time so was anyone in charge of them?'

'I saw no one taking responsibility, though I was told that the little boy was meant to be being looked after by his elder sister, but there was no sign of her either before the accident or during my time waiting for the ambulance. I don't know where she was and I can't tell you how old she might have been, but I was definitely told that she was in charge of her younger brother.'

'How soon after the accident did the police arrive?'

'I would estimate, because I wasn't timing them, fifteen minutes. Two cars came. The first contained one young officer; the second, about five minutes later, contained a male and female officer.'

'Did any of the officers attempt resuscitation?'

'No. To be honest they seemed more concerned with ensuring that traffic could flow freely around where I was sitting with the little boy and dealing with the profoundly shocked driver of the car. I told them that I had done everything to clear his airway and that despite repeated efforts I had been unable to locate a pulse or heartbeat for which I had listened with my head on his chest. They made no effort to remove his body from my arms where he lay cradled, and as I say, seemed much more concerned with ensuring onlookers were pushed back and traffic flowing to enable an ambulance to arrive. The paramedics immediately intervened, and I happily handed him over to them before going back to my friend's house to clean myself up.'

'And after that?'

'A police officer came to ask questions about what I had witnessed of the accident itself, which was nothing, and what I had done when I arrived at the scene.'

'Rabbi, thank you for describing the events clearly. Even though your behaviour was exemplary in every way, and you can rest assured about that, nevertheless, simply because you're Jewish and a rabbi, you may face hostile questioning at the inquest. The important thing will be that you tell the court everything exactly as you have told it to me. The issue of your being a Jew and a rabbi I will deal with. This is simply a tragedy for a family, for you it's the repeat of something dreadful to find yourself caught up in.

'My advice is to remain here in London until after Shabbat. A family that has been torn apart in this way often needs to hit out but sometimes later, before they come to court, they may well realise that their initial feelings, almost certainly based on guilt at having left the little boy with a sister who was negligent and unreliable, were entirely misplaced and probably being encouraged by a reporter who couldn't even get your name, your status or your synagogue right. I shall also be seeking to find out how the information, albeit mistaken, was passed on by the police. But, Rabbi, we are Jews!'

After their meeting with Mr Bloom, Elise made her way to North London to keep her appointment with Susie. She had already informed her on the telephone about what had happened so didn't have to go over it yet again.

'Let's not speak about the event and consequent circumstance that may or may not happen,' began Susie. 'Much more important is what is going on inside you and what thoughts you have as to why this could possibly have happened again. It doesn't happen to most of us even once, but now it is twice that a child has died in your arms.'

'With the assurance of Mr Bloom, my deepest feeling is a sense of a job well done. In a strange way, I am glad it was me that I was there, that I was in a position on both occasions to do this last act of kindness towards two children. I didn't apply priestcraft or say prayers of any kind, Jewish or otherwise, I simply served as one human being doing the best I could for another.'

'I am glad that you are able to rationalise in this way,' said Susie, 'but, as you will well know by now, that is not what I was asking.'

Elise smiled.

'But what if I was to reveal thoughts and feelings that are shocking, things that potentially at least, scare the living daylights out of me, what seems to be emerging beneath the surface like a volcano.'

'What you have described is a breakthrough and as you engage in your training you will always be looking out for such things in those with whom you are working. We've been together for a long time now and I would like to think that we have worked sufficiently well to provide you with the support you have needed to be where you are, but *perhaps*, and I use the word deliberately, because there is nothing certain about it, perhaps this is an opportunity as well as a risk with regard not just to your career and status but to the well-being of who you are in this world. So, say more.'

Elise remained silent for a little while before she spoke.

'I've always thought of this place with you to be somewhere utterly safe, and I think it so now. I'm in my early 30s, unattached, relatively wealthy through no achievement of my own, a rabbi and I have spent the last few years of my life as a student and now a teacher of ancient Jewish thinking. I am highly proficient, but when two children have died in my arms, when I spoke to Gail as she died along with her baby, what enabled me to be there and to do these things for people had nothing to do with my Jewishness, nothing to do with Talmud, the study of Hebrew and all those things I have devoted myself to throughout my 20s, it was simply my humanity. My qualifications and achievements, such as they are, were of no use. What I brought was a woman who did her best, because she shared the humanity of those with whom I was dealing.

'I am fortunate enough to be able to make choices that others cannot, but I'm not going to feel guilty about that. I never heard any voices from above calling me into anything religious, but I think I may have stumbled upon a voice, but one that I recognise as my own. I know this is just a beginning, and I am terrified by what the voice is suggesting, but I think it may be calling me to radical discontinuity.'

'In all my working years I've never heard change called that, but I suspect the voice you are beginning to hear can be trusted. When foundations shake, most effort goes into restoring them, shoring them up and ensuring that the original building is safer the next time anything causes them to move beneath the ground. What you call radical discontinuity is about demolishing, right down to the ground itself and even below to the very foundations and so, beginning again. Elise, I would urge you to listen to that voice, as Elijah himself heard it in nothing more than a zephyr after the tumults had ended, but do not underestimate the demands it will make.'

Janice had reported no protests outside the synagogue on Shabbat morning and Elise anticipated nothing untoward on her return home on the following day. Having dropped her stuff in the flat, she made her way to join Janice for lunch who was keen to know how her visit to Henry Bloom had gone.

'It was completely reassuring from a legal point of view but it's possible that the inquest will gain a larger hearing than last week's reports and there may be consequences not just for me, but for Jews in general. You know: the rabbi who passed by on the other side".

'But you did exactly the opposite.'

'But I didn't do First Aid, did I?'

'But you don't know how to, and any way in the story from the New Testament the person who did the really good deed was a Samaritan, and you are Samaritan.'

'Mr Bloom told me not to worry about the Jewish element. His basic instruction was to say only what I told him on Friday morning. I hope he's right.'

'What about the press? Might they come wanting a comment?'

'Oh, I shall handle them by only speaking Hebrew.'

'I wouldn't put it past you.'

'Oh, I'm not joking. I can speak colloquial Hebrew as well as anyone and that is all they will get. But Janice, I need a break before the start of term, and a renegotiation of my contract to allow me the time to undertake counselling training, allowing me an extra day off each week.'

'I think that's a great idea, Elise, and I think you'd be good at it. This is your first posting as a rabbi and it's assumed you will need to engage in further training, and training as a counsellor is an excellent idea. Will you continue teaching at *Leo Baeck*?'

'That's what I need a fortnight away to consider. I can't say more, because I have no idea myself, but a break allows time and space.'

'Sure, that makes sense. I'm about to fly home for three weeks, but would the last two weeks in August be ok for you?'

'Yes, thank you. There's no great rush.'

As she sat, not actually watching the television programme she had turned on, she knew there was no rush to change anything. She wanted to do the counselling course, had her flat and work, and knew that behind it all there was the considerable security of her investments, but she also knew that she had undergone a mind shift even though she had as yet no real idea what it might amount to. Over Shabbat, she was sure Jerry and Leah would have noticed her quieter than usual but neither would ever have tried to intrude – at least not yet. Her love and trust of Leah was considerable and although they were about to disappear for a summer holiday somewhere in foreign lands, she hoped Leah might come up and spend a few days with her on their return and before schools were back at the beginning of September.

The question of where single women rabbis go on holiday was perplexing, something she shared when she and Kim had met for a coffee in town to talk over the accident and how Elise was managing. After all that happened, Elise needed a complete break from Cambridge, and becoming increasingly aware, thanks to Susie, of the beginnings of a break from the false self she had succeeded in becoming to find her true self, her own voice. It sounded clever of course, but might take the whole of the rest of her life to accomplish – whatever it might be

Aunt Nancy

In the final week of Janice's holiday, with her own arrangements still not made, the opportunity to get well away from Cambridge came in the form of a wholly unexpected phone call from Canada, from Bracebridge, the town in which she had been born and lived up to the time of the move to England.

'Is that Elise?' said a voice with a Canadian accent.

'Yes.'

'My name is Penny Drury. I am the live-in carer of your aunt Nancy, and she has asked me to call you. I'm sorry to have to tell you that she is now receiving what is called end-of-life care because of bowel cancer, but she would like you to come to be with her before she dies, as you and your mother are the only two living members of her family and she does not want any contact with her sister. This is very short notice, but she has authorised me to book you two Business Class tickets on Air Canada for this coming Sunday. I really hope, Elise, that you can come because she says she has important things to say to you.'

Elise could hear a voice in the background, and then a different, weaker, voice spoke.

'Elise, please come. It's Nancy here. I haven't got long and it's vital I see you for your sake. There are some things you need to know which I don't think your mother will ever tell you.'

Elise didn't know what to say, and eventually only spluttered her reply, 'Yes, I'll come of course, Aunt Nancy.'

She could hear the phone being transferred back to Penny.

'Penny, you said two tickets. Who is the other for? My mother?

asked Elise.

'Definitely not!' she replied. 'It's because the relationship between Nancy and your mom broke down a long time ago that she insists she needs to talk to you. I don't know what about, in case you were wondering. She also thought it might be a source of support if you were able to bring someone with you. We don't know if you have a partner or even a husband, but Nancy thinks you should not come alone.'

'I'm not married, and my closest friend is away on holiday, but I'll have a think.'

'That's up to you, but Nancy thinks you should not come alone. I'll call you again as soon as I have confirmed your flight which should be within the hour. Air Canada will prioritise your tickets overnight, and I'll make sure you're met in Toronto. But, trust me, Elise, this means so much to Nancy and therefore to me too.'

'Ok. Let me give you my email address.'

'I have that. Now you should get packing. You'll be here for the start of the Fall.'

Once she had put the phone down, Elise wondered what had just happened, though by now she was sensing that unexpected things happening was what she might have to get used to. She had not seen her aunt since leaving Canada almost 20 years earlier, though assumed that her phone number and email address had been obtained from her mother, even though the sisters had never been close, and her mother had made no mention of being in contact with her sister.

Penny called back to confirm the booking and that tickets were being sent by courier to her flat, and the information that she would need to be at Heathrow by 6:00 on Sunday morning. This created a problem for a Jew as it meant she would need to stay overnight at the airport and travelling there on Shabbat, which at this time of the year did not end until after 8:00pm. But, she decided, this was a matter of urgent necessity, and what was the point of being a rabbi if she couldn't decide for herself what to do.

Elise sat back in her chair utterly puzzled. Yes, her aunt was dying, and probably soon, but why leave until now to communicate something clearly very important and then suggest she might need support? And who on earth could she take? And as she sat there, her mind desperately trying to think of anyone from the synagogue community, the name of Kim Woodhouse popped into her mind. On the last occasion they had spoken, Kim and she were sharing the difficulty of getting a holiday as a lone woman, Kim herself was divorced, and had mentioned she had nothing yet lined up. Perhaps she might like a paid-for trip to Canada. It was worth a try.

She rooted out from her diary Kim's phone number and called.

'Hello, this is Kim Woodhouse.'

'Hello, this is Elise Rosewarne.'

Both women laughed.

'Look, this is probably one of the most ridiculous phone calls you might ever receive but I wondered if you had yet managed to find yourself a holiday?'

'That's kind of you to call. The answer is that I'm going to go to Shrewsbury and spend a couple of weeks being spoiled rotten by my mum and dad. But your question doesn't seem to me ridiculous, so tell me more.'

'Is your passport up to date?'

'Yes, and now what you're saying has become more intriguing than ridiculous.'

'Ah well, just you wait.'

She told her of the phone call from Canada and how arrangements had been put in place for her to travel business class to Toronto on Sunday coming.

'Now I come to the ridiculous bit. I have been sent two tickets, as my aunt thinks I might need some support from a friend – for what she hasn't said – and so, Kim Woodhouse, would you like to come with me, all expenses paid, to Ontario with me on Sunday morning?'

'Are you kidding me?'

'No, Kim, I really am not. We've both been floundering about a holiday and where we will be going is so lovely at this time of the year with so many holiday-type things to do. And you've been so generous with your care following the accident, I just thought of you straight away. So, call your parents and tell them you're going a bit further west instead!'

'Oh, Elise. I'd love to. Wow.'

Arrangements for the flight and the airport hotel were all put in place by Penny and all that was required by the two women was to be driven to Heathrow on Saturday evening by Fergus, Kim's brother, who was a tutor in sociology at Trinity Hall. Elise was surprised to discover that Kim's brother was of a different colour to his sister. Kim told her that he was born of Sri Lankan parents, and had been adopted when her parents had thought they couldn't have children of their own. And then, almost inevitably with a ready-made brother waiting for them, two daughters followed naturally, Kim first and then her sister Polly, another academic, working in Wales.

Elise, an only child, had never had to share a room with another person, so found the room booked by Penny with two single beds something of a challenge, and wondered whether it would be the same when they arrived in Bracebridge. However, Kim didn't snore, and Elise slept well. The hotel staff woke them at 4:30am in good time for the shuttle at 5:30. Then they had to endure all the demands of security as they slowly made their way to the departure lounge and some coffee having been informed at the check-in desk that breakfast would be provided on the plane.

The two women luxuriated in the comforts of Business Class with good food on real plates and an initial glass of champagne once on board. This, they decided, was the only way to fly. Despite being tired they spent the first half of the flight talking and discovering more about one another, Kim fascinated by Elise's experiences in Israel and training to be a rabbi, and Elise by the story of Kim's awful experience of marriage before training to be a counsellor and psychotherapist.

Eight hours after leaving Heathrow, the Air Canada jet descended over Lake Ontario and then banked sharply to starboard to begin its final approach into Lester Pearson International Airport, where, inevitably, those is First and Business Class were given priority leaving the plane, reducing the amount of time Kim had to queue at the Immigration Desk. With Elise still having a Canadian passport she was waved through and set about collecting the baggage. Eventually the pair entered the arrivals hall where Kim saw a sign with the word "Rosewarne" on it and pointed it out to Elise.

'I know that man,' she said at once. 'It's Harvey Walter. He had, and obviously still has, the Bracebridge Cab Company.'

They walked towards him.

'Welcome home, Elise Rosewarne. You haven't changed and I would have recognised you anywhere.'

'Nor you, Harvey. This is my friend Kim.'

'I'm pleased to meet you, ma'am.'

'Thank you, and it's Kim, please.'

By Canadian standards the drive of about 120 miles north to Bracebridge was nothing. People would often drive there and back for an evening at the Theatre and think little of it. The roads were considerably less congested less busy than in England and setting cruise control on the car could mean you could travel at least 50 miles sometimes without needing to break or change gear. Harvey soon had them away from the airport and they settled in the back.

'I'm afraid your aunt doesn't look too good,' said Harvey as he drove.

'I feared that might be the case.'

'But her spirit is strong, and I know how much she's been looking forward to having you both come to visit.

Aunt Nancy lived in a big house just off McMurray St. From the front it gave the appearance of being single storey, but it was built into a rock face at the rear, so in effect had three levels and the views from the back were spectacular. Clearly, thought Elise, my aunt is not poor, but one look at her as she welcomed them emphasised that she was undoubtedly poorly.

'Oh Nancy, after all this time, and to find you looking far from well,' said Elise as she tenderly put her arms around her.

'Elise, Elise. It really is you. Oh, you can never know how grateful I am that you have come.'

'Aunt Nancy, this is my good friend Kim, and be careful what you say because she's a psychotherapist and analyses every word.'

Kim took careful hold of Nancy and kissed her cheek.

'Thank you for inviting me to come with Elise to be with you. I am so glad to meet you.'

'Well, dear ladies, it's probably just in time, but come on in properly downstairs. This is just a welcoming and storage area.'

Nancy gingerly made her way down the stairs and led the women into a room with two single beds and an amazing view.

'Oh wow,' said Kim involuntarily as she looked out from the window.

'It's not all you might imagine,' said Elise, 'from here you can also see the 118 Road West and the A&P Store.'

'It's called M&M now and not as good, though they do deliver,' said Nancy, 'but just over there to the right you can see Macdonald's. What else?'

They laughed.

'Now, would you like some coffee? The machine's over there and prepared. But being English you might prefer tea, so I asked Penny to leave some tea bags by the kettle. Would you do the honours, Elise? You'll see a lot of Penny as she's my live-in carer. She wanted to be out so I could welcome you myself, so she's popped out to do some shopping in Gravenhurst. She'll be cooking for us later. So, Kim, is this your first visit to Canada?'

'Yes, it's very exciting to be here.'

'You're probably just a little early for the Fall and its astonishing colours, and I guess this year I won't make it either.'

After their drinks, Kim said she would welcome a sleep whilst Elise stayed with Nancy, where soon they were joined by Penny, a woman of about 40, who clearly cared for Nancy with great kindness and skill. Elise at once thanked her for all the arrangements she had made for their journey.

'I'm just so glad you've been able to make it. It's still holiday time so you should be able to get in some swimming and maybe even some water-skiing, which Nancy tells me you were always skilled at.'

'Once upon a time, but I'm nearly 20 years out of practice.'

'I think the girls can manage steak tonight, Pen. What do you think?'

'I agree, Nan. I'll get them prepared.'

Elise had forgotten that Canadians were forever shortening their names and feared that by tomorrow she would be Eli, though unless they called her K, by no means impossible, Kim was safe.

Nancy and Elise reminisced about her early years in the town.

'Would you believe that as we came down the street, I recognised Phoebe Proctor with whom I was at school. She had two children with her. We used to call her "Big Red" because she was so tall and had striking red hair.'

'She's a nice young woman and seems happy, though I often say the word "seems" because if I've learned anything in this world it is that presentation can conceal substance, and often what is presented to the world is not quite as it is shown to be.'

'So, tell me about you.'

Nancy told her about her diagnosis of bowel cancer which had spread and was now inoperable.

'I am unlikely to make October, and although seeing you boosts my spirit, my body gets weaker by the day. I couldn't manage without Penny.'

'How wonderful then that she is here for you. Does she not have a family?'

'She's been going through a messy divorce in which, inevitably, only the attorneys are the winners. Her 12-year-old son lives with his father and new partner in Buffalo, across the Border and she doesn't get much chance to see him, but she's hoping that might change with the divorce settlement.'

Kim enjoyed the steak which was cooked perfectly and congratulated Penny on the sauce to accompany it.'

'Yeah, I guess not everyone likes the taste of moose, as it's strong meat, so the sauce helps it go down.'

Kim looked at Penny with open mouth.

'Did you say moose?'

'Don't you guys have it in England?'

'No,' said Elise, 'nor do we have coons and happily neither do we have skunks, other than those in parliament.'

They all laughed.

'We have both sorts,' said Nancy.

'What are coons?' said Kim tentatively, knowing that in England it was a term of abuse for black people.

'Racoons,' said Elise. 'Mind you, we do now have beavers but skunks you can keep.'

'Is it true that they emit a horrible smell?'

'Horrible? No way,' said Penny. 'It is an absolute stink, and it hangs around for a couple of days, and if you go upstairs and look in the closet, you'll find large containers of tomato juice. You have to bathe in it if you get covered, and it's the only thing that gets rid of the stink from your body and hair.'

'I'll assume you don't add Worcester Sauce, and thanks for the warning,' said Kim.

The Will

Bracebridge is set in the Municipality of Muskoka, sometimes known as Canada's version of the Lake District, and a resort for the rich and famous with their boats on the lakes and some very large houses. In winter it is a Mecca for skiing and skating and many other winter sports and activities. In summer, with the sea many hundreds of miles away, it was in effect a series of inter-linked lakeside towns with Bracebridge as the hub.

On the morning after their arrival, Nancy encouraged Elise to take the car and show Kim the sights which she was more than happy to do, reuniting her adult self with the places she had known so well and felt torn away from. In a café where they stopped, on a hot day, for an ice cream, Elise even met another former school friend and Kim watched with a smile as they chatted eagerly catching upon on what the years had brought.

Elise especially wanted to take Kim into a forest near the town to something she called "Duck Chutes", which, on hearing, led her to assume it was somewhere to shoot ducks. However, her spelling was corrected when saw a series of small waterfalls leading into a beautiful small lake.

'I used to go out in a canoe here and one day, further down the river I saw my first beaver swimming towards me. It was a wonderful moment. I often came here on my bike with a little picnic in my basket. I adored being alone here.'

'I can understand that. With the trees still in full leaf it's almost like a giant church containing this wonderful lake.'

'I'll see if I can get a canoe and you can go and see if you can see a beaver too.'

'That would be great. 'Has Nancy spoken to you yet about what it is that she's brought you here?' asked Kim.

'No. I guess we'll just have to wait until she's ready. I do know, however, how lucky she's been to obtain the help and support of Pen. I really like her.'

'Me too, and in all honesty that steak last night was lovely. Perhaps I could set up a business in England selling moose meat!'

The serious conversation for which Elise had been summoned across the Atlantic was clearly planned for the following morning. After breakfast Penny said she needed to head out for a couple of hours to see her parents, clearly an absence pre-arranged by Nancy.

'Nancy,' began Kim, 'if you want me out of the room, I can go and read.'

'I would like you to stay, please, not for my sake, but so that what I say can be heard by you as well as Elise.'

'Lovely Elise,' began Nancy, 'all this should have been told you before now by my sister, your mother, and from everything you've said since being back, I realise that you cannot have been told anything, so it's for me to tell you.'

'It sounds ominous, Nancy,' said Elise guardedly.

'All was well until you were 7 years old. Your home and school life went well. At that time your dad was an executive of a mining company out west, and he was often away, but what we only found out later was that he was involved in a major swindling racket and was making a lot of money which he hid from the government overseas. In addition, he had shares in the company for which he paid tax quite normally, diverting any possible attention from his other activities.

'And then one day your mom arrived home unexpectedly in the middle of the day and found him trying to engage in sexual activity with you.'

'Oh my God!' said Elise. 'I can't remember that. Perhaps it didn't happen.'

'I'm sorry to have to tell you, Elise, that it did. Your mom did not make it up and what she described was him attempting to rape you. She insists that she stopped him doing so. I'm so sorry to have tell you this and you needn't have known but for the things that followed.

'He persuaded your mom not to go to the police because he insisted that might also mean financial things about himself would emerge and that they would lose everything including their house. She spent hours in tears with me. You did what children in similar situations do; you suppressed the memory so successfully that you can't even recall it now.'

Kim moved to join Elise on the sofa and took her hand in her own.

'Do you want to stop for a break?' asked Nancy.

'No, please go on; I need to know everything.'

'From then on, your mom and I would never let you be alone with him, and you came to me after school. He was away more than ever, out in Calgary. But it all had a very strange effect on me. I was worried sick and one day as I was passing St Joseph's in McMurray St I went in. I'd never been in a Catholic Church before, but I felt it was a place where I could just sit and feel safe. I loved the colour, and so I returned frequently and eventually approached the priest, Fr Larocque, and was received, a Jewish convert to Catholicism. I do recall how appalled your mom was but for me it was a place of great comfort.

'In the following Spring I offered to take you with me to Toronto to see a performance of *Annie the Musical* which was on at the Royal Alex in King St and for us to stay over. It was Easter weekend and we drove down on the Saturday morning and went to the matinée performance.'

'I remember that,' burst out Elise. It was wonderful.'

'And do you remember what happened later?'

'No. Should I?'

'When of course you should have been getting ready for bed in our hotel, I took you to St Michael's Cathedral in Bond St for the Easter celebration which began at 10-00pm. We sat at the front and though you had never been in a Catholic Church before, let alone one this size, you accepted the candle we were each given without question and sat quietly as we waited for the service to begin. It lasted two hours but you took it all in without so much as a word. The colour and the music were impressive, but something happened to you during the service. I thought at first you were just exhausted and wondered whether I should take you out, but whatever it was clearly passed.'

What do you mean "something happened", Nancy?' asked Elise.

'I have no idea, but I looked at you and you seemed to be elsewhere, almost as if you were focussing on something behind what we were sharing that I couldn't see, and nobody else either as far as I could tell. I know that doesn't describe it but it's the best I can do.'

'How long did it last?' asked Kim.

'Long enough for me to begin to be anxious, but it might have been just a few minutes or even longer.'

'I've never recalled that occasion,' said Elise hesitantly, 'and as far as I can tell I never spoke of it to anyone from then until now, not deliberately because I share everything with my therapist, but because it was hiding somewhere inside. I recall the music and the colour, but surely the service lasted considerably less than two hours. My memory suggests minutes not hours.'

'Did you speak of it to Elise afterwards, Nancy?' asked Kim.

'Not then, not ever, and she said nothing to me, and neither of us mentioned it to her mom. And the strange thing is that afterwards you were just the same little girl everyone knew. Whatever had happened it didn't lead to you wanting to come to church with me.'

'Are you still a Catholic?' asked Kim.

'Oh, yes, and Fr Lee brings me Holy Communion here at home each week. I can't get to church nowadays.'

Elise looked as if she was deep in thought, but then said, 'So why did we leave the country?'

'Your mom came to see me and told me you were emigrating to England. She was in a real state, I can tell you. She told me the truth about your dad's crooked money dealings was going to come out within a short while, and she felt she couldn't cope with the shame of it and was fearful of the effect it might have on you. He also was keen to get right away.'

'But wasn't this a criminal matter? Didn't he have to stand trial?' asked Kim.

'No. It was the company that came under public scrutiny and revealed for its activities. The only ones arraigned were the Finance Director and the Company Clerk, both of whom went to jail, but the other directors were named in the papers with the hint that they had got away with things they shouldn't have. One of them was your dad. He got away in time and probably nobody in England heard a thing. So, I'm afraid your dad escaped justice for the crimes of attempted incest and theft on a grand scale.

'These are the things I needed you to know, Elise, before I leave this world which will be very soon, but I can at least do so knowing that despite all you are a very fine young woman and have survived it all.'

'Yes, but whether or how I can now escape the knowing will remain to be seen.'

'I can now see why you wanted someone to come with Elise,' said Kim. 'I'm here for you, Elise.'

They could hear from the noise in the kitchen that Pen had arrived back and spontaneously it seemed to all three that this had been enough. Elise said she need to get some fresh air and go for a walk. Kim let her do so.

At dinner that evening they were once again eating meat strange to Kim, and she decided to have the courage to ask Pen what it was.

'Seared elk in an onion sauce. Nancy and I love it.'

'Elk! That will test Waitrose when we get home,' replied Kim looking across at Elise, who was clearly enjoying the constant diet of meat which seemed to make up a huge proportion of the Canadian diet, but wondering two things, or possibly three, as they ate. The first led into the second. Her aunt knew that she was an ordained rabbi, and second, was this meat and the other things she was once again enjoying, kosher, with a third thought she was trying to avoid: did she care?'

As they completed the meal, but still at the table, Nancy

suddenly said, 'I need to let you know about my will as it will soon come into operation, and I wanted Pen here with us as she already knows everything.

'I can't imagine the house and its contents will be of any use to you, Elise, and I don't want it sold, so I have already set in motion its sale to Pen for a nominal amount of $1 which will be completed October 15. She doesn't wish to sell it but to continue to live here, and hopefully to bring her son to live with her. You have cared me for me over and beyond what anyone might possibly expect, Pen. You deserve this and much more.'

'Nancy, that's simply wonderful,' said Elise, 'and for you Pen, I do so hope it might be possible to get your son back. Bracebridge will be better for his health in every way than Buffalo. I take it he is Canadian.'

'Yes, he was born in the same place you and I were, here in Bracebridge.'

'Will it be a struggle to bring him back?' asked Kim.

'My attorney tells me that all is set for a hearing in mid-October sby which time I will be the owner of my own house, thanks to you, Nancy.'

'It will be nice to think my illness and departure from the world can do something so good. Besides the freezer is full of moose, elk and all those other things Kim has been greatly enjoying.'

They all laughed.

'As for the rest of my will, and Pen knows this and is very happy about it, in anticipation of your visit, Elise, I made some changes in the hope that you are as I have found you to be. I have set up a trust fund which will give Pen a monthly income of $10,000 for two years. I wanted it to be more, but you said that even one year would be unnecessary, but I have over-ruled you. It will allow you to train to be a nurse which I know you want to do and take away anxiety about managing this large house with you and Greg.

'However, the remainder will eventually go to you, Elise. I say eventually because transferring money across the Atlantic takes time and I am handing over the task to my attorney Mike Lynch, whom I would like you to meet before you go back, so I've made an appointment for you to visit his office tomorrow morning at

9:00. He'll be able to give you the details and explain the tax situation. He is also my joint executor with Fr Jean-Pierre Larocque, now retired as priest here but living close by in a sort of hermitage just off the 117 on the way to Baysville. He's hoping you might share lunch with him tomorrow.

'As I say, Mike will give you the details, but I think you should eventually receive something in the order of $2.5m – Canadian dollars of course. I hope you can make good use of this.'

'Nancy! I don't know what to say. Shouldn't you be giving it to a good cause here – the church or the hospital?'

'No, Elise. The majority of my assets are going to the hospital via Pen training to be a nurse, and she will continue to serve the church.'

'You're a Catholic too?' asked Kim.

'Yes. That's how we first met. I'm what's called a Eucharistic Minister. I help Fr Lee when I can. But, Elise, please understand that Nancy and I both think you should accept what is also Rosewarne family money because we know you will use it well.'

'Goodness,' said Kim. 'All this and elk too.'

They all laughed.

'Nancy,' said Elise, 'your generosity is overwhelming especially in the present circumstances.'

'Hey,' Nancy said in response, 'no sentimentality. Death's quite natural, you know.'

'Yes,' said Elise, taking hold of Nancy's painfully thing hand, 'it is, though the process of getting there is like all journeying. You almost wonder whether it's worth the effort.'

Nancy smiled.

'Yes, Elise. I know you know.'

When Elise had arrived in England almost 20 years earlier, she had found making friends at school far from easy, not least because academically she was well ahead of her year group and took her GCSEs and A-levels a year early. This left her with a year to spare before university and having heard an interview on the radio with the founder of the modern hospice movement, Dame Cicely Saunders, she applied to become an auxiliary nurse at St Christopher's Hospice, in South London, where Dr Saunders still worked.

The work had brought her face to face with the reality of death. Even in her first week she had been present at the deaths of two patients and assisted in her first "last office" in which she prepared a body for the mortuary, and then accompanied it to the basement and placed it into one of the fridges. She also met a lot of people she admired hugely, and she discovered that despite the nature of the work which was caring for the terminally ill in the final stages of their lives, it was a place of considerable laughter and friendship. Included in her time there was a three-month period working on nights which she enjoyed most of all because it gave her more time for reading and provided an extra day off each week.

She was therefore interested to see what the end-of-life care for her aunt consisted of. Before she went out of to meet her aunt's executors, a young woman doctor and a nurse called to see Nancy and to keep her topped up with the medication for controlling her pain. Elise knew about this from her time at the hospice where Dr Saunders had pioneered the use of diamorphine for the treatment of pain in the dying, titrated at a level to maintain a patent as alert and aware as possible. The medical establishment had been wary until then, as doctors knew that despite its analgesic properties it could suppress breathing, but the hospice movement had shown what could be done and Elise was delighted to see it had spread to Bracebridge, Ontario.

As they were leaving, by the car, the doctor said to Elise, 'Your aunt is a very special lady and has been keeping going for you to get here, but it wouldn't surprise me if she doesn't feel she can now let go, perhaps even whilst you are here.'

'I think you're right, doctor. I worked as a nurse in a hospice in England for a year and I recognise the signs.'

'Whereabouts?'

'St Christopher's Hospice in London.'

'Do you mean you actually know Cicely Saunders?'

'Yes, it has been my privilege to do so.'

'My own teacher in Montreal is called Dr Balfour Mount, and he has pioneered her work in Canada.'

'He was a regular visitor at the hospice, and I once had a conversation with him over lunch in the canteen when he discovered I was Canadian. I really liked and admire Bal.'

'Jeez! What a small world.'

'Well, thankfully so, doctor. The research undertaken by Dr Saunders from 1945 onwards into pain control is active here, thousands of miles away just 50 years later. But I'm grateful for all you're doing not just for my aunt but for those others in pain.'

'Thank you, Miss Rosewarne. It's appreciated.'

The plan for the morning was that Elise, and after the early call by the doctor and nurse, and at Nancy's insistence that Kim be with her, would visit the first of the two executors of Nancy's will, and then Elise would go on by herself to visit the retired priest, Fr Larocque, for lunch, with Kim being taken Pen out in a boat onto Lake Muskoka to one of the islands where they would have some lunch and then try their hands at some fishing. Elise had already noticed how close Pen and Kim had drawn to one another, and how often their shared bursts of laughter could be heard in the house.

It turned out that Mike Lynch, had first been a solicitor in Stockton-on-Tees before emigrating 15 years earlier. He informed them of the process the will and money transfer would go through.

'It could take at least six months, I'm afraid. After tax and all the other ways in which the Canadian government will attempt to rob you, I have worked out that you should eventually receive just shy of a £1½m give or take a shilling or two depending on the exchange rate at the time. The money market is not exactly settled right now.'

'A shilling, Mr Lynch! I approve. So much better than talking about the thing called "five p",' said Kim.

'Well, you know the first rule of progress, it always makes things worse. Did Nancy fill you in on the details of the arrangements with the house and Penny.'

'Yes, she did, with Pen with us as she did so.'

'Just in case you are concerned about Penny's probity, I can assure you that she is what you see, a good person who has gone through a huge struggle to get her son Greg away from her former husband. He moved to Buffalo because US courts would not allow him across the Border to someone with no home. I represented her at the divorce hearing and will be doing so again when we are going to allow Greg to come home after 15 October. She is well shot of that man whom she married too young. He was quite frankly a shyster, a claim I'm more than ready to present to the court in Buffalo based on evidence I've amassed since the last hearing.'

'Do you mean he was a lawyer. Shyster implies that,' said Kim.

'Oh yes, he acquired dubious qualifications following an on-line course from one of those many so-called universities in the States which offer get quick degrees. He set up an office here in town and began offering cut-price legal advice to those eager to cut their costs, which I understand. The trouble was that the advice got more into trouble and the authorities began to close in, so he transferred his business back to Buffalo, because he is an American citizen. Penny refused to go, and I know he was sometimes violent with her. It was all so very acrimonious, though

Penny never gave expression in my hearing to the contempt, if not hatred, she must have felt for the man. Nancy invited her to share her home when the husband sold theirs. I've now amassed enough evidence to have him removed from office, struck-off as it's known back home, and in doing so a number of individuals and businesses are very much hoping for compensation for all he stole from them.'

Mike told Elise that Fr Jean-Pierre Larocque, his fellow executor, was a somewhat unusual priest who lived alone in a small forest clearing.

'He lets me get on with Nancy's affairs and I just keep him informed, but he's extremely shrewd and very quick on the uptake. You'll like him, I'm sure, but he is odd, and his lifestyle unusual to say the least, but if you're lucky, going for lunch you'll be well fed.'

'Moose, Elk or maybe roast skunk?' said Kim with a laugh, knowing her own luck planned by Pen would be a treat.

The sun was shining out of a clear blue sky and for late August it was a hot day, as Elise drove the Buick towards the totally out-of-the-way location in which Fr Larocque was spending his retirement. Elise had been expecting a big man in a checked shirt with a grand beard, an archetypal lumberjack, but when the bungalow door was opened, she was met by a slight man wearing thick glasses and possessed of a lovely smile as he welcomed her into his house.

'It's a delight to meet you again, Elise. How you've grown!'

Elise was baffled and assumed he was just making small talk.

He indicated an armchair which had certainly seen better days, but which proved surprisingly comfortable. There was not a great deal of living space but everything needful seemed to be there.

'Now,' he said firmly, 'the first rule is that I am Jean-Pierre, and I am greatly privileged to have been asked by Nancy to be a joint executor of her will. She is a lovely lady, and I shall miss her, and this is the thing you might think very odd, I shall nevertheless be greatly relieved for her when she leaves this life, and of course we know it's going to be soon. Trust me she has been so well served by Pen to whom she is leaving the house and an income, and believe me, if anyone deserves that, it is Pen. So, before we continue, is there anything you want to ask me about the will in relation to your aunt and of course to my fellow executor Mike Lynch, who is an attorney of enormous integrity, despite being English by birth?'

Elise laughed.

'I can't think of anything to be honest, Jean-Pierre. My aunt and you two have sorted things out so very well. I do not believe that I have done anything to be the beneficiary of her will, but if that is what she wishes, then I will try to use it in the best way I can. How long have you lived here, Jean-Pierre?'

'I came to live here eight years ago, but I had been preparing before that and spending more and more time here.'

'Even by Canadian standards it's pretty isolated.'

'That was the aim, though at least in the summer months good people come and visit and get in my way, but I love to see them and hear all about their lives and their families.'

'I know enough theology to recognise that you didn't stop being a priest when you retired but do you still function as one?'

'I only attend the occasional requiem if someone I know and love dies, as I shall when Nancy leaves us, but I take no other direct part in church life.'

'I assume then,' said Elise, 'that you are fulfilled in other ways.'

Pierre gave her a long and thoughtful look.

'That strikes me as very perceptive.'

'But I'm interested to know what you are here for. You served as a Catholic priest, and as far as I can tell, you seem to have done it very well, but what now?' said Elise. 'Though if my question is impertinent, then please forgive me.'

'Your question is not in the least impertinent. I am however, struck by the fact that in all my time here nobody has ever asked it of me in so direct a form. I stand naked before your words. A great deal of what I do in the summer is working hard in the woods so that I can live in the winter when my limited farming can't be done. That was a hard learning curve when I began but I'm used to it now.'

'And in winter?'

'I wait.'

'But not for Spring, I imagine?' said Elise, somewhat surprised by her own words.

Before he could reply, Elise said, 'No, not that, is it, Jean-Pierre?'

Pierre smiled gently and shook his head.

'I've prepared some lunch but let me first get you a glass of my J-P special cocktail. As you're driving, Elise, you had better only have a little, but you might like it.'

Lunch was a tasty meat stew which Elise recognised as moose. Over such Jean-Pierre asked Elise to tell the story of how she became a rabbi.'

'How did you know that?'

'Have you not seen Pen's extraordinary computer skills at work? You should. As computers develop, she could make a fortune using those skills, but prefers to do nursing.'

Elise gave Jean-Pierre an account of how she had realised she was Jewish, her time in Israel and her study towards ordination. She was aware of how intently he listened, never interrupting, which she found a little unsettling.

'That is a powerful and very moving story, Elise. Thank you for telling it to me. And now I shall need your forgiveness if what I am about to so say is completely wrong, but I am aware that you have not told me the whole story by any means. You have described a route of growing awareness and study leading to the rabbinate, and I am inevitably impressed by your considerable learning, but none of that has made the woman sitting opposite me. You are considerably more than your achievements. Call it intuition or whatever else but you, Elise, bear upon your face more than you have told me, and though I'm hesitant to say so, I feel you have not told me the most important things about you, those that even now are shaping your life, perhaps in unexpected ways.'

Elise said nothing, considering Jean-Pierre's words. Finally, looking him straight in the eyes, she said, 'I'm visiting some old friends from my school days this afternoon.'

'I make a good meal porridge, if you can get here early in the morning, say 7:30?'

Terry

The conversation with the evening mainly consisted of Kim's accounts of her very first day fishing and the meal the results of her efforts. Clearly, she had enjoyed the day with Pen. Elise reported back on her afternoon meeting with former girls from school, now all women with kids, and with all sorts of stories to tell about the intervening years. About her meeting with Jean-Pierre she said little other than that she was returning in the morning to complete their conversations. She did notice the look Nancy had given her, though almost in response to the doctor's words of the morning Elise thought she detected a real change in Nancy's condition.

Pen had invited Kim to join for a morning trip to Gravenhurst to do some tourist shopping which she was delighted to accept, whilst Elise made the return trip back to Jean-Pierre's bungalow from which he came out to meet her.

'Bonjour Père Jean-Pierre. Quel beau matin.'

'Bonjour Elise. Oui en effet. Come in. I have some porridge on the go even on such a lovely morning.'

She followed him into the house and sat at the table, to which he brought and poured into a bowl something considerably darker in colour that the porridge she might have been eating at home, but once she put a spoonful into her mouth discovered how rich and tasty it was.

'It keeps me going on the coldest of days in winter, but I tend to have it all the year round. I get up early and it can be chilly first thing even on what becomes the hottest of days, as I am sure you

96

can recall. But this morning I want it to strengthen you because our conversation yesterday was far from complete, and I have to tell you something clearly no one else has ever told you, not your mother, nor your aunt. It is why she wanted you to come to see her, because she knew that you would never find out once she had died.'

Elise put down her spoon.

'Are you telling me that there's more even that I have been told already?'

'Please, Elise, eat your porridge. It will get cold.'

She looked up at her host and said, 'This is very good porridge, Jean-Pierre.'

'Priests don't only just keep secret what they hear in confession, there other things to which even the word confidential barely applies. But I shall risk telling you something which I have kept to myself for many years. I told you yesterday that I was meeting you for a second time, though it was only once before and you were a baby.'

'That was what you meant by my having grown!'

He smiled.

'Yes. And one day, not long after you were born, there was a knock on my door at the presbytery and before me was Hannah, your mom, holding you. I sensed at once that she was in distress and invited her in, but before she sat down, she asked me to baptise you.'

'What?'

'As a priest I was accustomed to baptising babies at risk in hospital. I could tell at once that this was a different sort of emergency, so against all the rules, and at the time I wasn't even sure myself why I was doing this, not least because I knew your mom was a Jew, but I served in the dual role (one I have never repeated) of being both sponsor and priest, and led her into the church. Once there I baptised you and, then, and even now this is the bit I least understand, I confirmed and anointed you with oil, and gave you a new name.'

'You did what?' exclaimed Elise, almost dropping her spoon.

'At confirmation we add the name of a saint, and I called you

Mary, though I'm not sure your mom took that bit in.'

'Are you saying I'm a Catholic?'

Jean-Pierre nodded.

'You have only me to blame, Elise.'

'And Nancy knows this?'

'It seems the only person your mom told was her sister, and to the best of my knowledge has spoken of this to no one other than to me, and even she doesn't know that I confirmed you.'

'But I'm an ordained Rabbi, a Jew, the daughter of a Jew.'

'Yesterday, you knew what I meant when I said my work here is to wait. Am I not right in thinking that waiting is also at the heart of your life?'

'But...'

'Allow me to say a little more. Until yesterday no one has ever understood what I mean by waiting. The church authorities most certainly did not, and it would not have been fair to speak of it to my parishioners. And then, yesterday, almost literally, out of the bright blue sky, there appeared a woman rabbi, who knew what I know, and I knew you knew.'

Elise sat silently for a while and then said, 'I've never told this to another soul, though there were witnesses who were as surprised at what happened as I was.

'I was working a late shift as a nurse at the hospice for the dying where I worked between school and university. In one of the four-bedded sections of the ward I noticed Terry was agitated. He had been a patient for a couple of weeks and usually as bright as a button. Without any particular warning after the evening meal, he became unsettled and kept sitting up in his bed and then lying down, so much so the nurse in charge put up the cot side so he could sit up more safely. His face suggested a measure of distress and I could see that this was having a detrimental effect on the others and yet we didn't want to put the screens round his bed. His evident distress continued for quite some time and was spreading to the staff too, so eventually I decided to go and on one of his lying down phases I placed the palms of my hands on his forehead and just wished him peace, though I used no words.

Elise paused again, almost as if she was relivi§ng the event.

'And within two minutes of my taking my hands away, he had stopped breathing and was dead. I think we were all taken aback, to say the least, but there were witnesses to what had taken place, and I had not imagined it. Nothing was said. I imagine each person took it with them to whatever they were doing when they got home. I can't recall doing anything other either. I went back to the nurses' home in which I was living and just got on with what I had to do in preparation for being on an early shift on the following day. It was so oddly matter of fact. The most important thing was that Terry achieved the peace I wished for him.'

'Did you pray for that peace?'

'I don't know what you mean by that, but I certainly didn't invoke anyone or anything. It was just Terry and me.'

'What authenticates what you've told me is the sheer ordinariness of your encounter and the way you simply got on with life afterwards. You simply accepted what had happened, responded appropriately, and then continued what you were doing.'

'Yes, and that's what I mean about waiting,' said Elise. 'I knew instinctively that what took place was not of my making. But there's more. You were quite right when you said I wasn't telling you everything.'

Elise described the two deaths of children at which she played no part other than holding each child as they died in her arms, waiting for the ambulances to come. Then she told him about Gail and her baby. By the end both she and John-Pierre were in tears, and he supplied her with a cloth for her face and reached for one for himself.

They sat in silence together.

Finally, Jean-Pierre spoke.

'Just after I passed my 63rd birthday, I received a phone call from the police to attend what turned out to be a murder in Port Carling. Someone had stabbed a man who had requested a Catholic priest. There's no priest at St Ann's, these days, so I was the nearest. He was in a bad way. It had been a fight in the holiday season – too much drink, I imagine. He was 17 years old and by the time I arrived, he was unconscious and had lost a lot of blood.

We were waiting for the paramedics but being a Saturday, there was only one team on duty, and they were attending on the other side of town. The supposed duty of a priest would be to anoint the dying man and say various prayers, but I felt unable to do so. Instead, I did what you did. I just sat on the sidewalk, took his head into my hands and did absolutely nothing. Perhaps people thought I was praying, but I was not aware of doing anything at all. I was just waiting, and I knew I was just waiting.'

Elise took hold of Jean-Pierre's hand.

'We had a psychiatrist who came to the hospice where I worked, a lovely man called Colin Murray-Parkes, who claimed that as he approached the bed of someone close to death, the patient said, "Don't just say something, sit there"!'

Jean-Pierre closed his eyes.

'Oh, Elise, that is my life. I've had to stop speaking, stop the torrent of words pouring from my mouth, trying to make excuses for the God I can no longer believe in, the God who is supposed to be all powerful and yet allows such terrible suffering, the God allowing religious people of all kinds to manipulate others to the advantage of their own small minds.

'Did you know that on 1st November 1755, there was an earthquake under the sea many miles from the cost of Portugal while many of the faithful were attending mass for All Saints Day. Forty minutes after the earthquake out under the ocean, the effects were felt in Lisbon, a tidal wave hit the city, resulting in many thousands of deaths, perhaps as many as 50,000 in a matter of minutes, very many of whom were in church. And you and I are meant to continue to excuse a God who allowed that and claim to and find meaning in it, the God who took your forebears and 6 million others to their deaths in the camps. But need I say more, for there is no such God as that, and you know it as well as I, Elise, don't you?'

Elise nodded.

'Oh yes.'

'As I nursed the head of the dying young man, I experienced what I can only describe as an encounter. It wasn't a religious event – I know what they're like – and no voices, but a strong assurance of safety. Once they had taken him away, I went home to shower and change, and then I proceeded with the rest of the day, almost as if it had been the most ordinary event.

'That was when I knew I had to end my work as a parish priest and needed to find somewhere to wait, no longer attending to the religious needs and wants of the community. I found this place, repaired it and made my plans. It took a while to get things ready, but in all that time, I was trying to understand what had happened and why. Eventually, I left the parish and came here to be alone.

'I waited for some sort of confirmation that I had done right and then one day in the Fall two years ago I was in the woods gathering branches for my winter fires, when suddenly it felt as if I was being held, and once again without voices of any kind nor any sort of vision, I had the same awareness I had experienced as I had held the victim of the murder. I had no sense of fear or panic, just the sense of being there and completely safe. And almost as suddenly, though it could have been minutes or even hours later, I looked down at the ground and continued what I had been doing.'

Jean-Pierre stopped speaking, and the silence between them seemed almost tangible as they looked at one another.

'Jean-Pierre,' said Elise eventually, 'you've had space and time to reflect on these things; so now, please, tell me about them and what it all means?'

'For a moment then, Elise, I thought you might be about to ask me a tough question!' he said, and they laughed together.

The Waiting Room (1)

'You live and work in Cambridge as did one of the greatest minds of the last century, Ludwig Wittgenstein at Trinity College, who wrote, and it could almost be intended for us, Elise, "Whereof one cannot speak, thereof one must be silent"'.

'Does that mean we have nothing to say, even to one another?'

'No. We know ordinariness has characterised all our experiences of what I have called an encounter,' he said, 'and here we are doing something very ordinary: having breakfast together. Most people in Canada are doing the same thing right now. Since I gave up the theological language in which I was schooled, I have devoted myself to endeavouring to find even some words with which to understand what has happened to me and, do you know, one conclusion I have come to is that having breakfast is just as likely to be a place of spiritual insight as an act of meditation or a religious act.'

Elise smiled.

'That reminds me of the great spiritual conversation I once had with a rabbi – in a full and noisy coffee-shop. But…go on.'

Jean-Pierre said nothing for a few moments, then stood and fetched a book.

'As a student of literature, I imagine you know Wordsworth's *Lines Composed a Few Miles above Tintern Abbey*? He read the book:

"And I have felt
A presence that disturbs me with the joy
Of elevated thoughts; a sense sublime

Of something far more deeply interfused,
Whose dwelling is the light of setting suns,
And the round ocean and the living air,
And the blue sky, and in the mind of man:
A motion and a spirit, that impels
All thinking things, all objects of all thought,
And rolls through all things. Therefore am I still
A lover of the meadows and the woods
And mountains; and of all that we behold
From this green earth;"

Is that what you think *we* might be talking about, Elise? Feelings that come from within in response to stimulus from without?'

'I love the beauty of the natural world, and even perhaps, as a nine-year-old in the cathedral, great beauty in the forms of colour and music captivated me. However, the death of two children, the murder of a young man, or the death of Terry are where both you and I have been encountered, as you put it don't fit Wordsworth's romantic schema. And I once had an experience, perhaps even an encounter, when I was on holiday for a few days in the Pennines, hills in the north of England. I was out walking alone in a remote place when suddenly the weather changed, and I was in fog, wind and rain. There was no natural beauty, but an overwhelming sense of, yes, I use your word, encounter. It was undramatic and without speech of any kind, and how long it lasted I couldn't say – seconds, minutes hours even – and then equally as undramatically, it was past. I don't think Wordsworth was describing that.'

'Perhaps what you and I are seeing is always there but of which we have the merest glimpse.'

'I might be able to think that but for the facticity, if there is such a word, not just feelings. I *was there* for Gail, for the two children, and for Terry. Your own account of the murder victim echoes those, but in each instance, I was there almost as if they were waiting ready for me.'

'Yes, I know, and it's impossible for me to disagree and I'm not trying to test you, because I'm questioning myself constantly, and your presence with me is the next and possible last encounter. I don't think we are talking about coincidence, Elise and neither do you. I think you were chosen, and I now know the same for me. I have a question for us though: doesn't being chosen imply a chooser?'

Elise stood up.

'Jean-Pierre, I need to stop, to attend to nature, not above Tintern Abbey, but in my body. My therapist tells me it's all to do with my vagus nerve.'

'How silly of me! The bathroom's through the door on the left.'

Elise followed the instructions whilst Pierre collected the empty bowls and removed them to the sink and began making more coffee. When Elise returned, she could see what he was doing.

'Don't you have any tea?'

Jean-Pierre laughed.

'It's clear you have been well and truly Anglicised. Yes, I keep some in for moments like this. Am I obliged to sing God Save the Queen as I make it?'

'No, but I'm sure it will be much improved if I make it!'

They sat more comfortably, away from the table.

'My friend Kim's brother Fergus, is an academic interested in chronicling and relating alleged contemporary religious and other experiences to those of medieval mystics. I have given thought to asking him what he makes of my experiences.'

'I can imagine his work is most interesting, and more medieval writings are being discovered, so we know more than once we did,' said Jean-Pierre. 'I have read some of these medieval mystics and learned much from them, and interestingly a great number of them seem to have been women. I can certainly understand why you might wish to share with him some of your own experiences.'

'I sense a "but" on the horizon.'

Jean-Pierre smiled.

'But,' he began, and smiled again, 'you have not described your experiences as religious, and what sort of consideration might an academic give to your encounters with Gail, Terry and the two children who died in your arms other than in terms of coincidence? And how would you react if, having listened to you, he dismissed your claims as fantasy? He will have met many claiming direct communication with various deities, some malevolent and others trivial. Do you want to be another interesting claim added to his files?

'You require no authentication from anyone, Elise, neither from Fergus or me and I have explained why, but I want to return to the question you dodged by needing to visit the bathroom. I asked if being chosen, which you and I know we were, implies a chooser?'

'Jean-Pierre, this is a hard question to answer, because the implications are considerable, and if I may say, made even more complicated by the fact that I'm a rabbi and a Catholic at one and the same time.'

'Yes.'

'If I say no, then it would be to deny my sense of having been there for a reason, and therefore regarding what I encountered as more or less coincidence and a figment of an over-active imagination. If I say yes, then what are the implications for the way I now live as a rabbi? And the worst aspect of all this is that I can't simply blame you for making me face these things. The question has long been there, and I knew it, and preferred to avoid it. But I can't endlessly visit the loo, or bathroom as you call it (though, I must add in passing, there is no bath!), to avoid the question. And if it's true that this morning there has been another encounter, and I have learned that many years ago you baptised and confirmed me (though I don't know what the latter means), you are the only person who can assist me face those implications, and I'm due to return home in a few days, and I have to make the most of being here.'

'Whoa there, Elise! First you find fault with my loo – what a bizarre word to use – and then choose to invest me with magic powers I don't possess. I came here to get away from people doing that to me.'

'Now you're avoiding *my* question. If what we are sharing is true, it means that what brought me here was not to be near to Nancy being told things I didn't want to hear, but to meet you again even though I didn't know we had already met. And here we are. But to return I need more.'

'I baptised you, Elise and, for a reason I didn't understand, then confirmed you, something only done in later childhood or for adult converts, never done at the baptism of a child, and gave you the name of Mary. It means that you are fully a Catholic.'

'Well, thanks for that! I can just imagine my next Shabbat sermon mentioning it! Jean-Pierre, I need more.'

"At the still point of the turning world, Neither flesh nor fleshless:

Neither from nor towards; at the still point, there the dance is ...

...Descend lower, descend only into the world of perpetual solitude..."

That may be all I can offer you, Elise. I return to these words from *Burnt Norton* again and again, more even than to the other Quartets. TS Eliot certainly wrote truly even if he didn't necessarily know what he was writing. Need anything be different? I mean that you have known these experiences and encounters not because you sought them, but because they happened to you as you are and have been, but I should warn you it's not impossible that you may be used again.'

'You're such a comfort, Jean-Pierre, I don't think! But what am I to do about that? I can hardly be a Catholic Rabbi?'

'Would you come with me? No one has ever seen what I am now going to show you.'

Elise followed Jean-Pierre along the passage into a small room with space for perhaps two people, but no more. The walls were a gentle pastel green and there was a small window. A small table stood at the end with a book and unlit candle on it, next to a stool.

'This is the waiting room. I spend at least two hours each day, just waiting, doing nothing and trying to think nothing. It's not Buddhist meditation nor that pale and sorry westernised imitation known as mindfulness. In silence, I wait. And today, my waiting has been rewarded.'

They stood together in silence. After at least ten minutes, though it may have been longer, as Elise lost all sense of time, she heard Jean-Pierre say, 'Now we must have some coffee and cake.'

He led her out of the room, though Elise had wanted to remain and even felt she could go on standing there for hours, despite the spartan conditions, or perhaps because of them. If this was religion, then it was nothing she had ever come across before.

Elise sat down with no idea of what time it might be. She watched her host making the coffee and then coming towards her with what seemed to be a rich fruit cake. As she took it, he said, 'It comes with a warning: I made it myself.'

She bit into the cake and nodded her approval.

'The Enlightenment set in motion a great change and change is now becoming the constant, but on its way here not threw out a great deal. Yes, we now understand considerably more about ourselves in terms of the body and the mind. Your companion, Kim, as a psychotherapist will understand a great deal about the latter, and I think we shall soon be learning a great deal more about how the brain operates. But I have come to rely more and more on the ancient and now largely discarded notion of the soul. The scientists and the psychologists will tell you it doesn't exist, that it's just a way of speaking about our experiences or even more likely, our fantasies.

'So, allow me to tell you about Marty. He was just 32 and had become a father three days before, who whilst making a drink in the kitchen, fell down dead of an aortic aneurism. Just two days afterwards I was saying mass when suddenly one of the altar candles exploded sending wax everywhere. Then the PA system we use in church began making bizarre noises before cutting out completely. There seemed no apparent reason, so I continued but then, equally unexpectedly, it burst into life again, at full volume. The people laughed of course, but I did not, because I knew that Marty, who was not actually a Catholic, was present and not yet at peace. So, on the following morning with just the angels and archangels present, I said a requiem mass for Marty and told him that he could now be at rest. That's not an exorcism, just the effect of the mass. There was no repeat and I said nothing to anyone, but I knew he was now at peace.'

'There were always prayers at the bedside at the hospice when someone died – "commending", I think they were called.'

'"Commendatory", probably, helping the person on their way, but not the body nor the mind in the brain. I experienced Marty's presence. It was real, and I was able to use the requiem to help him on his way.'

With the coffee mug in her hand and a piece of cake already eaten, Elise knew the time had come to gather what she would need to take away with her.

'I'm ready,' she said.

'And I am too. I can now let go.'

'You mean you are ready to die?'

'Of course, though I shall continue my daily vigil until the time comes. But you need not concern yourself with me. You have done the needful by coming here, and now you must return to the normality of your life. But Elise, you need the silence. Perhaps two hours each day is a lot to ask as you begin, but you should begin. It takes time to get the rhythm of the dance. I shouldn't trouble your brain with much reading about any of this and you mustn't trouble yourself with trying to believe anything. In Lewis Carroll's great story, the White Queen tells Alice to *make* herself believe things, claiming she could make herself believe six impossible things before breakfast! Lewis Carroll in the guise of Alice knew it can't be done, no matter how hard you might try, so don't try and you never know what might come.

'Just get on with your daily living as you have been doing. Be ordinary and nothing special. Don't get involved with religion unless you absolutely have to and always expect nothing but to go on waiting and, of course, loving. But Elise, I don't really need to say any of these things to you, because you know them.'

Elise put down her empty plate and finished her coffee.

'We might not meet again in this world, Father Jean-Pierre, and perhaps we don't need to. You were in my beginning and perhaps brought all this about, though neither of us shall ever know. I will read the Four Quartets again soon, because as I have sat here with you, they came into my mind with a clarity wholly lacking before.'

'Eliot, like you, was born on this side of the Atlantic and went to England. The final words of *The Journey of the Magi*, are just for me.'

'"I should be glad of another death"?' said Elise.

Jean-Pierre smiled.

'It's always interesting to discover what sticks in our minds. Now go. I shall miss the warmth of your presence, but much will remain.'

Elise stood.

'Am I allowed to hold you close, Jean-Pierre?'

'Why not, I held you in my arms at our first meeting long ago, so I should do so again at our last.'

They hugged for a long time, and both had tears on their cheeks.

Elise took a last look via the rear-view mirror at Jean-Pierre whose arm was raised in a wave, or was it a blessing?

She drove the Buick back to the normality of life and death in Bracebridge, though just what she was going to tell of her morning, she had no idea.

An End and a Beginning

Kim and Pen had obviously had a wonderful morning shopping, and had returned with gifts for Kim's family, and when asked, as they sat down to pizzas, Elise replied that Jean-Pierre and she had met and shared experiences from their work. It was true in so far as it went, and they seemed satisfied, though Elise knew from a look from Nancy that she at least knew better!

'I'm feeling guilty,' began Kim, as she and Elise relaxed on their beds for a post-lunch snooze, 'I'm having such a good holiday whilst your aunt is dying, and you've received pretty horrendous news from her about your father's attempted sexual assault. I feel I ought to be attending to you as you brought me for support, but it hasn't quite worked out like that.'

'A psychotherapist feeling guilty seems somehow inappropriate,' replied Elise with a gentle laugh. 'The reality is that I've had a lot of business to deal with from the past which I will have to begin working through when we get back. In the meantime, I'm so glad you are enjoying being here in Bracebridge, and I'm still hoping to get you into a canoe up at Duck Chutes. I guess much now depends on how Nancy is. I feel I have to give her as much of myself as I can, and perhaps freeing Pen a little to enjoy showing you why this area was so hard for me to leave all those years ago. So, please, Kim, continue to make the most of a holiday. You know your clients will be waiting for you, not to mention the new course. None of them can reach you here, so enjoy the freedom.'

'I am so grateful to you, Elise, and when we get back if I can do anything to give you support in dealing with what's come up here, you know you can rely on me.'

'Thank you.'

After their rest, Elise went in to see Nancy.

'So, you just had a nice chat with Jean-Pierre then, though it lasted four hours.'

'Perhaps it was more than just a nice chat.'

'Yes, he doesn't do them.'

'He cooks an amazing porridge and makes a great fruit cake. The most important thing was that he took all I had to say seriously, not just out of respect, as we might politely listen to someone chatting away, but because we were in tune together.

'We shared quite a lot about life as it has been. He's very happy there, and whilst I can well imagine how good a priest he was, I know just how settled and fulfilled he is living the life of a solitary monk.

'I conveyed to him that the happening you noticed all those years ago, Nancy, in the cathedral at the Easter service had sort of occurred again. He said that the reality of the experience didn't depend on particular religious beliefs and that if they come, they are to be received, and then give way, as they have done, to normality. And, of course, he told me how my mother had approached him and asked for baptism and how he had acceded immediately to her wholly unusual request, possibly binding him and me in a peculiar way.'

Elise said nothing about the unusual confirmation nor the name she had been given.

It had been a warm day and in the late afternoon as the temperature fell, Pen suggested that she take Elise and Kim to Duck Chutes, as she had been able to obtain the key to the shack up there, knowing it contained a canoe.

'Alas,' she said as they prepared to leave, 'at this time up there in the woods the mozzies will be hyper-active, so ladies, before we go we need to cover ourselves in lemon juice to keep them off.'

Smelling like odd cocktails the three women brought out the

canoe, and Elise had first go, delighted to realise her old skills were still active. She took the boat out of the lake downstream to where, many years earlier she has seen her first beaver. It was a lovely and special as she had remembered, and Wordsworth would have been moved at the way the sun played through the trees, the leaves of which were just beginning to turn.

It was next the turn of Kim, but she stayed close to the shore though clearly enjoying herself, and not least the ribbing she received from the other two. Pen had brought a little food and drink which they ate at the water's edge, and she spoke movingly of just how much she was longing to bring Greg here later in the Fall.

'I do think you guys should come again in the winter, perhaps over Christmas. Elise won't tell you, Kim, but I will, that she was a quite outstanding skier in her young days. I should think the skills would still be there, and I'd love you to come.'

'It sounds amazing from what you've told me, Pen, though I'm pretty sure I would be spending more time on my bottom than on any skis I tried to put on.'

Once again, Elise noticed a communication between Kim and Pen, unspoken but apparent.'

'You two have both been through difficult marriages, so it must be a huge help for you to share your experiences.' Elise said.

'It has. Sometimes the only real understanding about this sort of thing is possible with someone who has been through the same experiences,' said Pen, Kim nodding her head.

'That's undoubtedly true,' added Elise, meaning something quite different to what they were speaking of.

In the morning Elise asked Nancy if she could do her wash and brush her hair instead of Pen who sensed it was important that niece and aunt had some time together alone. She and Kim went out for a walk downtown to the bookstore Kim had expressed an interest in.

Elise had noticed that in the last 24 hours Nancy's condition had worsened and that she was now quite frail. Her voice her voice had quietened and assumed a gentleness almost like her own.'

'Have you recovered?' her aunt asked Elise now sat alongside the bed after all the personal care had been done.

Elise smiled.

'If you mean what I think you mean, then it might take me a lifetime. I didn't know, and how could I, but it's clear that my coming was for more even than being with you.'

'I am so glad you're here, Elise, but I also knew that the point of your being here was to link up again with the priest who baptised you.'

'Ah well, he didn't just baptise me, Nancy. He told me yesterday that after he baptised me, he did something he had never done before nor since, he confirmed me.'

Elise could see that Nancy had tears in her eyes.

'I was right. Your visit has been meant and now my part is over.'

'No. Your part has made a beginning possible, aunt. Jean-Pierre and I would never underestimate the enormity of your part in all this.'

'What name were you given?'

'Mary.'

'Elise Mary, my niece. Yes, yes, yes.'

Nancy closed her eyes and looked settled as she drifted off to sleep. Elise sat with her, wanting to be there for when she awoke again. Nancy's breathing was slow but even, though Elise knew that the diamorphine cocktail she was taking to deal with the pain would also in time completely suppress her breathing and allow her to drift away. She gazed at her with profound love in her heart.

She was suddenly aware of having fallen asleep herself in a room that was very warm but was now brought back by a moan from Nancy. As Elise looked, Nancy's face looked skewed up in what she assumed must be pain. She reached out her hand and placed it on her forehead and murmured words of comfort. Suddenly she realised what she had done, and looking and listening, she realised that Nancy had died.

The Waiting Room (2)

At the requiem mass for Nancy held on the evening before she and Kim returned home, Elise had glimpsed Jean-Pierre at the back of the church as the service began. As he had come forward to receive communion, he surreptitiously handed Elise a book. It was a collection of sayings of the so-called Desert Fathers of the 4th and 5th centuries who fled from the corruptions of the cities and their churches to live as solitaries, or in groups of monks, in the deserts of Egypt. He had highlighted the first two sayings:

Abba Arsenius prayed to God, and said, "O Lord, direct me how to live"; and a voice came to him, saying, "Arsenius, flee from men, and thou shalt live."

And when Arsenius was living the ascetic life in the monastery, he prayed to God the same prayer, and again he heard a voice saying unto him, "Arsenius, flee, keep silence, and lead a life of silent contemplation".

And so she had.

The locals, though few in number, thought her odd, no matter how pleasant she was, for who, and one so young, would choose to live an isolated life on the moors with frequent bitterly cold winds from the east and the ever-present threat of snow in winter? For Elise it could sometimes feel like the Canada she had left when she was 14, and she didn't mind the cold nor the snow. She still had her car and the roads up to her house were good as they had once been adapted for military vehicles when the RAF had been here. That was especially useful when she had visitors, though they were few. It was a long way from almost everywhere, but that is what Elise had sought and she never felt lonely.

She awoke at 4:30 as she usually did but from the first moment there was a note of excitement already within. Today Leah was coming to stay. Elise would drive into York to collect her from the train. It was not her first visit but she loved her closest friend and had prepared everything in advance.

Leah had been the first person told that she was not returning to the rabbinate, nor training to be a counsellor. As she drove from Scarborough on the A64 past Malton, she recalled that meeting, now almost five years earlier, and how expecting a negative response from her friend was delighted to be told that at last she would be able to do what she was meant to be doing in this world, even though at that stage Elise had no idea what that might be! This was echoed by Susie who gave her great encouragement to think creatively. The response of Janice at the synagogue had been less positive, perhaps understandably, as it meant she was she was left working alone, but they stayed friends and when the time came to leave the city, Janice had proved her friendship by all the help and support she gave Elise on move day.

Eastmoor had been an out-station from the Fylingdales Early Warning Station, but then abandoned, leaving in place a comfortable house and several outbuildings, most of which were still much as they had been left by the RAF. The base was just a handful of miles away, and Elise had been able to buy the house and land for an excellent price, mainly because no one else was interested.

The train was on time and the two women threw themselves into the arms of the others. It had been over four months since they had last met. One of the features of their close friendship was the capacity for total honesty and a shared delight in cream-filled pastries, so having put her luggage into the car, Elise led Leah to Betty's Tea Rooms in St Helen's Square, which was typically very busy in what was the run up to Christmas. They had to queue for almost half an hour in Betty's, but they talked ceaselessly, and the wait was worth it!

'You're looking a little more matronly, Leah. Too much good food?'

'And not enough exercise. I'm thinking of joining a Jewish gym to see if that will help.'

'A Jewish gym! Who would have thought it.'

'And they have a mikveh attached, so for women at the end of the periods they can exercise first and cleanse afterwards! I'm not sure the Orthodox approve, but who cares? But are you eating properly up in your eyrie?'

'I guess you'll find out when we get there, but I shop regularly and eat nourishing food though it's never easy cooking for one?'

'Dare I ask if it's kosher?'

'On my Jewish days it is, on my Catholic days it's not.'

'Oh, Elise, you are a scream.'

'I think I've worked out a good pattern for myself given how odd I am.'

'You've always been the most sane person I know – you know, a woman living alone on the North York Moors in a lonely and windswept place near the cliffs – what could be more sane?'

They laughed and decided on just one more cream horn each!'

Once at the house, Leah looked around her and smiled.

'As I said, lonely and windswept!'

'It's true that sometimes when I go out for my daily walk I get a bit windswept though I don't object to that, but I have never once in five years felt lonely. I get on well with myself, and with the local farmer and the occasional postman, though of course they think I'm barmy.'

'Do you have a television?'

'No. Besides which there probably wouldn't be a signal here. I do listen to the news on Radio 4 at lunchtime and some music on Radio 3.

'And are you still linked in with the Association of Solitaries, or whatever it's called?'

'The Fellowship of Solitaries it's called, and yes, though I'm what's called an Associate member as the others all call themselves

Christian, and I call myself nothing at all. But yes, we do communicate from time to time, and there are two Greek Orthodox nuns living near Whitby, in a remote ex-farm. One is in her 80s and fierce so I don't have a lot of contact, but their little church is certainly very beautiful with its icons and candles.'

And what about you, Elise? Are you still feeling the same level of commitment to being here and being all by yourself, and doing whatever it is you feel called to do.'

'It's more a case not doing, or at least I try to achieve that. On one or two days in the past five years I've even managed it.'

'Once or twice in five years? That's not what I would have expected to hear.'

'You're just a hard taskmaster, Leah Jacobs. If I told some of the solitaries of history that I had managed it once or twice in my silence, they would accuse me of an unlikely boast!'

That evening the food was a mushroom risotto followed by what Leah thought might be porridge oats with pieces of fruit, but which Elise called Granola, and onto which she poured fresh, albeit unpasteurised milk from the nearby farm.

After their supper Leah brought Elise up to date with news from the synagogue and the girls' school, in which Elise was greatly interested. She loved the family and so many of the others at the synagogue community amongst whom she had learned so very much about Judaism. She noticed however that Leah had said little about her husband.

'And what of Jerry, Leah? You've hardly mentioned him.'

'You may recall from my last visit that we'd had a difficult time on our summer holiday. Jerry seemed so withdrawn and I had to do most of the entertainment for Ruth and Sarah, which isn't like him. But it's got worse in the last couple of months. He's not like himself. He's irritable with the three of us, even over small things and the girls have noticed it.'

'Is it work?'

'I don't think so. He has a good balance between the hospital and his private work, mostly with Jewish patients, so he gets variety, not to mention a lot of money. I just don't know what it is, other than knowing it's something.'

'Does he still attend synagogue?'

'You know how assiduous he was when you were living with us in not just attending but being involved in community life in so many ways. And suddenly he has stopped. He hasn't been on Shabbat for quite some time.'

'What about Yom Kippur?'

'He stayed home of course but didn't go to the synagogue. And I don't think the new Rabbi would want to risk asking if anything was wrong; she's not the sort to challenge a man, and certainly not a hospital consultant.'

Elise laughed.

'Then why is she a rabbi? It's ok, don't answer. But perhaps you might suggest he sees someone like Susie. If there's something he's not attending to inside him, he may need help getting to it. I know I did.'

'The problem is that he is a consultant, and as you know many consultants think highly of themselves, and would not dare to dare to admit need. I suggested it just once ever so gently, and almost had my head bitten off.'

'That doesn't sound like the Jerry I knew, and perhaps indicates that he recognised you were nearer the truth he doesn't want to face.'

'He's also withdrawn from me over the past year, sexually I mean, so his inner difficulty, whatever may be the cause, is having a negative effect on our life together, and the girls ask me what the matter with him is.'

'If the rabbi won't talk to him, have you asked him directly why he has stopped going to synagogue?'

'I did, just two weeks ago. He shrugged and said, "Things change" and left it at that.'

'Well, yes, I am the last person on the face of the earth to claim that things don't change, but I wasn't married.'

'Oh Elise, your change was earth-shattering for many of us,' said Leah with some force. 'It may have been complex for you but to turn your back on the rabbinate and in effect, Judaism, and then to claim you are also now a Catholic, was utterly disturbing to those who knew and loved you. And you can't say buying a remote house on a cliff edge in Yorkshire was just a phase you were going through. We all thought you were mad and many of the community in London and Cambridge accuse you of betrayal and apostasy. And did it not play a part in your mother's illness?'

'The only people I felt I could rely on when it all came about were you and Susie. I know you must have felt the pain, but you remained utterly constant in your love which I needed and have continued to do so. From that I derived so much strength. And Susie gave me the courage.'

'Do you see her?'

'No though I would love her to come as she inspired me to make the big change we both knew was necessary, but enabling an ordinary relationship with someone who's been your therapist and in effect knows everything and one or two other things is not easy.'

'And what about your friend Kim, who you took to Canada. Are you still in touch?'

'Mostly by letter. You'll recall that only three months after we returned home, she returned to Canada, to Bracebridge, and is in practice there. She and Penny seem to be so very happy together. She let me know about the death of my former priest friend Fr Jean-Pierre. I cried and cried, which is, I suppose, odd, because he and I met him just three times and one of those was when I was a baby.'

'He was the person who made you a Catholic?'

Elise laughed.

'I think becoming a Catholic involves a lot more than that, but yes, he baptised me, and then we met again, and set me on this course of life. Kim said he had been found by two walkers in the woodland he loved, and I'm sure his was a good death, but as I say, I cried and cried, which I didn't when my mum died. The hospital called me, and I left at once but, perhaps just to spite me, mum died shortly before I got there. I stayed in her house until after the funeral. With her will was a letter to me, in which she expressed her sense of a failed life – failure to protect me, to leave my dad when she knew he was a crook, forcing me to leave my homeland, and not telling me anything about her Jewish identity. Last of all she apologised for never telling me about my baptism which she said she did in the hope it would serve to protect me. And she ended the letter by saying that what I was doing up here proved that she had at least got the baptism bit right. That amazed me. She left everything to me, so all in all, my dearest Leah, I'm a wealthy person with little idea what to do with it.'

'Elise, are you a Catholic?'

'I've always been one even when though I'm also Jewish through and through. When I fill in documents, I now put my name as Elise Mary Rosewarne, which is almost hilarious because I have discovered that there is an Anglican solitary nun living just outside York called Sister Elsie Mary. I haven't met her of course, as we're both solitaries and, by definition, we don't meet, but she sends me nice cards to which I always reply.'

'What an odd coincidence. Oh, sorry, you don't believe in coincidences, do you?'

'Leah, dear heart, indeed dearest heart whom I love, you know I don't do beliefs of any kind, but I do know that when our old Rabbi Samuel brought you and I together it was meant to be.'

'And I know that too, I don't need to believe it!'

Leah

When Leah woke up, she could find no trace of Elise other than a note by the kettle saying she would be back in time for breakfast at 8:00. Slightly late, Elise arrived at the back door wearing a green overall.

'I've been doing the milking! Do you not recall that from your previous visits?'

'I have to say I'd forgotten.'

'I'm there every morning now, and even if I say so myself, I've become remarkably proficient. When Jim had flu, I did it by myself on a couple of mornings.'

'But doesn't it disturb the pattern of your day, your silence I mean?'

'No. I rise at 4:00, have a quick cup of tea, dress and spend about 10 minutes in my silence room, and then cycle to the farm. I come back, shower and eat but as a special treat to you I'm making our porridge first, and then I'll have a shower. The smell will do you no harm though I don't notice it now even though when we're done there's usually no small amount of slurry to be removed and the parlour hosed down. As a special treat because you're here, Jim was finishing off this morning.'

'Oh!' said Leah. 'I've just realised this is a dream, and in a minute I'll wake up and find myself still in bed.'

Elise laughed.

'I think if you catch a whiff from my overall before I take it off and put in the wash, you'll know it's not a dream, though in a way for me it is part of the dream I am living day by day. Doing the morning milking has become a natural part of my life now.'

'Do you have to do it twice a day?'

'Jim does, but in the afternoon, he has a farmhand who helps him, though Jim says I'm much better than him.'

'Do they know what you're doing here? That you're a Catholic rabbi living as a solitary?'

'Better than anyone, Leah, and in fact only you, know that even I'm not all that sure what I'm doing here other than following the promptings.'

'That's a good description.'

'Yes, I'm rather fond of it. It doesn't make me sound too ridiculously arrogant claiming anything more. Even after five years I can't do that for myself, let alone for anyone else, though there is one thing I have come to understand, and perhaps it's the only one so far. It is that although I live alone much as other solitaries do, I am not alone. I am bound up with the whole of humanity because I'm part of it and whatever it is that I know here, it doesn't belong just in special places such as this. What I know is that it is everywhere, and we all live within it. As a solitary I am bound up with others in a way I don't understand but which keeps me here, not for my sake but for others.'

'I'm not sure I understand,' said Leah.

'That's how it's meant to be, Leah. So often our attempts at understanding are attempts at grabbing power and self-importance. Just look at the history of religion everywhere. Power and self-importance cannot find a hold here, and that is why in a funny way the solitary is one with powerless people everywhere. Perhaps that's why it's been so many deaths that have brought me to this place where I can confront life and death with no distractions.'

'If that's an attempt at helping me understand more, then you've failed.'

'That goes without saying as any solitary can tell you.'

Elise had now shed the overall and was in a sweater and jeans. Leah could see how well and strong she looked, and for the first time could see that this odd life had, perhaps unexpectedly, made her more obviously physically attractive than once she had seemed. And at 39 she was still a young woman, though Leah smiled to herself when she considered what sort of man could take her on, unless of course it was Farmer Jim venturing into bigamy!

'This is unusual porridge,' said Leah as they ate together, 'tasty and enjoyable, but unusual.'

'Yes, it's what I call meal porridge. I make it myself based on a something I once had in Canada. It gets me through.'

'I notice you've bought a rather fancy coffee machine.'

'I haven't taken a vow of poverty, you know, nor for that matter of chastity or obedience, though I volunteer my obedience, so why not have the means of making good coffee? I buy the beans and grind them myself. So, can I in interest you in a cup? And over coffee you can tell me all about how being head of the maths department is going.'

After a prolonged breakfast, Elise put the washing machine on and then said she would now disappear for a while and that possibly they might go for a walk later. Leah took advantage of Elise's absence to do some reading, something which her work and two teenage twin daughters did not often allow.

Walking towards the cliffs and the many thousands of different types of seabirds that almost drowned their conversation, Leah once again began to speak about Jerry.

'There was or is, I should say, a registrar, called Joan, though by now when Jerry mentions her, she's "Joanie". Jerry spoke highly of her from the first and when I met her in the department, I could see people thought well of her – obviously on her way up though still in her early 30s, and very pretty. There was a conference in Hanover for ENT specialists and Jerry told me all his team would be going, but by accident I discovered from one of the nurses I spoke to when calling Jerry at work, that only Mr Jacobs and Miss Wainwright were going. I gave Jerry an opportunity to tell me this by mentioning the trip, but he didn't change his story. Just the two attended, and even on his return he persisted with the story that the whole surgical team were with him.'

'Did you not challenge him?'

'No. Cowardly, but I thought to myself that I still love him and we need him, and that I didn't want to risk that for what was probably nothing more than a sort of mid-life silly fling with a girl more than 20 years his junior. It struck me that he had most to lose, because surely this sort of thing couldn't be hidden from colleagues, even if the lady in question does not boast about her catch. So I said nothing and once I'd set out on that path, it's difficult to stop.'

'Have there been other excursions?'

'Doctors are always attending events of various kinds, especially consultants, many of which involve weekends away, and that means being away for Shabbat. I'm not sure the lady in question is Jewish.'

'Oh Leah, my dearest friend,' said Elise stopping and taking hold of her hands, 'I'm so sorry for you and the girls, because they are the ones who suffer most. I know from the car-crash of my parent's marriage that what you're going through must be really scary. How long has it been like this?'

'The Hanover conference was more than three months ago. Since then, his lists have seemingly become longer and keep him later, and sometimes he says he stays over at the hospital as if he were a junior on call.'

'Surely he realises you are aware of what's going on. Jerry's not stupid.'

'But just possibly he thinks I am.'

'And we both know you're not. I regret to say that he would not be the first man who getting older, has his head turned by a young woman. The male menopause I've heard it called. Apart from telling me have you mentioned it to anyone else – the rabbi for example?'

'As I mentioned last night, she's so young and inexperienced that I wouldn't want to say any of this to her and not altogether sure she would want me to. So, the only person I can speak to has to be a hermit on the North York Moors!'

Elise laughed and continued to walk holding Leah's hand as they did so.

'I hope you know that I would always want to be there for you. You, the girls and Jerry too, matter so very much to me after the ways in which you loved and cared for me, that all you say hurts me so very much. But it would appear to me from the absolutely safe eyrie I occupy with all these seabirds, you can either continue as you are, saying and doing nothing, perhaps in the hope that it will end and that he will come to his senses, or you can be proactive, first of all so he knows you know, and then that you are not prepared to let it continue. I think you should expect him to deny it, but he needs to know you know his denial is a lie.'

'Elise, you live as a solitary on the North York Moors, how on earth do you know about this sort of thing?' said Leah with a laugh.

'I haven't always been a weirdo! Like you, I was a Samaritan for quite some time, and I have used my eyes and ears to learn, but more than anything else I'm a human being, and knowing how I would operate an adulterous affair makes me think how Jerry might.'

'And do you wonder if you will ever have someone special in your life, and I don't just mean friends like me.'

'There are no other friends like you, Leah. All I know is that here I am and will remain unless I'm prompted to do otherwise. You know because I have told you that Fr Jean-Pierre made it clear to me that his and my calling, if that's the right word, was to wait in silence, and so in silence I wait even though I don't know what for.'

'Perhaps you should advertise yourself as someone who can listen to others and encourage their own waiting.'

'No chance. I would draw the wrong sort of attention which I don't want. No, I wait.'

'And you're suggesting I should now *stop* waiting and do something about my situation.'

'I want only the best for you and the girls, though I want only the best for Jerry as well, and he will never do better than with you.'

They shared the Friday night meal at the beginning of Shabbat with the customary lighting of candles and prayers, though Elise had told Leah she did not keep it as different from any other day for each day to her was holy. As they ate, Leah said, 'Elise, it's no use telling me you don't think about what you are doing here in this life. I can't believe that, so what are you thinking?'

'Simply, I think of myself as someone who lives according to inner promptings – I've told you that, and Susie, who in psychotherapeutic terms was no pushover urged me to follow them. I really do try very hard not to think in any kind of religious or philosophical way about what I'm doing because I know I just don't have the words. All I have is the experience which requires no external authentication, and I would like to hope it's growing as each day passes similar to the sort of awareness that others have tried to describe from aeons ago, sages, wise men and women, desert fathers and mothers, mystics of all types. I also read a lot of poetry aloud for relaxation but here, Leah, out on the edge, I'm as free as the birds on the cliffs that fly out to sea, and I'm as happy as anyone can hope to be, especially when my wonderful Leah comes to stay.'

'Are you still Jewish, Elise?'

'Leah! I'm shocked. You now that I can never cease to be Jewish. My mother was Jewish so, q.e.d I'm a Jew, and proud to be, but I no longer feel bound by one of the various forms Judaism has adapted and adopted. Cows have to be milked on Shabbat, but every day for me is a day of rest in the arms of HaShem or whatever other name is given to what people sometimes call God but which, like the name "Jesus Christ," are strangely most often used as swear words without people thinking what they are saying. As Jews we are wise to say HaShem, the Name, and as a Jew I refer only to Yeshua, "Jesus Christ" being the Greek translation used by Paul to try to convince Gentiles that this new religion he created was not Jewish nor he himself, hence his own change of name from Saul. Do you not know the doggerel "Roses are reddish, Violets are bluish, if it wasn't for Christmas, we'd all be Jewish"?'

'There are others such as "How odd / of God / to choose / the Jews" to which someone replied: "But not so odd / as those who choose / a Jewish God / and hate the Jews". I repudiate nothing but seek to live without needing to describe me or the Reality that seems to know me.'

Barbara

With the half-term break over, once milking and porridge were finished, Elise drove Leah into York, though even on a Sunday morning the traffic in the centre of the city was considerable.

'You know my daily routine but if ever you need to call me do so. If I'm out leave a message on the answering machine and I'll call you back. Just tell me the times when it would be best do so. You know, my dearest Leah, that I invest so very much love in you and the girls, and in your errant husband too, so please take good care of that investment.'

'Thank you for letting me stay. You send me away with so much to consider, but with the sense that however odd it might seem to some, you are in the right place.'

'Let's just agree that I'm in the right place for now. Who knows, for both of us, what might become known?'

On Christmas Day as a special gift for Jim, Elise undertook to do the milking herself. The cows had been kind and Jim had made a real effort to allow her to do so without sneaking a quick check. He and Audrey invited her for lunch with their children and grandchildren, at which for the first time since arriving here she actually had a drink of sparkling wine. She enjoyed it so much she realised why in the history of monasticism so many monks had made wine!

Less joyous was a phone call from Leah to say that she had finally confronted Jerry about his affair. He had replied that it wasn't an affair but the preparation for marriage, and that he would be moving out and moving in with Miss Wainwright ("he actually called her that, Elise", Leah had said). The synagogue community was shocked by the news, but Leah had quickly become aware that such things were considerably more common than she had perhaps realised even within the community.

At the year's turning, Elise felt profoundly sad about the tidings from London. But worse was to come just three days into January. When Kim had informed her that she was emigrating in the eventual hope of marriage to Pen, she had mentioned that this news had plunged one of her clients into considerable distress. Barbara, she had said to Elise was an unhappy person who had become very dependent on her, and perhaps she had allowed this to continue unchallenged for too long. In her last letter from Canada, Pen said she had mentioned Elise to Barbara as someone she might occasionally talk to about matters of faith, which had not pleased Elise, but since then she had heard nothing, so thought it was unlikely now to happen. Until 3rd January.

The call came just as the light began to fade in the mid-afternoon.

'Hello, it that Lisa? My name if Barbara, and Kim who was my therapist, gave me your number and said I could call you if I needed to do so.'

'Hello Barbara, my name is actually Elise not Lisa, but I'm afraid I can't be of much help to you. I am not a counsellor or therapist, and I don't have the sort of skills Kim possessed.'

'She told me you were a Samaritan.'

'I was, though I gave that up more than five years ago.'

'Oh, but I bet you were good. You have the loveliest voice, so comforting.'

'As I said, I've not worked at the Samaritans for a long time though I'm sure you could call them, and they would be able to help you.'

'I think it's too late for that.'

Elise at once felt alarmed.

'What do you mean by too late?'

'Too late for me. I've lost everything. I had a husband, and still technically have, but he's not interested in me, and I suspect he has someone else. He's a policeman who works in the armoury, handing out guns when needed. He's a horrible man. My two children have grown up and gone away and I hardly ever see them, even at Christmas they didn't come. And of course, I lost Kim whom I really loved now some years ago and I miss her terribly. I'm sure you can understand why anyone might love Kim. And she's moved to America somewhere and is getting married. I loved her so much because she really cared for me as me even though I'm worth very little in this world. No one loves me and that's why it's too late for things to be different.'

'That sounds like it's been a pretty tough Christmas for you.'

'The last couple of years, Lisa, have been just awful and now it's supposed to be a new year and frankly there's nothing new to look forward to, just more of the old. And now it's too late.'

'Barbara, you keep saying it's too late. Please tell me what you mean by too late. It's important.'

'No, not any more, nothing is important.'

'Where do you live, Barbara?'

'In a place called Littleport. It's near Ely where there's a big cathedral.'

'Yes, I've been to Ely. It's lovely. Would it help if I was to get someone to call and see you, so you could talk these things over? I live hundreds of miles away.'

Elise was thinking she might ring Fergus and see if he could suggest someone to call in on Barbara, a vicar say, or just anyone.

'No, I've told you, it's too late.'

'Barbara, please tell me why it's too late,' said Elise, now beginning to think the worst.

'I've taken some tablets. It's too late and I don't want to go on. I'm finished.'

'What tablets have you taken, Barbara?'

'Something to stop the pain.'

'Barbara, have you taken paracetamol?'

'Good for pain, they say, so I've taken enough this time to stop the pain.'

Elise felt Barbara's voice was becoming weaker.

'Barbara, let me get you some help. Let me call you an

ambulance and get you to the hospital, to the Princess of Wales in Ely. It's just down the road from you and they will have there in a very short time. They can help you.'

'You don't know what it's like. No one can know what another person's pain is like. And it's too late for anything to stop that pain. My life ended some time ago.'

There was a pause in which Alice could only hear the sound of breathing.

'Barbara, please keep talking to me. Tell me about your children. They haven't died and owe everything to you. Tell me about them.'

Again, there was only silence.

'Barbara, please keep talking and tell me your home address so I can get help to you.'

'I've taken 60, will that be enough?' came the faint reply.

'It will make you poorly and you will need help to recover, but perhaps with your recovery you can begin again with your children, begin again with your life.'

Elise now knew what was to follow. Jean-Pierre had warned her. That moment had come. She knew Barbara was going to die.

'Barbara, can you hear me?'

There was only silence. Elise understood the effect of paracetamol, that it would render her unconscious, possibly inducing a heart attack but certainly kidney and liver failure. Even if she was to be found soon, her chances of survival were slim, and Elise could only hope she would be allowed to die without medical interventions of horrendous kinds.

She kept the telephone line open for a further half hour but could hear nothing. She hoped Barbara was on a bed where she wouldn't fall and inflict further wounds upon her poor body. Elise sat in absolute stillness just waiting. There was nothing. She replaced the telephone on its cradle. Outside it was dark, and a wind had arisen. She felt profoundly pained by the events of the past hour and then began to think that this simply was not fair, that she did not want this calling, if that is what it was, having to deal with what had happened again because in some way necessity was laid upon her.

She picked up the telephone again and dialled Leah's home

number, desperately hoping that she might be back from school. The call was answered by Ruth, one of Leah's twin daughters, who was so excited to hear from her "aunt" Elise. Her mum was not yet home but expected soon.

'Aunt Elise, did you know about daddy, that he has left us?'

'Oh my darling, I'm so sorry to hear that. It's a horrible thing for you and Sarah to have to live through.'

'It's more horrible for mum really and she cries a lot. But he had become quite horrid at home. He lost his temper so often and didn't want to help us with our homework and stopped attending synagogue. It's ghastly for mummy but me and Sarah are more relieved not have him here. He wasn't the daddy you knew when you lived with us. I think you should come and live with us again, aunt Elise. Please. We could do with you here because you always brought such happiness with you. Oh, here's mum. "Mum",' Elise could hear Ruth shouting, '"it's aunt Elise".'

'Oh Elise, Elise, I'm so pleased to hear from you. The last couple of weeks have been simply dreadful. Jerry has gone.'

'Yes, Ruth told me.'

'And he's been so cruel and spiteful, openly comparing me with the new lady in his life in every sordid detail. It's been so terrible and eventually, just before the end of last term, on a day when he was out and staying out overnight, I made his stay permanent and had all the locks changed. I packed his clothes and toiletries in a couple of suitcases and had a courier collect them and deliver them to his department at the hospital in the hope of causing maximum embarrassment. Since then, I have only communicated through a solicitor.'

'I feared this, Leah, when you were here in the autumn and I suspect you knew even then that this might come to a head. I can only hope his supposed new life is everything he thinks he no longer needs, you know; his children, his community, his identity as a Jew but above all the love of a wonderful woman who has never failed him.'

'Oh, he could provide you with a list of my failures as a wife and woman, Elise. Miss Wainwright as an ENT specialist clearly specialises in other things besides! It isn't just his head that has been turned, as he has made abundantly obvious to me in explicit detail I had no wish to have to endure.'

'I was going to say that I can imagine, but the fact is I can't.'

'It's so wonderful to hear from you Elise. I fear Hanukkah was not exactly a time of light for us though my mum and dad came to stay over the holiday period, which the girls loved. They have been wonderful. I even had a tiny idea. Next week the girls are going to Austria skiing with their school, and I wondered whether you could bear for me to come and be with you, perhaps watch you milking and just be able to talk together about all the sorts of things we have spent so many hours in the past doing. The school head has told me I can take off such time as I need following the breakup of my marriage.'

'Leah, I can't tell you how much I would love that. As for the cows, when Jim and I have finished milking we have to engage in the shit shifting; it sounds to me that after what you've just been through you would be an expert!'

Leah laughed.

'Thank you, Elise, I can't wait to come. And are you ok?'

Elise thought back to the recent phone call with Barbara.

'I'm fine, of course,' she said. 'Life goes here as normal: wind, rain and the sea birds – what more could I ask?'

It hadn't struck her at the time when her call with Barbara had ended, but the words she had use were reminiscent of the words she had heard so often when patients died at the hospice, commendatory words as Jean-Pierre had reminded her, but, working away inside her head was the realisation she had used those words rather than those of the Kaddish which as a Jew, let alone as a rabbi, she would have used. She stood up and in Hebrew recited the prayer:

אבל: יִתְגַּדַּל וְיִתְקַדַּשׁ שְׁמֵהּ רַבָּא. [קהל: אמן]

בְּעָלְמָא דִּי בְרָא כִרְעוּתֵהּ וְיַמְלִיךְ מַלְכוּתֵהּ בְּחַיֵּיכוֹן וּבְיוֹמֵיכוֹן וּבְחַיֵּי דְכָל בֵּית

יִשְׂרָאֵל בַּעֲגָלָא וּבִזְמַן קָרִיב, וְאִמְרוּ אָמֵן: [קהל: אמן]

קהל ואבל: יְהֵא שְׁמֵהּ רַבָּא מְבָרַךְ לְעָלַם וּלְעָלְמֵי עָלְמַיָּא:

אבל: יִתְבָּרַךְ וְיִשְׁתַּבַּח וְיִתְפָּאַר וְיִתְרוֹמַם וְיִתְנַשֵּׂא וְיִתְהַדָּר וְיִתְעַלֶּה וְיִתְהַלָּל שְׁמֵהּ

דְּקֻדְשָׁא. בְּרִיךְ הוּא. [קהל: בריך הוא:]

לְעֵלָּא מִן כָּל בִּרְכָתָא בעשי"ת: לְעֵלָּא לְעֵלָּא מִכָּל וְשִׁירָתָא תֻּשְׁבְּחָתָא וְנֶחֱמָתָא

דַּאֲמִירָן בְּעָלְמָא. וְאִמְרוּ אָמֵן: [קהל: אמן]

:יְהֵא שְׁלָמָא רַבָּא מִן שְׁמַיָּא וְחַיִּים עָלֵינוּ וְעַל כָּל יִשְׂרָאֵל. וְאִמְרוּ אָמֵן

[קהל:אמן]

עושה שָׁלוֹם בעשי"ת: הַשָּׁלוֹם בִּמְרוֹמָיו הוּא יַעֲשֶׂה שָׁלוֹם עָלֵינוּ וְעַל כָּל יִשְׂרָאֵל

וְאִמְרוּ אָמֵן: [קהל: אמן]

And then in English said:

*"May God's great name be praised throughout all eternity.
Glorified and celebrated, lauded and praised, acclaimed and
honoured, extolled and exalted ever be the name of thy Holy One,
far beyond all song and psalm, beyond all hymns of glory which
mortals can offer. And let us say: Amen."*

She stood in silence and waited, and perhaps only the wind
outside, now causing the rain to lash the windows, repeated the
Amen.

In the middle of the next day Elise received a long-distance
phone call from Canada.

'Elise, it's Kim Woodhouse here. I apologise for calling and
disturbing your peace and quiet, but I wanted to pass on some sad
news. Do you remember me mentioning one of my former clients
called Barbara, who lived in Littleport. You may also recall that I
had suggested she might call you if she needed to do so. I just
wondered if she ever had.'

'Just once. Why?'

'It's just that last night I had a phone call from her husband to
say that she had been found dead from a suspected overdose and
had left a note asking that I be informed. Obviously, I shouldn't
have off-loaded her on to you but if she only called once I feel a
little relieved. Anyway, it's very sad.'

'Yes, always. But tell me about you.'

'Pen and I are very happy, still in McMurray St and I've managed
to build up a significant practice, whilst Pen is still nursing. Greg

will soon be leaving us for university in Montreal. He's a fine young man and we shall miss him, though not having constantly to tidy up after him. And you?'

'As before and settled here on the edge. But please remember me with affection to Pen. From the start I thought you were made for one another, and I'm delighted it has worked out. But, Kim, thank you so much for calling.'

With the certain knowledge that Barbara had died, and for the first time in her five years, in the waiting room Elise suddenly felt lonely and vulnerable.

Verbazingwekkend

On the following morning, after milking and breakfast at the farm with Jim and Audrey, instead of returning home to the waiting room, Elise helped Jim and the vet, a Dutchman called Pieter, do one of the regular sessions of TB testing. Living in a designated Low Risk Area, and never having yet had a cow test positive, this only took place once a year. Four days earlier the vet had injected each of the cattle twice in the neck and was returning this morning to check each cow for any reactors. The implications could be considerable and for Jim and Audrey, but also for Elise concerned for them and her favourite cows, these four days were tense. If any reactors were found they would have to be slaughtered and 60-day restrictions placed on the movement of animals, plus the loss of all milk which might have come from any reactor, which would mean the loss all milk. Happily, on day four, all were clear, and they could all breathe again.

'It's unusual to find a young woman working on a farm out here in the middle of nowhere,' said Pieter as he and Elise washed their hand under a tap in the yard. 'I had thought at first you must be Jim's daughter, but even a Dutchman could tell your accent was not local.'

'No, I live a short distance away and began helping Jim a couple of years ago now. I come to do the milking with him each morning. I greatly enjoy doing so.'

'I assume you don't live alone out here in the wild.'

'Then Pieter,' said Elise with a smile, 'you should be careful with your assumptions. I live alone in a small house I bought from the

RAF five years ago.'

'You have lived here alone for five years!' exclaimed Pieter. 'Verbazingwekkend!'

'I can manage Arabic, Hebrew, French, Greek and Latin but I do not recognise that wonderful sounding word.'

Pieter laughed.

'It is the Dutch word for expressing amazement, to say that I am flabbergasted, but I am even more so that you have mastered so many languages, though I can't imagine you get much chance to practice them here.'

'Whereas, of course, there must be a thriving community of Dutch farmers hidden away in the North York Moors!'

Pieter laughed again.

'I'm part of a practice in Whitby. Posh tourists sometimes say Yorkshire people speak "double-dutch", which I know is not very polite but as far as I know I'm the only person who speaks "single-Dutch".'

'Not your own family?'

Pieter smiled.

'Like you, I live alone. My wife, who came from Whitby, died of ovarian cancer less than two years after our marriage, and I have remained in the town though perhaps in time I shall return home.'

'Where is that?'

'I come from near the town of Leiden and studied to be a vet in Amsterdam.'

'I am so sorry to hear about the death of your wife. What was her name?'

'Julia.'

'You must miss her.'

'More time has now passed than we were married and for much of the time she was sick. I could not have wished for longer given how she was.'

'Even so, it is a loss not just of her presence but the possibilities inherent in a marriage of years, of sharing, of children and so much more.'

'You have lived this loss also?'

'No, but I have spent much time with the dying and the

bereaved.'

'You are a doctor or perhaps a nurse?'

'Would you have time to come and have some lunch with me?'

Pieter did not hesitate to accept.

Elise cycled up the road and Pieter followed slowly in his van. Once inside Elise made herself a cup of tea and for Pieter a strong coffee from her machine which he admired. Sitting down with their drinks he looked round the room.

'Your furnishings suggest someone of purpose – no television but fascinating books, and chairs and a sofa designed above all for comfort. It is not a spartan existence as shown by the paintings you have on your walls, reflecting a recognition of beauty.'

'They are only copies.'

'But copies of important art. And among them two from the Netherlands.'

'Most people associate the Renaissance with Italy, but your countrymen have produced wonders in every sense of the word.'

'Have you ever visited?'

'No.'

'May I ask you a question?'

'You want to know what on earth I am doing living in isolation in such a place?'

'Well, yes. I can tell you must be a person of considerable stability, able to withstand the silence of the years and able to retain such warmth as you have already shown me, and not just me, as Jim and his wife have told me how much they value you. He said he sometimes even lets you do the milking by yourself. This is not usual.'

'Do you find the unusual difficult?'

Pieter smiled.

'Not at all. But I imagine there is a story behind your being here.'

'I think you would laugh if I was to tell you.'

'I am intrigued by some your books as I look at the titles. You have books I would not expect to see anywhere other, possibly, than in the home of a scholar not just of languages but of Jewish literature in particular.'

'I used to teach Hebrew and Talmud.'

'Good heavens!'

'Possibly,' she replied with a grin.

Pieter laughed.

'But you're Canadian, I think.'

'You have just earned your lunch, Pieter,' said Elise, laughing. 'Yes, I lived in Ontario until I was 14 but I'm trying to acquire the double-Dutch of Yorkshire.'

'But what on earth was a young and lovely, if I may, Canadian, doing acquiring the expertise to teach Talmud, let alone Hebrew, now abandoning it for a solitary existence.'

'Hey, it's not completely solitary. I milk the cows each morning!'

'Probably more communicative than Jim, though married to Audrey, he probably doesn't get much of a chance to get in a word edgeways.'

'She's lovely. I adore her and she's a bastion of the local Women's Institute, though so far, I have resisted her attempts to enlist me!'

'Then you are wise as well as clever,' said Pieter with a laugh.

Elise rose.

'I will get us some bread and cheese, and also some fruit.'

Pieter went over to the bookcase and looked more closely. In addition to titles obviously in Hebrew, there were names and titles he did not recognise: *Meister Eckhart, The Desert Fathers, Spinoza* and poems by names wholly new to him, *GM Hopkins, Elizabeth Jennings and Peter Levi*. He took out one book and saw an inscription which almost took his breath away. When Elise came back from the kitchen, he held up the book and said with a tone of almost incredulity, 'This says you are *Rabbi* Elise Rosewarne.'

'Yes,' she said, putting cheese and bread on the table.

'Verbazingwekkend, or even more so!' said Pieter.

'That really must be double-Dutch,' said Elise. 'Please come and sit and allow me to pour you some water. I regret I have nothing stronger.'

Pieter walked to the table and sat down, speechless and with eyes wide open, staring at Elise. Eventually he said, 'I'm wholly at a loss for words.'

'Then there is hope for you,' said Elise with a grin. 'The philosopher Wittgenstein, you may recall, said something to the effect that silence is always preferable to words when faced with what can't be described.'

'But...a rabbi! What on earth does that mean and I'm afraid you might just have to use words to tell me.'

'Pieter, I'm still struggling to find the words to describe it to myself.'

'But might you be willing to do so, to wrestle with the words, for me, or is that an entirely inappropriate question? You may struggle with an answer, but I'm not even sure what questions to ask?'

They both laughed.

'In philosophy the real art is determining the questions, which I suspect always is much more taxing than finding answers,' she said.

'Well, let me ask a simple one of fact. The inscription describes you as a rabbi and you do not deny that, but where, out here on the edge of the world, is there a synagogue or a community you serve, other than Jim, Audrey and their herd of Friesian cattle?'

'Good Dutch cattle, I'm sure you would agree,' said Elise.

'No milk yields to match them, but do they need a rabbi to help increase them?' said Pieter with a smile.

Elise picked up her bread roll and broke it in half.

'Six years ago, as you would have seen from the date of the inscription, I was ordained as a rabbi in Leo Baeck Rabbinic College in North London, where I was also on the teaching staff, and I went to serve the Reform Synagogue in Cambridge. Shortly afterwards following a visit to Canada to see my dying aunt, I abandoned the rabbinate and bought this place and have been living here alone since then. On my visit to Canada, I had the surprising discovery that following my birth, my Jewish mother had taken me to the local Catholic priest and that he had baptised and confirmed me. Those are the simple facts for which you asked. Please eat your lunch. You need the energy.'

'To listen to this story, I agree!' Pieter said, smiling.

Desperately trying to think what to say next, he broke his own bread roll and took some cheese.

'It's unpasteurised,' said Elise. 'I make it myself.'

'I'll take the risk!' he added, not entirely sure what he meant by it.

'But what do you do here, apart from the morning milking?'

'I have spent five years trying to pursue being rather than doing, though of course I have to eat, so once a month I go shopping in Scarborough, and I ensure there is order in the house and garden in summer. Above all, I am here to be silent and to wait.'

'What are you waiting for?'

'Perhaps for verbazingwekkend!'

'Your accent is good.'

'I have a quick ear for languages.'

'There is so much more I would love to know, Elise, but I also have patients waiting for me between three and six, but tomorrow is my day off. May I return in the morning and cook you some breakfast after milking?'

'I would like that very much, Pieter, but Pieter what? I don't know your name, and I have already told you just about everything about me and would like to know more about you.'

'I know that you have not really told me anything more than bare facts and I am intrigued enough to want to know more, if that is, you are willing to tell me. But as a bare fact I'm Pieter Westenberg – it means "west of the mountain", which is odd given that we have no mountains in the Netherlands, just a few hills.'

'Then it seems we are both a little odd which is a great relief. The door will be open. Just come in and make yourself at home. I'm usually back by ten o'clock though I then need a shower.'

'I would imagine sausage and bacon are not on your menu',' said Pieter with a laugh.

'I will eat whatever you cook for me. Here I normally just eat home-made porridge but I do make good coffee.'

Pieter stood.

'I don't know that to say,' he said.

'What is the Dutch for Until Tomorrow?'

'Tot morgen.'

'Tot morgen Pieter Westenberg.'
'Shalom, Elise Rosewarne.'

Elise cleared everything away and sat on her sofa. She knew she had to prepare the spare room for Leah's arrival but needed first just to sit and be still, as best she could, because she knew something had happened. Following the phone call from Kim and the news about Barbara (though it was not really news to Elise) she had instinctively known that the appointed time for her total withdrawal into the silence of waiting was over. She need not return to the waiting room, the transport had arrived.

Prachtig

By Saturday evening, just two days on from the TB testing results day, Pieter knew that his own waiting was now over. He looked at the photograph of his wedding day to Julia on his sideboard, and still thought of her constantly with love, but had never ceased to recall her diminution and pain of her long illness and death. Yet now, he felt he had begun to heal in the presence of this most odd and quite wonderful woman he had encountered, wholly incongruously, in a farmyard. He understood little of what she had endeavoured to tell him of her unusual, rather than bizarre, story and its possible meanings, but that mattered little to him. He only knew he came alive again in her presence and although he was more than a little scared of her capacity for what she called purposeless being, he felt certain, already, that he wanted her to spend the rest of his days with him. And he also knew that she felt the same.

The last thing Elise wanted to do was to cancel Leah, even though it would inevitably limit the time she could spend with Pieter, and given the circumstances of the breakdown of Leah's marriage to Jerry, it was hardly an ideal time to tell her closest friend that she was in love, but on the other hand she could almost barely wait to share the news.

Since their Thursday lunch, Elise had not returned to her waiting room, nor returned to the intense practice of silence which had characterised her life since her encounters with Jean-Pierre now more than five years since. Kim's call, confirming Barbara's death, which she sure Jean-Pierre had intimated in some odd way, had led to the first feeling of loneliness, something quite new. And then on the morning after, what she had been waiting for arrived.

Elise had never been in love, except perhaps in a detached sort of way with Jean-Pierre and had never been kissed properly until darkness was falling on the Friday afternoon, as Shabbat was beginning, when she and Pieter had sat together and held one another on the sofa. He had been gentle and understanding as he kissed and drew her close to him. She had spent a long time since breakfast endeavouring to describe her way of life and how things had fallen into their unusual place, and amazed that he was clearly making every effort to understand and not pretending to do so when he did not, something she was reassured by. He was not pretending anything, and neither was she, and that, as she understood, was the only basis for their being together.

And then it had been his turn. He spoke about his childhood in Holland, about his love for animals and how he chose to be a vet rather than a doctor which his parents and schoolteachers were hoping he would do. He had met Julia when she came for a year to the vet school in Amsterdam though it was only after they had both qualified and she was working in Whitby that he accepted an offer to come and work alongside her in the practice. Even then it had taken time for the colleagues to become friends and more. They had known one another for four years before they had married. It was just over a year afterwards that she was first taken ill with the cancer that was to take her life six months later. Now, at 39, the same age as Elise, he had been widowed four years and assumed that he would not now meet anyone to take the place of Julia, and indeed thought no one could. And he was right, because as he now realised, Elise was not even a little like Julia and would have no wish to take her place. Elise most definitely was Elise and no one else.

This morning, she had come to his home, and almost the first thing she did was to take hold of the wedding photograph.

'Oh, Pieter, how beautiful was your Julia, and how wonderful you look together. The pain of losing her will always be with you.'

'And you, Elise, are the bringer of healing. I don't think you seem even remotely interested in bringing religion of any kind, and indeed you told me yesterday you are not religious, but I feel I am feasting on the fruits of your waiting in silence.'

'I was waiting for you, but it had to be at the right time. It was only after I had been informed of the death of Barbara for certain, that I knew my waiting time was complete, and you were there. Of course, it might have been Jim or one of the cows that I fell for, but it was the most *prachtig* you.'

'You're pretty wonderful yourself,' laughed Pieter, impressed by the correct use of a Dutch word he hadn't taught her.

After lunch they walked hand-in-hand along the harbour. It was a cold day, and the east wind was threatening snow, but they didn't seem to notice.

'I shall have to drive to York tomorrow as soon as I have finished milking, to collect my friend Leah who is coming by train. I would love to give her the surprise of her life by bringing her home to you. Might that be possible?'

'I am on call from midnight tonight to noon tomorrow, so of course, if it means I can see you and meet your best friend. Should I arrange to have a defibrillator on hand in case the shock is too much?'

'No and the only mouth-to-mouth you are allowed is with me.'

'Will she be expecting a kosher diet?'

'I wouldn't give her pork or lobster, but she's been often enough with me to be housetrained. And besides which, she's Reform.'

Leah was desperate to talk, though Elise had to give much of her attention to the roads as the threatened snow had arrived overnight and was still falling.

'Ruth and Sarah have arrived safely though I could have been spared considerable expense by bringing them here to ski,' began Leah, as they by-passed Malton, now having to travel slowly. Elise knew that the road to Scarborough would be relatively ok but thought that the road to Whitby, being higher, might be more difficult, but knew for certain that the track to the farm would be especially treacherous. She did notice with some considerable pleasure, however, as she drove with great caution, that another vehicle had left tracks ahead. Eventually they reached the farm but could go further and she could see Pieter's van at the farm, meaning it was on foot from here.

'Oh gosh,' said Leah when she saw the van, 'some poor vet has had to come out in this weather.'

'Such self-sacrifice,' replied Elise, with a grin Leah did not understand. 'They must really love what they do.'

The trek up the hill was demanding for Leah, and though the snowfall was continuing it was lighter than earlier.

'It's alright for you,' she said, noticing Elise seemed more determined, 'you're a Canadian and used to it.'

'Well, we're almost there.'

As they approached the house, Leah suddenly stopped and said, 'Elise there's a light on and I'm sure I saw someone briefly at the window.'

'It's unlikely to be a burglar; it's against union rules to burgle in snow because of the tracks in the snow. Let's go and find out.'

Approaching the front door, it magically opened, and there stood a tall, fair-haired good-looking man with a broad smile.

'Welcome Leah. Elise has been so looking forward to your arrival and so have I.'

Leah was dumbfounded and did not move other to give a quick glance at Elise.

'Oh, I'm so sorry, Leah, I forgot to mention that Pieter the vet would be here and cooking our supper.'

'Pieter the vet?'

'Hello, that's me, I should have introduced myself, but you don't have to stand outside in the snow. Come in, dry off and get warm. I have a good fire on the go.'

Leah walked in hesitantly and looking back at Elise as she did, almost walked into an armchair.

'Elise,' she said, 'what's going on?'

Elise laughed.

'I thought you might be surprised but I took the risk anyway, just for the sheer joy of seeing your face, which is a real picture. So, yes, this is Pieter, and he is a vet, and we are in love.'

'Oh!'

Leah looked at both in turn, each with as wide a smile as might be possible on a face.

'What I really mean is "Wow", she added hurriedly. 'And by that, I mean that I have not heard such wonderful news for a very long time. And even in a matter of seconds I feel such a sense of joy that I might explode.'

'Oh, don't do that, Leah,' said Pieter, 'I'm but a humble vet and might put you back in the wrong order.'

All three laughed. Elise helped Leah off with her coat.'

'I'm sure what you need is a cup of strong tea,' said Elise to her friend who had by now sat down. 'I will make it as Pieter is Dutch and doesn't understand the art of tea-making.'

'I have acquired the art of tea drinking, however. I've had to. Every farmer insists on pouring it into me.'

He sat opposite Leah.

'That is how I met Elise, on the farm here, we were testing cows for TB, and then something happened.'

'Yes, it would have to be like that for Elise.'

Pieter smiled.

'You and I are the only ones who could say that. She has told me a great deal of what it is that has brought her here and a quite astonishing story it is too. What are the chances of meeting a rabbi in a farm on the edge of the North York Moors helping test cattle after having milked them, and then discovering that she's also a Catholic and has lived an almost solitary existence for five years engaged in what most people would regard as some form of contemplation for four hours a day? And then, what might the chances be of a Dutch vet falling completely in love with her, and then making the even more astonishing discovery that she had fallen in love with me? I should have visited a bookmaker and made a fortune.'

'You will have that too,' said Leah.

'I'm not sure what you mean,' said Pieter, somewhat puzzled.

Elise had come back into the room with a teapot, cups and milk.

'I haven't got round to that,' said Elise.

'Round to what?'

'My fortune. Well, it's not an absolute fortune, but it's enough.'

'I think I should have said nothing,' said Leah.

'Not at all,' replied Elise, pouring the tea. 'I really didn't think it was important enough to mention until we had spoken of other things, but what Leah means, Pieter, is that thanks to my father and my aunt, and more recently my mother, their deaths have made what might be called quite wealthy.'

Pieter turned to Leah.

'I really didn't know, honestly. Every time I'm with Elise is a surprise, so this shouldn't come as some kind of shock, though it does.'

Elise laughed, came over to Pieter and kissed him full on the lips.

'I'm glad you love me just because I am as I am. With you I am rich beyond any money that might be in a bank.'

'Stop, Elise, or else I shall be in tears,' said Leah, 'and you should put some whisky into my tea, or better just give me a large whisky with a little tea in it.'

They laughed, as Elise handed Leah her tea and then sat on the sofa with Pieter.

'Oh Leah, forgive me not telling you until now. How it didn't burst out of me at the station when you got off the train I don't know, but I have so wanted you to share in our joy.'

'Did you really meet in a farmyard?'

'Oh yes,' said Pieter. 'On the first occasion we just worked together with the farmer, but when I returned to check the cows, it happened.'

'I had known the evening before that my time of waiting had come to an end, and I'll tell you why later, and then Pieter and I began to talk and that was it.'

'It's really quite wonderful, but ever since you came into my life, Elise, you have brought wonder with you and of course, sometimes astonishment.'

'The word you are looking for,' said Pieter, 'is verbazingwekkend.'

'Well, I don't know what it means, but it sounds exactly right!'

Jewish Fish and Chips

By evening, it had finally stopped snowing and although Leah had expected that Pieter would be staying overnight, she was surprised that once supper was ended, he made himself ready to walk down to where his van was parked.

'I'm on call from midnight,' he said in answer to her unanswered question, 'and I have morning surgery tomorrow. Given the snow it might take until midnight for me to get back, but I'll try my best. I'm hoping the snow plough has been at work on the main road, but hopefully Jim will have used the shovel on his tractor to clear the lane or the milk lorry won't be able to get through.'

'I'll come down with you,' said Elise. 'I have my skis.'

'This lady has no limits,' said Pieter to Leah.

'Since meeting you, Pieter, I realise that the only one previously missing is now provided for.'

'I will see you sometime soon,' he said shaking her hand, which was wonderfully formal. 'I am just delighted that you are here, and I am sure you will have much to discuss. She may get you on to skis.'

'I'm not sure Sarah or Ruth would be impressed by their mother returning home with a broken leg from North Yorkshire whilst they have been skiing in Austria, so perhaps I'll just watch.'

Elise's face was bright red when she arrived back, removed her skis and stood in front of the fire to get warm. In the meantime, Leah had restored a measure of order to the sitting room. She could see that Elise's red face was not just the product of the cold but a kind of excitement that was working outwards from inside.

'It must feel so odd, Elise. For five years you have maintained a rigid discipline of control over every aspect of your living, observing long periods of solitary silence, and now, all at once you have emerged, dare I say, like a butterfly from a chrysalis.'

'I was never unhappy in that chrysalis but leaving feels like a butterfly must feel – a wholly unanticipated freedom and joy. I have often laughed with Jim and Audrey, and when visiting shops have sought always to be cheerful, but when the moment came on Wednesday and I knew for certain of the second suicide, of Barbara, for the very first time I felt a sudden and quite acute loneliness. And so, on the following morning there was Pieter. To say that it was meant would be to claim that the universe was arranging things around me, so all I can say is that in a very real sense I just knew everything had fallen into place. I'm sure Jean-Pierre, and perhaps our own Rabbi Samuel, would allow me to say that without further comment.'

'And yet, despite your disclaimer, all I can say is that meeting Pieter has confirmed my hopes for you, that one day you would meet the right person and you have, and at the right time. No more deaths and waiting, Elise, please!'

'I have abandoned my waiting room and am already using it as a store room. I have spent many, many hours in there, so you might think leaving it would be extremely painful, but once the train arrives, you leave the waiting room behind and forget all about it.'

'But you won't be forgetting what you have learned in these years. Whatever now lies ahead for you and Pieter must also include some attempt on your part to give expression to all that you have experienced. Don't you owe that to others?'

'I'm not sure, and besides it's far too early to make any sort of decision, but now I want to look forwards not back, not least because so much of what I leave behind remains largely unspeakable, a word we mostly use to describe something terrible, but which in my case has been so constantly rich *because* beyond my grasp. If I now attempt to put it into words, it may be that I would be going wholly contrary to everything I've been about and which has brought me here, and more, importantly, here and now, and brought Pieter to me. If I couldn't speak of it whilst I was in its midst, there's going to be no chance of doing so now.

'And I rather think Pieter is aware of that,' said Leah. 'It seems to me, however, that you and he have both been waiting, you for the second telephone death, and he since the death of his Julia. Gosh, I wonder what will follow.'

The telephone rang and Elise answered it.

'That's just great...of course, we shall enjoy that...twelve o'clock it is... and I love you too.'

'Anyone I know?' asked Leah.

'The main road was clear and he's home safely. He has suggested a fabulous fish and chip restaurant for us to have lunch with him tomorrow. After milking I shall try to persuade Jim to use the tractor to clear the road from the farm to here, but it will give us a chance to sample Whitby's best.'

As she lay in bed, Leah thought back on that phone call. Part of her, because of an almost superstitious grasp of all that Elise had been about, had dreaded it being the police to say there had been an accident.... She stopped herself from thinking and was glad Elise had put an electric blanket on her bed. Elise had once told her that one of the medieval solitaries had written words later used by TS Eliot: "*and all shall be well, and all manner of things shall be well*". She was so glad for Elise, but it served to heighten her own sense of the loss of love and the betrayal of a partner, something that felt like an experience of death. She knew that once Elise was back from milking, she would need to speak these thoughts to her as the only person she could speak to, but the emptiness within was surely not unlike that silent void of which Elise had lived for so long.

There had been no further snow overnight, and to Leah's delight, when she heard an engine on the lane outside and looked from the window, she could see Elise in the cab of the tractor alongside the farmer as they shifted snow.

'Have you told your farmer or his wife about the big change?' she asked once Elise had shed her overall and come to the breakfast table for porridge made by Leah according to instructions left by Elise.

'He saw the van yesterday of course, but he's not the sort of person who would poke his nose into the doings of others, but I managed to avoid Audrey this morning, because she just might!'

'Would you mind?'

'Mind? I'd be overjoyed. Good news is for sharing surely!'

With careful attention as she drove, the trip into Whitby for lunch was running on time. The town was quiet at this time of the year and Elise needed to do some shopping before they met up with Pieter.

'I am here for you first and foremost this week, Leah,' said Leah as she was parking the car. 'You matter so very much to me, and I always miss you when you have to go back and although this time I have another distraction, Pieter and I have already agreed that we shall have a great deal of time together after you have returned home, so you must be my priority whilst you are here.'

'I am more than willing to share him with you when possible. I like him very much and I want to share in your joy. He has work so we can spend all that time doing what we wish, but as much as possible please include him in what we do. That will make me much happier than thinking that having just come together I could be a cause of your being apart.'

'Oh Leah, that is to typically generous of you, but tell me, does it hurt you seeing us so happy together given all that you have been and still are going through?'

'Not hurt, but perhaps envy. Once upon a time that was how it was for Jerry and myself, and has been throughout many years. I keep trying to work out where I have failed, what I could have done for our marriage to be better.'

'But it isn't just a matter of you and Jerry, is it? He has abandoned real and genuine care for Ruth and Sarah. I'm sure he will meet his financial obligations but that's not what being a dad is about nor what they need or want. Every day will fail them when he is not there, and he has also openly flouted the religion he professed so ardently. It's not so long since they each had their *bat mitzvah* in which I am sure he will have given great encouragement, but now what he has done repudiates that support that was there for them on that occasion and in the formative years of their teens to come.'

By now they were walking towards their meeting place with Pieter, and when they saw him, both waved enthusiastically. Once they had given their orders for lunch and received their cups of tea ("as compulsory with fish and chips, as white bread and butter", said the Dutchman!), Elise decided to continue the previous conversation.

'We have been reflecting on the way in which Leah's husband has possibly betrayed the trust not just of his marriage vows to Leah, but his responsibilities to his daughters in terms of their life as Jews in the community.'

'That must be so hard, Leah, for them to understand. Jewish identity is so very important. It's considerably more than just a matter of fulfilling certain religious activities. This I have already learned from your friend Elise, who is a great teacher. Ruth and Sarah, however, do at least know of their Jewish identity and heritage, unlike their aunt Elise from whom her Jewish identity was concealed until she was a student. That will always stand them in good stead, and they cannot lose that identity, as Elise cannot. Once a Jew always a Jew, and they will pass that on to their children.

'That is not to underestimate what it means that their father has let them down, but there are still many days ahead in which he may redeem himself provided he too does not forget that he is a Jew. He doesn't shed that just because he has behaved badly, just as when I make a mistake, sometimes a serious error, in my work, it does not mean I cease to be a vet, just that I learn and do not repeat.'

The waiter arrived with three plates of enormous fish, chips and mushy peas, together with a plate of the heralded ready-buttered bread. As she looked down at the feast before her, she said aloud,

'*Barukh ata Adonai Eloheinu, melekh ha'olam, hamotzi lehem min ha'aretz.*'

'And the fish, chips and peas,' said Elise before she and Leah dissolved in laughter.

'Leah said the prayer of thanksgiving for the bread from the earth, and I felt the need to add the rest', she said by means of explanation to Pieter who had enjoyed the laughter.

'Being Jewish sounds like a lot of fun.'

'Well, it can be,' said Leah, picking up her knife and fork, 'but not so much because of the religion and that goes with it but because in a real way it is simply about affirming life. That is why we do not say "Cheers" when we drink but "L'chaim" – to Life.'

'There is a passage in the New Testament book of John,' added Elise, 'in which Yeshua, or Jesus as he is mistakenly known, says he has come to bring life and life in all its fulness. That Jesus truly is Yeshua the Jew.'

'In which case,' said Pieter,' he would enjoy this meal.'

'Of course,' said Elise, 'and he chose at least some fishermen to be close followers, including the man after whom you are named.'

'Oh no, wonderful Rabbi. I am named after the great artist Pieter Bruegel the Elder. My father is a leading expert in early Dutch and Flemish art, and what is more I am a direct descendant of the great man through the van Kessel side of the family, Hieronymus van Kessel the Younger (also a fine artist) having married Pieter's granddaughter Paschasia.'

Elise stared open-mouthed at Pieter and then said, 'I shall need to extend my Dutch vocabulary, but verbazingwekkend!'

By Thought Never

True to their word, Pieter and Elise did not give Leah any grounds for thinking she was being deprived of the attention and love she had come north to seek in her days with them. As a thaw had quickly set in, they had been able to do some walking together and both knew that sometimes it was doing this that enabled serious talking to be done, when they weren't gazing intensely at one another in the confines of a sitting room.

Elise took Leah to Rievaulx to see the ruined Abbey which she loved and showed her too, the large Catholic Church and School at Ampleforth.

'If you have children, Elise, would you want them brought up as Jews or Catholics?'

'Don't you think the likelihood of children at my age is pretty small and probably unwise?'

'No, I don't, and I can't think of two people who would be better parents: one, the descendant from outstanding artists, the other, a Catholic rabbi. The combination would be fascinating.'

Elise laughed.

'Do you think I should go and see a doctor to see if having a baby might be possible at 39, or 40?'

'You could always ask a vet!'

'He might think I'm wholly jumping the gun. We've only known one another for a week.'

'Elise, anyone could see he's not just besotted with you, and you with him, but that you both know deep inside that in some strange way, and you're more used to this sort of thinking than me, that this is meant to be. There is nothing more to say, though actually, Elise, there is, well two somewhat delicate things.'

'And clearly only my best friend will have the temerity to ask them, so go on.'

'Are your periods are still happening and regular? You have been living an irregular lifestyle, so it is not an entirely inappropriate question if you were considering whether or not to become pregnant.'

'Yes, they are, regular as clockwork, and I have a feeling I know what the second question will be. You want to know if I will know how to perform in bed. Am I right?'

'To the best of my previous knowledge, you are still a virgin.'

Two boys from the school passing by, as they walked out of the great church at Ampleforth, hearing this, turned, gave the women a peculiar look and one another even more perplexing looks. Leah and Elise laughed.

'They're Catholic boys, so they're quite use to virgins conceiving!' said Elise, causing Leah to almost fall over with laughter. 'But yes, I am, but with frequent cycling and sanitary products being what they are, I'm hoping I shan't have too much to fear.'

'The only thing you should fear is your lack of experience and knowledge. Hopefully Pieter will help provide what you need, but I beg you, having not just my own experience to draw on but that of so many calls to the Samaritans from unhappy women, be wholly open about what you want and need to know. Ask Pieter – do not be too shy. Sex can be wonderful but for many women it is not so because truly they just grin and bear it rather than being proactive. Please don't lie back and think of Dutch and Flemish masters!'

Elise was herself now the one unable to stop laughing.

'I'm not joking, Elise. There are pleasures as yet unknown before you, but they have to be sought out. It strikes me that when you take me to the station tomorrow, you should go into Smith's in the city and buy Alex Comfort's *The Joy of Sex*. It's more than 30 years old and perhaps there are more recent books geared specifically more to women, but I think you should at least have perused its pages.'

'Yes. I'll do that. What a good job I have someone so close to me who can say these things. Occasionally when I was a Samaritan and far too young I too had conversations with women who had run into difficulties. I knew even less than every one of them, but I recall Chad Varah telling us to read that book so that when people called we could advise and help them. I was far too embarrassed to go into a shop back then and besides which soon I would be training to be a rabbi.'

'I think our new rabbi could do with improving her reading. Rabbi Samuel was so grounded and understood about sex – and he never called it "sexuality" which is such a sanitised term.'

'Yes, it's like the horrible word "spirituality" which now means anything at all, however nonsensical but might I return the compliment and ask you about sex?'

'Yes, I miss Jerry in bed. Even at our advanced age we could still bring merriment and joy each Shabbat night, and sometimes in between. But obviously he needed more and turned to his young colleague, twenty years my, and his, junior. I hope she doesn't kill him. As for me, well, let's agree I get by. I sent for something by post, which arrived discretely wrapped in brown paper, but I could tell from the look the postman gave me as he handed it over at the door, that the shape of the package was not exactly as disguised as I might have hoped.'

Elise laughed.

'And?'

'It works, but it's not the same.'

'And if Jerry was to come, tail between his legs, wanting to return, would you welcome him?'

'Regardless of what was between his legs, I now think the answer would be no. It's too late. The hurt to Sarah, Ruth and myself is already so intense that I'm not sure it can be healed. And if his new relationship did collapse and I would think it's more than possible if, for example, she got her own consultant's post in Newcastle or somewhere a long way away, and no longer needed the leg up he has provided for her, then he would be very mistaken were he to imagine that there would be a home available to him.

My solicitor says that having left the matrimonial home he will be at a great disadvantage. The mortgage is paid off and the house is in my name, which we did for tax reasons way back.'

'Leah, we have known each other a long time, and yet never had we had a conversation such as this.'

'Well, you were a single woman training to be a rabbi and then a solitary woman living mostly as nuns do. It never occurred to me to mention sex, but now we're sharing such intimacies and you have returned to the human race, I can dare to tell you something that's happened to me and perhaps underlies why I won't be taking Jerry back though you may disapprove.

'Leah, my loveliest and best friend, there is nothing you could ever tell me that would bring about my disapproval.'

'This might. I went to see my solicitor after Jerry left, and found a good reason to go back within a couple of days. On the second occasion I was asked if we might go out for dinner together, and to my astonishment I said yes, and so we did.'

'That's wonderful, Leah. I totally approve.'

'Ah well, I haven't told you yet the full story.'

'Go on, I can hardly wait.'

'My solicitor is called Ursula.'

Elise's eyebrows shot up.

'Dat is geweldig' she said, smiling broadly. 'It's Dutch for "That is wonderful". Pieter taught me. But tell me more.'

I hope there are no more schoolboys listening, but she has passed my case over to one of her colleagues because it would not help if anything came to court and it was found that my solicitor and I were in some sort of relationship. She's 47 and has also been through a divorce five years ago, but I think she seems taken with me and I with her and on the night before I left to come here with the girls already on their way to Austria Ursula stayed over and shared my bed.'

'There's no harm in sleeping in the same bed, is there?' said Elise, feigning an old-fashioned look of disapproval.

'Absolutely, rabbi, though the best bits, to misquote Stevie Smith, are when waking not sleeping.'

'And here you were, giving advice to me. Did you need a book?'

'No need. Women know.'

Elise thought for a while.

'Do you know, our conversation today would be hilarious if it was on the radio. But Leah, as a rabbi I give you my absolute and total blessing, and as a Catholic I know you won't be using contraception! In the words of something I heard recently, it's win-win!'

Most of the journey back was spent in shared laughter and also reminiscing about their friend and former rabbi.

'He always said the essence of faith and marriage had to be found in honesty,' said Elise, 'and that too often when it began to lessen so did the reality of the marriage. But he also said that when we are older, we are not the same people we were when we were younger, and we should be gentle with ourselves as we change. Recognising change and the opportunities it brings is maturity, or at least I hope it is, otherwise I should be locked up in a mental hospital, which many of those who have known me probably think should have happened a long time ago.

'Leah, my love. We both are moving on and we should welcome with open arms those who now come into our lives, especially those who come bringing love, and with them those parts you imagine I can't imagine and need a book to teach me!'

'I bring with me Ruth and Sarah,' said Leah. 'What realities of the past five years, the isolation, the dead children, the suicides and the recognition that these were meant to be part of your life are you going to take into your new life with Pieter? I hope I'm not being unkind when I say that in these past years you've had an on-going relationship with Jean-Pierre. Will you be taking that into your new life?'

'I have no idea and not sure how I can know but on the day before Pieter entered my life, I knew for certain that the previous way of living to which I know I had been called was now completed. I was being released, you might say, though my cell was not a prison cell, but the only way I could prepare myself for the joys to come. I have no idea what that means but I knew for certain on the next morning as I stood next to a man and a herd of cows, that the new life had begun. Why worry about the meaning?

Perhaps the role to which Jean-Pierre was convinced I was called was like the part someone adopts in a play, and when that play is over, so is the role.'

'Elise you were never playing a role. I think you owe it to others to try at least to express for them something of all you have been through, just as the medieval mystics did in the few writings that have come down to us.'

'"He may well be loved, but not thought. By love may He be gotten and holden; but by thought never" – the unknown author of medieval *The Cloud of Unknowing* wrote that. How different the world might be had these words been heeded by the religions of the world since then. I have no idea how I would begin to do what you say, and besides which, now is not the time, but perhaps when I know the time is right, if ever it is, I might try to write something however slight, to encourage others to know what I know, that I was chosen, and that Jean-Pierre pointed out to me that if I knew that, then I must also know there is a chooser.'

'Even to write that would be to say so very much.'

'Maybe, but not yet, but now tell me more about Ursula. I'm dying to hear everything about her.'

'Well...' began Leah and spent the remainder of the journey in full flow.'

Gale

Every vet in practice at the time could tell you where they were on 19 February 2001 when they heard that Foot-and-Mouth Disease had been detected in Essex and Northumberland. It heralded almost seven months in which over 6.4 million cows and sheep were slaughtered, mostly in the fields where they had been grazing minutes earlier, and in which vets had to play a major part, though during the epidemic soldiers, slaughtermen and others with a licensed humane killer from hunt kennels were drafted into the killing fields. On the moors the sheep and cattle disappeared, and walkers were forbidden.

Pieter Westernberg and his colleagues had not become vets to kill animals in such numbers but their orders from the Ministry were clear. In the evenings, at home, he was often extremely downhearted, and it took all his wife's efforts to keep him as hopeful and positive as possible. There were considerable movement restrictions across the Dales where he and Elise now lived, having bought a practice a year after they had married, and to which they had moved with their precious daughter, Grace, just a month old. Now, with Foot-and-Mouth behind them, Pieter was once again enjoying his work and the hills once again boasted sheep and cattle, whilst Elise was pregnant again. This would be number three. Julia (suggested by Elise, the name of Pieter's first wife) had joined her sister two years afterwards and now, so the scan revealed, another sister would be joining them soon.

Elise was treated as an old mum-to-be, though as it was her third pregnancy and there had been no previous problems, the midwives mostly let her alone, now in the sixth month. In any case she would only just be 47 if the new baby was on time, and she and Pieter had decided that three would be enough. They lived in a large stone cottage next to the surgery, though Pieter's work was mostly with large animals on farms, the small animal work done in the main by the two female colleagues he employed. Therefore, spending most of his days with the ever-complaining men on their farms, he delighted in his womenfolk at work and at home.

For Elise, with a husband and two, soon to be three, tiny children, the solitary life lay long behind her, and she never once found herself hankering after it. She also loved the life of the village and had now mostly shed her Canadian accent and to an unknowing visitor could almost sound like a native, even if a slightly posh one!

She knew the old joke about the technical term for Jewish babies that have not been circumcised – "girl", but she was producing Jewish women capable in their turn of passing on the heritage. Not that she practiced any aspect of her former Jewish life, nor that of her Catholic past either. The girls had not been baptised and there were no plans to change this, at which Pieter's mum, Fiene (which was a diminution for Jozefien), feigned shock. She was now living with them, and she and Elise had rapidly become close and in wanting to share in childcare allowed Elise some space to do what she still wished, which was to join one of the local farmers two mornings a week to share in the milking and to be out on the hills walking hand-in-hand with Pieter. They could almost climb Penhill blindfold so often had they made their way to the plateau at its summit with its views over to the North York Moors and along the length of Wensleydale to the Pennines beyond.

Elise's only sadness from the early part of their marriage was that she was fated never properly to know Pieter's father, Heinrijck, an acknowledged expert of early Dutch art. She and Pieter had married one another in Leiden just five weeks after their cow-side meeting, and though they had spoken briefly after the wedding, at which Heinrijck had warmly welcomed her into the Dutch family, whilst they were on their honeymoon, he had become unwell and within a short time had died of pancreatic cancer. Elise had met the family again, this time at a funeral, and it was then that she suggested Fiene come and live with them in Whitby. It was only when they had moved with a new baby that Fiene had come and was now established as part of the family. The girls loved her and she the girls.

The most frequent visitors were Sarah and Ruth Jacobs who loved playing with and caring for the girls, but also enjoying the Dales and taking walks with their "aunt" Elise. Their mother, Leah, and partner Ursula, regularly came to stay and Elise urged them to leave London and come north and suspected that one day, perhaps soon, Leah might do that. "I will at least have a rabbi close by", Leah had commented when Elise pressed the case for a move. Her visits, however, always threw Fiene into a panic on the question of her dietary needs, even though Leah always insisted that being Reform she would eat anything.

Pieter and Elise had often spoken of her time in solitary reflecting on what it all meant.

'I often felt I was being guided by some words of a Russian hermit, "Keep your mind in hell and despair not". I never lost sight of the many deaths that took me into solitude, and in the face of so much suffering in the world I strove daily not to despair. It was only on the day before you came that I felt despair and acute loneliness for the first time with the death of Barbara, and knew, my work was done.'

Elise never wavered in her understanding that what had happened was in accordance with the Chooser who had chosen her even though she had no idea why that should be or even what she really meant by it but not remotely troubled by this. She often turned to Eliot and Little Gidding:

You are not here to verify,
Instruct yourself, or inform curiosity
Or carry report. You are here to kneel
Where prayer has been valid.

It had always been prayer, of course. She knew that though never mentioned the word even to Pieter, not least because as with the word most often used of the Chooser or HaShem (on her more Jewish-minded days), it was abused in so many words. Eliot had continued,

And prayer is more
Than an order of words, the conscious occupation
Of the praying mind, or the sound of the voice praying.

She had no doubts that it had been real, though it took some time for Pieter to accept that Elise had responded to some sort of initiative outside herself and was sceptical for a long time about the existence of the Chooser. As he said, he was very much the product of a very secular Holland, its school and universities.

Two things changed this. First and foremost was knowledge of this woman he adored, the mother of his children, a help and playmate in so many ways, (not least in bed, which at first had perplexed him as she maintained she had no previous experience though later confessed to having been instructed by Alex Comfort!). But Elise, he knew, was the most stable, able and trustworthy person he knew. That his scepticism she fully understood and did not feel in any way slighted by it, also made a great impression on Pieter. He knew she didn't need anyone else to validate or authenticate what she knew, and it didn't disturb her that he could not do so.

'To be honest,' she had said one day in the first year of their marriage, 'if I was you, I would think as you. do. That is in part why I speak of it to no one other than Leah and you. I neither expect nor need require any vindication of my knowledge, nor need to inflict it upon anyone else.'

'That, my dearest Elise, is the greatest obstacle to my scepticism. Most religious people seem to need the approval of others to endorse their own beliefs. You deliberately avoid speaking of beliefs as such, reject them as worth very little, and seek no external authentication, and that's my difficulty, because it makes me think you may just be right.'

The other change came about through the influence of his mother. Fiene had taught at the Amsterdam School of the Arts and had become interested in the life and writings of 17th century

Jewish man who had been excommunicated (though she knew that was not the right word) from the synagogue in the city and had spent the remainder of his short life grinding lenses for the new wonderful world of microscopes and telescopes, which Fiene thought a wonderful parable for what this man had done. He was known to philosophers as Spinoza and although his writings are held to be difficult had they always appealed to her because he seemed to be giving the whole of himself to God, if that was the right word, without any religion. When Fiene had told Pieter about him, he at once began to wonder how akin this story was to that of Elise.

Elise had never mentioned Spinoza to Pieter, or anyone else, but had long-since regarded him as her predominant inspiration, her patron saint. This came as a surprise to Pieter. The two women to whom he was closest knew something so very important about one of his own countrymen that he knew nothing about, and that furthermore he had been brought up just a few miles from where the philosopher had lived following his banishment from Amsterdam.

'Spinoza has mostly been ignored by modern philosophers,' Elise had said, 'as they have reduced meaning to nothing more than the analysis of language. He was way ahead of them. He was a great man, though to be fair when I say that I'm biased because another Dutch man is my life and lodestar.'

'I had been jealous for just a moment until then,' said Pieter with a broad grin, 'but do you think along the same lines as he did?'

'We are both Jewish and have moved on from that, though he was never a rabbi. He had no choice as he was issued with what is known as a *herech*, a terrible curse. I received a different sort of command, but we were similarly exiled and had to start from scratch in our involvement with such reality as we knew. I have never used even the limited language he does when writing of the Reality he and I knew for fear that it will inevitably be misunderstood and reduced under the impact of most peoples' religious lack of imagination to nothing, but I know what he means though to say his writings are difficult is to understate massively.'

This conversation strengthened in Pieter a sense that in

marrying Elise, he was drawing close to Something, but like her neither had any idea what it might be nor needed to have any idea. Elise told him that the only idea he should have, was to have no idea at all. He liked that, and it consoled him as he had to engage with the terrible times he and so many others lived through during the Foot-and-Mouth epidemic.

Elise was interested to learn just how much Fiene knew about Spinoza and hoped that she might possibly take her on a pilgrimage to the places where the great man had lived and worked. Having been married to a man who had given much of his life to the study of art, she endeavoured to link something of her knowledge of the writing of Spinoza to art itself.

'As an Irish poet said of poetry, if I knew where art comes from, I would wish to live there,' she had said to Elise one day as they were out in the village with a pushchair apiece.

'Of all people, Feine, knowing Spinoza as you do, surely you know that you already live there. We are ever *in-God* as Spinoza says and can never not be.'

'That's the very first time I've heard you say the word God.'

'I'm only reporting Spinoza's *Ethics*. I never normally use the word; that's perhaps the Jewish bit of me still functioning. Jews never speak the word, but what he said was true. I'm not a solitary any more and neither do I spend four hours a day in what some might call prayer or meditation, but I don't need to because I know everything is *in-Ha Shem*, to use the Jewish colloquial word.'

'Did you enjoy working as a rabbi?'

It was the first time Fiene had ever spoken of it and produced a laugh from Elise.'

'Will it make sense if I say that's like asking a long-distance runner if they enjoyed doing the first 100 metres? At the time it meant a lot but very quickly afterwards I knew I was made for something else, but I don't regret it in any way and I'm not planning a Wensleydale synagogue.'

'Dare I ask this?'

'Go on, my mother.'

'You've never called me that before.'

'I love you as my mother, Fiene, in a way I could not the Jewish

164

woman who gave me birth, so ask whatever you wish.'

'I was going to ask whether if the girls had been boys, you would have circumcised them?'

'Tell me, are there any easier questions I might try first?' said Elise, laughing, but knowing that the question had taken her unawares. She thought for a moment.

'I am Jewish by race, because my mother was and her mother before her and so on. Your granddaughters are also Jewish because that's how it works, and though I am quite thrown by your question, I think the answer would be that yes, I would have done so or had others do it. In that way the Jewish identity of the boys would be clear to them always but whether girls or boys they must always be exactly who they are in themselves.

'Although I take no part in any religion including the Jewish, I am proud to be a Jew, as probably Spinoza was too even after he had been cursed. It can't be cursed away, and I am descendent of some who died in the Shoah, as Jews call it, the Holocaust. I do not sing or dance about it, but it's also who I am, or at least it is still there inside and can't be erased.'

'And though I am not Jewish, Elise, I am so moved that you called me mother, so perhaps I qualify as an honorary Jew working upwards from daughter to mother.'

'Well, Fiene, I do know that only Pieter and the girls are closer to me than you.'

'Oh my goodness!' Fiene suddenly exclaimed. 'I've just had a thought. Please don't tell me you circumcised Pieter.'

Elise laughed so much, both Grace and Julia woke up and stared at their mother.

'It's ok, Fiene, I am Reform!' she said as her daughters joined in with smiles.

The weather outside was wild but the new daughter's birth was as trouble-free as her sisters' before her, and like Julia, she was born in the Friarage Maternity Centre in nearby Northallerton. Up to that moment Pieter and Elise had been undecided about names but on this day, given both the weather and the beginning of Elise's encounters, Pieter said she should be called Gale. This had occasioned a certain merriment when forms were being completed after her birth as they had to spell out the name and, even more, when the midwife on duty had asked Elise for her religion.

'Jewish,' she had said, 'Gale is a member of a chosen people.'

The midwife looked uncertain.

'I am Jewish, as are Gale's sisters, and as my mother was and their grandmother and their great grandmother all the way back to the Promised Land. But I am also a baptised and confirmed Catholic.'

The midwife turned from uncertainty to complete confusion.

'There's only space for one religion. I'll just put C of E to be on the safe side.'

Had it not been for the recent birth of his third daughter, Pieter felt he might have died laughing, and the midwife made a rapid departure.

'So, my end truly is as my beginning,' said Elise, trying to contain her husband's laughter. 'From nothing to Jewish, Jewish to Catholic, Catholic back to Jewish, and now back to nothing once again.'

'But Gale's birth, my darling, is another beginning and we have so much to look forward to.'

'I know, but such a long journey, as Eliot would say, "the ways deep and the weather sharp", but at least I now know that I have been led all this way for birth and that fills me with such joy.'

'You have been chosen for this, Elise Mary Westernberg, so I thank the Chooser.'

'That's more than I know, Pieter, my darling husband, and as the great Wittgenstein might have said if he'd come from Yorkshire: "If tha knows nowt, say nowt!"'!

PART TWO: 2008-09

Aishe

So many of the friendships between women begin outside the school gates in the afternoon. Dropping-off times in the morning tend to be hasty events to be concluded before other essential tasks have to be performed, but in the afternoon, there is a steady trickle of, mostly, mums who assemble in advance of the end of the school day. Pieter always enjoyed doing the dropping-off part, but Elise knew he was much happier if she did the gathering, when his work as a vet made him unreliable. Fiene, Pieter's mother was always happy to deputise, but Elise preferred doing it herself as an opportunity to meet different people and to catch up on town gossip, though to her disappointment the latter was often limited! Grace at 7 and Julia 5, meant that she now had only Gale with her in the daytime after at one time having had three under five at home, at which time Fiene had been so helpful.

Elise noticed that a young Indian-looking woman had joined the mothers from the start of term but that either she kept herself apart or was not included, so on the third afternoon of the first week, Elise decided to approach her.

'Hello, I'm Elise, I suspect you may have one of your children in the school for the first time or, and this is quite possible, I've sufficiently combined blindness and stupidity and just have not seen that you've been coming for years!

The woman laughed.

'No. You're quite right, my little boy has just started school this week. I'm Aishe Harman and I am so very pleased to meet you...er...'

'Elise...Elise Westernberg.'

'They're unusual names, and can I detect a faint trace of something North American?'

'What a disappointment! I was hoping to sound truly native by now.'

Aishe laughed.

'But you're quite right. I am Canadian by birth though I've lived in this country since I was 14.'

The children were coming out and a beautiful little boy approached.

Hello, Raj, how was school?'

'It was good, mama, and I have a friend called Julia.'

'That must be my Julia as she's in Reception too,' said Elise, 'and indeed here she is with her big sister. Hello, you two, this is Mrs Harman, Raj's mummy.'

'Raj is my friend,' said Julia.

'And I am hoping Raj's mummy is going to be friends with your mummy, Julia,' said Aishe.

By now, Grace had joined them.

'Oh, you have two children,' said Aishe.

'Three,' replied Elise. 'The youngest is at home with her Oma.'

'What is an Oma?'

'It's the Dutch word for granny. She's Oma Fiene, and like our daddy, is Dutch,' said Grace. 'She sometimes brings us to school.'

'What a wonderful family you have. A Canadian mummy and a Dutch daddy and living in Wensleydale.'

'And a Dutch Oma,' added Julia.

'Yes, of course.'

'Raj's daddy is a doctor,' said Julia.

'Our daddy's a doctor too – an animal doctor,' said Grace.

'Of course,' said Aishe, 'I do know your name. We took our cat when he was poorly to the vet, and I noticed the name then. How stupid of me.'

'And I take it that Dr Harman is your husband,' said Elise. 'I collected a prescription for my mother-in-law and saw the name.

You haven't been here long, have you?'

'My husband began work in August, so just six weeks now.'

'We should meet for coffee or whatever. Is that possible?'

'I would love that.'

'Give me a call. I've got a card here with my mobile number on it.'

'What about after the school run in the morning? I'm not working tomorrow.'

'Yes, that would be great!'

It was another triumph of the school gate friend-making club!

Being nearer to Aishe's house, they went there together on the following morning.

'I can't tell you how pleased I was that you came and spoke to me,' she said. 'Other than in restaurants there are not many people who look like me round here, so I shall have to get used to being ignored, or until my status improves once they know I'm the doctor's wife.'

'Or until they discover what a lovely person you are,' replied Elise. 'Where did you move from?'

'Tan was a GP in Cardiff and we both felt like a major change from city life, so we came here.'

'Is Tan short for something?'

'Yes, for Tanvir, but he's used the shortened form ever since he was a student. We use his second name as our surname which would otherwise be Patel. I'm sorry to say that there is still prejudice we have had to contend with.'

'That I understand only too well, as I'm Jewish.'

'Really?'

Elise could hear the astonishment in her voice.

'Yes, 100%.'

'I didn't anticipate meeting many others from my own background here, but a Jew. Wow, and how long have you lived here?'

'Seven years. Grace was one and we'd just lived through Foot-and-Mouth which was a tough time for Pieter, my husband.'

'I assume he's Jewish too.'

'No. I'm sure there must be some Jewish vets in this country, but Pieter isn't one of them.'

'What about the children?'

'I have three girls and as the children of a Jewish mother, they too are Jews, but by race rather than religion. In essence being Jewish doesn't immediately mean observance, and we don't.'

'In which case that's like us. We are Indian by racial origin, and both sets of our parents were professional people in Uganda, until thrown out by that monster Idi Amin. They came to the UK. Tan was born in Portsmouth, and I emerged in Caernarfon.'

'You're Welsh?'

'And very proud to be so, especially when they play England at the Millennium Stadium.'

'And do you speak Welsh?'

'It was compulsory at school but very few people spoke it in Cardiff and with not using it I regret to say it is fading rapidly.'

'That a great shame. I'm a language nerd. I read Middle Eastern languages at University and still have some Latin and Greek from school. Apart from being a full-time mum, do you go out to work?'

'I'm a community speech therapist, which is how Tan and I met when he came to Cardiff to read medicine.'

'And you enjoy the job?'

'It's such enriching work. I worked a lot with children in the city but here I shall be visiting mainly those recovering from CVAs.'

'Enriching, but surely also very demanding?'

'I think all work with patients is demanding, just as I imagine your husband finds having to deal with the owners of pets.'

Elise laughed.

'Oh yes! Though he prefers work with large animals, and he drives up and down the dale every day and loves it. Most small animal work is done by his two associates.'

'Going back to what you were saying, I always thought being Jewish meant a great deal in terms of day-to-day living?'

'*Being* Jewish means everything to me; *Doing* Jewish is different. However, when younger I became a rabbi.'

'You're a rabbi? Does that mean you do circumcisions and the like?'

Elise laughed.

'When I mention to anyone I'm a rabbi, that's always the first thing they think of. But yes, I am still a rabbi which is to say that I have had passed on to me the authority to teach and perform such things necessary for a community, including the act of circumcision, but I have never performed one, and there's not a great deal of call along the banks of the Ure for my services.'

'And no synagogue?'

'They are as rare as Hindu or Buddhist Temples in Wensleydale!'

They both laughed.

'So, if I might ask, if you're rabbi, however did you meet and marry Pieter, a Dutch vet in North Yorkshire – though I'm assuming you're married.'

'We met when we were both 39. I was single and he was a widower. I was helping a farmer friend getting his cattle tested for TB; Pieter was the vet. It was love at first Friesian!'

Aishe's eyes opened wide with amazement.

'We married in Whitby Register Office very soon after we met.'

'I've seen it on the map.'

'You should pay a visit. The fish and chips are quite magical! With your Indian background and the name of Patel, I assume you are Hindu rather than Buddhist in origin.'

'Yes, but not something we practice though, ironically, now being two generations on from India I have more interest in understanding what it might mean to me, though I haven't made a great deal of progress so far.

'Hinduism predates Judaism considerably by at least a thousand years.'

'Yes. Many Hindu myths are ancient.'

'In the 5th century BCE there was an unusual mental leap called the Axial Age that gave birth to Taoism and Confucianism in China; in India, Hinduism, Buddhism and Jainism; in Persia, Zoroastrianism; and of course, Judaism when the first Biblical writings were made. Christianity and Islam came much later and are both heretical developments from Judaism. Sadly, all these traditions have mostly only left conflict behind them, though not yet here in Wensleydale. '

'What does it mean for you to be Jewish?'

'I still study the Talmud, which I first did living in Jerusalem, but less and less as time goes by. Besides which, and if this doesn't confuse you nothing will, I am also a Catholic.'

'A convert, do you mean?'

'It's a long story but I am Jewish by birth though I didn't know that because my parents didn't want me to know it until I discovered it when I was a student. Neither did my mother ever tell me that as a baby I was baptised and confirmed as a Catholic by the priest in the town in Ontario where I was born and lived until we came here when I was 14. I didn't discover this until after I had become a rabbi when I went to visit my dying aunt who still lived in the town, and I met the priest.'

'You're right, I am confused. So, what does all that make you?'

'It makes me simply me – Elise Mary Westernberg.'

'A rabbi called Mary?'

'Mary was the Greek translation of the Jewish name Myriam, which they misused as they did with the name Yeshua, allegedly her son, to convince Gentiles that this new religion was not Jewish.'

'So are you more Jewish than Catholic?'

'I've never practised any form of Catholic religion though there are aspects of it I value highly. It was done to me, remember, when I was a baby, as some men complain about the missing bit of their penis. Being Jewish is simply a fact, though having chosen it as an adult, I retain a strong affinity with aspects of it.'

'And your husband?'

'Pieter is simply the most wonderful man in the world and we share so many things, but religion is not numbered among them.'

'That's also mostly true of Tan and myself. He has been formed and shaped by a scientific and secular mentality, not that he is isn't also very caring and loving, but his Hindu roots mean nothing, and anyway we came out of Africa, not India. Our parents on both sides were never practising Hindus. But, as I said, for the first time I have begun to read stories of Indian culture and history, and I include in that the Buddhist traditions too.'

'Judaism has always flourished in the context of storytelling, much more than through attempts at giving it intellectual expression. The first rabbi who cared for me only ever told stories and my kids would tell you that is what I do all the time.'

'Then they are lucky indeed.'

'But although you and I have very different roots, we share a common history of being uprooted by hatred. My great grandparents died in the Holocaust, and my grandparents sought exile in Canada, and your parents had to flee and find a new home. Storytelling goes on.'

A Hebrew Lesson

'How's your new friend Aishe?' asked Pieter at breakfast a couple of weeks later.'

'Working today. She does three days a week.'

'Her husband does four and is never on call, unlike your friendly neighbourhood veterinarian.'

'You wouldn't swap though.'

'Certainly not. Besides which most doctors are not anywhere skilled enough to be vets. Yesterday I performed major gynaecological surgery on a cow with a prolapsed uterus, turned obstetrician when a sow was stuck in the process of birth-giving, cardiologist for a horse with an uneven heartbeat, and scientist when testing a new tup for his sperm count. My first call this morning is to tend to a donkey with what seems to be a broken leg and this afternoon Heidi and I are operating on a cat with a dislocated jaw and a dog with cancer. I am GP and multi-disciplined Consultant in one.'

'And the best daddy, son and husband in the world,' added Fiene, who had come into the kitchen mid-conversation.

'It's hardly surprising,' added Elise, 'with five women supporting him here in the house and two adoring female colleagues at work.'

'I'll have you know,' said Pieter laughing, 'that you lot simply offset my days which are mostly spent with smelly and grumpy male farmers.'

'You love them,' said Fiene. 'They may be smelly and grumpy but it never seems to stop you going into the farmhouse for cups of tea, freshly-baked scones from the farmer's wife, and long chats about everything under the sun.'

'These days, mother, that is what is called networking, and is most important to running a business.'

'There are no scones or farmers' wives for poor Dr Harman,' added Elise.

'Nor performing procedures in pouring rain, snow, mud, outside in the freezing cold at night and frequently getting covered in what comes from inside the bowels and bladders of my patients.'

'And Aishe doesn't have to cope with the smells that accompany you into the house,' added Elise, 'but perhaps she doesn't share her life with a man who is so clearly fulfilled in all he does and whom I love.'

'Oh mummy,' said Grace, who had crept into the kitchen unseen, 'don't be soppy at the breakfast table. Can I have some porridge, please, Oma?'

'Of course,' replied Fiene. 'Is Julia dressed yet?'

'Don't be silly, Oma.'

Breakfast conversations repeated almost daily!

With the two older children in school and Gale in nursery, Elise went into the room she used as her study. She lit the beeswax candle as she always did and sat in the comfortable armchair. The candle was for the Presence, and as happens with all rituals had now become automatic though on this morning she gave it her full attention.

Her Jewish self would never name what she preferred to call שְׁכִינָה, Shekinah, the Presence. In earlier days it might have been HaShem, 'the Name', which Jews use to speak of what is too holy to name, though for Elise ever-present. She had spent five years living as a solitary on the North York Moors with only the Presence for company, a period which had ended only on the day before she had met Pieter on the remote farm where she helped out with the milking. She never spoke of it to anyone other than Pieter, Fiene and her closest friend of many years, Leah. She would need considerably more than just a speech therapist to know how she might possibly give expression to it in words.

That thought reminded her that she, Fiene, and Aishe were due to attend an event in the local church hall, of something that was called *Alpha*, to which Aishe had received an invitation for herself and friends to attend. Had Aishe not asked Elise to come, wild horses would not have dragged her there, and Fiene said she would come too. It was meant to be a meal of sorts at which the local vicar would also speak with the intention of winning participants on a six-evening course which as far as Elise could see from the internet was a Christian evangelistic outreach course which it claimed was sweeping the country.

Looking at the candle in her room she knew instinctively that if anyone was going to speak religion, by simple definition it must be literally non-sense, and she would only go if Pieter was available to read the stories and put the children to bed. For that to be the case, the animals of the Dales would have to be on their best behaviour.

Aishe had been invited, she had presumed, being the wife of one of the doctors, and possibly because her skin colour might have suggested she needed saving! She agreed with great reluctance but had been told it was going to be just like the harvest supper she and Tan had attended as special guests two weeks earlier.

The meal was simple – a jacket potato and salad, with apple pie for dessert. Elise estimated there must be about 40 present, mostly women The master of ceremonies was the vicar, Tony Reynolds, a man in his mid-40s who gave Elise the impression of being too smiley and trying too hard. As the meal began, he had introduced a man called Bruce who had apparently come from a church in York and who would say a few words later.

The meal passed against a background of something described as music, but which Elise assumed was part of the process leading up to the talks, consisting of what sounded like religious words sung by a group who had come with Bruce – his backing group, a thought which made Elise smile.

'Ladies and gentlemen of the Dales,' began the vicar. 'Thank you for being here this evening and I hope you have enjoyed our meal together at what we hope will be the start of a voyage of discovery over the next few weeks and beyond. Most of you will know that *Alpha* is sweeping the country at the present time, as more and more people find through it new meaning and purpose for their lives. So I'm especially glad to have with us Bruce, who is the leader of many *Alpha* courses from his base at St Michael-le-Belfry, the well-known church in York. So, Bruce, please speak to us.'

There was a smattering of applause.

'Thank you, Tom...' began the man.

'Tony,' said the vicar interrupting him.

'Sorry, Tony of course. Thank you for inviting our outreach team to be with you this evening. Yes, it's true, lives are being transformed by *Alpha* all over the country and across the world. We're not selling anything, but our church in the city is packed every Sunday morning and evening with young people and others who look around them at the world and wonder what's going on, and whether their lives have meaning.

'I've spent years studying the Bible in depth, and like many others have discovered it to be the key to deepening our understanding of the meaning of life. So much religion has become obsessed with accommodating itself to the latest thing in a desperate and mostly forlorn hope that it will appeal to people, whereas we have filled our churches using *Alpha* by realising that the challenge is for us to fit the pattern intended by God. It's as if we are aware that in just about every aspect of our lives we are wearing the wrong clothes and can't understand why we feel so uneasy all the time.

'We all know the message "For best results, follow maker's instructions", and that is what we are beginning this evening, something which will be enjoyable and local to you in this community, something to transform the ways we look at the world. So please accept our invitation to give it a go. You have nothing to lose.'

He sat down, and Tony stood again.

'We begin a week from tonight here in the hall. Has anyone any questions?'

A couple of people asked whether they needed to bring anything with them and were told everything needed would be provided.

'Can I ask a question?' said a woman sitting near the front.

'Of course,' said the vicar, uneasily, Elise thought.

'As with some others here who are farmers, we lost all our sheep and cattle during Foot-and-Mouth in 2001, and then two years ago my fifteen-year-old son died of leukaemia after a long period of awful illness. Will your course of six evenings really deepen my understanding of the meaning of life as you claim?'

'I'll take this, Tom,' said Bruce, standing, once again getting the vicar's name wrong.

'I'm sure everyone here will sympathise with your loss and one of the great consolations must be the love of family and friends. It's my sure conviction that in this *Alpha* course and beyond you will come to discover God's eternal love for you, and that even in the face of your terrible loss you will be consoled and strengthened by that love. After all, God's own son died on the cross, so he understands.'

'Oh, so that's alright then,' said the woman sarcastically. 'Our farming livelihood destroyed and my only son wasting away before our eyes for months. What sort of God-love is responsible for that?'

'I'm sure your son passed into something glorious.'

'He didn't pass anything. You make it sound like an exam or the driving test he was never old enough to take. He suffered greatly and your God did nothing to help.'

'In the Old Testament there is the quite remarkable book of Job which tells how all his farm animals and all his children died. It tells how he came to know and love God even after all that and I believe that this course will share that good news with you, that in this course you will find strength.'

Elise could take no more and raised her hand. Bruce pointed to her, and she stood.

'Most of us here know Mrs Satterthwaite and all she has been through, and we know she is far too pleasant a person not to object to being patronised as you have just done. We know too she has no need to find strength from the sort of nonsense you've just come out with.

'Please tell us, from your years studying the Bible in depth, what you make from your comparisons of the Hebrew Masoretic Text of the book of Job put together from diverse sources over 300 years, with the Greek Septuagint, together with the Aramaic and Hebrew scrolls found at Qumran. I imagine too, that you must have compared them with similar texts from Mesopotamia and Egypt.

'From all your years of studying the Bible in depth I'm sure you are familiar with this and recognise that Job is not one book but a compilation, so I wonder if you can explain the ending, of which I'm sure you know the Hebrew is quite complex showing an attempt to unite diverse sources, of the contradiction that Job first repents for blaming what Jews call HaShem for all the bad things that happened, but then says he doesn't repent at all. Please help us understand that contradiction in the Hebrew of chapter 42, from your years of studying the Bible in depth.

'Oh, and a final point you didn't mention, was that Job begins with a wager between HaShem and הַשָּׂטָן, properly translated as "the adversary" and not simply transliterated as Satan, and ends with Job receiving even more animals and children than he had before as some kind of recompense for all he had endured. That wouldn't have been much of a consolation to the children killed at the start of the wager, and please try explaining to Mrs Satterthwaite and countless numbers of other farmers in the Dales how it is that their rewards from on high seem even slower than the government in providing compensation.'

She sat down to a burst of applause, Bruce left standing at the front like a beached whale.

'The problem of suffering has been addressed by many greater men than me over the years on the basis of their study of the Bible. They, like me, look to the cross of Jesus as God's reply.'

He seemed pleased with his answer.

'As Mrs Satterthwaite said earlier,' said Elise,'"That's alright then". But just out of interest I take it your knowledge of that comes from your reading of Η Καινή Διαθήκη?'

'I'm not sure what you're referring to.'

'It's what "The New Testament" is in the original Greek in which it was written with which it would appear your years of Bible study in depth did not include.'

Tony the vicar, shot to his feet.

'And am I to assume that you *do* have a command of Hebrew and Greek,' Tony said, accusatorially.

'Yes! Why on earth would you think I would speak publicly about something I know nothing about?'

Tony blanched.

'Er, yes, well, what a stimulating evening with which to begin our journey of discovery. We have much to look forward to. A special thanks to the ladies who prepared the meal, and to Bruce and the team who have travelled from York, and I wish you all a good evening.'

Aishe, Fiene and one or two others near Elise and could barely contain their glee.

'I've never heard such sanctimonious crap,' said one of the women whom Elise recognised from outside school, 'but I think you've done everyone here a great service, Mrs Westernberg. Thank you.'

Elise walked forward to speak to Betty Satterthwaite.

'I hope anything I said wasn't inappropriate.'

'I was just so glad you were here, Mrs Westernberg. I've often had to say that to your husband when he comes to one of our beasts or sheep, but tonight it's you I want to thank. Pieter always brings skill and learning and clearly his wife does the same.'

'The idea that your courage and strength is insufficient I found simply insulting.'

As they walked up the street outside, Elise felt obliged to apologise to Fiene and Aishe.

'I just couldn't sit there without saying something.'

'You said something alright,' said Fiene, with great pride in her daughter-in-law. 'I've never heard you say anything like it before. I loved it.'

'Me too,' Aishe added, 'I can't wait to tell Tan.'

A Greek Lesson

Over the course of the following few days Elise received thanks from a number of those who had been present at the meeting and more than a few who had not but knew of what they called, with evident approval, her "put-down" of the vicar and his attempts to flood the town with notices about Alpha.

She was less than happy, however. It had never been her intention to humiliate anyone and was feeling that after years of silence she had spoken in public in such a way as to make people think she had done something clever. One evening about a week after the meeting and with children in bed, she expressed her regret to Fiene and Pieter.

'You need feel no guilt,' said Pieter. 'Those who have heard about it on the farms have all told me how indebted Betty Satterthwaite was to your standing up and defending her. And from what you told me it wasn't the vicar here whom you addressed, but the guy he had brought to speak. You know as well as I that evangelical Christians love being persecuted, as I'm sure he imagined you were doing.'

'That's true, Elise,' added her mother-in-law. 'And you were not rude or showing off, just revealing that he was not quite as clever as he wanted to appear.'

'I suppose so,' admitted Elise, 'but it's the first thing I have ever said in public about anything even remotely religious since I stopped working as a rabbi, and I don't ever wish to do so again.'

'I only wish that a lot of people who feel obliged to sound off in public would say the same thing,' said Pieter. 'Please don't feel troubled, my darling. You acted in defence of someone else, not advertising your own cleverness, though of course you are seriously clever. What you did was entirely appropriate, and I am proud that you said what you did.'

Elise smiled, but her anxiety was not mollified and wondered if she should make an effort to apologise to the vicar. Pieter knew her well enough to read her face.

'Oh no, you don't,' he said.

'Don't what?'

'Don't even consider apologising to the vicar. I know how your mind works. If you were to say sorry to him, it would only encourage him to pass it on to his fan club and claim the high ground again.'

Elise laughed.

'You know me too well. Ok, I promise.'

However, as things turned out she bumped into the Revd Tony Reynolds on the following morning as he was entering, and she leaving, the small supermarket in the town.

'Oh, it's you,' he said in a far from friendly or forgiving manner. 'Thanks to you last night there were only five people at the meeting, after 43 came last week. Weeks of planning and prayer had gone into this, all ruined by someone showing off her cleverness.'

'I think, Mr Reynolds, if there was a ruination it was not of my making, but that of your speaker. He couldn't remember your name, he made claims in public founded upon ignorance in the face of someone who had recently lost a son and a whole community who knew the realities of Foot-and-Mouth. You weren't here then, were you? To be honest I'm disappointed that even five people turned up last night. Your brand of religion attempts to use the natural fears of being human, that there is actually no daddy in the sky to protect them from the vicissitudes of living, to manipulate them psychologically, and on the basis of profound ignorance even of your own founding texts. I assume you at least can read the Greek of the New Testament.'

'You are welcome to your opinions, and I think you will find that modern translations provide us with all we need.'

'All Imams read the Quran in Arabic, all Rabbis read Tanakh in Hebrew and, honestly, I think you would greatly benefit from being able to read the New Testament in the original. It's written in what's called Koiné Greek, which is straightforward and so avoids having to learn vocabs to do with battles and philosophy. If I've ruined your plans for *Alpha*, it was not my intention to do so, I just couldn't sit and let that man say things that are simply untrue and patronise Betty as he was doing.'

'But how do you know any of this?'

'I read Hebrew and Aramaic at university and studied Talmud in Jerusalem.'

'But that suggests you are Jewish.'

'Yes, of course I am, as are my three daughters, two of whom attend your church school.'

'But there is no synagogue.'

'That's reserved mostly for men. Women are too wise to subject themselves to masculine religion,' said Elise with an ironic grin.

'That's the opposite in most churches. The women come and the men stay away. But how do you know Greek?'

'I have always found languages easy, and I did Greek and Latin at school. The Greek of the New Testament is easy compared with Classical Greek. You should give it a go and I would be very happy to help. I used to work as a tutor in the Jewish equivalent of what you would call a theological college.'

Tony said nothing for a few moments and was clearly thinking hard.

'Ok. I would like that. But I don't even know tour name.'

'Elise...Elise Westernberg. My husband is one of the vets here.'

'So that is how you knew quite a few of the farming people at the meeting last week.'

Elise handed Tony a card.

'My mobile is the best one on which to get me. The landline would take you through to the surgery.'

'And to think I only came out to get some milk,' he said.

'Yes. Things happen in life in all sorts of strange ways. It's obviously a dangerous thing to go out for milk first thing in the morning!'

Tony laughed.

'So it seems. When can I call you?'

'Give me the chance to get home at least,' said Elise with a laugh, 'and in the meantime I'll look out a book we might use together.'

'Thank you. May I call you Elise?'

'If I can call you Tony. You don't look even remotely like a Tom!'

Tony laughed again as they shook hands.

Pieter was at work when she arrived home and Fiene had returned from taking Gale to nursery, and when Elise told her that the vicar was coming for Greek lessons, she began at once to laugh.

'Oh, Elise my lovely daughter, nothing you do ever surprises me. A week ago, you were making yourself his sworn enemy and now he is to be your student. Does he know you are a rabbi?'

'I thought I'd save that. In the first place he has to come to terms with a Jewish enclave in his parish he didn't previously know about, and one that has already ruined his evangelistic plans and planted two Jewish girls into his Christian school! I thought that was quite enough for one trip to the shops to buy milk.'

Fiene laughed again.

'And will you give lessons in Sanskrit to Aishe?'

'I'd love to learn Sanskrit and read all those wonderful Vedic and Hindu myths which are so important.'

'How do you mean "important"?'

'Myths tell us so much about ourselves and when I read them, I strive to listen behind the words of the stories to what they tell us, from as far back as seven thousand years, what they knew about what I know. In that sense they are much more my contemporaries than poor Tony and his evangelical cohorts.'

'You'll tell him that of course!'

Elise laughed and made them both some coffee in the latest of many coffee machines she had acquired over the years, even including her time living as a solitary. There was no excuse for bad coffee, she often said, and now the kitchen was overwhelmed first with the noise of beans being ground and then the aroma of freshly made real coffee. Fiene loved it.

Pieter had been out since the early hours performing a caesarean on a cow that simply refused to give birth in the established way, and so was in the kitchen and smelly when Tony arrived for his first Greek lesson.

'Come in,' said Peter, 'and don't mind me. I've been in the bovine equivalent of a labour ward, so I may stink a bit. I'm Pieter and you must be Tony. Elise has been looking forward to meeting with you again. I think she felt bad about the effect of what she said at your course meal.'

'She made quite an impact and I've put the course on hold for the time being. But she needn't feel bad. Perhaps it was for the best.'

Elise came into the kitchen.

'Hello Tony. I apologise for my smelly husband. Coffee?'

'Yes please. I imagine you must get used to the amazing things he does, but I'm impressed.'

'It was cows that brought us together, but that's another story.'

She showed Tony into her study whilst she made the coffee and he looked at her books, though his eye was immediately caught by a photograph of Elise and a bearded man, both of them wearing some sort of official garb. When she returned, he was still looking at the photo.

'That's Rabbi Samuel with me at my *Semikhah*. He's a wonderful man.'

'What is whatever you called it?'

'My *Semikhah* – you would call it ordination I suppose.'

'Do you mean you are a rabbi?'

'Yes.'

'I've met you just three times and each time you have surprised, if not actually shocked me. It's no wonder you were able to speak so authoritatively at the meeting, and the range of your books blows my mind. How many languages do you speak?'

'These days only English though married to a Dutchman I'm striving to learn Dutch. I don't *speak* any of the others now, as there's not a great call for them hereabouts, but I'm at ease with Hebrew, Aramaic, Latin and Greek. But as I told you before I have

the sort of mind that can handle languages easily but I'm relatively
dyscalculic. Our brains differ considerably in what we can and
can't handle, so let's see how yours manages Greek, but first, if
you will, tell me something about you and how you got to become
vicar here.'

'I've only been ordained for three years and this is my first
parish. I used to work as an electrical engineer for ICI in Leeds,
and then experienced a conversion and later began training for
ordination.'

'Where did you do that?'

'At home. It was a three-year part-time course during which I
continued at my job and did my studying in the evenings and at
the weekends. On some weekends I met with others near
Huddersfield where the course was run from, and each year we
had a weeklong summer school, a bit like the Open University. I
was ordained in York Minster and helped out in my local parish
church, still working for ICI, and then it was suggested I might
come here to become what is called a stipendiary minister.'

'That must be quite a change.'

'It is.'

'Do you pray?'

'Gosh, that's almost like asking about my sex life.'

'I won't ask you about that,' she answered with a smile.

'Well, yes, of course. Each morning and evening I read the
services from what's called Common Worship.'

'What about meditation or being silent?'

'In my evangelical tradition our focus is upon hearing what God
is saying each day through the words of scripture. We are
suspicious of anything that smacks of Buddhism or anything like
that.'

'Ok. Well, let's turn to the study of Greek. I've got a book here
which is designed for Christians learning Greek. We should begin
with the alphabet which is a series of symbols each of which has
to be learned before anything else, but once you can make a start
with learning to read and recognise the sound of each, you'll
quickly be reading some of the gospels. Paul's Greek contains
vocab not found in the gospels, something Christians don't usually

ask why, but I will leave that to you. When I read him, I recall that he also was a Jew, though abandoned it and even changed his Jewish name to something more acceptable to Gentiles.'

For the next half hour Elise took Tony through the Greek alphabet and introduced him to the first sentence of John's gospel which, before he left, he could read the words with which, in English, he was familiar. He was pleased with himself and clearly pleased with Elise.'

'You're a good teacher.'

'You can judge me better after we meet again, and I can find out how much homework you have done.'

'That sounds somewhat ominous but please let me thank you and say how wonderful it is to be taught how to read the New Testament by a rabbi, even if I don't quite understand why a rabbi is living here in the Dales and without a synagogue.'

'When you know more Greek you will learn that συναγωγή means a gathering of Jews, not a building, much as I imagine you tell people that a church is a gathering of those called together, in Greek ἐκκλησία, not that building at the bottom of the High St. So, there is a συναγωγή here in this town consisting of myself and my three Jewish daughters.'

Tat Tvam Asi

Her conversation with Tony taught Elise a great deal about the ways in which many forms of religion function. It had served to illustrate perfectly a recently published book she had read by a psychiatrist-neuroscientist called Iain McGilchrist, which set out in considerable details the ways in which the two hemispheres of our brains function, with a clear distinction between the more analytical and controlling left side in contrast to the right which looks at things in a wider perspective, and from where art, music and beauty evolve. She had in her years of solitude learned to shed book learning and logic in order to know the Presence, which was inaccessible to the left side of the brain which would have sought to turn it into a religion with order and control, speaking of something simply which was nothing more than a projected image in the sky of human rulers on earth. That something was all the gods, deities and divinities she utterly rejected as void of content and meaning. It was why, she assumed, Jews spoke of HaShem (the Name) rather than using any other word, as she thought only of שְׁכִינָה, though of course she knew well enough that Judaism too was so very often just like the other religions with divisions and hatreds.

Tony, an engineer thought totally along the lines of the left side of his brain and his religion inevitably bore the same hallmarks. Evangelical religion was the epitome of left-sided manipulation and control, a religion of the book, the supreme example of a religion of words, strict order and control.

She knew this sort of religion very well, for she had thrown herself into it with a zeal from the first moment she had begun living as a Jew as a student, becoming a highly regarded authority in the study of Talmud as she trained as a rabbi, which itself meant more and more words. Her religion had been simply the Jewish form of Tony's religion of the book.

She had to be shocked out of this by her close encounters with death, and a wholly unexpected meeting with Jean-Pierre. Being with him for just a few hours in his woodland retreat had shaped the rest of her life, beginning with the life of a solitary for five years on the moors by the North Sea.

Her closest friend of many years, Leah, was coming to stay at the weekend, together with her partner Ursula, and Leah's two daughters Ruth and Sarah, up for a few days from London. Elise hoped she might get the chance for a one-to-one with Leah, who with Pieter and Fiene, was the only other who knew in depth what it was she had been doing for the five years spent in isolation, being her only visitor. A naughty part of herself was tempted to email the vicar with a note that this weekend, with four more Jews in his parish, the numbers attending her συναγωγή would be doubled, and then, reluctantly, thought better of it!

Two days after the first Greek lesson, Elise and Aishe met for their regular morning coffee on a morning when Aishe was not working.

'So how was the Greek class?' said Aishe with a grin.

'What he told me filled me with alarm, to be honest, Aishe. Here he is running a local church and presumably ministering to people at crisis moments in their lives, for which he has received next to no real preparation or training.'

'You're kidding.'

'He trained part-time, mostly at home, whilst continuing to do his full-time job, for less than three years. A basic BA with the Open University lasts six years, and from what he told me unless someone seriously blotted their copy book, there was simply no chance of failing. Rabbis do five years' full-time training.'

'You exposed the lack of serious training at that meal, said Aishe.'

'I looked up on the Internet the curriculum he followed on his course. Three months each on the Old and New Testament, in translation of course. He and so many other of his fellow evangelicals, apparently taking over the Church of England in a desperate hope it will bring in more people, use all sorts of unintelligent gimmicks of which *Alpha* is the latest fad.

'What worries me though, is that in teaching him Greek I'm not challenging his predominant analytic way of operating, just worsening it when he comes to see it as another tool to be used in the same way as the others, something with which to impress and enhance his alleged authority when he preaches.'

'I know from my own reading', said Aishe, 'the importance of myth and stories forming and shaping our ways of being and inducing a response, but never being told how to receive the stories. They are not stories then which should be responded to however we are.'

'Aishe, I could learn a great deal from you, and would love to share together some of the ancient myths of your own Hindu forebears and Buddhists, though I also learned long ago that the most important aspect of our lives as human beings cannot be acquired from any amount of information from the left-side of our brains. It is with the right-hand side with which we need to hear stories.'

'Elise, you never speak, other than in the occasional aside or hint, about what was clearly something of enormous importance in your life, but I've been with you often enough in your study to know that the first thing you always do is to light your lovely beeswax candle for no purpose other than what I think is recollection, acknowledging something or someone.'

Elise looked intently at her friend, and then smiled.

'Tat tvam asi.'

'Until I met you, Elise, I would never have thought twice that to say "Thou art That" was even remotely meaningful, and though you have never engaged me in any kind of religious dialogue, I seem to have intuited something, or perhaps enough, to make me want to respond.'

'That is the only way, Aishe. Our poor vicar and his fellow evangelicals are simply abandoning all that the right-side of their brains could teach them and serve as a guide, and like the rest of the world have become hooked on linear knowledge.'

'Can't you subvert him?' said Aishe with a laugh.

'The Emperor heard of the wisdom of one of the Desert Fathers in the 4th century and travelled hundreds of miles to visit him. But over three days the old man said nothing. Finally, the Emperor left in disgust. The disciples of the old man protested that he could have had a great influence on the Emperor, to which he replied, "If he cannot learn from my silence, he cannot learn from my words"!'

'What a wonderful story,' Aishe said with her eyes wide open, 'and there are similar stories told also of the Buddha.'

'I think it's much the same with music and art. An analytic approach to either might be impressive, but it doesn't make you hear the music or see a work of art. That can only happen when it happens. The great American dancer Isadora Duncan was once asked the meaning of dance she had performed, and replied, "If I could explain, I wouldn't need to dance!".'

'I was wondering what our husbands would make of what we are speaking of. Tan is totally scientifically-minded and the very possibility of our earlier conversations he would regard as simply the result of psychological conditioning which he believes causes all religion.'

'And I would almost totally agree with him. A great deal of religion comes out of peoples' needs and longings, with an almost endless supply of people willing to provide it to them with the only cost being their integrity and the closure of their minds to other possibilities. That's why I gave religion up a long time ago and have no wish to return.'

'What about Pieter?'

'He too grew up in a totally secularised world in Holland and, as with Tan, is scientific in all his work, but tells me that he increasingly relies on intuition when working with animals and farmers alike.'

'We haven't known each other long, Elise, but already I value our friendship so very highly. Perhaps one day you might even dare to trust me enough to tell me the story of what I think you know and never speak of, though that in itself already tells me a great deal.'

Elise looked at her friend for a while, and then said, 'William Blake was asked if at sunrise he saw a round disk of fire somewhat like a Guinea coin, to which he replied, "O no, I see an innumerable company of the Heavenly host crying Holy Holy Holy is the Lord God Almighty". This cannot be taught or learned from any number of books, and I think you know how I have no interest whatsoever in the things people say they believe or even worse, believe "in". But Aishe, I feel the same joy as you in our friendship and all we might have to offer one another. I know so very little of what you bring with you in your DNA. You might have been born in Wales, but your roots lie deep in the Indus Valley. That makes you so very rich, for those roots go back long before my own Jewish roots.'

Aishe stood and went for a book that had been resting on the dining table. She sat down and opened it.

'I was reading this last night, and I don't know why it affected me so, but is seems to apt for what you are saying. Yes, this is it. It's from the *Kena Upanishad*:

"There sight cannot go, speech cannot go, nor the mind.

We cannot know, we cannot understand. How can one explain It?

It is other than all that is known. It is above the Unknown.".

'That's how it is, isn't it Elise?'

Elise nodded her head and smiled at her friend.

'There is a story of Francis of Assisi who sent his friars out to proclaim the gospel but to use words only if absolutely necessary! I think Aishe that we already speak the most important things to one another without words.'

'Yes, I know.'

'And shall continue, though I must go now, as I'm collecting Gale from nursery, but is there any chance you could bring Raj over on Sunday morning to play, and for some brunch, to allow you to meet Leah, Ursula, Rachel and Sarah?' Tan too. Doctor and vet can compare notes.'

'Alas, it's his morning for playing golf and he's just joined the Richmond club, but as a golfing widow I'd be more than happy to come and so I imagine will Raj. He talks about Julia ever such a lot when he comes home from school.'

'She does the same. They have formed a close link.'

Having collected Gale from nursery, they made their way home, Gale chatting nineteen to the dozen in her pushchair, demanding the attention of her mother, when Elise received a surprise phone call from the farmer's wife she had defended at the meeting, Betty Satterthwaite.

'Mrs Westernberg, please excuse me calling you, but can I come and see you?'

'Of course.'

'I won't tell you the reason over the phone but it's important.'

'Can you come this afternoon? I pick up the children at 3-30 but any time after 2-00 will be ok.'

'Yes. I'll come then. Thank you so much.'

Even as Gale chatted on, Elise wondered why Betty Satterthwaite wanted to come and talk about something too important to mention on the telephone?

She looked up at the sky, which was darkening and threatening rain, and soon the clocks would go back, and it would be getting dark by 4-00. For Pieter winter meant more hours in freezing cold barns and remote stone outbuildings with inadequate lighting. Doctors on their golf courses, she decided, didn't know they were born!

Two Days In October

Elise knew that almost all the wives of farmers she knew (and she was well aware that in the Dales though most "farmers" were their women-folk shared fully in the work but still called "farmers' wives") inhabited two worlds for which they dressed differently, as it was with Betty when she arrived. Elise had known her most often in her farming gear when she came to pay the vet bills, but today she looked totally transformed with short blonde hair, make up and expensive clothes in which she looked very attractive.

'Thank you for agreeing to see me, Mrs Westernberg.'

'Please call me Elise, and may I call you Betty?'

She nodded and smiled.

'You know that Luke, my son, died of leukaemia. He was 15 and very poorly for more than a year before he died. That was just two years ago this past August.'

'I think we all remember that, Betty.'

'When he arrived just over a year ago, Tony Reynolds, the vicar, called to see us, well me really, as my husband won't have anything to do with religion. At first, I thought it was very kind of him, though I later learned that he had been told I had once been a regular attender at church, and I think he was trying to get me back. He called in quite a few times and was always very kind, then one day suggested I call in on him at the vicarage so he could show me a particular book, though he could have brought it to show me at home. So, I did.

'Hughie, my husband, had become so very bitter, what with Foot-and-Mouth and Luke's death, I must confess I was feeling very lonely, and so ...'

'I think I might be able to guess,' said Elise, interrupting.

'Yes, we ended up in bed and this became something that happened every week. I don't know whether you know his circumstances, but he's married and has two children, but they still live in the house he has in Leeds. His wife didn't want to leave and come to a vicarage, and I suspect doesn't share his religion-thing.

'Anyway, this went on until a couple of months ago, when he suddenly decided it was wrong and had to end it. I was devastated and that was probably why I said what I did at that awful meeting when you massacred the pair of them. I was so glad. But then, yesterday he saw me in town when I was doing some shopping and suggested a cup of coffee. To be honest I wasn't totally sure of his motives, but he said he wanted to apologise for what he had done and that he could understand why I had asked the question I had at the meeting. Then he hinted that perhaps we could pick up the pieces and begin seeing one another again. I told him that he had cooked his goose and that I was pleased he had been made to look so stupid at the meeting.

'That was when he told me that in point of fact he was meeting regularly with you now, and that, though you kept it a secret, you were in fact yourself a church minister. So, I felt I should come and tell you about it all. I don't want you hurt as I have been.'

'Thank you, Betty. I am not having any sort of relationship with Tony, though he came once just last week, for a starter class in Greek. Nor am I a minister, as he said. Did he not tell you that I am Jewish and considerably more knowledgeable than he, even about the New Testament?'

'Jewish?'

'Oh it gets worse, because I am, or more correctly once was, a rabbi. He didn't tell you that I imagine?'

'No. He sort of implied that what happened between him and me was taking place with you.'

'It is not. He must be fanciful indeed if he thinks one Greek lesson is opening the bedroom door, when not only am I devoted to Pieter, I also live with his mum and our three Jewish girls.'

'He was very convincing when I thought he was showing me care.'

'Well, as you said you were very needy and appreciative of his attention, in other words extremely vulnerable and I'm afraid his own needs led him to take advantage of you.

'I have two concerns. The first is for you, and the second for others who might be in a vulnerable position. I took a great deal of pleasure from the way you exposed his ignorance at the meeting.'

'It didn't take much, I can assure you. But would it help to talk it over with someone who's specially trained to deal with what is actually sexual abuse?'

'Was it abuse? I did enjoy it, after all.'

'Jews think sex is something to be enjoyed, but, Betty, you're a person of considerable courage, and have had to be as you have had go through hell with the illness and your loss of Luke, but there is still the question of what you called your loneliness and your isolation. The opportunity to talk it through and find what it is you want for the rest of your life might make a considerable difference to you. I don't know if you know, but the death of a child very often precedes the breakup of a marriage.'

Hughie couldn't manage without me. If I was to leave him, I honestly think he would shoot himself.'

'Has he said that?'

'Yes, a number of times.'

'That's why you should find someone, definitely not a vicar by the way, who could be there for you to try and see what might be possible rather than being a slave to someone else's threats.'

'A counsellor, do you mean? Can't you do that?'

'I do mean a counsellor, but one who is specially trained to do that sort of work with you. I am not a counsellor. I haven't been trained, though I once regularly saw a counsellor over a long period and from her received the impetus and support to change my life completely. And you could easily tell your husband that it is bereavement counselling.'

'And what about Tony? You said you are also concerned for others in a vulnerable situation.'

'It's clear he needs help and urgently. He should not be working as a vicar and living apart from his family, though I would imagine there's more that than just a difference of opinion about religion. But can he be stopped?'

'I'm sure he must, for his own sake, no less that of others. He will need to be reported to his higher authority, a bishop or someone. I don't know how it works in the Church of England.'

'But he's a hypocrite.'

'Yes, but in certain circumstances all of us fall short of our highest alleged ideals. Perhaps a while back you would never have thought you would commit adultery.'

Betty's hand shot to her mouth.'

'Oh my God, that's what it is, isn't it?'

'Betty, you are the victim of exploitation, and you must never forget that. It is a very serious matter in someone charged with responsibilities of care in a public office.'

'Does that mean you intend doing something about it?'

'I have a solicitor friend coming tomorrow with whom I would like your permission to recount what you have told me, someone who can advise us what we might do to help prevent other women being taken advantage of by Tony, and not least for his sake too. He will cause a major scandal eventually, and for his own sake and that of his family we must do all we can to help him.'

'Thank you, Elise. And I'm so pleased what happened with me isn't happening with you, as he slyly implied.'

'Give me a day or two, Betty.'

Pieter and Fiene noticed how distracted Elise was on that evening even though she had to prepare the rooms for the weekend visitors due on Friday and the evening meal she wanted to produce for them.

Her sleep was disturbed so when she rose at 4:30 on one of the two mornings a week she went to help a local farmer with the milking which she loved and he more than appreciated, she felt already tired. She was always invigorated by her contact with the animals and when the time came to muck out after the milking felt that the task was appropriate for what she was going to have to do with Tony!

She arrived home shortly after 9:00, the children already dealt with by Pieter and Fiene, had a shower and set about bed-making. Just to add colour she also felt her period starting. Mercifully (for Pieter?) she had never suffered greatly from PMT, but at 49 wondered when this monthly visitation (allegedly the result of a curse on Eve for chatting up a snake in a garden which she thought was somehow disproportionate to the original offence!) would start to end. She had begun child-producing late, at 42, 44 and 47, so perhaps her body thought there might be the chance of another and at 49 Pieter had lost none of the longings that made bedtime so good for both of them (she keenly making up for lost time having only begun at 39!), but enough was enough they had decided and in the previous year he had received the minor surgical attention they both hoped would keep the number of their girls to three!

She was longing to see Leah. She and her former husband, Jerry, had provided her with a home and a nest in which she could learn what it meant to be Jewish. Then, as her life changed after the five years "in the desert" and she had met Pieter, Leah's marriage had ended amidst much acrimony, leaving her with Sarah and Ruth her twin daughters. Most surprising of all was when she told Elise that she was now living with Ursula, also Jewish and the solicitor who had taken Leah through her divorce. The couple had moved north two years ago, and Ursula had joined a legal practice in Harrogate and they lived in a tiny place called Pateley Bridge, which allowed Leah and Elise to meet as often as possible. Sarah and Ruth were still flat sharing in Hackney, Sarah studying medicine and Ruth reading law, both at Kings College. Amusingly, they still insisted on addressing her as "aunt Elise" which she adored!

It wasn't going to be a Shabbat Friday evening meal tomorrow, given that neither Fiene nor Pieter were Jews, and herself and her own girls not observant, but nevertheless she wanted it to be special for them. It was not often in Wensleydale that there would be 8 Jewish women together to begin Shabbat!

With her preparations complete, Elise was about to sit down to have some lunch and the chance of a nap, when into the kitchen came Heidi, one of Pieter's colleagues.

'Elise, I am a bit concerned because Annie hasn't turned up for work and though I phoned her there's no answer. I just wondered whether she might be poorly. When you live alone it can't be easy if you get flu.'

Annie was the practice cleaner.

'No, and it's most unlike her not to call in if she's feeling poorly. Do you think I should pop round and see her?'

'I should do it really,' replied Heidi, 'but we're up to our eyes in surgery, but if you could that would be great.'

'Of course,' Elise said and went to get her coat.

Annie lived just five minutes away and when Elise arrived, she could see that the curtains of the ground-floor flat were still closed. She knocked on the door a few times and called through the letterbox before knocking on the window of what she thought might be the bedroom. But there was no reply. By now Fiene was back from nursery with Gale and came to join Elise.

'It doesn't look good,' said Fiene.

'No,' replied Elise, 'and I suppose I ought to call the police but if she's unwell in bed, the sight of Constable Halliwell bursting into her home might terrify the living daylights out of her. The fanlight in what must be the lounge is open slightly. Perhaps I can clamber up and use it to open the window below.'

'And go in? Elise you are not a young girl.'

'Thank you, dearest mother, for that reminder, but let me at least try.'

She brought the rubbish bin to the window and carefully mounted which gave her immediate access to the small window which she easily opened and then by stretching was able to flick open the latch on the larger. Now she climbed through the window, by which time a group of about five people had gathered to watch and Gale was entranced by the sight of her mother doing gymnastics!

Elise gave a quick look round, opening the bedroom door and seeing the bed properly made before going into the kitchen. All seemed well and it occurred to her that perhaps Annie had gone away somewhere, and then something made her return to open the bedroom door wider. That was when she saw Annie's body on the floor beside the bed, with tablets and containers lying around her.

She knelt and touch Annie's leg. It was cold and already Elise could see that Annie was dead.

A Lawyer Intervenes

When Leah and the others arrived for the weekend on the following morning they were surprised to find two police cars outside the surgery though there didn't seem a real sense of urgency, and led in by Elise found three police officers sitting round the kitchen table drinking tea and chatting with Fiene.

Once in the kitchen where they had put their bags down, the officers seemed to take the hint and made ready to leave.

'Thanks for the tea and cake Mrs Westernberg senior,' said Constable Halliwell to Fiene, and thank you, Mrs Westernberg junior for inviting us in. I only hope yesterday's discovery wasn't too much of a shock. I'll get your statement typed up for you to sign but obviously there's no rush and I'll call in with it on Monday.'

'Thank you, John, you and your colleagues handled it very well. I suspect I've had more experience than the three of you with the dead having worked in a hospice a long time ago, but they worked with great sensitivity. Please pass that on.'

'Now then, look what has come in through the door: four lovely ladies I am so very pleased to see.'

'What's happened, Elise and where are Pieter and the girls? asked Leah.'

'They're visiting some alpacas. We thought it best to get them out whilst the police were here. As for what had happened, yesterday afternoon I was alerted to the non-appearance of the lady who cleans the surgery and went to find out if she was ok – she lives just 200 metres away – and when I got inside through an open window, I found her lying on the bedroom floor completely cold and surrounded by tablets of various kinds. One of the local GPs was called and he confirmed that they were all prescription tablets from them, and happily none from us. It looks like suicide but of course there will be an inquest in due course.'

'A shock for you, aunt Elise, all the same,' said Sarah.

'But the best possible cure is the arrival of you. So if the police have left any, let's get some cake and cups of tea on the go.'

'Already on the way,' said Fiene.

With the children back, and Pieter in the surgery talking with his two colleagues, Elise had to spend some time completing the preparations for the evening meal, and it provided an excellent opportunity for Leah to join her.

'A suicide – who would have thought it? Please may it not be the beginning of five more years of solitude,' she said.

'No chance of that, but how could I not think it significant?' replied Elise.

'Well, you see significance in all sorts of terrible things, my beloved friend.'

'I suppose I am always looking for meanings, but this suicide may just be what it is, a tragedy, and nothing more, though I do have something in my mind I didn't mention to the police.'

'Elise! You are impossible!'

'And that's why you love me and I love you, but there a couple of things I need space to talk over with you, perhaps in the daytime tomorrow and for one of them I might ask the help of Ursula.'

The events of the previous day did not serve to cast a shadow over their celebratory meal in the evening. Although Julia and Gale were in bed before they began, Grace stayed up with them and clearly enjoyed the adult company which included much laughter. As the only man, Pieter also loved being with these delightful ladies and amused them with one or two stories from the farms that made their laughter almost hysterical at times. He had worried that the discovery of Annie's body would have affected Elise, but knew enough from all she had had told him that as in previous encounters with death she had an overwhelming sense of peace afterwards, and clearly it seemed as if she did so tonight.

Because Saturday was the silver wedding anniversary of the farmer with whom she worked twice a week, she had offered to do an extra shift by herself to allow him to enjoy a morning lie-in. When she had made the offer, she had forgotten it coincided with the visits of her friends, and therefore had to get up at 3:30 to ensure she could be back in good time for a later breakfast. She loved working with the cows by herself, enjoying the skills she had acquired over the years, not least because she had no time for thinking about anything other than these particular ladies and their needs. Mucking out and moving slurry was the least delightful part of the job but at least she knew she had nearly finished by then, and as she left the parlour and turned off the lights knew had done a good job. Now she had other matters to concern herself with.

Sarah and Ruth wanted to go to Richmond as they knew Saturday was market day; Grace and Julia would be taken by Pieter to their Saturday Club held in the local Rugby Club; Gale therefore had all the attention she might want from her mother, Leah and Ursula, and was happy!

Elise (freshly showered), Leah and Ursula took their coffee mugs into the sitting room with its wonderful view over the Valley down to the river, whilst Fiene was busy in the kitchen baking, which she did every Saturday morning.

'Leah mentioned there was something I might be able to help with,' began Ursula. 'If I can, of course I will, and I assume it must be something at least quasi-legal.'

'Thank you, Ursula,' began Elise, and went on to tell the story, first of the meal and meeting in the church hall, and then of the visits, first of all of Tony Reynolds for a lesson in basic Koiné Greek, but then of Betty Satterthwaite, whom she called Audrey.'

'And then yesterday, when I had just found Annie's body and was waiting for the police, I noticed on a side table a copy of the church parish magazine. There's nothing odd in that in a small town I thought at first, but then I remembered that Annie was not a church member, and looking again at the magazine I noticed that there was a small piece of writing on the back cover. It said "So enjoyed my visit. See you again soon. T xx".' And in the light of what Audrey told me, I was immediately concerned.'

'You didn't remove the magazine, I hope,' said Ursula.'

'No. I left it as it was. And when it came to making my statement, I didn't make mention of it, not least because what I knew from Audrey might compromise her, and also because of course it could be interpreted entirely innocently.'

'Elise, do you feel you *should* do something, or are just wondering aloud about something that might happen in communities quite often? Do you remember Sir Humphrey Appleby in *Yes, Minister*, saying that at one time adulterers were stoned, whereas now they get stoned and commit adultery?'

Elise and Leah laughed.

'The thing is', continued Ursula, 'that although as Jews we come from a tradition that did once stone adulterers to death, and we know it is still practiced in some Islamic countries, it is not *per se* a crime unless coercion is involved. Your friend Audrey admits she enjoyed the experience until it was peremptorily ended and may see in you the basis of some sort of revenge. His suggestion that you were meeting with him may have been deliberate as a means of showing off, and the writing on the parish magazine is undoubtedly more than capable of innocent explanation.

'On the other hand, if Audrey has told you the truth, I can't think that any church authority would require more to set in motion the process of suspending him, but the established Church of England has set in place all sorts of legal obstacles in the face of what might be a false claim, and for understandable reasons. Would the vicar be willing to answer questions about this if he denies or suggests that the nine-month relationship clearly showed how much she approved?'

'H'm, and this is why I wanted to seek your advice.'

'I haven't advised you. All I've done is present you with things that need to be borne in mind. From what you have described I think people should be protected from his own needs overcoming his capacities to handle them, and of course you and I share the same sense of foreboding about the sort of evangelical religion that the churches imagine is going to solve all their problems which operates by offering something entirely bogus.'

'Spoken like a true and unbiased lawyer,' said Leah, laughing. 'It's why I love so you much.'

'And it's why I need your mathematical brain to keep a close eye on all the money I screw out of people who I manage to convince need my services at great cost.'

All three women laughed.

'Tony is unhappy,' said Elise. 'He is living physically apart from his wife and children but also, I imagine, intellectually or as he would see it, spiritually apart from them as he seeks in something ultimately futile the salvation he longs for having clearly lost any sense of it elsewhere.'

'Spoken like and true and biased rabbi on Shabbat morning in the synagogue!'

'Leah! What an outrageous thing to say!' said Elise, laughing.

'But what are you going to do, Elise, if anything? I know you, and I can't imagine you will let sleeping dogs lie.'

'I live in this community and the well-being of women I know is quite possibly at risk from someone whose own needs are in danger of overflowing in such as way as to cause pain. It's one with his religion – all about his psychological needs.'

'And presumably,' added Ursula, 'an institution so desperate so solve its own problems that it allows someone now living apart from his family, and without offering proper support as they didn't offer adequate training. I understand what you are concerned about, Elise, and I share your concern at the personal level. All I was saying earlier was to highlight some of the pitfalls that may lie ahead if you want to take it further. But I would say one thing in the way of legal advice, that you say nothing to the police about the handwritten note on the parish magazine. If they notice and pursue it, that's for them to do. You would be treading on very thin ice otherwise.'

'What strikes me,' said Leah, 'is that you need to verify Audrey's claim in some way. Years ago, we had a rabbi, before Rabbi Samuel, who told me that he was experiencing the nuisance of fantasy projections from certain women in the community. It's something to do with the role and the appearance of being wise and learned. In other words, when Tony first came to see her, was he doing his pastoral work and then found himself drawn into living out *her* fantasies? It's worth considering before you decide to act.'

'And everything you've both said is why we need friends and those who can speak the truth without fear or favour, and in your case, Ursula, without fee!'

'Oh sorry, didn't I mention my Saturday fee?' she replied with a grin.

'I'll have you know,' said Elise, 'that this Shabbat morning gathering of three Jews is what we know as בֵּית כְּנֶסֶת, a synagogue. If you're not careful I shall insist on a plate left by the door for your contributions!'

Having been told by Leah, that Elise wanted some time alone with her, Ursula took herself and Gale off into the kitchen with Fiene whilst her Oma got on with the baking which was smelling more enticing by the minute.

Elise suggested that she and Leah went out for a walk near the gallops at close-by Middleham, where there were a number of racing stables, but which would be peaceful today as trainers and grooms would be away at various racecourses on a Saturday. As they crossed the delightful 19th century Middleham suspension bridge, Leah asked why this was known as Wensleydale when the river was the Ure and other dales known by their rivers.

'It used to be called Yoredale apparently, but the answer lies in ancient history when the now tiny village of Wensley was an important town with some 700 inhabitants. It was granted a market charter in the 13th century and for a hundred years afterwards, was the only market town in the dale. It therefore gave its name to the dale. Sadly, a terrible plague struck the village in 1563 and many of its residents died and it never fully recovered and remained a small community in which I go to do the milking twice a week and did this morning as a special treat for the farmer on his silver wedding though to be fair I never checked that his wife wanted him in her bed longer than normal. But I enjoyed having the cows to myself and that's all that matters.'

Leah's Revelation

It was a mild October day with a gentle west wind as they went out onto the gallops with their white rails erected to accustom horses to what they would see on a racecourse.

'Are we safe?' asked Leah.

'Yes. Tomorrow morning would be different. And just look how lovely the dale looks from here. I often come up here with Gale on my back and walk whilst she talks.'

'She looks the spitting image of you, whereas Grace and Julia are definitely Pieter's offspring.'

'That's so reassuring, Leah!' said Elise, with a laugh. 'But yours are looking so good. Do they keep in contact with Jerry?'

'They don't mention it, but I think and hope so. The new wife has a consultant's post in Guildford, and they live somewhere in Surrey. He now only does private work in the Nuffield.'

'And you certainly give the appearance of being happy and settled with Ursula.'

'If I have managed to make her as happy as she makes me, and she says the same, then it's not appearance only. And I can tell that you and Pieter are still as totally enthralled with one another as you were from the very beginning.'

'Yes, not least because he is still loving his work. He enjoys being out on the farms and never seems to mind being called out, which his two colleagues more than welcome. He's put together a good team.'

'Now they've lost the cleaner.'

'Yes. Annie fitted in well and worked hard. We shall miss her. The job meant so much to her and although she didn't ever talk much about herself it seemed to provide her with something that was otherwise lacking. I feel rather bad that I didn't pick up the signals of what may have been a deep unhappiness.'

'Did you have much contact with her? You don't often go into the surgery I would imagine.'

'No. Pieter and his staff knew her very much better than me. He told me last night that he had sensed she seemed distant and unusually uncommunicative in the last few days, though Heidi and Fran reassured him that they had noticed it too, to the extent that Fran had asked her if everything was ok, but that she said she just had one or things on her mind. And then – yesterday!'

'And you're troubled, aren't you, by this vicar.'

'He's vulnerable himself so more than capable of damaging others. '

'He needs counselling,' Leah said, as they continued their walk along the gallops, carefully watching their steps where the horses had gone into the softer ground, 'but for you to be more involved would be like where we are walking – full of potential for tripping up.'

'And Audrey? What do I say to her?'

'Elise Rosewarne! – for that's how I still think of you – you don't know how to say anything about the most important thing in your life history, so I recommend you say as little as possible to anyone, including Audrey. You're not a rabbinic divorce court.'

Elise stopped and turned to her best friend.

'I love you, Leah Jacobs. All through, what others no doubt saw as lunacy, and of course may have been, you are the only who stayed with it, with me, as I went through five years living in what I now think of as my solitary refinement. From the start, and I don't suppose you know how any more than me, you understood completely.'

Leah smiled and took Elise's hand in her own.

'I'm holding your hand to stop you falling on dangerous ground, and perhaps now, at last, after many years of trying to make sense of it myself, I can now possibly tell you why I knew what you were doing was completely right.

'Even when I was a little girl, I had a very strong sense of what you call the Presence, the closeness, almost intimately close, of HaShem. Of course, I would never have ever dared speak of this to my parents, the rabbi or anyone else, even our dear Rabbi Samuel, but it remained with me, almost but not quite tangible. I didn't think it was providing me with anything – protection or achievement or anything. And long ago you taught me something I've never forgotten because it's been more than borne out by my experience. You said once that HaShem or the Presence is not there to be believed in, and not even worshipped, but to be known.

'I burst into tears when I saw that film about the Scottish runner Eric Liddel, *Chariots of Fire*, when he said to his sister that when he ran, he felt the pleasure of God, and I cried because I knew exactly what he meant. And so you see, I've always known what you meant when you spoke to me of knowledge not just as a feeling but considerably more, but about which our words cannot cope.'

'Yes. "Words strain / Crack and sometimes break, under the burden" as Eliot wrote,' said Elise, now holding Leah's hand tightly.

'Being Jewish helped, because we don't ever speak the Name, HaShem, and there were times before you came to live with us when I feared I was possibly experiencing some form of mental illness. It was most odd when you first came because it was perhaps the only time I experienced a powerful sense that having you come into our life was meant to be. My enduring sense of the Presence has not prompted me to do anything particular as has been your experience.'

'And this enduring awareness, is it still there?'

'Yes!'

'I love the way you said that, as if I was a total idiot for even asking the question.'

'Elise, my dearest friend, you're the only person in this whole world I've ever said this to, and it's taken me into my late 50s to do so even though I've known this day by day since I was a child, even though I knew that you knew this of yourself. It has almost been like a guilty secret I'm scared of facing.'

Elise threw her arms around Leah.

'I want to sing הָבָה נָגִילָה as loud as I can, such joy do I feel.'

'I rather think you and I singing *Hava Nagila* would frighten the horses, were there any – we're not the best singers in the world. But the important thing is that now you know what has drawn us so closely together. I could also cry with relief. How often I've wanted to say something but didn't know how.'

'Perhaps we should consult my speech therapist friend Aishe, whom I met at the school gates in September. Her son and Julia are in Reception together and great buddies, I've invited them to come and meet you for brunch in the morning.'

'You've mentioned her a couple of times on the phone.'

'Although she was born in Wales, which I suppose is not totally her fault though obviously sad – as I have told her and which made her laugh – she is Indian in origin, though her parents lived in Uganda until they were thrown out by Amin. She's married to one of the GPs in the town and we get on well, though despite having no direct experience of religion, I sometimes sense in her DNA a something of the Vedic myths in that, despite her job, I think she is more concerned with what cannot be spoken, something we both understand.'.

'Is the husband coming too?'

'No. Golf, apparently, and I don't mean the car he drives.'

The two women walked back down the gallops at little more than a crawl, hand in hand.

'I feel so happy about what you have told me, Leah. Now I know why I needed to say so little to you about my five years on the edge of the cliffs – you already knew.'

'There were times when I even contemplated coming to live with you, but the girls needed me, and at first so did my errant former husband, but as I said earlier, I have never known any sense of being directed as you were, other than the day we welcomed that lovely young student into the life of our family.'

'That truly was a great day for me too and you'll never know just how much I received from you – an incredible amount of love and teaching by example of what it meant for me to be a Jew.'

They walked in silence for a further minute or two before Leah halted.

'Elise, was it merely coincidence that once again you have been drawn into a suicide and on the day before when I was coming to be with you? Is it possible that this is a new beginning in some way neither of us can imagine?'

'I suppose I hope it is merely a coincidence, though my own experiences have suggested otherwise, but I now have three wonderful small children and I could not begin to think anything other than of my responsibilities of caring for and loving them, Pieter and Fiene. Though, I will admit that when I awoke very early this morning to go to do the milking, just for a moment the thought did cross my head. Mercifully my dear friends, the Holstein-Friesians demanded all my attention!'

As they reached the car, Elise's phone rang.'

'Is that Mrs Westernberg?' said an unfamiliar man's voice.

'It is.'

'Hello. I'm Detective Sergeant Colin Moule, from Northallerton CID. I would like to ruin your Saturday afternoon by coming over to ask you about a couple of things that have arisen in our attempts to understand the apparent suicide of your near neighbour. I don't suppose it will take long and it doesn't concern your discovery of her body, but I would appreciate a little of your time, please.'

'Of course. I'm out now but will be home soon and should be around at about 4:30. Would that be any use to you?'

'It would be grand. I'll see you then. Oh, and it's milk and two sugars,' he concluded, although Elise could hear his smile!

'Most mysterious,' she said to Leah, as she told her the details of the call.

'Yes, you wouldn't expect CID to be involved in what was assumed to be a straightforward suicide.'

'Unless they have found something that makes it less straightforward. I await developments,' she said getting into the car.

The morning activities had gone well for everyone though they had all had their lunch by the time the two Gallopers returned. Elise told Pieter about the phone call.

'That's most odd because you barely knew Annie Driver. Why

on earth would they want to speak to you rather than myself, Fran or Heidi, or one of the nurses who also knew her?'

'I will have to wait until 4:30 to find out. In the meantime, I must spend some play time with the girls or they'll fire me and replace me with Sarah and Ruth.'

'And has your time with Leah been good.'

'Quite wonderful, which I will try and tell you about later, perhaps in bed, though after my extremely early rise this morning, I may not make a lot of sense and then drift off.'

'You don't mean you might be talking double-Dutch do you?'

Elise put her arms around Pieter's head and drew his face and lips to hers.

'You told me about double-Dutch on the day we met, and do you know I love you now not just no less than I did on that day, but even more than I could ever have thought possible.'

'Even more than the cows?'

'It's a close-run thing, but yes!'

In the privacy of the kitchen, they kissed. Without their noticing, Fiene came in and smiled at the sight.

Shortly before the policeman was expected Ursula asked Elise if she would like her to sit in with her.

'You told me about the relationship between the vicar and the lady you called Audrey. This may have nothing to do with that whatsoever, and having a solicitor present might generate suspicion but it might be helpful for a friend to be with you.'

'I think that's a good idea. Let me see what he wants to talk about first and if need be, I'll come and get you.'

DS Moule

DS Colin Moule was a clean-shaven pleasant-looking man in his early 30s and arrived in an unmarked car, for which Elise was grateful. However, on arrived he said he had asked PC Halliwell to join them. Elise knew and liked the red-haired John and his wife, Deirdre, one of the other mums she saw at the school gates.

With John present, and mugs of teas and freshly baked scones in the hands of the policemen, DS Moule began.

'At the moment we are treating the death of Miss Driver as unexplained. A post-mortem was carried out yesterday and found sufficient tablets in her system to account for her death, but there was also a significant quantity of alcohol. The pathologist has placed the time of death about midnight on Thursday night but that the period in which she was unconscious before that may have been as long as four hours.

'Oddly there was no sign of a bottle or glass or an unwashed container of alcoholic spirit in the house or in the bins. It would be odd to say the least for someone intent on a suicide to take tablets, wash them down with alcohol of which we can find no trace and wash up before settling down to die.'

'Are you suggesting there was someone with her?'

'It's a possibility we much consider. Forensics will make a full search tomorrow for any evidence of another person and you will have to let us have your own fingerprints so we can exclude them. But the reason we have wanted to talk to you is because of information John received this morning from a farmer's wife living outside the town who came into fetch fish and chips at about 7:00 pm on Thursday for herself and her husband. This lady rang John to say that she had seen a man near Miss Driver's house door as she passed in the car. She also said that she was certain who it was, and that the one person who might understand why she felt this was suspicious, would be you.'

'Are you talking about Betty Satterthwaite, Colin?'

'Yes, I am.'

'In which case may I go and bring in my friend Ursula, who's here for the weekend? I've already spoken to her about my contacts with Mrs Satterthwaite because I wanted her advice as a solicitor. I would like her here though not as my solicitor because I don't need one, but as the friend with whom I've spoken already about this.'

'Yes, no problem, Mrs Westernberg,' said Colin, 'though can I just clear up one thing we learned from Mrs Satterthwaite. Should I be addressing you as *Rabbi* Westernberg?'

Elise laughed.

'In this country, titles, especially military ones, seem to live on after they cease to be meaningful. However, I gave up being a rabbi in Cambridge after just one year almost 15 years ago. So, it would be entirely inappropriate for you to use it. I would prefer Elise.'

'Thank you. You're right about titles though. There's no shortage of retired colonels and generals in North Yorkshire, I can tell you, who still insist on their former ranks given when addressed.'

Elise left and returned with Ursula who introduced herself to the two officers.

'I'm here primarily as Elise's friend not her solicitor, so please call me Ursula.'

Colin nodded and smiled and then turned to John.

'When news spread,' said John as it does rapidly in communities such as this, about the death of Miss Driver, I had a call from Betty Satterthwaite.'

'Not Audrey?' Ursula asked Elise, puzzled.

'I didn't need to tell you her actual name earlier,' replied Elise, 'but it is Betty.'

'She told me that she had seen a man near Miss Driver's house on Wednesday evening, whom she recognised as someone with whom she had been until recently having a relationship which she openly described as sexual. She told me that she had told you, Elise, all about this, having discovered from the man that you had once been a rabbi, or as she had initially thought a church minister.'

'Yes, she told me that, and the only person in this community apart from my family who knew this was the man she was seeing who had come to me just last Monday for a lesson in New Testament Greek.'

'She said he had implied he was getting close to you,' said John.

'She told me that too, but a lesson in Greek is not a euphemism for anything else. I told him that I was a rabbi because he had experienced a considerable put-down by me at a public meeting when it became clear that he didn't have the first idea what he was talking about in terms of the Bible and was using it to manipulate others.'

'Yes, she said something about that too.'

'The man she claimed to identify and with whom she said she had been in a relationship was the vicar Tony Reynolds,' said Colin.

'I don't know about her claims to have seen him near Annie's house on Wednesday night because I haven't spoken to her since, but she told me she about her affair with the vicar. She said she was concerned that I might be his next conquest.'

'What do you know about him?' asked Colin.

'I know he is a married man living apart from his wife and family who live in their marital home in Leeds or somewhere near there. I know too that for the job he has been given he is seriously under-equipped in terms of what I think he should have been taught, but that he is by training an electrical engineer.'

'And when he came last Monday for his Greek lesson, did you feel that he was interested in you as a woman, as a potential next candidate for his attentions?'

Ursula was about to intervene, but Elise pre-empted with a simple, 'No.'

'However,' she continued, 'and I forgot to mention this when I made my statement yesterday, John, I did notice when I was in Annie's house after I had called the police, a copy of the church magazine with a hand-written note on it. I wasn't aware that Annie had contact with the church though I dare say the church delivers its monthly magazine to houses other than of its members.'

'Did you recognise the handwriting?'

'No. But I can recall what the note said: "So enjoyed my visit. See you again soon. T xx", and it occurred to me that the T might well be Tony and the double x entirely inappropriate.'

'When Betty came to see you, did she tell you that she claims Mr Reynolds had broken off her relationship?'

'Yes.'

'And did it occur to you that in coming to talk to you she might have been doing so out of a wish for revenge by dirtying his reputation with what she might have thought was a fellow professional religious person?'

Elise gave him the nearest thing to a dirty look she was capable of.

'Gosh, no, it would never have occurred to me, Detective Sergeant! Of course I did.'

'And she confirmed that to me,' added Ursula.

'Yes, I'm sorry for that,' said Colin, blushing slightly. 'So having dealt with facts, dare I enter into the area, entirely off the record, of your opinions of the reliability of Mrs Satterthwaite's account and your thoughts about Mr Reynolds.'

'If I was Elise's solicitor,' said Ursula, 'at this point I would advise her to say nothing.'

'It's ok, Ursula,' said Elise, 'an opinion is just that – an opinion. Yes, in the main I think Betty's account to me was as truthful as her account to you, John. I know that hell hath no fury like a woman scorned, and I'm not denying that there might be an element of that, but I thought she was telling me the truth.

'As for the vicar I'm not in any sort of position to comment on anything other than that his performance at the church meeting I attended was dire, but as I think all evangelical Christians have profound unaddressed psychological issues, and anything other that could be interpreted as biased.'

Colin laughed.

'As was once said "You might very well think that, I couldn't possibly comment",' said Colin.

'He's out of his depth intellectually, that is a fact. Whether he is out of his depth emotionally, separated as he is from his wife and family, is not for me to ascertain. What part he played, if any, in the death of Annie, is for you to resolve. If he did indeed have a sexual relationship with a bereaved woman over a nine-month period, then he has not committed a crime *per se*, but should not be allowed to continue in his job, and just possibly that's what he wants – a way out!'

'Thank you, Elise. What you've said has been very helpful in painting a fuller picture. Looking around your study I doubt anyone would be likely to charge you with intellectual weakness. One final thing. Will you be meeting the vicar for another Greek lesson?'

'Doesn't that in part, depend on you, DS Moule? Though I gather from Elise he is due here on Monday morning,' said Ursula.

The two officers smiled as they rose to leave.

'What do you think will happen?' Elise asked Ursula after the policeman had gone.

'It will very much depend on what forensics. Tomorrow, I imagine the vicar will be left to get on with his work. They won't want to alarm him or the people at his church, but he is undoubtedly what they call a "person of interest".'

Returning to the early Saturday evening household Fiene had produced an evening meal for them all.

'I don't know what I would do without you, my mother dear.'

'I love you calling me your mother, because I rejoice in your being my daughter, so it works both ways, and whilst I can, I will do all to enable you and Pieter to do what it is you both have to do.'

'There's nothing I have to do, save love and care for my family.'

'Maybe, and maybe not,' said Fiene enigmatically.

Sunday morning brunch was a noisy affair. It was raining and very windy so Tan had decided to abandon golf and came with Raj and Aishe. The children played in one room, Raj and Pieter took refuge from the monstrous regiment of women in another, whilst Elise, Fiene, Aishe, Sarah, Ruth, Ursula and Leah managed to continue several simultaneous conversations in the kitchen and dining room.

'I was devastated to hear about Miss Driver,' said Aishe to Elise, 'and Tan heard from one of his colleagues that you were the person who found her.'

'We were concerned that she hadn't turned up for work as usual and her curtains were drawn. I volunteered to call and see if she was ok, but when I couldn't rouse her, I turned burglar and climbed in through an open window. It's so very sad and although I barely knew her because she worked in the surgery, I know how much the staff in there will miss her.'

'I can't imagine what it must have been like for you to find her there.'

'I suspect that I had prepared myself when I entered in the way I did, but it's not a nice experience to find someone like that, though I'm not entirely unused to the reality of death.'

'Can I ask something personal about it?' Aishe asked. 'When you found her, did you offer prayers of any sort?'

'No. There were practicalities to be dealt with – calling the police and an ambulance and notifying Pieter and the others.'

'What sort of prayers did you have in mind, Aishe?' asked Leah, who had been listening.

'I've no idea and I'm not saying that I thought you might. I was just wondering. Sometimes shock can prompt us to behave in unpremeditated ways and it struck me that someone who once was a religious professional might react in some sort of religious way.'

'Yes, I can understand that,' said Leah.

'And,' said Elise, 'I was really nothing other than a religious amateur. I didn't function long in the job, and in any case, I don't think prayers in any situation is anything more than something we do to make ourselves feel better, and would do nothing for Annie. I felt at ease without them.'

'I imagine there will have to be an inquest, though such things can take ages, but a verdict of suicide will surely be straightforward,' said Aishe, though she noticed the odd look Elise gave Leah as she said so.

'As you say, these things can take quite a while,' said Leah. 'Ursula is a solicitor and the time things can take in the legal world is something that drives her quite crazy.'

The conversation had moved on.

Monday Morning

On Sunday afternoon Leah and Elise had safely delivered Sarah and Ruth to York Railway Station, allowing them further time together to talk.

'During your time in solitary I know you sometimes listened Radio 3,' said Leah once they were free of the horrendous traffic that characteristically snarled the centre of the city even on a Sunday, 'do you still do so?'

'Not as much as I would like. Living with Fiene, Pieter and children means that I'm constantly interrupted in the most wonderful and welcoming of ways when I fondly imagine I should try to write something or listen to the radio.'

'What sort of writing?'

'Oh, you know, about what I share with my dearest friend, almost my sister, who took almost 30 years to tell me a great secret.'

'Gosh. I can hardly believe someone might that do that to you,' said Leah, smiling.'

'What is most difficult when I pick up my pen and you try to use your tongue, is avoiding the knowledge that anything written or spoken by either of us, will be received as some form of psychological aberration.'

'And has that thought not occurred to you too?' asked Leah.

'No more than once a day.'

'The odd thing is that although I've often feared of it myself, I have never thought it of you.'

'Well, if it's any consolation I think the same of you. For me the most authentic aspect of what you told me yesterday is that it has taken so long for you to dare to tell me.'

'But I was a Jewish mathematics teacher with a husband and twin daughters. I have always been able to understand how it could be that you were forced by what you knew into isolation on the North York Moors, as befitting a rabbi who has mystical experiences – if that's what I dare call them – but I lived in Hackney!'

'Yes, and that's why I know what you've experienced is real and not a dream caused by eating blue cheese before you go to bed. After all, is it not quite likely that the Presence should be known and encountered in the midst of city life? You already know that my own deepest encounters were in the mess of two children killed by cars, two suicides, and a man in great anxiety as he died. My spiritual guide, Fr Jean-Pierre, experienced the Presence holding in his arms a young man murdered in the street. So to me it seems perfectly sensible for a teacher of maths, a wife and mother, to be encountered there in the midst of the ordinary, and it just might be possible that the reality of the Presence is always there but most people are unable to know it is so.'

'If that is so, then I can't think how it has happened to me.'

'Perhaps it's akin to having an ear for music or an eye for art. Yes, we can learn a great deal about both, but I'm convinced that there is a world of difference between knowing about and knowing as you and I might claim we know. It's not any sort of intellectual thing and perhaps the less we think about it, the better. But it doesn't matter why or how, does it? Perhaps the only thing that does matter is what we do with it. What we have been given is not a toy to be played with though I truly think it can be enjoyed. It is of course holy, but that shouldn't mean it's not part of our daily living – surely as Jews we take for granted the holiness inherent in the ordinary.'

'But the Presence took you into five years of living almost wholly isolated. Why?"

'It meant I was full so of nonsense I needed it to be emptied out. That's why I call it my solitary refinement. But, Leah, I've said this before, and I think I know it even more now, I was never once lonely in all those years, even in the four hours a day I spent in the waiting room doing and endeavouring to think nothing. Until, of course, that last night. On that night I was slightly terrified to be there alone for the first time, and then on the following morning I met Pieter and knew the time had come to move out of the waiting room onto to what was to come – and wonderful that has been – my wonderful husband, our three daughters and a quite amazing mother-in-law who has become my mother in every way. I sometimes laugh to myself that it was worth the wait.'

'And what now, Elise? Does it not strike you as significant that you were the one to find the body of Annie?'

'I have no idea because most significance is only seen in retrospect, and it was just three days ago. Since then, I've been doing what I do as a mother and wife and being with my dearest and truest friend. Perhaps its retrospective significance has to do with your presence here not mine at all.'

'Well, I would be lying if I didn't say that in the middle of last night I woke up in a sweat fearing that might be so.'

'We just have to wait.'

'And have you thought about the fact that you have a Greek class due tomorrow morning with Tony?'

'Yes, and I want to ask a favour of you and Ursula. I know you will want to get home before dark, but might you stay at least until I have met with him. He's due at 10:30.'

'Happily. Ursula asked Pieter this morning if she could possibly go out with him on one of his farm visits in the morning. Apparently, he's turning dentist to a horse in Masham, where the brewery is.'

'That's settled then.'

Elise and Aishe met outside school.

'Thank you for yesterday. Tan so enjoyed the time he spent with Pieter. In fact, he came back and announced that there was no way he was clever enough to have been a vet and is hugely relieved not to be in veterinary general practice! And Raj loved playing with your three girls and was so impressed by Gale that he asked me last night if he couldn't have a little sister too!'

'Might you?'

'I wouldn't want to go through IVF again and though wonderfully it gave us our lovely son, it was one hell of a struggle.'

I hadn't known that.'

'What made Tan laugh was when Pieter told him he had been trained to administer AI on cows – IVF in other words – and that he had an 85% success rate. I only managed to keep a pregnancy at the fifth time of asking.'

'Oh Aishe, someone who has had no trouble conceiving, such as myself even at the age of 39 when I had my first sexual experience cannot possibly know what you have been through, and that of course makes Raj so very special, though he is also a very beautiful boy. Your struggles have been richly rewarded.'

Almost exactly at 10:30 the front doorbell rang, and Elise admitted Tony who immediately gave her what she thought of as his insincere vicar-grins.

'I've been working hard,' he said, sitting down in her study.

'That's good. Language learning is difficult for some people as not everyone has the sort of brain that can make much sense of storing lists of vocab, nouns and verbs for easy access, but they have got to be done. So how far have you got?'

'I can do all the present tense of λύω, though why do we start with a word that is hardly found in the New Testament?'

'It's because it's a perfect verb, what is sometimes called a simple verb. It obeys all the rules. Most other verbs vary in complexity so it's best to begin with λύω. And what about reading Greek, even if you can't yet translate it?'

'Yes, I've been doing that although I'm pretty sure I haven't got the right pronunciation.'

'No one has. We cannot know how the writers of ancient texts would have spoken the words, and we cannot know how much in translation into Greek the original Aramaic allegedly spoken by those in the gospels has been lost.'

'Allegedly? Are you implying that the words of Jesus as recorded were not spoken by him?'

'He certainly did not speak in Greek, so they have gone through some process of transmission on their way into the texts we have now. Even his name has been translated from the Hebrew יֵשׁוּעַ, Yeshua, which I imagine was done to distance the new religion being advanced across the Mediterranean world of Gentiles from its Jewish past. And I don't know how much of what he might have said has similarly been sanitised. I would not like to have to translate the Aramaic I know into Greek, because it's not simply a matter of changing word for word but seeking to translate so many nuances from one tongue into another without changing the original intent.'

'No one ever taught us this. I have always believed that what has been handed down is a reliable transmission, that God would not allow otherwise.'

'That is a belief, but beliefs are not the same as evidence. No one can be convicted of a crime on the basis that someone *believes* someone is guilty. I suppose that what I am saying, Tony, is that if you are serious about learning Greek, you at the very least should also consider some of the complexities involved with regarding any ancient text as somehow bypassing normal human process.'

Tony sat back and sighed.

'Do you, Elise, think it possible that in the face of complexity we too easily seek explanations that satisfy our inner needs rather than engaging in the toil of understanding?'

'That's a good way of putting it.'

'In my previous work as an engineer I operated based on knowledge. Just believing something must be the case, because nothing else could account for it, only showed a lack of thoroughness and determination to do the hard work demanded.'

'And how do you think that compares with what I am suggesting as an engagement with the complexities of handling ancient texts?'

'It's not just ancient texts that are complex though. As a former minister yourself, even in a different tradition, you must have had to live with the complexities of how congregations receive what is written, mostly without ever using a commentary.'

'Complexities and compromises certainly in terms of the public work, but even more those within, as who we really are, what therapists call the true self, comes up against the inner longing for security and sense of well-being. It's not easy.'

'That started for me about five years ago. I met someone on a work weekend conference whom I so admired. He clearly had total peace of mind and told me he was a Christian and explained the fundamentals of his beliefs. I was certainly searching for more at that time. Both work and home life were very far from stimulating, even boring and repetitive. My role was to bring in the money. I stayed in touch with this man, and he arranged for me to meet someone locally who continued the initial process of what I came to think of as my conversion.

'That rapidly became a new energy within me, and it wasn't long before the suggestion was made that I might consider training to become a minister. At that time, and perhaps still, the Church was looking for people with successful careers to train for the ministry on one of the new part-time courses. I went forward for selection and got through.'

'What did your family make of this?'

'Not a lot. Barbara never shared any of this with me, but it gave me meaning and purpose, an energy I had lost. I hoped she would see that, but it hasn't happened. The perilous state of the Church of England has led to more and more people like me being ordained and, in my case pushed into my own parish after a very short time. It's hoped for by many as the great evangelical revival of our age, though so far, the fruits are not all that obvious.'

'Let's not talk about the bigger Church, Tony. We might more profitably talk about what is happening here with your own life and work. If that is, you wish to.'

'You're easy to talk to, Elise, and though all you say from all you know scares me somewhat, I can't help wondering...well er...if you haven't said something important to which I should attend.'

At that point Elise heard the doorbell ring and outside she could see the car that DS Moule had come in on Saturday. Leah had gone to answer the door, and soon she heard the policeman's voice ask if Mr Reynolds was here. On hearing Colin, Elise stood up and went out into the hall, and led him into her study.

Questions

'Mr Reynolds,' began DS Moule, 'I would like you to come to the police station with me so you can assist us with our enquiries into the death of Miss Anne Driver.'

Before Tony could reply, Elise said, 'Can't you ask your questions here, sergeant, unless of course you're wishing to caution him?'

Colin and Tony looked at one another, almost as if to see which of them would blink first.

'Yes, of course,' said Colin, reluctantly.

'Tony, I have a solicitor friend staying with me whom Colin met on Saturday; would you wish to have her here with you?'

'I'd prefer it if you were allowed to stay.'

'Colin?' asked Elise.

He nodded.

'Forensic examination of the house of Miss Driver has shown three sets of fingerprints. Most belonged to the deceased. Others to the same person who entered through the window and found her body, which we know was you Mrs Westernberg, though we shall need to check that by taking your prints. The most important prints are the others. Do you think, Mr Reynolds, that the other fingerprints might be your own?'

'I don't know how many visitors Annie received but I certainly have called to see her and have no reason to deny that.'

'Were you in a relationship with her?'

Tony, somewhat sheepishly, looked at Elise.

'No.'

'Ok, but were you hoping you might be in a relationship with her.'

'I thought she was a lonely person who might be able to make friends at the church, so I was trying to encourage her to come along and give us a try.'

'When was the last time you called to see her?'

He looked up and pursed his lips as if struggling to recall.

'I think it was on Monday. Yes, I am sure it was.'

'At what time would that have been?'

'Mid-afternoon, I suppose. I don't write down every person I call on nor the time when I have done so.'

'So where were you heading at about 7:00pm on Wednesday when a witness claims you were outside Miss Driver's house?'

'I was there to put a parish magazine through her letterbox. I didn't go in and I didn't see her.'

'Was there a light on?'

'I didn't look to see.'

'We know, and Mrs Westernberg also already knows this, though not from us, that you have been having a sexual relationship with a married woman who had been recently badly bereaved that lasted about nine months, which involved regular sex in the vicarage, and which you ended a couple of months back. Can you confirm that?'

He nodded, and then said, 'I'm not proud of it but it happened more or less as you have said, though it's not a crime so why have you raised it?'

Colin ignored the question.

'Did your visit to Miss Driver on Monday include any sexual conduct?'

'No.'

'Would you say you were close to her?'

'Inevitably when people share things about themselves you feel a little closer to one another.'

'And had you spoken to Miss Driver about your own situation as a man separated from his family?'

'I was there primarily to listen to her.'

'And had you spoken to Miss Driver about your own situation as a man separated from his family?' repeated Colin.

'I imagine so, yes, though I most wanted to share with her something of the reasons why being part of the church might enrich her life.'

'When you last met with her, on Monday as you maintain, did you drink any kind of alcoholic beverage with her – beer, wine, spirits.'

'Of course not, I don't drink.'

'You're not supposed to commit adultery either! Do you have alcohol in your house?'

'I keep some for visitors – wine and sherry.'

'Miss Driver, it would appear, shared your alleged teetotal lifestyle and yet forensic tests have shown that there was alcohol in her blood at the time of her death even though she did not, unlike you, keep any alcoholic beverage in her house, nor was there any bottles or containers found in her bin. That suggests that the third set of fingerprints belong to whoever brought alcohol into her house, removed all traces of it after she had drunk and then took away the container in which it came. Were you that person?'

Tony looked at Elise and then back at Colin.

'Look...I...alright...I'm not cut out for this.'

Before he continued, Colin turned to Elise.

'Mrs Westernberg, I wonder if you could ask your solicitor friend if she could join us?'

Elise left and returned with Ursula. Colin immediately stood up.

'Anthony Reynolds, I am not satisfied from what you have told me that you have not had some involvement with the death of Miss Anne Driver. You do not have to say anything. But it may harm your defence if you do not mention when questioned something which you later rely on in court. Anything you do say may be given in evidence. Do you understand what I am saying?'

Tony looked up at Elise with his eyes wide-opened and with panic written all over his face.

'Yes, I suppose so.'

'What are you intending to do now, sergeant?' asked Ursula courteously.

'I shall ask for a car to come and take Mr Reynolds to the police station in Northallerton, where he can be fingerprinted, and checks made to verify his accounts under the caution I asked you to witness.'

'Mr Reynolds, when you reach the police station my advice to you will be to ask for a solicitor and they must provide you with one before further questioning takes place, unless you wish in the meantime to make a statement that will enable the police to check out that what you have said is true or will enable them further to find out the truth of what happened to Miss Driver.'

Tony sighed and looked completely defeated.

'There's no need. I will tell you everything now, and I hope you both,' he looked at Ursula and Elise, 'will remain whilst I complete the picture with the missing pieces of the jigsaw, and frankly I am just so relieved to be able to do so.'

Over the next ten minutes Tony spoke of the loneliness he felt and fear that he made a huge error in coming into the church and breaking away from his family. He told about his relationship Betty Satterthwaite, about the break-up which he said had come about because he was feeling guilty, but then of how he had met Annie on the market one Friday and had suggested he might call. She was single and he on the road to a divorce and thought she might make a good partner. On Monday last, for the first time they had intercourse and was hoping for the same when he called to see her on two evenings later. He took a bottle of wine, and he knew she was terribly distressed by what had happened on the Tuesday because she had phoned him and asked him not to see her again, but had hoped that by sharing a drink she might change her mind and even persuade her in to bed once again. But he soon realised there was little chance of this, and it was clear to him that the drink had made her sleepy, so he washed up the glasses and took the rest of the wine away.

'She was sleepy and sitting on the sofa when I left.'

Silence followed.

'Sergeant,' began Ursula, 'I am a witness to this confession by Mr Reynolds. If what he has told us is true, might I suggest that I accompany Mr Reynolds to Northallerton, and sign an affidavit that I was a witness to the confession?'

'And given his position in the town, might it be possible for me to bring Ursula and Tony in my car rather than in a marked police car?' said Elise.

'Mr Reynolds has made a confession to an involvement in what may be a serious crime. I have to take him for questioning, but I am perfectly happy for his solicitor to come with me as I do so.'

'Then I will follow, to bring you back, Ursula,' said Elise.

Tony looked at Elise and smiled.

'I am glad it's over. You know why.'

'Yes, I do, and I'm glad for you too.'

'Religion is very odd,' said Colin, as they all put on their coats prior to departing.

'Mostly because it seeks easy answers to complex questions that cannot be answered, and to square that circle it has to engage in the most ludicrous mental gymnastics.'

Once at the police station, Ursula first made an affidavit confirming that she had been present when Tony had made his confession, and then joined him in the interview room where she said she could not represent him as his solicitor and that before any further interviews could take place, he had the right to request a solicitor, possibly being provided by the church authorities. Tony said he was perfectly happy to make a statement reporting his confession without a solicitor being present.

Elise was asked to provide her fingerprints using a scanner to compare them with those found in the house after her break-in. The more pressing matter for her was to make two telephone calls to numbers given her by Tony.

The first was to the Bishop of Ripon, who was something called an 'area bishop', a man called Gerard Allen.

'The Bishop of Ripon's office', said a secretarial voice.'

'Good afternoon. To whom am I speaking?'

'Katie Williams, the Bishop's PA.'

'I need to speak to the bishop urgently.'

'I'm afraid that won't be possible as he is in a meeting in Leeds this afternoon and not to be disturbed.'

'Ms Williams, I have told you the matter is urgent and when he learns about it, he will want to know why you did not interrupt his meeting, I can promise you that. All you need to know is that one of the vicars in his area has been arrested on a very serious matter and is currently being held in a police station and requires immediate legal representation.'

'And you are?'

'I am Rabbi Elise Westernberg and I am in the police station. I will repeat just once again that this is an urgent matter requiring immediate attention.'

'I will telephone the bishop at once. Please can I have your phone number and I will ask him to call you at once.'

Elise gave her number.

'Are you able to say where this priest is being held?'

'Of course, as I am there now, but I will give this information only to the bishop or his legal representative.'

'Ok. I will call him now.'

It took almost ten minutes for a call to come through. It was a different female voice.

'Is that Rabbi Westerham?'

'Westernberg.'

'Oh, I'm sorry about that, Rabbi. The Bishop of Ripon is tied up in a Diocesan Finance Meeting and has asked me to take your call.'

'And you are?'

'Helen Grossmith, the assistant diocesan secretary.'

'Ms Grossmith, you need to let the bishop know that it is quite likely that the evening newspapers will get to know that one of the bishop's priests is in very serious trouble relating to the death of one of his parishioners. That man needs urgent support from the person who is supposed to be his pastor. That is all I can say to you. Only the bishop will do.'

'Thank you, Rabbi. I will report back.'

It was only a couple of minutes before Elise received another call.

Hello. Is that Rabbi Westernberg? I'm Gerry Allen, the Bishop of Ripon.'

'The Reverend Tony Reynolds is under arrest and being held at Northallerton Police Station in connection with the death of a female parishioner with whom he admits having had sexual

intercourse two days earlier, and whom he further admits to being
with and plying her with alcohol in the hope of a further sexual
activity, even though she had asked not to see him again. She was
found dead on the following day, with an initial assumption by the
police of suicide. Mr Reynolds was seen at her house in the
evening though at first denied it.

'I should add that he has also admitted a nine-month long sexual
relationship with a married woman who recently lost her teenage
son to leukaemia. It is quite possible that he will be charged with
contributory manslaughter, and he needs you not to be discussing
finance, but to be with him and providing him with legal
representation.'

'Thank you, Rabbi Westernberg. How are you involved?'

'I am a retired rabbi and live in the town. I offered Tony lessons
in New Testament Greek when it became obvious that your
institution had placed an inadequately trained man into a position
where he was forced to live away from his wife and family. He
talked to me about his profound unhappiness and almost total lack
of support. I then learned about his adulteries and then came the
information about the alleged suicide and his part in it.

'I travelled with him here and have remained since his arrest.
You should be here, bishop. One of your flock has gone astray and
I gather you like to seen holding a shepherd's crook. Well, now
you need to use it.'

'Yes. Thank you, Rabbi, for your care. I will arrange for a
diocesan solicitor to attend at once and I will leave immediately.'

'Thank you, Bishop,' said Elise.' 'After all it was for this rather
than finance that you were appointed ἐπίσκοπος, assuming you
can read Greek. Finally, Tony has asked me to inform his wife of
his arrest which I shall do now.'

The phone was answered quickly.

'Barbara Reynolds.'

'Mrs Reynolds, my name is Elise Westernberg and I am calling
at the request of your husband Tony, to let you know that he has
been arrested and is being held at Northallerton Police Station in
connection with the death of a woman with whom he had entered

into a sexual relationship. I have informed the church authorities and they have promised urgent legal representation, but whatever the outcome, Tony will not be able to resume his life in his parish.'

'How are you involved?'

'I am a retired rabbi and knew Tony slightly and he confessed in my presence to the police to his involvement in the death of this person.'

'Oh well, there we are,' she replied. 'Thank you for letting me know. Is it likely to be in the newspapers?'

'I should think so, especially as all this will emerge at the inquest or trial if there is to be one.'

'If you speak to him again, please let him know that any thoughts he might have of returning here his is wholly out of the question.'

The call ended abruptly.

Apart, Alone, Silent

Although Elise could well appreciate Tony's relief, arriving home she did not feel sorry for him. Ursula told her that DI Moule had told her the post-mortem report made it clear that the volume of alcohol he had given her contributed to her death alongside the medications she was taking, and the question remained as to whether she had intended suicide or taken too many tablets because of the effects of alcohol, or more worryingly, whether he had plied her with alcohol knowing that she would also be taking tablets which might bring about her death, and look like suicide.

'I think it highly likely he will charged with something or other and taken into custody this evening,' Ursula said as Elise drove them back.

'I think he's been in a prison for some time already so he may feel at home,' said Elise. 'What he has done is dire, but the Church has a great to answer, especially the current evangelicalisation, if there is such a word, which it seems to be beset by. It is dangerous, just a plain unintelligent manipulation of vulnerable minds. Jews don't do this reaching out and conversion thing.'

'After all, who would want to be a Jew if you weren't one already?' said Ursula.

By school-time on the next morning word has spread, not least because someone in the police system had informed the local tv news and an item had appeared on *Look North* on the previous evening. Elise's involvement was not known so she quickly separated herself from the gossip and brought Aishe back with her for their regular Tuesday morning coffee.

'It's a great shame that you've been dragged into this,' said Aishe, as she tucked into one of Fiene's tasty fruit scones.

'Early this morning I milked half a herd of Friesian cattle and that helps me settle everything in my mind.'

'Why only half?' asked Aishe with a puzzled frown.

'Because there are two of us. It's called a herringbone parlour and the ladies are on both sides with us in the alley between and below them.'

'Isn't it a bit mucky? I mean don't the cows...?'

'They do indeed, but I quickly learned the art of recognising when to move and fast.'

'However did you start doing this? I can't think it was in rabbinic college?'

'I spent my first three years living alone with minimal contact with others, apart from necessary shopping. I had got to know the farmer's wife when I went to collect my milk and eggs, and then one day, as I watched him milking, I asked if he could teach me. So, for the remaining two years of my solitary life, I did the milking with him, and even occasionally completely by myself, each morning. When we moved here, I went to see one of the local dairy farmers and offered my services. My test lasted just one morning session, and I was in. I have never asked for payment though he regularly asks, but I ought to pay him for the privilege. I just love doing it.'

'And for five years you were mostly living alone? However did you withstand it?'

'My friend Leah, whom you met on Sunday, came and stayed for a few days each year, but otherwise it was just me.'

'*Only* you?'

Elise smiled.

'I did sometimes listen to classical music on Radio 3 but not often, and of course I did some reading about other solitaries in the past, not that there have been many Jewish ones, but certainly medieval Christians, most often women, and hermits in the Orthodox churches, but towards the end I learned a great deal from reading about Buddhist and Hindu solitaries.'

'But was it only you there, Elise? What I mean is that the first thing you did as we came in here was to light that beeswax candle. So, was it only you out there on the edge, Elise Westernberg?'

'One of things I sometimes said to my students when I was teaching Talmud was "You're not asking the right question", and that is what I say now to you, every though I sense and am moved by the possibility that you might ask the correct one!'

'That's too enigmatic for my poor brain.'

'So, stop using the left side of your brain which is seeking something logical, easy to place and evaluate. Instead consider the whole picture.'

'That's difficult because I would need at least a little more information about how it was, being so apart, so alone, so silent.'

'So, ask.'

'Well, most people these days are terrified of silence and need a background of constant noise. Was it like that before you went into what you call solitary refinement?'

'Yes, in the sense that I found that I could concentrate better against a barrage of sound, often in a coffee shop where I often used to study languages. The noise was an effective barrier against all those internal voices that tempted me to do almost anything other than what I was doing and served to focus my attention. Paradoxical.'

'When you were in your house on the moors, near the cliffs, what sort of thinking did you engage in without the constant stimuli we live with now?'

'Getting some measure of control over the nonsense of my thinking took at least two years of sustained and much-repeated effort.'

'And this is a question I've been wanting to ask you and haven't dared to do so, a bit like the one I asked the other day about whether you prayed after you found that poor lady's body, but in your five years did you have a regime of whatever daily religious activities rabbis and Jews in general engage in?'

'When I went to live there it had already become clear that I had to leave all those things behind. I wasn't living a monastic life in the catholic sense, with the day divided by services, or the weeks, months and years by a calendar. I observed neither Yom Kippur, the holiest day of the Jewish year, nor Christmas. I was stripped bare of the accoutrements, physically and mentally, of religion.'

'Was that hard?'

'Not even slightly. I had only come to the realisation of Jewishness was I was a student, so it wasn't completely ingrained in me, and my Judaism was also more intellectual than anything. I no longer kept the food laws, for example, and although life was austere, I made sure my food was not!'

'So, what did you do?'

'I would like to be able to say I just was, and just being became my aim, something I know some forms of Buddhism would understand, but it neither sounds easy and mostly wasn't. I practised it four hours a day, usually in two sessions.'

'So why were you there?'

'Oh Aishe, I can't yet offer any sort of answer to that question, and the beginning of an answer would involve a series of long, complex and mostly bewildering stories, which we should perhaps leave to another time. I've been thinking for a while that what I needed was a speech therapist who could enable to me to say at least something about the essence of what I've been describing the peripheries of to you.'

'We didn't cover that in our training,' said Aishe, allowing both women to laugh gently.

'And believe me when I tell you it wasn't in my training to be a rabbi either, because of course it cannot be taught because, as yet the words have not been formed. But perhaps when I can learn something of how you function in helping people return to speaking, it may be that you can also my teacher helping me to learn to speak.'

'And if it has to remain silent?'

'Then, teacher, you will have to help me learn silent speech.'

'Perhaps, Elise, we can learn together.'

Elise had said nothing to Aishe about her repeated discoveries that almost all Buddhist writings now flooding the self-help market in the UK were worthless. In the main they offered learning techniques which would empower them and make them more capable of overcoming the negativities that many people were more than aware of inside themselves. Perhaps the latest fad of *Mindfulness*, adverts for which were outnumbering even those for *Alpha*, could help people caught up in the whirligig of modern life, but she knew this sort of commercialisation had nothing to do with her own experience of solitude. It was sold much as cosmetics were, enhancing ourselves to make us achieve more of what we want.

As she reflected on this once inside her study at home, her candle flame flickering, she knew that her fundamentals of Judaism protected her against the nonsense of much *western* Buddhism, especially in its Americanised forms. She was sufficiently well-read to know that in the Buddhist homelands of the Far East, Buddhism for the masses was little more than superstition and never included meditation of any kind and smiled to herself whoever she saw the countless adverts on the internet for Buddhist paraphernalia, as if they served any purpose other than lining the pockets of those more than willing to encourage people to buy things of no spiritual value in the fantasy that they were.

For lunch, she, Fiene and Gale set out for Northallerton where they would feast on luxury sandwiches in Betty's, followed by their monthly visit to the supermarket.

As she drove past the police station, she wondered how Tony was getting on. She had not expected to hear anything other than in the form of gossip, and although she understood and even welcomed Tony's release from the mental confines of church life, she knew enough to realise that if he was spending even one night in custody it would be a terrible shock. But if, as Ursula had suggested, he would be released on bail, where could he go? All she could hope was that the church would stand by him and provide help, although her knowledge of how institutions function gave her little grounds for optimism, though perhaps one calling itself Christian might be different.

'Twice in two days,' said Fiene. 'I imagine this is a happier visit than your last.'

They were sitting in Betty's and enjoying watching Fiene enjoying a sandwich.

'Was it helpful having Ursula with you?'

'Definitely.'

'I like her very much and because she's a little nearer me in age than Leah, we got on well. She told me she was the daughter of Orthodox Jews, and that Leah was Reform. You must explain the difference to me sometime. She also said they still strive to keep a modicum of Jewish life at home in Pateley Bridge, keeping Saturdays as sacrosanct and endeavouring as far as possible to keep Jewish food laws. That's not something you have done, is it?'

'When I returned from my world-changing visit to Canada I resolved to abandon all religious practices, even my Jewish ones. I wanted to begin my solitary life with what is called *tabula rasa* – a clean slate, if you like. If I took a previous mindset with me, I felt it would threaten the absolute mental austerity that was being asked of me.'

'You were astonishingly brave, Elise, to do what you were setting out on, though knowing you now as I do, it doesn't surprise me in the slightest.'

'I wasn't wholly devoid of my Jewish experience however, Fiene. I was constantly aware of the dangers of intellectual idolatry and adultery which so easily beset mankind especially when it manages, as it does again and again, to forget history.'

'Oh dear, I'm afraid that's a bit too clever for me.'

'I suppose what I mean is the same as TS Eliot's "humankind cannot bear very much reality". We opt for what are mostly fantasy figures in whom we invest magical properties: Buddha, Mohammed, Moses, Jesus, Guru Nanak or their secular equivalents, and even worse we tend nowadays to combine them and use a bit of this and a bit of that.'

'And that's what you mean by intellectual adultery, "a bit on the side"?'

'That's very an impressive colloquialism for a Dutch women to use.'

'In the light of the past few days are you surprised?'

Just after 5:30 whilst the children were having their tea, Elise's phone rang.

'Rabbi Westerbang?' said a voice Elise had heard before but couldn't immediately place.

'This is Elise Westernberg, yes.'

'Oh sorry. This is Gerry Allen, the Bishop of Ripon. We spoke when mercifully you rescued me from a tedious finance meeting, but more especially rescued Tony Reynolds, for which I must thank you.'

'How is he?'

'He has been released on bail pending further enquiries, and I was allowed to take him back to my own house in Ripon rather having him taken to prison.'

'That's good.'

'My reason for calling is to say that he has to go back to Northallerton Police Station tomorrow and I'm then hoping to take him to the vicarage to collect clothes and other things he needs, and I did wonder whether I might call in and see you to thank you face to face.'

'Ok. Anytime between children delivering at 9:00 and collecting at 3:30 will be fine. My husband has the veterinary practice here and we live in the cottage adjoining the surgery.'

'I look forward to that.'

As she put down her phone, Elise was far from sure she did.

A Dead Horse

At about 2:00am she and Pieter were woken up by the phone. There was a problem with a mare in foal at one of the stables and the vet was required. As often happened, after Elise had woken, she struggled to get back to sleep. Pieter, she knew, when he returned would be asleep in seconds. Sometimes the radio could send her to sleep but not on this morning. In any case, she would be getting up soon as it was a milking morning.

She was going over in her mind the forthcoming visit from a bishop, and then returned to her conversation on the previous day with Aishe. They had not known each other long but from the beginning Elise felt a communication with her that hinted at the possibility that she might be able to tell her all about her time in solitude, though she also knew that in so doing she would be taking an enormous risk. It was not that she thought Aishe would rubbish what she said, because already she knew and trusted her well enough to know that would not be the case, it was much a matter of describing a reality that she had not fully shared even with Pieter and Fiene, Leah being the only one who knew everything.

Her recent conversation with Leah had thrilled her heart and now she knew she could speak far more intimately with her about what she had come to know, but unless Aishe knew as Leah had described the reality of the Presence, anything she said might simply be like casting stones into a river, never to be seen again.

Pieter returned just as Elise was getting out of bed and was looking downcast.

'I lost the foal, though if they had called me an hour earlier it's possible that I could have saved it. When I got there it was stuck but in such a way as not to allow me to do a Caesarean, and when finally, I managed to get the foal out, because it was breech it had in effect drowned in its mother's amniotic fluid and there was nothing I could do. They were devastated as both dam and sire were top class and they were hoping for something special, and when we examined it, they had lost something that looked superb.'

'Was it her first foal?'

'Yes. I'm not sure what they'll do with her now. She probably can't race again so I imagine they will look to sell her.'

'They won't want her destroyed?'

'You know I never put down a healthy animal. Whatever they decide, I imagine they won't tell me. So have you managed to get back to sleep?'

'Too much on my mind, I'm afraid, but I'll get it all cleared away like I do when I'm cleaning out the slurry once I'm finished with the ladies.'

'You really love that, don't you?'

'Yes. I'm not sure quite how it fitted in with my time in solitary, but I know it did.'

'Would you be interested in going on a course to qualify as an AI inseminator. You'd be good at that.'

'Pieter, my darling husband, I love being seen in my underwear by you, but I don't want Wensleydale farmers doing so.'

'It would brighten up their lives. It does mine.'

'Meneer Westernberg, it's time you went back to bed, and I went to the parlour.'

'You're very sexy when you speak Dutch.'

'Sleep well,' said Elise with a naughty grin.

On milking mornings Fiene took the children to school, allowing Elise time to get back, showered, dressed and get some nourishment. On this morning, having had no more than three hours sleep she was feeling ready for bed again by 10-00am and hoped the visit from the bishop would come soon so she might get the chance to catch up for an hour in the middle of the day.

The doorbell eventually rang shortly after 11-15. Gerry Allen gave an appearance to Elise of being what she would call "smarmy", and like all the vicars she had ever met, smiled far too much. She led him into her study and then sought a coffee for them both which Fiene, who was about to collect Gale from nursery, brought in.

'I can see from your books that you were well-equipped to give Tony and the chap from York the roughing up he described,' he said with a grin.

Elise did not return the smile as she sat down.

'It was not so much that they had not expected a Hebrew and Aramaic scholar in a Wensleydale town than that what they said was both offensive to people there and highly unintelligent, whilst making unsubstantiated claims as to their authority to speak. It might even be described as the bullying of a recently bereaved woman who had recently been dumped after a nine-month sexual affair with the vicar.'

'That was of course regrettable.'

'Do you mean because of the damage inflicted on her and the community or that there was someone there able to stand up and reveal what charlatans they were, and which is, I read from the internet, part of a movement in the Church of England you and many other senior clerics personally endorse.'

'Charlatans is not a word I would ever use of those who have been properly trained to do a difficult job.'

'Tony did a part-time three-year course, mostly from home, exactly three years less than a basic BA with the Open University, in which the Biblical texts were covered in just two sections of three months each, without any knowledge of either original language. After two years "helping out" in his local parish (his words) you appointed him as vicar here, even though in doing so you were effectively allowing him to break up his marriage without any on-going care following this collapse of his marriage. He was not properly trained, Bishop, and neither was the imported *Alpha* salesman with him. Charlatans is exactly the right word.'

What training did you do to become a rabbi?' he replied, almost accusingly.

'Four-years full-time study of Hebrew and Aramaic at

University, including a year studying Talmud in Jerusalem, followed by three further years full-time Rabbinic training in London where I also became a tutor in Talmud, plus, as many potential rabbis do, three years of psychotherapy.'

Elise saw him blanche.

'Well, they met their match certainly.'

'But how many others get away with an alleged authority to manipulate people with the inhuman deceits of Saul, also known as Paul, and of course, Jean Calvin, upon whose writings *Alpha* is based? I have read both volumes of *The Institutes*, so I do know all about Calvin's theology! And what astonishes me about *Alpha* more than anything is that like Christianity itself it is based on the writings of a renegade Jew and makes so very little mention of Yeshua who lived and died a Jew, and whose followers before Paul with his new Gentile religion, remained observant Jews.'

The bishop gave a small laugh.

'I'm glad I wasn't the speaker on that evening.'

'But do tell me, Bishop. How do *you* account for what has happened to Tony?'

'My failure, our failure as a church, perhaps our desperation as a church in serious decline, in which we simply cannot afford the cost of providing full-time training for all nor wish to divide families by frequent house and school moves. Tony came with experience as a senior engineer, a responsible position, and we have been encouraging people with different life experiences to offer for ordination, and especially women.

'I didn't know him through his selection and training process but looking through his file I can see how positive he reported the question of his wife not yet sharing his faith, and when I approached him with a view to going full-time here, he gave me complete assurances that his wife needed to remain to see the children through school.'

'You checked that out with her?'

'There seemed no need to do so as he convinced me all was well.'

'When he appears in court will you be pleading guilty to contributory negligence.'

'We are hoping that there will be no charges brought.'

'And to become a bishop, what was your own training for the job?'

'I read Botany at Exeter, before moving into Town and Country Planning for ten years. I then spent two years full-time in theological college in Cambridge, where I learned how that form of training, especially for older candidates, can adversely affect family life. I became a curate and then a vicar in Derbyshire before being invited to become Bishop of Ripon.'

'You had just two years in which to combine Biblical study, Christian doctrine and history with acquiring the arts of pastoral care and preaching. That was quite a heavy load.'

'But you will know yourself that learning on the job teaches more than anything else.'

'Of course, but didn't Yeshua as recorded in Matthew Chapter 7, echo Psalm 11, when he said that without proper foundations buildings have a tendency to fall when the weather changes?'

The bishop smiled.

'I must not take up more of your time,' he said, clearly readying himself to stand.

'Will you also be calling on Betty Satterthwaite with whom Tony committed adultery to apologise?'

'From what Tony has told me, I'm not sure that would exactly be of help to her.'

'Tell me before you must rush off, Bishop, about your prayer. I ask the question of all clerics I meet because I'm interested.'

'Not a question I'm normally asked as a bishop, but I read the offices each day, morning and evening, and I try to have a quiet time with the scriptures on at least two mornings a week so God can speak through them to me. But I am very busy. Laborare est Orare after all.'

'St Benedict did not actually include those words in his *Regula*, and a better rendering of the intent of the Rule is *Ora et Labora*, by which he meant that monks having spent the early hours of each day in silent and common prayer took their prayer out with them into work, rather being a substitute for prayer. Still, what do I know, I'm just a retired rabbi?'

As he put on his coat the bishop said, 'I very much like your beeswax candle, if my nose is to be trusted.'

Thank you. As I'm sure you realise it is שְׁכִינָה.'

'Indeed,' said the bishop leaving the study and waving briefly to Fiene as he passed the open kitchen door on his way out.

'What did you say the candle was, naughty girl?' she said.

'I gave it its proper name. It means the Presence.'

'He had no idea what you meant.'

'You shouldn't have been listening in.'

'I've given Gale her lunch and put her down for her rest. She gets so tired at nursery. I kept the kitchen door open in case you shouted out and needed assistance. As he left, he raised his hand to me but I rather think he was not waving but drowning.'

'Fancy you knowing Stevie Smith's poem.'

It's one of your books. It took me a while to realise that Stevie Smith was a woman, but I like her poetry not least because I can occasionally use it to keep my daughter behaving herself!'

'It will be like water off a duck's back to the poor man. Just like Tony, he's stuck in a job that will get worse the longer he stays, poor thing, and he has to ignore what he would perhaps regard as my siren voice.'

'Perhaps he should have inserted beeswax into his ears.'

'So, you've been reading Homer too.'

'You always say how brilliant he is, so I thought I'd give it a go, though to be honest Elise, the Odyssey is more fun than the Iliad.'

'And is also about a long journey home. I love it too, but don't tell my Greek teacher at school who might order a whipping for saying that!'

'Nonsense, I'm sure he loved you.'

'He was a sweetie. I was his only Greek student though some others did Latin and Ancient History with me. Do you know, I should have told the bishop that those training to be vicars or whatever they are, all need a grounding in the Greek classics before ever going to work in a parish, but I would have been wasting my breath. What a ghastly job he's got though Pieter was up in the night and unable to save a foal, but unlike the bishop at least he's not actually flogging a dead horse!'

A Sort of Answer for Aishe

Half-term and chickenpox sweeping the school had meant a break of two weeks since Elise and Aishe had been able to speak together. So it was with some relief that they managed to get one of their coffee chats together.

Aishe began by asking what if anything, Elise knew about the fate of Mr Reynolds since his disappearance from the town and its church.

'PC Halliwell telephoned me to let me know that investigations into the death of Annie were on-going and that Mr Reynolds was assisting them in their enquiries whilst he remains on police bail. More than that I'm sure they won't tell anyone including me. I suspect he won't be returning here.'

'I was told by a church member I met that he's resigned as vicar.'

'I can only hope that the church authorities who got him into the mess his life has become will care for him adequately, though I have my doubts.'

'As you were the person who found her body, will you be required to give evidence at the inquest?'

'There has already been an inquest opened at which identification was given, and immediately closed by the coroner at the request of the police but will enable her funeral to take place though I have no idea where that might happen. It's now in the hands of her sister and brother. I sincerely hope that I shall not have to give evidence when the main inquest takes place. All I did was find her body, but my dread will be if the court refers to me as Rabbi Westernberg, rather than Mrs.'

'All it would need is for some smart Alick solicitor to focus on the Jew who humiliated him in public and who was then instrumental in finding the dead body, and before long the tv cameras would be at my door unleashing waves of the anti-Semitism which lies just beneath the surface of British life.'

'Aren't you being slightly paranoid, Elise? This is a very different world, in which even my brown skin has been accepted without demur even in this community. You ceased being a rabbi a long time ago, and you've told me yourself that you're not bringing up your girls to practice the Jewish religion.'

'I ceased functioning as a rabbi a long time back – that's true, though a rabbi is someone who has been given authority to teach, so I am still technically a rabbi. In terms of practising a religion, you know I don't, but my girls and I are Jewish. They cannot shed that because it's as much a part of their permanent being as the beautiful brown skin of Raj is to him.'

'But you've told me that you don't believe in God.'

'I don't. How could anyone believe in such a thing given the suffering and misery of so many on our planet in the immensity of space. But Aishe, I'm sure I've told you that as far as possible I don't have any beliefs, because I regard beliefs as essentially worth nothing, because they are two a penny, and mostly the result of the need to believe something, anything, to make them feel better. Evidence is different.'

'Yet I have seen something very different in your own life. Yes, I recognise the truth of what you say about beliefs, but you have undergone a process, extreme one might say, that to my eyes obviously continues to fashion (if that's the right word) your living. The most you say is the word Presence. But is that not a belief?'

'My five years in solitude were all about shedding beliefs and seeking something other, though I discovered, paradoxically, that it was the Other that discovered me. If I could say anything to my fellow Jews it would be that HaShem is not there to be believed in but known in the absence of beliefs.'

Aishe held back any reply she might have been about to make and was endeavouring to make a huge mental readjustment. Elise could see it was happening and said nothing. Perhaps two minutes passed before Aishe spoke again.

'That means...that means...that I've suddenly been able to hear what you are saying, as I might with one my patients recovering from a stroke. Oh Elise, I shall need time to allow this to sink in deeper. But perhaps you can begin to help by telling me why it is that you still insist on setting your life upon your Jewish background.'

'I will tell you a terrible and true story. There was a witness to this, who after the war became an ordained pastor of the church in Germany.

'In early 1944 as the Russians were advancing, a guard of SS men armed with submachine guns were leading a small group of Jews westwards to an extermination camp before the Russians could rescue them. One young woman had fallen 50 yards or so behind the main body, mainly because she was exhausted in the last stages of pregnancy, was carrying an infant in her arms and dragging a child of about eight by the hand. One of the guards noticed that she had fallen behind the rest and returned to her. His first action was to knock her over the back of the neck with the butt of his submachine gun. She fell face down on the road and began to vomit. When it was clear to the German that despite a barrage of kicks to the stomach, she would be unable to get up, the man shot her with a short burst of fire and left her corpse on the road with two children screaming and scrambling over it.'

Elise paused and looked at the shocked face of Aishe.

'That story and so many others are why I remain proud to be a Jew, proud to be one of a despised people. It's also why I cannot believe in any kind of deity who might intervene and does not, and who is concerned only with which form of religion we choose over another. How could any sane or moral person believe that?

'Some time ago I had a series of close involvements with deaths in ghastly circumstances, more than could be accounted for as simply coincidences. It was in a meeting with a Catholic priest in Canada that I knew I had to try and come to terms with the reality of suffering and death, and that is why I was led into five years of solitude. The story I've just recounted was ever before me, but I also knew that I had not to take with me into that solitude any of

250

the beliefs that people, including my own Jewish people have wrestled with, as they considered the Holocaust, in which my own great grandparents perished. I had to stop thinking completely, and Aishe, I am telling you something known only to Leah, Pieter and Fiene, that I had five years in what I described as the waiting room.

'Clearing out ideas and explanations and thoughts, as any real Buddhist monk would tell you, was extraordinarily difficult, but I was determined by keeping before me the deaths to which I had been drawn. Apart from my two years of milking cows and occasional visits from Leah, I lived completely alone and for almost all that time in silence, apart of course from the constant noise of the sea birds and the wind, a noise I adore anyway. I was there to wait and wait, never feeling lonely or fit for the madhouse. It was not my belief in anything that kept me there but simply knowing that I had to be there.'

'And what you were waiting for – did it come?'

'It was another close accidental involvement with a death that revealed the time in what I call my solitary refinement was ended. On that evening, for the first time in my five years, I felt lonely and fearful. And on the following morning a Dutch vet called Pieter Westernberg came into my life as I helped my milking partner get his cows tested for TB. We both knew at once that we were in love. His first wife, Julia, had died of cancer just a short while into his marriage and he too had been waiting, albeit in a different way. And so, it was cows that brought us together, and like your own Hindu forbears, I now regard them all as sacred!'

Tears were coming down the cheeks of Aishe as she strove to smile at Elise's little joke.

'Oh Elise, what can I say? I feel so totally privileged to have heard what you have just told me and in all honesty I am quite stunned by it and have no idea how to respond, other than to say, and this could be totally fantasy, that as you spoke I had a most odd feeling that my own time of waiting had also come to an end, though honestly I have no idea what that can possibly mean.'

'That's how it's meant to be, and you must always strive to remain in that place because it's the only true and safe place to be. You and I must never fall into compartmentalising or turning such knowledge into a religion. It means an austerity of the left-side of the brain which will revolt and demand our obedience and must not be heeded.'

'But how…what…? I don't know what to say or think?'

'That's the left side insisting on your attention, and it will be a struggle at times, Aishe, but we can support one another.'

'But Elise, in the light of all you have told me, what meaning is there in your renewed encounter with death in the suicide of Miss Driver?'

'Oh, don't you start!' said Elise with a grin. 'That's exactly what Leah asked me, but the question is left-sided, the longing for a place for everything, and there isn't. Aishe, my dear friend, please strive not to try and make sense of this. Meister Echardt, a German mystic of the 13th and 14th centuries wrote that for the sake of HaShem we have to take leave of HaShem (though that's not the word he used of course). The reality of Presence I know, but only by not thinking.'

'You have spoken about the two sides of the brain, but it's not possible to shut one side off, presumably because they must work together. So how does left side of your brain handle the realities of life such as in the terrible story you told me earlier?'

Elise thought for a moment.

'Two ladies were overheard talking on a bus. The first had described this or that, and the other replied "Be philosophical. Don't think about it". I love that story, but your question is fair enough. When I consider the systematic murder of six million of my fellow Jews and as a Jew it's always somewhere inside me and was during my five years alone, I have learned to accept I can't work it out logically, which the left-side of our brains demands, and how it might be allowed to fit with the logical longings of the religions. I focus wholly on what I have come to know, not logically but by experience and don't ever attempt explanations, because whatever the attempt, they will be wrong.

'So, of course, I cannot talk about this, because inevitably all words and their proliferation cannot express things beyond words.'

'Yet you have spoken to me.'

'Yes, and gladly because I intuit a capacity within you to receive what I am saying. I suppose I am taking a risk, Aishe, but I have already in a relatively short time come to trust you completely. Although Pieter and Fiene know the story of my solitary refinement in terms of how and what and where, and both accept all I have said to them, it is only Leah and now you, with whom I feel a kinship beyond words that allows me to risk words to describe what I know as שְׁכִינָה – Presence.'

Aishe's earlier tears had returned and were now coursing down her cheeks.

'And how do I live with this, Elise? It is so momentous.'

'As my wonderful Canadian priest said to me, don't do or be anything special, just get on with normal life day by day with Tan and Raj, but always beware the temptation to turn it into a religion.'

A Nativity Conundrum

It was inevitable as Elise had anticipated, that once her Jewish children attended a Church school, there would be a clash, and the forthcoming preparations within school for Christmas were threatening to bring this to a head.

Last year, Grace had been a sheep in the school nativity play and her sister, Julia, was reprising her big sister's role. But this year, being such a good reader, Grace had been chosen as one of the two narrators – of the Christian Christmas Story!

On the application forms before admission Elise and Pieter had agreed that they should write "Jewish" for religion, but it had never been picked up by the headteacher and never referred to again, even when repeated for Julia. Not that this was altogether surprising as it was the only Primary School for miles around and they took everyone. Perhaps it had been assumed that at Primary level this hardly mattered as the actual Christian input was never all that great and Elise assumed that it probably had no long-term deleterious effect on any of them. "Hands together, eyes closed", which Grace recounted as the practice in assembly, Elise thought nothing to be concerned about, but Grace, a Jewish child, reading a New Testament reading about something Elise knew was in any case a pure invention written as much as 100 years after the alleged event, about which even the two stories as they appeared could not barely agree on was different..

What troubled her most was the Greek name of Jesus instead of the actual name of יֵשׁוּע, Yeshua. She wanted the children in school to know that this was a Jewish baby with a Jewish name. Pieter suggested she just let it pass and regard it as just an enacted fairy tale as most of those attending would treat it anyway, something mostly for mums and grans to ooh and aah over. But there was streak in Elise she had previously, and probably conveniently ignored, that thought this a matter of principle. She decided to discuss it with Leah when the next spoke on the phone which they did two or three times each week.

'"A matter of principle"? Oh Elise, that doesn't sound like you.'

Elise laughed.

'Are you suggesting, Ms Jacobs, that I have no principles?'

'As if I would dare!' replied her friend. 'But it's not the first word that comes to mind when I think of you, because there are other words I would use. You are the most determined person I know, single-minded when you need to be. Without a doubt you are also the most loving person I know, but "principled" doesn't fit you because it suggests a mind-set that is angular in ways that you are not. Principled people write to newspapers, and you would never do that. Nor could I ever see you in any kind of protest march, not because you don't care, but because you're wise enough to recognise that not every fight is worth engaging in, and few are.'

'You do know how much I hate you when you're right, don't you?'

'As long as you continue to love me.'

'Oh, Leah, my love for you is not constant, it is ever-growing.'

'Even when I say that you should just go along and listen to Grace reading her part of the story? You know as well as I that nativity plays at Christmas have nothing to do with Christianity, however much the church likes to tell everyone they do. Christmas began in mid-November in Harrogate, and even here in Pateley the Christmas Tree is up. It's not a religious festival but a purely commercial one.'

'But am I failing Grace, Julia and Gale if I just go along with it? You know that I didn't know I was Jewish until I was 20 years old because my parents hid that from me, and I don't want to do the same for my own daughters.'

'Then perhaps you can begin to do this gently and almost indirectly by celebrating with them Hanukkah, the loveliest and least doctrinal of Jewish celebrations. After all it commemorates an actual event in history which is more than a nativity play does. Besides which I'm sure Grace is excited about the play, so to allow her to do that and then discover the feast of lights, can only enhance her young life. And even more, I'm pretty sure that if you speak to the headteacher about how Jews celebrate Hanukkah, you might even find it possible to get it included in the diversity curriculum.'

'Oh Leah, now I hate you more than ever.'

'I'll take that as a compliment then. Have you heard anything further about your vicar?'

'No.'

'Have you been called to give evidence?'

'No. I get the impression from our local policeman that it's being downgraded and will almost result in a verdict of suicide.'

'Allowing the vicar to get off scot-free?'

'It will depend on the evidence presented by the police.'

'I take it he has not returned as vicar.'

'No, but there has been a development of sorts. You will remember that he had admitted to an affair with the woman I named as Audrey to you.'

'Ursula explained that it wasn't her real name.'

'Well, Pieter came back from a farm visit this week and overheard two men discussing the lady in terms that claimed she is getting something of a reputation for putting herself around, if you take my meaning. She told me that one of the reasons she was so devastated by the breakup with the vicar was that she missed the sex she was enjoying, as well as the feeling of being wanted even if only for that, which was more than her husband did. The death of a child can do this to families.'

'But possibly it has woken her up and she can see possibilities she could never see before.'

'She told me her husband had told her he would kill himself if she left him for someone else. I've never met him, but Pieter has and says he's one of the most curmudgeonly farmers he knows and that's saying something, knowing farmers around here.'

'I can't imagine how I would respond to the death of Sarah or Ruth, but perhaps like all parents I have considered it as a possibility and wondered how I would survive.'

'Going back to my days as a rabbi, I remember being with someone who said of the death of her husband that it had completely shaken her faith in HaShem. I expressed my concern for her, but I wanted to say that she had believed in HaShem knowing such things happened to countless others, so what sort of belief was it that everything was to be cast aside when it happened to her.'

'True, Elise, but not everyone has our knowledge of the Presence. Knowledge cannot prevent bad things happening, either to those close to you or yourself, but you are sustained all the same. Equanimity describes you more than principled.'

'Gee thanks! I'll bear that in mind.'

Elise looked up the date for Hanukkah which varies each year according to the Jewish Calendar. This was Hebrew Year 5769 (2008 to everyone else) in the month of Kislev. Hanukkah would run for eight days from sundown on 21st. That would mean it was in the school holidays and run across Christmas Day, though of course as a family they would have a tree and presents as would everyone else, but it ought to be possible to run it in parallel. But she would need to talk this over with Pieter and Fiene.

She had to explain to them its origins in the rededication of the Second Temple in 164 BCE after the overthrow of the invader Antiochus Epiphanes of the Seleucid Empire which stretched from modern Turkey as far as India. From her study of Talmud, she knew that from early days candles were lit on each of the eight nights of the celebration, which why it is also called the festival of lights. She suggested that she acquire a simple Menorah, the candelabra with eight branches and that they could take turns in lighting the next candle on successive days, but wholly without prayers or anything else, other than the giving of chocolate coins.

'I love this,' said Pieter. 'My wife and my daughters are Jewish, and I cannot think of anything better for introducing this to the girls. After all they will have to endure the nativity plays at school and I think this will mean much more to them, and something that grow within them.'

'I totally agree,' said Fiene. 'Elise, I am privileged that the woman I call daughter and who calls me mother is Jewish, and so are my three granddaughters. I think this will be a wonderful way of celebrating this with the girls. As they grow older, they will choose to use every aspect of who they are as their lives will determine, but I cannot but think this is an excellent way to start. Clever you.'

'Oh no, Fiene. The credit is wholly due to Leah. She suggested it.'

'You are so very close to her,' said Pieter with what she thought was possibly a knowing or, at least, an enigmatic smile.

'Actually, when she suggested it, I told her I hated her because I had not thought of it.'

'I understand that, my darling. I hate Heidi and Fran too when they're right and I'm wrong at work, even though I love them both.'

'And of course it doesn't happen very often,' said Elise with a grin.

'Hardly ever, of course, which is why I mostly work with large animals and leave the small ones to them, meaning I work alone and so they're not there to correct my mistakes!'

Elise decided that this year at least she would not suggest to the head that the school might incorporate a recognition of Hanukkah into the school year, though she knew that some attention was given in the curriculum of various feasts and celebration of other religions, apart from Judaism. So far, the knowledge that she was a rabbi was limited to just a handful of people. If she was to tell the head and she wished to make use of Elise to help plan something, she feared it might have a wider circulation, something she did not wish, not least for fear that her girls might be on the receiving end of anti-Semitic hostility which she knew lay just a little below the surface in British life.

The Nativity Play took place in the school hall, in the absence of a vicar to welcome the school into the church. Of the children she could tell that Gale, whom she held throughout, seemed to enjoy it most, especially when her sisters were either visible in a lambskin or telling the story. Fiene took photographs and Pieter cheered at the end. Elise loved it too and worked hard at suppressing the conflicting thoughts that arose as the narrative proceeded. She thought back to her own former Rabbi Samuel, now in great age and recently bereaved of his beloved partner. He would have said something to her in the form of an amusing rebuke such as "Principle, Schinciple, Elise" and left it at that. Yes, Schinciple, was exactly that, and as they walked home together after the play, she looked at her excited and joyful family and considered herself a fool!

By coincidence, at lunchtime on the Friday before Hanukkah, , Elise had a phone call from Detective Sergeant Moule asking to drop by and inform her what was happening in the matter of Tony Reynolds. As the Festival of Lights, drew near she wondered whether she might be about to confront darkness!

Festival of Lights

Elise had heard nothing about the matter from PC Halliwell, and gossip at the school gates gossip had turned to other matters, which in the run up to Christmas was not surprising, so she was pleased to welcome Colin Moule into her study, plying him with coffee and some sort of special Dutch Christmas log called a *Banketstaaf* made by Fiene. Elise was addicted and after eating some, Colin said he could understand the addiction!

'I must apologise for not letting you know what is happening in the case of Tony Reynolds. The simple reason for that is that it was taken out of my hands and dealt with by my superior once it became clear that the Bishop of Ripon and lawyers from the diocese of Leeds were involving themselves in the matter.

'However, this morning he appeared before magistrates in Northallerton, the Crime Prosecution Service having agreed that there is sufficient evidence to charge him with gross negligence manslaughter and perverting the course of justice. In clearing away evidence before he left, it seems certain that she cannot have known what he was doing, and that therefore it is quite likely that he had either made her drunk with sexual intent and then abandoned her in that state, or worse, knew she had taken an overdose of medication, and did not seek help. The magistrates have committed him for trial, and he has been released on bail. However, after the hearing, his solicitor made a statement to the journalists present that they would contest the charges, not least on the basis that Mr Reynolds had been undermined in his work by a rabbi who had humiliated him and a guest speaker at a public meeting, something that had left deeply disturbed and feeling under duress when he made his original statement in the house of the rabbi where a houseguest, a Jewish lawyer, colluded with the rabbi to bring about his arrest, and it was no accident that the person who discovered the body of the deceased was the rabbi herself. This therefore made it quite likely that she was the one who cleaned up in such a way as to point the evidence at him.'

Elise sat back in her chair and said nothing for a few moments.

'And that was the lawyer appointed by the Church of England?'

'Yes, and done, no doubt, to bring about maximum publicity in the run up to Christmas.'

'You mean like that nasty Jew, King Herod, who ordered the baby boys of Bethlehem to be slaughtered?'

'Something like that. However, the CPS had heard all these claims, and rejected them utterly before authorising his charge. You have nothing to fear from these claims other than adverse publicity, which is why I wanted you to know as soon as I could get here.'

'Might I have to appear in court at the trial?'

'You should seek legal advice on that though I doubt it, as the evidence against him offered by PC Halliwell and myself that at no time did he act under any duress, is considerable, but when cornered he may lash out. It has been known.'

'Christmas Day is on Thursday. One of my daughters was the narrator in the Church of England School Nativity Play, and another a sheep. We have a Christmas Tree and Father Christmas will be bringing presents. I suspect a visit from Orthodox Jews might not find evidence that I am a rabbi, so if anyone from the Press comes, they are welcome to all that.'

I have no doubts, Elise, that you can handle this, but I would still recommend legal advice.'

'It is of course anti-Semitism, to which at various times in my life I have been subject, but I will speak to my solicitor friend, the one with whom I was allegedly in collusion in a Jewish conspiracy, but honestly, Colin, whilst I'm not pleased about this, it really is nothing. At the end of the day, Tony is aware that I know about his long-term adultery, and that there were at least 40 witnesses at that public meeting who will affirm that I only corrected textual errors and if the two men felt humiliated, that was because they put themselves into a position in which they misused the Biblical record in an attempt at manipulation. But I am profoundly disappointed in the Bishop of Ripon. I thought better of him than that he should permit church solicitors to make such a statement which is blatantly untrue.'

'There is going to be quite a while before the trial begin, so this will disappear from public view and what is said after a hearing is sometimes forgotten at a later stage. So don't lose too much sleep.'

'My three daughters and I will be celebrating Christmas in the next few days, but all four of us are Jewish, and will also be celebrating Hanukkah at the same time. Jews have learned never to sleep too soundly when hatred is around.'

'I can't imagine anyone wanting to hate you, Elise.'

'The Nazis did not hate individuals, they hated Jews.'

Pieter, Fran, Heidi and the other staff members were out for the Christmas lunch, so when Colin left, Elise immediately telephoned Leah and told her everything.

'Do you remember long ago when there was adverse publicity about the little boy killed by a car, when you ran to him and held in your arms as he died, you were told to make contact with a barrister in London who handles Jewish matters?'

'Of course.'

'Well Mr Bloom is no longer with us, but when the whole matter of my divorce was being dealt with, I was given excellent advice from one of Mr Bloom's team, a Mr Lionel Nivern QC. I think you should call his chambers immediately and I'll give you the number, though it's Friday afternoon and Shabbat begins in less than an hour's time, but someone will take your call, I'm sure.'

Leah gave Elise the number.

'I'll call Ursula at once,' added Leah.

Elise dialled the number which was answered by the clerk of chambers.

'My name is Rabbi Elise Westernberg and it is likely that I about to be subject an anti-Semitic attack in the local press following a bizarre statement made after a hearing in a magistrates court in

Northallerton.'

'Rabbi, I will put you through at once to Miss Levin. Mr Nivern has already left the building.'

Elise tried as briefly as possible to inform Miss Levin, who had asked if Elise was happy for the call to be recorded.

'Ok, Rabbi. Whilst you were speaking, I looked you up and saw that Mr Bloom once advised you on a similar matter. We are closing soon for Shabbat, but please first give me the news outlets you think will prove a nuisance.

Elise named the local newspapers and the two television news channels.

'Ok. I will make a couple of calls and Mr Nivern will be in touch on Sunday. In the meantime, Shabbat Shalom and a happy Hanukkah.'

What it was that Miss Levin did, Elise never knew, but no one came to her door and the tv news reported nothing about the court hearing. The only thing she did hear was from Ursula who said that she knew of Miss Levin's reputation and that clearly so did some of the major news channels!

For Elise on that evening when the first of the Hanukkah candles were lit by Gale, who was almost overwhelmed with excitement at being chosen before her big sisters, recalling the moment when the Maccabeans had overthrown the tyranny of the Seleucids and the Temple restored, was a moment of greater significance than she had possibly anticipated. It raised for her a question she had not considered greatly either in the Waiting Room or since: the relationship between her knowledge of the Presence and her Jewish identity.

Pieter and Fiene had been shocked by Colin's revelations and were urgent in wanting to know how best to support Elise.

'It's our daughters and your granddaughters with whom we should most concern ourselves. The possibility of bullying at school can't be overlooked if these stories become widespread.'

'We should arrange to meet with the head after the holidays and discuss it,' said Pieter. 'Teachers will need to be alert.'

'Possibly,' said Fiene, 'but, given that nothing has been said yet, and may not be according to Ursula given the intervention of the lawyer in London, might it not be best to do and say nothing either to the school or to Grace. Doing what we did tonight with the lighting of the Hanukkah candles is just part of the way this family celebrates this time of the year, together with all the Christmas events we share with everyone else. Other houses will have other traditions and if we were in Holland that would certainly be the case. Grace is very proud of her Dutch heritage, but if we suddenly get obsessed with her Jewish heritage it might cause her a heightened anxiety she can well do without. And that will be the same for Julia and Gale as they grow. They loved tonight's candle lighting as they loved it when we dressed the tree. Just let it be as natural as that.'

'Yes, mother,' said Elise, taking hold of Fiene's hand. 'As usual, yours are words of wisdom and we should heed them. What do you think, my darling Dutchman?'

'I spend most of my days at the mercy of wise women at home and at work, so how can I say anything other than Ja hoor.'

Early on the Saturday morning as she sat in her study, the only light coming from the candle of the Presence she found herself more than anything needing to be with Aishe. If she spoke to Leah, as most naturally she would do, she knew that both being Jewish and alive to the Presence might occlude her thinking, and that on this morning what she most needed was a speech therapist to help form her words and thereby reveal the shape of her mind.

She sat for almost half an hour in total silence both without, as it was before the girls were awake or the adults out of bed, but also within as she had learned in her years alone. The candle continued to burn – שְׁכִינָה.'

The Saturday morning before Christmas with all its activities made it impossible to meet with Aishe as Elise had hoped, but she and Raj were going to pop in for a cup of tea in the afternoon, an invitation strengthened by the promise of a piece of *kersttulbjand*, a Dutch cake which Elise thought even better than the *banketstaaf* Christmas log enjoyed by Sergeant Moule of the previous day.

'Do you do Christmas in Dutch or the English way?' asked Aishe as she ate her cake in the kitchen with the four children tucking in to theirs.

'A little Dutch,' answered Fiene, 'in that we gave the girls little gifts on December 5th. In Holland that is the big day of present giving rather Christmas Day. It is the eve of the feast of St Nicholas who gives his name to Sinterklaas, so in this house he calls in early with a little something for each one and then returns on Christmas Eve.'

'But we also light special candles, one each night, which we started last night, Oma,' said Grace, sitting at the table with them.

'Is that Dutch too?' Aishe asked Fiene.

'No,' said Grace, 'it's called Hanukkah and it's because we're Jewish as well as Dutch and English.'

Elise caught Pieter's eye as he too enjoyed his mother's cake, and they gave one another a little smile.

With the children playing, Elise and Aishe went into the study where Elise brought her friend completely up to date with the news about Tony Reynolds, but also about the statement made after the hearing.

'There was nothing on the news last night,' said Aishe.

'Perhaps there won't be, but you can imagine that I have anxieties for the girls.'

'I think your daughters are growing up to be more than capable of looking after themselves, besides which at school they are best known for being the vet's daughters, more than yours. They are greatly envied for that!'

'And I am the vet's wife, so that must make me acceptable too,' laughed Elise.

'Of course, and I am the doctor's wife, so despite the colour of my skin I've been invited to join the WI.'

'My envy knows no bounds. They haven't asked me, and I've lived here much longer than you.'

'Hey, if you think I'm flattered by being asked you'd be quite wrong. I made some jam for the Christmas Fair and they assumed that made me eligible. I'm not joining, saying that it might cause conflicts with some of them being my husband's patients. You're different. I know how much people like you as a member of the community but are slightly wary of your reputation for being very clever, which doesn't say much for me!'

'Ah well, I need to talk with you for I'm struggling with my speech again.'

'I charge double on Saturdays.'

Elise laughed and then said, 'But does it cost less than everything?'

A Little Giddy

"'A condition of complete simplicity
(Costing not less than everything)
And all shall be well and
All manner of thing shall be well..."

It was Aishe speaking, and she continued, 'Your friend, Eliot,' said Aishe, 'the very end of the Four Quartets. I've been reading him thanks to you. Of course I don't understand a lot of it, but I learned that bit, and you told me that the part which speaks of all being well comes from a medieval solitary woman. I've been holding on to that.'

'I do too.'

'But what amazed me when I first read the poems was that in the third he mentions Krishna, who was the incarnation of the god Vishnu. Isn't it odd for an Anglican American to refer to a Hindu deity?'

'It is known that he was familiar with the *Bhagavad Gita* and in earlier drafts the references also included a mention of a hermit in the East, and of course in Burnt Norton there is "the lotos rises quietly, quietly, in a Cotswold Garden", and in his earlier work *The Wasteland* there are clear indications of his reading of Asian literature. But like all writers he was inevitably something of a magpie, picking up things here and there to make use of.'

'But Elise was there something in particular you wanted to talk about or, more especially, need to discover how to say?'

'My beloved Pieter and Fiene both know a great deal about my time alone, now quite some time back, and to be honest I speak of it very little to them now, but their knowledge lies mostly dormant, respecting me. Overall, I think it's fair to say, they now give it little consideration, and quite rightly so. Leah is quite different because in a very different sort of way, wholly unrelated to me in any way, she herself manifests to me a knowledge of the Presence. It doesn't make her in any way especially religious, although she and Ursula maintain a pattern of Jewish living more than me.

'But I have been reflecting on my Jewishness, not least in the context of the events of the past few months since the meeting in the hall to launch *Alpha*, though of course I fear I caused it immediately to sink on its first outing, as with the Titanic.'

Aishe laughed.

'With the girls growing I want to know how much if anything I can say to them about what it might mean for them to be Jewish.'

'You mean as well Dutch and English?'

'Yes, I was really amazed to hear Grace say that. But in meeting you, my dearest Aishe, I have quickly come to recognise that you recognise what I have spent so long engaged with, and you have no religion, Hindu, Jewish or Rastafarian. It took the best part of five years to rid me of religion but with my daughters I find myself puzzled.'

'But need you say anything? They know and love you, and almost certainly Grace will suspect you're slightly loopy lighting your candle every time you enter this room, but let it be, let it be – oh forgive me, I sound like a Beatles song! You have often told me that some philosopher, whose name I can't recall, said something to the effect that what can't be communicated can't be communicated.'

'Ludwig Wittgenstein, and he was certainly an oddball, but he was right. Oh, Aishe, perhaps I need a new process of refinement, not like that of my previous five-year isolation, but just as real, to strip away the layers of nonsense I so easily wrap around myself.'

'It's not nonsense trying to find a way of communicating to our children something of the depths inside us. So, I have had an idea, prompted by something I heard on the radio, which, were you to agree, would require the help of Fiene and Peter, but I wondered if you and I might travel to Scotland to stay for a few nights at the Tibetan Buddhist Centre in the Borders? In addition to offering courses, they welcome visitors who just wish to go and be, possibly joining the community for silent meditation for an hour in the morning but otherwise free, and free of home constraints for just a while to clear our heads.'

'To be refined, you mean?'

'Possibly.'

'My parents want to come and stay, and they could look after Raj and Tan who, both being men need looking after. They would enjoy that because my mum is the best cook in Wales.'

'Aishe, that is a great idea, and we would have the chance to spend more time together than being the mums of young children and your work allow. My old Rabbi Samuel liked visiting Temples and Retreat Houses so I know he would approve. I will mention it to Pieter and Fiene and see what they have to say, but thank you for mentioning it, but even more for being you and helping me keep on the straight and narrow.'

The tentative idea received a warm welcome from Pieter and his mum, and they discussed it a little over a late brunch on the Sunday morning, during which Elise received a phone call from Mr Lionel Nivern QC.

'Good morning, Rabbi, I hope I'm not disturbing you but before we shut down for the holiday period, I wanted to let you know that Miss Levin handled the Press on Friday with considerable alacrity, so you need fear nothing further. The statement by the solicitor from the church was blatantly anti-Semitic and wholly contrary to the evidence presented to the magistrates. I have already contacted the Bishop of Leeds, who is the head of the diocese, to register our official complaint about the solicitor they used. He said he was shocked to hear what was said and would investigate.'

'How on earth did you get him on a Sunday morning?'

'Ways and means, and we were at Oxford together. I have his personal phone number. It's possible that you might receive an apology at some stage but it's a busy week before him. So put it all out of your mind.'

'Thank you so much, Mr Nivern. I remember an almost similar conversation with Mr Bloom many years back'

'I was his junior as Miss Levin is mine. It is my certain belief that she will have an important part to play in protecting us all in years to come.'

It was the Bishop of Leeds himself who called Elise before 10:00 on Monday morning. She had just returned from the morning's milking, something which always gave her pleasure and after a quick shower and change of clothes was sitting with the children eating porridge when her phone showed a number of which she recognised the dialling code as coming from Leeds.

'Is that Rabbi Westernberg?'

"Yes, I am Elise Westernberg, as I prefer to be called.'

'My name is Gregory Haddenham, and I'm the Anglican Bishop of Leeds. I have been informed that someone employed by this diocese made a deeply offensive anti-Semitic statement following a court case on Friday, which was fortunately not reported in the media because of an intervention by a barrister in London. I want unreservedly to apologise for that statement. Our senior legal officer has told me that because it was the last day before the Christmas break and the appalling case straightforward, that the most junior member of the team had offered to attend the hearing. Trust me, his Monday morning when he thought he was on holiday will be far from comfortable.

'My colleague the Bishop of Ripon, has told me that far from plotting against Reynolds, you were offering him lessons in New Testament Greek in your own home. He made me laugh, when he went on to tell me that in encountering you, he came up against a quite formidable theological and linguistic mind which left him thinking he himself ought to be doing more serious study!'

'Languages have always come easily to me, Bishop, and though I don't make much use of them now, my Hebrew is still sufficiently active to recognise when the Tanakh is being misused, and if you've studied classical Greek, that of the New Testament is a doddle.'

'You don't work as a rabbi now though?'

'At 4:30 this morning I began milking a dairy herd in the village of Wensley, which I do two or three mornings a week, and if I feel

any sort of urge to preach, and I don't, it would be only to these
ladies I know so well and who are more than willing to deliver the
contents of their bladders and bowels upon me!'

The bishop laughed.

'I ceased operating as a rabbi a long time ago, to devote myself
to a long period living as a solitary on the North York Moors,
engaging in encounter with what Jews call HaShem. After five
years I knew I could stop and on the following morning met and
immediately fell in love with the vet who had come to do TB
testing on the farm where I also used to help with the milking.

'We have three daughters and shortly after foot-and-mouth
bought the veterinary practice here. I still study Talmud as a hobby,
as I once did full-time for a year in Jerusalem and later taught it,
but small children, friendships and the wider family of this town
mostly take up my life, other than my abiding concern above all
else with שְׁכִינָה, which is the Hebrew word for Presence.'

'The Bishop of Ripon told me about the candle in your study. I
think he was deeply moved, which makes what happened on
Friday doubly shameful. Might I dare to suggest we meet face-to-
face? I am not merely intrigued by your story, that would be a rude
thing to say, but I am drawn to it and would welcome the chance
to hear more.'

'I would be very glad to welcome you but only if it is unofficial
and, in effect, a private visit.'

'I would like that too. I will consult with my diary and suggest
a few dates, if I may.'

'Of course. Thank you for calling, Bishop, and for the apology
on behalf of the Church to a Jew. In the meantime, may I wish you
a happy Hanukkah and a happy Christmas.'

'And you. Shalom.'

It was just three days into the New Year that Pieter received an
early morning call to say that Hughie Satterthwaite had been found
dead earlier that morning having shot himself in the mouth with
his 12-bore and they need him to come and check on the state of
the animals. As it was a dairy farm, and cows need twice-daily
milking he told PC Halliwell that he would bring Elise with him

in case she was needed to do the milking for which she was well qualified. It was well known in the town that she was milking on a nearby farm regularly and John gave his agreement.

It was still dark and frosty when they arrived at the farm where there were three police vehicles and an ambulance outside on the road. Pieter and Elise were waved through along the track. Elise said she would wait in the car until Pieter indicated she was needed, but that took less than five minutes. Hughie had obviously killed himself without attention to the cattle.

Her first task was to survey the parlour which was not the most modern, and then she went out to where the cattle were becoming increasingly agitated as they waited. It was going to take quite some time but once she opened the gate, they began to make their way in.

'What do you want me to do?' asked Pieter once he had checked on the other livestock.

'Get me someone to come and help. This place is somewhat antiquated, and it will take ages if I have to do it myself, and when you've done that, set in motion the redistribution of the herd by checking their health and providing movement certificates.'

Pieter returned to the car having informed John Halliwell of what Elise had said.

'Leave finding someone to me,' said John. 'There's a few retired farmhands who will respond.'

'Ok. I can't do a health check until after milking, but I'll begin to ring round and see if local farmers will be willing to take a few more beasts, otherwise we're in real trouble. They have to be milked again this evening and tomorrow morning and so on. Even my wife can't manage that, and in any case, she has her own responsibilities for milking tomorrow morning in Wensley.'

As he was returning to the milking parlour, he bumped into Tan Harman who had obviously been called.

'Not a pretty sight, Pieter,' he said.

'I can imagine.'

'Most of his head is missing but I would imagine it's a straightforward case of suicide. Poor man. The police said he never got over the death of his son.'

'What about his wife?'

'She's in the house but you should warn Elise that she's asking for her.'

'For Elise?'

'Apparently so. She's in a state of shock and I'll get Christine Goole, her GP, to call in and see her, but it's your wife she wants.'

'Does she know she's doing the milking?'

'She's been told.'

'I'm sorry you had to deal with that, Tan. Not the best way to begin the new year.'

'Thanks, but all I did was confirm death which didn't take a lot of doing and keep my eyes away from the head and neck area. I've made then cover them. The people I'm most sorry for are the funeral director and his assistants. Their task is horrible to consider.'

'And then of course the questions that inevitably follow a suicide.'

'Are you implying there's more to it than the death of his son?'

'I'm not implying anything, but the suicide of farmers is on the rise everywhere and this will make a further addition to that number. I imagine the problems being faced by farmers will have to be considered when they seek to make sense of this.'

Pieter went on to the milking parlour where Elise was already hard at work.

'John Halliwell is trying to get you someone to come. I'll need to do a health check on them when you've finished. The alternative will be for me to send them all to slaughter which I'd prefer not to have to do. I'm going to ask Heidi to come and help me. In the meantime, Betty in the house is insisting that the only person she wants to talk to is you, so when you've done here, John wants you to go in and see her, if you're willing.'

'Of course I will. You know that.'

'Yes, I told him you would.'

'This is a mess in just about every way.'

The Aftermath

John Halliwell had summoned two experienced former farmhands, both of whom were experienced in milking and they turned up within 20 minutes.

'Hello, Mrs Westernberg,' said a man known locally as "Old Gem" though nobody seemed to know what he was really called. 'I've come to relieve you, and Pete Sanderson should be here very soon. Bad business, and this place is a bit out of date, but you've done a grand job.'

'Thanks. I'll wait until Pete gets here but then I've got to go in and see Betty as she wants to speak to me.'

'Aye well, I know Luke's death affected Hughie badly, but I don't think she's exactly helped.'

Elise shook her head and they each gave the other a look that spoke volumes.

Pete Sanderson arrived ten minutes later and took over from Elise.

'Thanks for coming, Pete.'

'That's alright, Mrs W. I imagine Pieter's having to work out what to do with the livestock. We can probably put together a rota for milking for a day or two, but this lot will have to be moved.'

'He's already on to it. When you've finished, please keep them in the yard rather than letting them back into the barn. He will have to do a health check before they can be moved, and one of his colleagues will be coming to assist him.'

'You're quite a pair, you two. Not many could do what you do.'

'The cows I normally milk are not my financial concern so I can do it simply because I find it such a satisfying thing to do.'

'Even when you get covered in shit?'

'You get used to it, as you know.'

'Aye, but since I stopped working our lass says she doesn't miss the stink.'

Elise laughed.

'Old Gem's already at work so I'll leave you to it.'

Elise walked towards the farmhouse where an over-eager constable she didn't recognise at first barred her entrance.

'Constable Halliwell said Mrs Satterthwaite wanted to talk with me.'

'Oh, I'm sorry. You must be the vet's wife.'

He let her in.

Betty was sitting in the kitchen close to the Rayburn, keeping warm, and looking into space, as Elise opened the door and came in. Betty looked up and smiled.

'What have I done, Elise? What have I done?'

'I assume you didn't shoot him.'

'No, though they've tested my hands and arms to see if I did. No. The bang woke me, and I knew what he'd done because he hadn't come to bed. I called the police before I could bear to go and look, and when I did take a look, I almost died. It was terrible beyond words. His whole face and the back of his head had gone – and I did that.'

Elise pulled out a chair and sat down close to Betty.

'Tell me what happened last night because I assume something must have done.'

'He'd been to the market at Hawes in the afternoon and I hadn't seen him when he got back; he must have gone straight to do the milking. It was at about 8:00 that he came in. He looked dreadful; his face was so angry I thought he was going to hit me.

'He yelled at me that he'd been made the butt of jokes at the mart, "utterly humiliated", were his words, and wanted to know if there was any truth in what had been called Betty's "Artificial Insemination" – AI – what your husband does for our cows.

'I am so ashamed now I know what he's done, because I had just had enough of his anger and bitterness towards me and everyone else, so I told him that I'd been left by him when I most needed him after Luke's death, so I was more than willing to accept love from wherever I could get it. I told him about my affair with the vicar and then with Len Grogan in Swaledale. "They showed me the love I needed, not you", I shouted at him. I think I knew then what he might do, as he'd warned me in the past as you know. But, do you know, Elise, what I think in the end drove him to fire the gun was not what I had done, but because he'd been laughed at.'

'It's less what you did, Betty,' said Elise. 'And much more the cruelty of those who made fun of someone in an extremely vulnerable position. That sense of being laughed at, humiliated in public, on top of the dreadful depression he had been in since Luke's death – that was why he killed himself.'

'But it'll all come out at the inquest.'

'Not necessarily. There's no doubt that he has taken his own life and that no one else was involved. He was so very unhappy and a changed man, according to Pieter, after Luke had died, and which of us wouldn't be. I very much doubt that anyone would begrudge your longing for comfort and love which he couldn't give you.

'Hughie died inside some time ago, and that was the second death you had to cope with. What happened early this morning was just the outward last stage. You will get only understanding from everyone in this community, and one or two farmers who were at Hawes yesterday will be the ones who will have to live with the guilt of what they did.

'But there are some practicalities to deal with. Pieter and Heidi will be up after milking's done – Old Gem and Pete Sanderson are finishing off – to see what fettle the beasts are in, because unless you're wanting to take them on, and I suspect you're not, they will have to be moved, either to other farms in small numbers or to slaughter. They can get a milking rota together for a day or two, but they have to go, and you'll need to think about the sheep though they're ok for a day or two, the same with the fowl. But most important of all is what you need to do. I'm far from convinced that staying here, at least for the next few days, is a good idea so, unless you can think of a better idea, throw some clothes into a bag and come home with me and stay for a day or two until you will be able to think more clearly. There's bound to be a lot of activity here moving cattle, and one thing and another, so being with us will be ideal.'

'I can't ask that of you, Elise. You've already done so much for me, you and Pieter, including this morning.'

'Actually, Betty, you didn't ask me. Truly, I think being away from here at least for a day or two is essential and you won't get a better offer right now.'

'I'll have to leave anyway. We're tenant farmers and that includes the house.'

'Come on, let me help you get some things together and you can come into town with me.'

Pieter had already contacted the local branch on the NFU to see if some of the cows could be taken by others at the same price as Betty would get if they went to slaughter which was considerably less than farmers would need to pay for them at auction. He made the point that speed was of the essence as the herd also included some in calf.

Once milking was over, he and Heidi went through the whole herd as quickly as possible and found that all were in a healthy enough state to allow them movement certificates. He also made provisional contact with the abattoir. The sheep he would attend to later and as almost all were in lamb, more easily relocated. The fowl, however, would have to be destroyed, because of the possibilities of cross-infection.

Arriving back home, Elise found that Fiene had taken the children to school and the nursery, so she sat Betty down in the kitchen, made he a mug of tea and prepared some breakfast for them both.

'Have you got family elsewhere, Betty,' asked Elise, as she made porridge.

'I have an older sister, Joyce, in Bedale and my younger brother, Eddie, lives in Darlington and works on the railways. I'll need to let them know before they hear it on the news.'

'Well get something thing into you before you do anything, and then I'll show you your room and you can make your calls. I imagine PC Halliwell will want to call in and see you.'

'Don't leave me by myself when he does that, Elise, please.'

'I won't.'

'I imagine everything is now going to come out – Tony and my relationship with Len Grogan. Oh God, what have I done?'

'I'm not a lawyer, Betty, but I can only think the coroner will return a verdict of suicide following a period of intense depression consequent on Luke's death. The only reference to you might come when it emerges that what pushed him over was being laughed at Hawes Mart yesterday. Those who did that will have uneasy consciences for a long time – or at least I hope they do.'

'And me too. I was the one who had the affairs they were laughing at.'

'And you, Betty, lost your son just a short time ago and have been struggling to find a way to survive without the love and support of your husband ever since. It wasn't his fault he couldn't cope after Luke's death, but he couldn't, and you knew you wanted to.'

'You're a good person, Elise. This is the second time I've come to you in a right mess, and you've been wonderful both times.'

The door opened and Fiene came in and immediately went and held Betty close to her and said nothing. Eventually she kissed her on the cheek and smiled at her.

'You're perfectly safe here, Betty. Pieter will take care of the farm, but Elise and I will continue to look after you here.'

'Oh, Mrs Westernberg, thank you so much even though I don't deserve it.'

'I'm called Fiene, it's short for Jozefiene, as I assume Betty is for Elizabeth.'

'Yes, though until I met Hughie, I was always called Beth, which I much prefer. My sister and brother call me that.'

'I was once given an extra name,' said Elise, though I don't use it.'

'What is it?'

'A name translated into English as Mary but was the name of the Jewish mother of the Jewish man you know as Jesus, and I call Yeshua.'

'Oh.'

'Oh indeed!' said Fiene. 'Look, let's get you to your room and then into a shower, and a change of clothes. Practical things are especially important at times like this. Elise and I can make any phone calls you want, and let people know what's happened. You shouldn't have to be doing that.'

'Thank you. I'll get you the numbers for my brother and sister, but Elise, someone urgently needs to let Len know what's happened.'

'Yes, I'd thought of that. Let me call him. Just tell me what I need to know.'

'He's ten years older than me and lives with his daughter, Jane. He was divorced five years ago, and he farms on the far side of Muker, he has goat milkers and sheep.'

'He sounds an interesting man.'

'He is and he also knows me as Beth,' said Betty, as she handed Elise a list from her bag with the numbers on it.

Fiene led Betty, upstairs whilst Elise went into her room, lit her candle and sat at her desk and before picking up the telephone looked at the names and numbers. Perhaps Betty had already written the list for herself that morning since Hughie's death, but surely the numbers would have been on her phone already. Or had she been working towards this? Elise decided to leave that as a puzzle for now and began to make the three calls.

'Hello. Is that Mr Grogan?'

'Aye.'

'This Elise Westernberg, the wife of Pieter, the vet from Wensleydale.'

'What can I do for you?'

Elise told him what had happened without adding anything further.'

'How's Beth, and where is she?'

'Here at the surgery, having a shower and changing her clothes, and waiting for the police to come and take a statement.'

'Please her tell her that I shall come and collect her from you this afternoon, and that she's to come here. I'll care for her, and I don't give a fig for what anyone might say. She's very special.'

279

'Mr Grogan, I will tell her straight away and I imagine she'll want to speak to you as soon as she can.'

That, Elise thought, was the best of all possible news and she went up at once, even whilst Betty was in the shower to tell her.'

'Oh, Elise, thank you, thank you.'

Back in her room, Elise made the calls to Betty's brother and sister. PC Halliwell called for Betty's statement and later she left for Muker with Len.

In bed that night after what had been a demanding day, Elise told Pieter about the list of phone numbers.

'She told me once that Hughie had told her that if she ever left him, he would shoot himself. What do you think?'

'It's not our job to speculate. Tomorrow, I have to ensure the cattle are moved and the chickens collected for slaughter. That's my job and yours is not to engage in too much thinking. Isn't that what you are meant to be about?'

You're a very rude Dutchman and I adore you.'

A Visitation

Elise didn't mind the Bishop of Leeds coming to see her, but she wasn't exactly excited by it either. His PA suggested a date and time that would cause maximum inconvenience as it was school home time, but she said yes.

She had also spent a few mornings with Aishe planning their visit to the Buddhist Centre which from the map, seemed to be in the middle of nowhere, which Elise thought appropriate.

Aishe had been concerned about Elise's involvement in yet another suicide which she now knew had been so influential in beginning and ending her solitary refinement, as she still insisted on calling it.

'I have no idea whether my involvement with the two the suicides of Annie and Hughie, is anything more than coincidental. You know that my spiritual guide Fr Jean-Pierre told me that whatever might be, the living out of an ordinary life was essential, and so that's what I've been doing.

'However, this afternoon the Bishop of Leeds is calling in. I think he's been attracted by the novelty factor of a woman rabbi in the Yorkshire Dales, but he might have news of Tony.'

The bishop arrived on time and was dressed in casual clothes. He was in his early 60s, bald and with what Elise thought was a kindly face.

'I'm sorry for the clash with your children coming home. My wife and I are on our way to Durham for a few days away.'

'I hope she's not outside in your car.'

'She'll be fine there.'

No, she won't,' said Elise. 'Please go and bring her in. My mother-in-law will make her some tea and a piece of Dutch cake, which she may now have to withhold from you for treating your wife so badly!'

The bishop went and brought in his wife whom Fiene rescued from his cruel hands, and he was led into Elise's study. He was at once struck by the lit candle and the photograph of her *Semikhah*.'

'That's Rabbi Samuel Green with you unless I'm mistaken. I met him a few times at the BBC and of course heard him on the radio.'

'Yes, he was my first rabbi and guide who taught me more than anyone else that HaShem is present in every circumstance, including that of a meeting of a rabbi and bishop in the Yorkshire Dales, though it sounds like the beginning of a joke. But please sit down and tell me first what you know of Tony Reynolds.'

'He's living in Mirfield, near Huddersfield, with the Community of the Resurrection, a sort of religious order he encountered a little during his training. We don't yet have a date for the trial, but the CPS are pressing on with it. He knows how stupidly he behaved, but we both know, and probably you better than me, that what happened flowed out of his loneliness here and the break-up with his wife. We also made a serious error of judgement on the basis of a lack of knowledge about his circumstances when he was appointed.'

Fiene came in with tea and cake, and also offered the bishop an enigmatic smile.

'We are a composite family,' said Elise, catching her mother-in-law's look. 'I'm Canadian, my husband and his mother, whom you've just met, are both Dutch. I am a rabbi and once taught Talmud which I studied in Jerusalem. After I became a rabbi on a visit back to Canada, I discovered that when just a few days old, I was baptised and confirmed as a Roman Catholic. Pieter, who owns the veterinary practice here, and I have three Jewish daughters who attend the C of E school. Finally on two or three mornings a week I leave very early to do the milking with a farmer up the dale, that being my favourite hobby. What about you?'

'My goodness. How could anyone compete with that? I'm seriously boring in comparison. After Oxford where I read French and Spanish, I taught for several years at Winchester College, not exactly your typical secondary school, before heading to a place called Cuddesdon, near Oxford, to train for ordination. I was a curate in Reading for three years before spending five years as the Anglican chaplain in Paris. I came back to be Archdeacon of Cheltenham and was appointed as Bishop of Leeds seven years ago. I'm now in the House of Lords and take my turn at leading prayers and attending, plus a member of innumerable committees and I have a special brief on matters to do with inter-Church relationships. No milking I'm afraid.'

Elise gave him a smile.

'Tell me about your praying.'

'Goodness. I hadn't expected a question like that. Well, what can I say other than that because of my busy life I rely very much on the prayers of others to sustain me, though I strive not to miss saying Evening and Morning Prayer from the Book of Common Prayer, and endeavour to ensure my wife and I get away at least once a fortnight for a walk in the countryside. I find that strengthens me a great deal. But may I return the question and ask you?'

'I had five years as a solitary on the North York Moors, and you will hardly be surprised to know that has shaped and fashioned my life since then.'

'There have not been many Jewish solitaries, or Christian ones for that matter.'

'There are probably more than you know because the essence of being solitary is that you don't broadcast your existence. My external contact was limited to one friend who came for a few days twice a year, the local farmer who taught me how to milk which I did every morning for my last two years, and a visit to the supermarket in Scarborough once a month, otherwise I lived quite alone.'

'Were you living a sort of monastic lifestyle?'

'No prayers, no religious observance of any kind. I was there to wait in silence and that is what I learned how to practice. My *lectio divina* consisted of Eliot's *Four Quartets* and the *Apopthegmata Patrum*, in the absence of the Canadian Catholic priest, himself also a solitary, who having directed me to this, departed this life. My life was equivalent to the title, though not the content, of a book by someone called Brother Lawrence...'

'"The Practice of the Presence of God",' said the bishop interrupting.'

'Yes, though I never use the *G* word you have spoken because it is so abused by religious and non-religious alike that it is now wholly devoid of meaning. Occasionally, if absolutely pushed, I will use the Jewish term HaShem, but even to say that is to distort all I have come to know.

The bishop sat quietly, reflecting on what he'd just heard.

'But what about now? With three children and a husband I assume it's some time since you abandoned the solitary life.'

'What I came to know in those five years in what I call solitary refinement, is just as real to me now as then. When I met Tony Reynolds and the wonderful world of *Alpha*, plus even your colleague in Ripon, I was left profoundly disturbed that Christian teachers and leaders are mostly not rooted in prayer but in busyness. I find it hard to understand how you can offer much to anyone, without spending at least an hour each day in silent prayer. Out of what do you possibly dare to speak to others? Please excuse my directness, but I am only a distant observer.'

'There is no need to apologise.'

'What I have come to know emerged from close personal encounters with tragedy and death, with an ever-present awareness of the Holocaust, in which my great-grandparents perished, and living in almost complete silence (with a background noise of seabirds, as I was only 100 years from the cliffs where they nest). I discovered I had to shed religion completely, though I recognise you belong to a religious tradition I know so little of and what I say may be of little use to you.'

'The idea of an interventionist deity, which underlies my religious tradition is not something you accept, even though it runs through the pages of what we call the Old Testament?'

'It took me the first two years of struggle to shed all my previous beliefs and I have no concern for the beliefs of others because they are formed more by inner needs than awareness of an outer reality.

'I'm not sure what to make of you've told me, Elise, other than that I'm somewhat in awe of it. I reckon it has an austerity that most people would find challenging or more likely, disturbing, and in the modern Church of England, which easily echoes those words of EM Forster about "Poor little talkative Christianity", would produce mostly blank expressions, though from that wing of the church now in the ascendancy, an absolute rejection.'

Elise shrugged.

'I am reminded of some words of the former Archbishop Runcie,' the bishop continued. 'He compared the Church to a swimming pool, in which all the noise comes from the shallow end!

'But if I understand what you have said aright, this is not about some kind of reformed Judaism based upon the Biblical revelation so much as about direct experience of the divine which would mean a radical shift within each of us. Do you know the writings of the Welsh priest-poet RS Thomas? He spoke about God, if you will excuse my use of the word, being found more in absence than in anything presented or offered by religion. I find he speaks to me.'

'Yes, I have a close Welsh friend who introduced me to his writings, though I prefer those which are the product of his observations of farming communities, those to do with Iago Prytherch. They resonate with me here. Later, he increasingly wrote of what the Christian tradition calls the negative way, the apophatic, to use the Greek term, but nevertheless still holding hands with what my own former religious tradition calls HaShem. You may think I'm being obtuse, but even he still didn't let go of what must be let go of.'

'Well, not obtuse, Elise, but certainly disturbing. No wonder Gerry Allen came away from his meeting with you feeling somewhat shaken. And yet, here is the paradox. You're not some sort of weirdo ascetic or even a misery guts such as everyone says RS Thomas was, but the mum of three small girls who goes milking cows two or three times a week.'

He shook his head in apparent disbelief.

'You've given me a lot to think about,' he said.

'I hope not, because that's exactly the opposite of what I would wish you to have heard from me!'

'I usually finish a visit to someone by offering to pray with them, but I think this is not the right time or place.'

'Again, quite the opposite. This is the place of encounter and I for one have never stopped what you might think of as prayer from the moment you came in. My candle is not some sort of religious artefact. As I told your colleague from Ripon, it is שְׁכִינָה'

'Presence,' said the bishop.

'Though I cannot take the candle with me to the milking parlour, that also is the place of שְׁכִינָה, as also playing with my children and making love with my husband. Rabbi Samuel told me that a rabbi came across a couple having sex in the synagogue. He was outraged that they could do this in front of the holy Ark. They said to the rabbi that if he could tell them where the presence of HaShem was not to be found, they would go there and do it!'

'That is a wonderful story though also very scary. But what is the Hebrew word used when the glory has departed?'

'You are thinking of אִיכָבוֹד, *Ichabod*. The Hebrew means "without glory", but it does not mean without Presence, for even there it can be known, even in the camps of the Holocaust.'

The bishop looked ready to leave.

'I can't begin to thank you, Elise for all you did for Tony Reynolds even when you knew the part he had played in the death of your surgery's cleaner, and I must apologise again for what was said by the diocese's junior solicitor. Most especially, thank you for your time here with me. Oh dear, I was about say "God bless" – a bad habit!'

Elise laughed.

'And I could give you a rabbinic blessing, but I probably can't remember the words, so touché.'

The bishop's wife was chatting still with Fiene and two if the children in the kitchen.

'Did Elise tell you that the family is descended from Pieter Breughel the Dutch artist?' she asked her husband.

'Nothing would surprise me in this house,' he said, as Elise showed them to the door and waved them off.

Elise returned to the kitchen.

'How was that?' asked Fiene, as Elise turned her attention to Grace and Julia.

'Like most religious liberals he is a flirt. He likes a little bit of this and a little bit of that, including just a little bit of a poet or two. It's exciting for a moment, before returning to what is familiar and completely safe. As I say: a flirt.'

A Visit

When Leah heard of the possible visit to Samye Ling, the Tibetan Buddhist Centre in the Borders she immediately asked if she might come too, which thrilled Elise, and Aishe said she would welcome the chance to get to know Leah better. The visit was arranged after the half-term holiday and after the inquest into the death of Hughie Satterthwaite.

The police investigation was somewhat perfunctory, not least because here seemed little point in looking beyond the prolonged period of depression following the death of Luke to account for it. The coroner was therefore easily able to allow a verdict of suicide, given that his officer had become aware that he might have been pushed over the edge by comments made at the sheep market but that it wasn't possible to be sure of this nor who might have made them.

Betty Satterthwaite was already calling herself Beth Grogan, and let Elise know that she and Len were planning a quiet wedding in Richmond after Easter. It seemed to Elise the best thing for her to start a completely new life in a completely new dale, for though they were but a few miles apart, Swaledale and Wensleydale folk were as different as the two breeds of sheep bearing their names.

Leah offered to do the driving and took them via the A66 across to Penrith and then up the M6 and A74(M) to Lockerbie before taking the slow and twisty side road north towards Eskdalemuir and the Temple complex, which showed itself with garish statues and a golden building against the backdrop of the beautiful green hills above the river.

They had booked a room for three and unloaded their baggage

before going for a walk round. They were immediately attracted to the Tibetan Tea Rooms and the chance to do what the English always most need to do which is to sit down, drink tea and, though sitting, find their feet.

'If you don't like colour, you're definitely in the wrong place' said Leah, 'especially the colour red.'

'It's not my favourite colour and I'm not wild about the gold,' added Elise, 'but it's quiet.'

'It's a Monday in February, so I imagine it gets a lot more visitors when it warms up,' added Aishe.

After their drink they walked over towards the Temple area, which was still in the process of being transformed into a massive quadrangle but now consisted of steps leading up the doors, where they had to leave their shoes before entering.

Inside it was a mass of golden miniature statues of the Buddha across three walls with a whirling electronic prayer wheel running constantly. There were seats for those not able to adopt a cross-legged position, which Elise knew she would definitely be choosing when silent meditation time came. There were benches presumably for the monks, some of them raised, but once again the place was characterised by waves of colour hitting the eyes. In the middle was a raised seat, almost like a throne, presumably to be occupied by the head monk, who was apparently known as Rinpoche.

As they left the Temple it was beginning to get dark.

'I must say,' said Aishe, 'I really liked the colour in there.'

'That's your Hindu DNA emerging,' said Elise with a laugh. 'What about you, Leah?'

'I suspect that my reaction, given the tradition from which you and I have come, is to think it a little over-the-top, but I look forward to spending more time to get to know how everything functions. Things might become a little clearer to me then.'

'Yes, I certainly have never experienced anything quite so in-my-face in any other sort of synagogue, church or temple, but I'm not here for the colour or the statues but for a chance to understand what and how I can learn from those who have made this their home in the Buddhist tradition.'

At the evening meal which was vegetarian and simple, they saw several monks and what they took to be nuns in their saffron robes sitting amongst others and chatting. It did not possess the quality of Elise's waiting room silence, but she was more than prepared to wait and experience the hour-long meditation at 8:00 the following morning.

Elise slept well but was awake very early, dressed quietly and went out into the dark, frosty morning. The setting was idyllic though the place wholly out of keeping with the land around it. She wandered down towards an area where she had seen some animals on the previous evening and at once recognised the familiar signs of milking, though disappointed to discover that they no longer farmed yaks! What she hadn't expected to see were goats waiting to enter a special-sized parlour – a lot of goats, some with kids alongside.

Because of rules about biosecurity, she wasn't allowed inside but could see enough to recognise what was so familiar from her years in the parlour. She had seen in the dining room notices that goat's milk was used exclusively at the Centre, and in the shop that goats milk cheese and soap were on sale. Clearly it was a small industry doing well.

The goat's milk porridge warmed her up before she made her way to the Temple for the hour-long meditation where she was soon joined by Leah and Aishe and several others mostly young, who in contrast to these "seniors" were taking to the floor, planting their bottoms on cushions and crossing their legs. Ahead the members of the monastic community were on either side in their robes and in the centre seat there was a large bald-headed man, more in a robe of gold than red, who was, Elise assumed, the Abbot or Rinpoche. Outside, a handbell continued to be rung summoning all and sunder to abandon their shoes at the door and enter. When all was ready there began about five minutes of what Elise presumed was Tibetan signing, a deep moaning noise from the community (or the *bhikkhuni-sangha* as it was technically know being made up of nuns and monks, though it was generally *Sangha* for short) and most of the young persons present. The sound was deep-throated and gravelly, not easy listening but neither unpleasant. Then there began 55 minutes of complete silence ended by the Abbot striking a gong.

The three friends decided to go for a walk along the banks of the river.

'My bum hurt after about half an hour,' confessed Aishe.

'My legs went to sleep,' added Leah, 'and after that I couldn't focus on anything other than on them, but for you Elise, it must have been a return to something completely familiar.'

'It's almost ten years since I came out of the waiting room and in our house, there isn't a great deal of silence, but I slipped straight back in and time flew by. Don't forget I spent two hours in total silence at a time, twice each day, so it was a little bit like meeting an old friend.'

'How on earth did you manage that?' asked Aishe, to whom Elise had never spoken much of what had characterised her daily routine in her solitary eyrie.

'If I'm honest, it took me three years before I could still the lunatic voices in my head telling me, in Eliot's words, "that this was all folly".'

'I've not found them in the *Four Quartets*.'

'They come from *The Journey of the Magi*, which he wrote earlier. So, it doesn't surprise me to hear about your bum and legs. I'll leave you here for a year or two and by then they'll be feeling better!'

They laughed.

'Oh, but did my head fill with lunatic voices!' said Leah, 'But what amazed me when I opened my eyes was the stillness of the monks and so many of the young people, though I was relieved when it ended, that some of them found their legs had gone to sleep and they struggled to stand, not the members of the community though.'

After coffee in the Tea Rooms, they had volunteered to do some work in the kitchen and dining rooms, Leah and Aishe helping prepare lunch whilst Elise mopped the dining room floor with two young Scottish girls, both of whom were more than ready to supply reasons for their stay. For both it was a gap or interim period in which to consider what they wanted to do afterwards. Neither seemed attracted to becoming a nun!

Elise was late into lunch and saw her friends at a packed table engaged in happy chatter so collected her food and sat alone, but not for long as another straggler, a monk in his saffron robe came and asked if he might join her

'I'm Bahuputtikā Soṇā,' said a gentle Scottish voice.

Not a monk but a nun!

'I'm Elise, and I'm delighted you've come to sit with me. My two friends are over there on the noisy table!'

'Is this your first visit?'

'Yes.'

'And how are you finding the place?'

'Culturally speaking it is a shock to the senses, but I very much enjoyed seeing the goats being milked and the quality of the silence in the Temple.'

Soṇā laughed.

'That's a most interesting combination I've never heard before, but you must have been up early to see the milking.'

'I didn't go in because I know about biosecurity, but I was most interested because at home I milk cows two or three mornings a week. Hence, I'm used to getting up early and have been for years.'

'You're a farmer?'

'No. I'm a full-time mother of three girls under eight and I have a husband who's a vet.'

'That explains why you enjoyed the silence,' said Soṇā with a smile.

'No, it doesn't,' said Elise, with a smile.

'That's an enigmatic comment. Can you expand on it?'

'I will, but first I want to ask you about your own involvement with silence in becoming what you are.'

'That's a most unusual way of asking why I became a nun and I'm more intrigued than ever. I will tell you because the question frankly amazes me in the way you have put it and leads me to ask whether you have an involvement with silence you might be willing to share, but Elise, I'm not sure this is the best place to do that. I have some work to do straight after lunch, but I could be free after 3:00, and we could either go for a walk or I will find us a room where we can talk in private.'

'I would like that, but perhaps we can prepare by just telling one another what we did before we discovered silence. I am a Canadian by birth, who moved to England when I was 14, and after studying middle-Eastern languages in Israel and London, though I didn't actually discover I was Jewish until I was twenty, then became a rabbi, believe it or not, in Cambridge.'

'Wow,' replied Soṇā. 'I can't match that, trust me. I grew up in a lovely seaside placed called North Berwick, east of Edinburgh, studied English lit at university, and then became a teacher in Stirling. I was engaged to one of my fellow teachers but broke it off when I could envisage only catastrophe down the line because of the amount he drank. That was when I paid my first visit here out of curiosity and then, aged 35, I came to stay for a year which has extended to six so far.'

'Where does your heart lie in the literature you studied?'

'It ought to be Robbie Burns, Walter Scott and Ian Rankin but, though I don't say it aloud, I'm wedded to the very English Jane Austen, the poetry of John Clare, and that of your fellow North American T S Eliot.'

'He has played a huge part in my life, Soṇā, and I shall be more than happy to share that with you later.'

'Good. So now tell me about your three daughters.'

They chatted together as they completed their meal, and both knew that waiting for them later were things of import. Elise decided to return to their room for a nap which lasted over an hour before Aishe returned and woke her.

'I like this place, Elise. You may be right about it being somewhere in my DNA. I even like the bizarre statues and I'm stunned by the stupa and all the flags. Not at all like where we live.'

'I think, Aishe, that might qualify as the greatest understatement of the year!'

Bahuputtikā Soṇā,

Soṇā had suggested that they meet outside what is known as Johnstone House, originally the cottage where the first Tibetan exiles had come in 1967, and led her inside to a quiet room on the first floor where they wouldn't be disturbed.

My Buddhist name, Bahuputtikā Soṇā, is taken from one of the original nuns taught by the Buddha. Before I came here, I was Rachel, but I like my new name.'

'Rachel's a good Jewish name,' said Elise with a smile. 'Although Jewish by birth, my mother took me at just a few days old to be baptised and confirmed as a catholic where I was also given a new name – Mary, not wildly original, though Jewish not Catholic.'

'So, let's do what is either paradoxical or contradictory and talk about silence,' said Soṇā.

Elise smiled.

'To become a nun, you have an initial testing period of a year before temporary ordination, followed by a series of renewals of the vows until you and the sangha are ready to make a life ordination. However, after my first ordination I asked if I might go to Holy Island.'

'Lindisfarne?'

Soṇā smiled.

'No. It's a tiny island just off the Isle of Arran used as a Buddhist retreat. It takes ages to get there and in bad weather there's always the danger of running out of supplies. I spent three years there, mostly by myself in one of the dwellings, though each day we had corporate meditation as we have here and one meal together.

Sometimes our Abbot here came to offer us teaching, but most of my time there was spent alone, and in winter it was dark.'

'Was the essence of your time there the study of Buddhist teaching?'

'Yes, and long periods of meditation, though we also had to do practical work to keep the place functioning and clean, taking turns in doing the cooking.'

'What would you say was the aim of that prolonged period of meditation and teaching?'

'In the first place a coming to terms with the profound muddles we each carry within us, and learning to put them aside as hopefully we grew towards what is sometimes called single-point meditation, but above all *Samadhi*, the utterly absorptive contemplation of the Absolute that is undisturbed by desire, anger, or any other thought or emotion that comes from the ego.

'I won't pretend that it was an easy three years, especially as I had been so used to being among lots of people with whom I was now not in contact, but it was such an important time and why I wish to continue in the life on which I'm set, and even daring to do a little teaching to some of the many who come on our courses and who are striving to live as Buddhists in the world.

'But I can imagine that what I have described is very different from how you became a rabbi, and then entered into what sounds from your hints something I have not associated with Judaism. Or have I got that completely wrong?'

'I was a rabbi, but more especially and wholly unrelated to that I'd had a series of close involvements with deaths which when I went back to Canada to visit a dying aunt, I shared with the Catholic priest who, I then discovered, had baptised me when I was a baby. He was now living in a remote woodland retreat as a solitary and said he'd been waiting for me ever since the moment of my baptism more than 30 years earlier. I already knew that I was not going to the rabbinate on my return, but Fr Jean-Pierre went much further and said he was passing on to me the mantle of living alone in what he called, and I followed, the waiting room.

'I went to live completely alone in a house abandoned by the RAF on the North York Moors by the cliffs overlooking the North

Sea, and that is where I stayed, living as a solitary for five years.'

'Five years? But how did you manage?'

'I went to the supermarket once a month and filled the freezer and lived simply. My closest friend, Leah, who's here with me, came for a few days twice a year, but otherwise the only other contact I had was with the nearby farm where I went to collect milk and eggs, and then in my last two years I learned how to milk cows and I did that extremely early each morning. For the rest of the time, I was simply waiting, but had to do so in absolute and total ignorance of what I might be waiting for.

'I had a small room containing only a stool and a candle, and there I remained for four hours a day doing what you were striving to accomplish, to rid my brain of the nonsense I had spent more than a few years acquiring, which included my Jewish religion and all other philosophies. I was there to wait.'

'I assume your Canadian priest gave you instruction on how to be in silence from out of his own Christian contemplative traditions.'

'No. I met with him just twice, the first a brief encounter and the second, on the following morning, lasted four hours. There is no Jewish tradition of silent prayer or meditation. Judaism is an extremely noisy religion, which gets by mostly through argumentation one with another over this or that detail of Torah or Talmud. I never studied in hushed libraries but in gatherings in which texts were constantly read aloud and argued over. And although I knew there were Christian contemplatives and I did read a little of some of the medieval mystics as they are known, mostly women interestingly, I received no teaching.

'Oddly, until the very last day I was never lonely, and it was only then, by an unusual further encounter with a tragic death, that I knew my time to leave had come to leave the waiting room. I should not have been surprised then, that on the very next morning, when as I helped the farmer get his cows in place for TB testing, I met and fell immediately in love with the Dutch vet, and he felt exactly the same! We married and have the three girls I told you about at lunch.'

'But are you still Jewish?'

'It's like being Scottish; you could live in Italy, dress and eat as an Italian, but you would still be a Scot. I'm Jewish because it is passed on from mother to daughter, and so are my three daughters, but I do not practice any aspect of Judaism or any other religion, but I know certain things and live with them day by day.'

'May I ask what they are?'

'My friend Leah who is with me here, knows and understands based on her own experience. My other friend is on the way to that knowledge and coming here will I think take that forward. My husband and his mother, whom in a real way is my mother too, know that I know but do not know themselves even though they respect my experience at face value. And now, because I take seriously the apparently accidental encounter you and I have had today as what Jung calls synchronicity, I feel it is safe to tell you even though the experiences that brought me to this are wholly different to your own.

'In my study at home, I keep a candle lit because it is what Jews call *Shekinah*, a Hebrew word almost impossible to translate, the nearest approximation to which is The Presence.'

'Do you mean God?'

'No. I never use that word for a lot of reasons, and I am clear and have been throughout, that I cannot and don't believe in such a possibility. How could there ever be such a thing given the world as it is? And I share that with you, don't I?'

'Yes, Buddhists do not believe in God. But therefore, what is *Shekinah*?'

'I have no idea. Isn't there a saying that if you meet the Buddha in the road, you must kill him?'

Soṇā smiled.

'Indeed, there is. Elise, I am inwardly reeling at your story. I had begun practising meditation before I came here and in my first year was extensively taught, and even in my three years of silence there was input regularly bring provided. Yet you had nothing other than an encounter with a priest who clearly had a unique bond with the Jewish baby he baptised and for whom he was waiting to return. I can feel myself tingling in astonishment.'

'I feel the same, Soṇā. Dare I say it is possibly like twins separated at birth suddenly encountering one another? Perhaps our languages are different, but we have lived alike and know what is inside the other.'

'What you did in your five years of solitary vastly exceeds my own time in the silence of Holy Island.'

'It wasn't always silent as I lived to the accompaniment of squawky seabirds.'

'That was so for me too! But what does this mean? I live as an ordained nun in a sort of monastic community, and you have a husband and three daughters, yet both of us have lived something extraordinarily similar.'

'Not only that, but my dearest friend Leah, has only recently stunned me by telling of her own awareness of *Shekinah* from her childhood as intimately as I know it after five years alone spent waiting. I alternate between rejoicing and feeling peeved that it came for her so naturally.'

'I should love to meet her.'

'If that is possible, given your responsibilities, then I am sure she would love to hear all you have told me. The Jewish teacher Yeshua told his followers not to cast their pearls before swine nor give dogs what is holy, and I can assure you that in speaking of your experiences to Leah you would not be doing that. She does still practice aspects, though only some, of Judaism. But truly Soṇā, this is quite overwhelming, and want I really want to do is to cry.'

'I shall ensure I can have time available in the morning from 10:00 onwards. Please come to *Purelands*. It is the white building 400 metres along the road and slightly up the bank. It is the place we use for retreats but there are none this week. Our nuns and some of our women volunteers live there. But in the meantime, I will endeavour to get our farmer to meet you before milking in the morning to provide you with a biosecurity suit and boots so you can actually go in and see the milking close to, and maybe even assist or teach him.'

Elise laughed.

'Now you're talking, girl!' said Elise.

Elise joined the others in the Tibetan Tea Room and began to give thought as to how she could communicate anything of her time with Soṇā. She was sure that Leah would understand, but neither did she want to exclude Aishe. As it was, Aishe was the one who wanted to share something of her own day with Elise and Leah.

'I had a conversation with a man who lives here on a permanent basis with his wife, called Alistair Murray, who is the director of the teaching courses, and who travels all over the world teaching Buddhist meditation and practice. I told him I was interested in getting in touch with my own Indian spiritual roots. He directed me to some books at first but then said he had some time available as this is a quiet time of the year, and so we spoke about how to work towards the practice of meditation. He then suggested I meet with his wife, Martha, herself a meditation teacher, in the morning, so I will go to see her. They live within easy walking distance.'

'I can drive you, if you would prefer,' offered Leah.

'Thanks Leah, but the walk will do me good.'

Elise smiled as this cleared the way for her to speak to Leah about their possible plans for the following morning a little later. For the moment she said nothing but enjoyed the chat with these two dear friends whose company she so loved, but at the back of her mind the memory of an extremely important afternoon.

Three Sisters

Elise turned up at the milking parlour before the goats, so keen was she to see the operation close to. One of the monks she had seen on the previous day in his saffron robes was attired quite differently now and handed her the kit to wear and showed her where to change and wash. He didn't speak much but he could tell that she was more than used to the processes involved in milking, and within a short time allowed her to put the cups on to the engorged teats of the ladies who were greedily engrossed in their supply of food.

Once done, she asked about feed, yields and the time when kids were taken away from their mothers to allow maximum milk supplies, and the inevitable question to vegetarian Buddhists about the fate of kid billies, and wasn't wholly convinced by the answer that they all went to good homes, for those good homes would presumably eventually want them for meat production Her own dairy work accepted the harsh realities of livestock born male!

Even after the joys of milking she was able during meditation to enter again into the silence she had known so intensely years back and when the gong sounded, she had a profound smile on her face.

She had managed to find a short while alone with Leah on the previous evening, but their morning walk towards *Purelands* mostly consisted of Elise recounting early morning visit to the goats!

'Why is this place named as it is?' asked Leah as they sat down together after Soṇā had shown them round and they were sitting drinking tea.

'The Pure Land is the name of the realm that many Buddhists hope to be reborn in, but also the name of a form of Buddhism popular especially in Japan where it is called *Amida*.'

'Are there many different forms of Buddhism?'

'There are different routes but the same destination.'

Leah smiled.

'I wanted to ask you, Elise,' continued Soṇā, 'following our talk yesterday, if you think what you call *Shekinah* is the same as I described as the Absolute?'

'My simple answer is that I have no idea, not because I'm not interested in you or the things we shared yesterday and hope to continue, but because in entering into my waiting room I not only shed past involvement with religious and philosophical ideas, but also future ones. What I mean is that I didn't put down one heavy load only to pick up another at a later date.'

Soṇā smiled.

'That is a quite remarkable austerity of mind, one that I'm not sure most of us could ever manage.'

'I make it sound easy, but it was attained only through painful struggle, and I've managed to retain it with remarkably little effort. I genuinely do not find my mind is given to speculation.'

'I don't think Elise is being rude to you tradition when she says that,' added Leah.

'I would never have thought that, not least because to me it sounds wholly consonant with the asceticism you practised in the waiting room. You didn't spend your time wondering what it might be that would come, and when it did, you haven't spent your time thinking how it might have been different or even improved on.'

'The supreme paradox however, Soṇā, is that I had to engage in that ascetic task, and you have had to become a nun and spend three years also more or less in silence, whereas Leah has known this from the beginning.'

'Yes, that seems unfair,' said Soṇā.

'I only rejoice that Leah and I share being at the same destination and I no way begrudge the fact that I had to hitch-hike, and she came by Rolls Royce!'

All three laughed.

'Perhaps what is different is that I suppose I feel still on a journey,' said Soṇā, 'and that I have to shape my life accordingly, convinced that my travelling will take my whole lifetime and perhaps beyond. Hence my commitment for life as a nun.'

'It's not so totally different, though,' said Leah. Both Elise and I live with *Shekinah* but it has also to be lived out within the circumstances of our daily living. I still seek to live it with some abiding attachment to the Judaism I have known all my life but now in the context of having been a teacher, wife, mother, divorcée and now living with a partner called Ursula in a place called Pateley Bridge. For Elise, it has had to be lived in encounters with tragedy, and to an extent still is, but above all in the love of a family she could not possibly have anticipated on her last evening in the waiting room. But the important things for us both, is that we go on living with what we know.'

Soṇā had closed her eyes and was clearly giving a lot of thought to these words.

'It would be presumptuous of me to be even slightly critical of what you both have come to know, and it goes without saying that I rejoice for you and with you. My only observation from the context of my own knowledge, if I dare use that word, would be to ask whether it is enough?'

'Oh Soṇā,' said Elise, with an urgency that surprised both women, 'I have been dreading facing this question for some time and I've had to travel a long way to find someone with the temerity to ask it.'

'Elise, I have no right to ask it of you, for I have had the uncomfortable thought since we spoke yesterday that I should be looking to you for guidance for my own journey.'

'Please stop, my dear friends,' said Leah suddenly. 'I shouldn't be here. You are talking of things way beyond my ken.'

'No, please don't go, Leah. You are the one who has accompanied me through the harshest of times. You are the only one who knows and understands everything. You are שְׁכִינָה too, and I will continue to need you with me, as I wish also to be with you, but with you too, Soṇā, also שְׁכִינָה. You are both my sisters. In whatever might follow, and as always, I simply have no idea

what that means, and probably shouldn't have, I need you both –
please!'

'My darling Elise,' said Leah, taking her hand, 'we have been
together for so very long, I would never abandon being there with
you and for you.'

'And I too,' said Soṇā, 'I also feel you are my sister, though I'm
troubled that I should have asked the question.'

'Please don't be. In fact, Soṇā, be glad that you have done so. I
have been avoiding it far too long.'

'Just hang on a moment, Elise,' said Leah. 'You and I have both
known that something was going to happen, and I even warned
you when you found Annie's Driver's dead body on the day before
I arrived to stay. And as if that was not enough Betty
Satterthwaite's husband shot himself, and the person summoned to
see her was you.'

'Actually, Leah, I was called to milk the cows, but I'm not
denying what you are saying. Oh, Soṇā, I'm going to have to tell
you the whole story.'

As quickly as she could, Elise gave an account of her
involvement with the first suicide of Gail, the deaths of the
children, her experience whilst working in the hospice, and the last
suicide which marked the end of her time in the waiting room.

'Since then,' she concluded, 'my whole existence has been my
family and our life, and then just a few weeks ago the two suicides
of which Leah has spoken. Leah did warn me, she's quite right.'

Soṇā had tried, as Elise spoke, to conceal from her face any sort
of reaction but by the end she could no longer hold back the
intense feelings that had been rising inside.

'I'm gobsmacked!' she said, raising her hand to her mouth.'

'Is that a technical Buddhist term by any chance?' said Leah,
hoping gently to lessen the intensity of their conversation.

They all laughed gently.

'I don't think there is any Buddhist term for what I have just
heard, nor do I have the faintest idea how to respond. I don't think
I could have survived that degree of close, intimate involvement
with death, and when you add to your commitment to hold on to
the realities of the Holocaust destruction of your great-

grandparents and six million others, I know I could never have done what you did in your waiting room. But I can see why you might want to feel it's all behind you, living with your constant and powerful sense of *Shekinah*, but Leah has underlined my question now that I know about the two suicides: is your work over and if not, now what?'

'Tibetan Buddhists have suffered hugely and Samye Ling has come into being because of Tibetan exiles forced from their homeland. They must have been sustained in this by their practice, and I can't imagine you haven't given thought to this, so how do they, and you, respond?'

'The word *Karuna*, a Sanskrit term, is held to characterise our response to whatever comes, and it is usually translated as Compassion. If our meditation does not lead us to that, it is pointless. Many young people come here but as I listen to them, I often feel uneasy about the way in which Mindfulness which many of them seek to practice is now being primarily promoted as the means to heightened self-improvement. What is the point if we do not develop Compassion to all living things?'

Elise and Leah said nothing.

'But you have said things that cause me profound concern, to which simply saying *Karuna* is inadequate.'

'I would never have wished to do that Soṇā, believe me,' said Elise, 'and Compassion is never inadequate and often extremely costly.'

'I know, but there is also the question of seeking to discern what is the basis upon which we seek truly to live our lives.'

There was silence again.

'The story you have told, Elise,' continued Soṇā eventually, 'moves me so deeply that I almost feel as if my equilibrium has shifted.'

She looked at the two women and smiled.

'That,' she said, 'is what I imagine an earthquake must feel like, and then the task is to recover and build again.'

'I know so very little about Buddhism,' said Elise, 'but it strikes me that your words must surely resonate with its deepest insights into the way our human minds operate – isn't impermanence an important aspect.'

Soṇā looked intently at Elise.

'I am thinking of recommending you to be our new Sangha teacher. You say you know none of the theory, but you have spent five years in a silence very few Buddhists have done and you speak out of knowledge and experience of the fundamentals of our 2,500 years of tradition.'

'Oh, Soṇā,' said Elise with a laugh and dismissive gesture with her hand. 'I wish no more than to be with my family and friends, in which I include the cows I milk.'

'Yes, I know, but if you did but know it, that is the very essence of Buddhism.'

'Oh no. I've already got two religions I've had to shed. Trust me, I do not need another.'

'What we think is often quite different from what we are. But we must now pause our time together as obligations are upon me, the first of which is our lunch which we shall miss if we do not leave at once.'

Into The Night

Aishe's morning had been rich in wholly unexpected ways as Martha Murray had introduced her to patterns of meditation she might explore, rather than offering her any sort of Buddhist theory, though had said that practice was the way into a deeper understanding of what it was her own life had become.

Aishe was such an attractive person in so many ways that the friends were more than able to share in her joy that something important had clicked for her both in terms of her DNA, but also in the present.

It was easy for Elise and Leah to listen to Aishe's account of the morning primarily because it meant they did not have to speak further about their own morning, not least because neither had the first idea how they might have done so.

Outside it was raining and had turned cold, but Elise decided before it was dark to wander round the whole centre with its odd statues, prayer wheels, the room of a thousand butter lamps and the resting place of the ashes of so many who had died, on show in glass compartments, including those of animals. It struck her that Buddhism, like all religions, was one of many parts though how she could hold together things she regarded as bizarre with the conversations she had been having with Soṇā, she did not know.

It was the intensity of the conversations, rather than the early morning milking to which she was quite used, that left Elise desperate for bed, and so deeply asleep that she didn't hear her two companions coming later. But she was wide awake shortly after 1:00am, having heard voices coming from the foot of the stairs up to their room, one of which she recognised as that of Soṇā. She then heard footsteps coming up the stairs and quickly left her bed to anticipate a possible knock on the door. Before her stood Soṇā in a jacket and jeans.

'Elise, I need you to come. Please dress and I will explain.'

Elise threw her clothes on, though struggled in the dark with the laces on her shoes, before quietly closing the door behind her and joining Soṇā below.'

'We need your help, and I can hardly believe what I am going to ask of you, but come out to the car and I will tell you.'

The rain had turned to sleet and threatened snow as Soṇā led Elise to a Land Rover parked outside into which they clambered.

'It's a mile away. They're a young couple. Scott the husband works in our gardens and until the last few weeks, his wife, Gemma, was a course co-ordinator here, managing people when they arrive and being available to respond to their needs. She stopped when she reached the eighth month of her pregnancy and gave birth at home yesterday to a baby boy. However, the birth was far from straightforward, and the midwife thought they were going to lose him. Last night his condition worsened. It seems he a serious lung condition and the plan is to move him later this morning to Edinburgh.'

'Scott and Gemma are both Buddhists and have been for some time, but with this peri-natal problem something inside themselves, quite understandably, has caused them deep anxiety about what will happen to Tomas if he dies.'

'I'm not sure I understand.'

They had arrived at a cottage up a muddy lane.

'They want Tomas baptised. Perhaps their parents are putting pressure on, I don't know, but it is what they want. The midwife is here, and she told me she is more or less certain Tomas will not survive, so he cannot be baptised in Edinburgh and the nearest priest is in Lockerbie. Elise, as I understand it, only a Christian can baptise another and they don't have to be a priest or minister. You are a baptised and confirmed catholic, and I would like you to baptise Tomas.'

Without a moment's hesitation, Elise said, 'Of course I will. Let's go in.'

The couple, who were in their mid-30s looked utterly forlorn, Gemma holding her baby to her breast with the midwife close by.

'I'm Elise. I am a baptised and confirmed catholic and it would be the greatest privilege on earth for me to baptise Tomas.'

'Oh, thank you so much,' cried out Scott, and Elise could see tears coursing down the cheeks of Gemma as she held Tomas close.

Elise turned to the midwife, whom she recognised as another of the nuns from the monastery.

'Please can you get me a small bowl of water and then allow me to make a blessing.'

The midwife returned, at once Elise placed her hands over the water and in Hebrew quietly said words she just about remembered for calling upon HaShem to looks favourably upon an item, which was the nearest she could think to a blessing on the water.

'Gemma,' she said gently, 'will you allow me please to take Tomas from you, just for a moment.'

She nodded and Elise knelt to take the baby into her arms, suddenly remembering twice before having done this for two children, before standing by the small table where she had blessed the water in the bowl. She looked at his wrinkled face which was blue, the result, she assumed, of his inability to breathe properly.

'By what name shall I baptise him,' she asked.

'Tomas Scott,' said Gemma at once.

Elise, holding Tomas in the crook of her arm, took a little water onto her fingertips and placed it onto the forehead of the infant.

'Tomas Scott, I baptise you in the name of the Father, and of the Son and of the Holy Ghost.'

She raised him to her lips and kissed his forehead, before once again handing the baby back to Gemma, who was sobbing, as was her husband. The midwife and Sonā had watched in stunned amazement, and they too were in tears.

'Oh, thank you,' said Gemma, 'thank you so very much.'

'Please will you allow to remain here with?' asked Elise.

Gemma nodded at once.

'Please.'

Elise turned to the midwife-nun.

'I think we could all use a cup of tea. I know I do.'

Outside the sleet had turned to snow and was falling heavily. Soṇā went to help make the tea.

'Tomas is such a beautiful baby. Would you like me to take a photograph of him?' asked Elise.

'Oh, please,' cried Gemma, 'that would be wonderful.'

Elise's mobile was basic, but she managed to take photographs of the baby's face and then of the couple with him.

'I will endeavour to get someone cleverer than me to send these to you. I'm useless when it come to anything practical.'

'To us, Elise, you are amazing, literally a God-send.'

Elise smiled.

It was clear that Tomas was not long for this world and gradually over the next hour his breathing became more irregular and shallower; at about 4:00 it stopped completely.

At the time of knowing about the death of Barbara, the moment when she knew her time for leaving the waiting room had come, she recited for Barbara the Kaddish, but now she felt no need to do so, nor did Soṇā or the midwife-nun suggest Buddhist prayers. Instead, they all sat, Gemma still holding Tomas, at first in complete silence and then the newly-bereaved mother gently sang a beautiful Scottish ballad, in which the two nuns and Scott joined, Elise humming almost inaudibly.

They sat like this until almost 6:00, saying little, until they heard a vehicle arrive outside. It was an ambulance which had fought its way from Lockerbie in the snow.

When the paramedics came in, the midwife said to Scott and Gemma that they would now have to surrender Tomas's body to them as there would have to be a post-mortem and inquest. Gemma's face registered shock.'

'It's alright, Gemma, 'said Elise. Tomas is completely safe, and the law is such that we must agree. I'm sure they will care for him and that soon you will be able to see him again, though in any case he is no longer here.'

The woman paramedic took hold of Tomas.

'Och, he's so beautiful,' she said, as she prepared to carry him outside into the ambulance. There were details to be given before they could set off back into the wild of winter.

'We should leave too,' said Soṇā, looking at Elise. 'You will need to let some people know, I'm sure. I doubt anyone will get through easily this morning, but perhaps family and friends can get here later.'

'Thank you, Soṇā, for finding Elise and bringing her. I'm so sorry you've both lost your sleep but for you to have been with us was a gift for which I shall be eternally grateful.'

She came forward, put her arms around Elise and held her tight.

'Thank you, Elise,' she said quietly, 'and your voice is so beautiful and gentle.'

Scott too came and kissed her, though neither did the same for Soṇā, presumably because she was a nun and that sort of contact forbidden.

Outside it took quite some time to clear their vehicle of snow, but eventually they were aboard and Soṇā began the perilous journey back.

'According to the Buddhist text *The Last Rites of Amitabha*,' said Soṇā as she drove, 'the dead body is not touched or moved until it is completely cold, as the soul does not leave the body immediately once breathing ends. Poor little mite, he was cold even before he died.'

'Will the community give them support in their bereavement?'

'Yes, and I expect their family will also.'

'Were you surprised they asked for baptism?'

'I stopped being surprised when you walked into my life, Elise, but you did not hesitate when I asked you.'

'*Karuna* – Compassion. Isn't that what you taught me is the end of all our exploring? But once upon a time a new-born Jewish baby was taken to a catholic priest for baptism, and he did so immediately. I shall not have to wait for Tomas as that priest had to wait for me, but when I let Leah know, she will totally agree with me, that this is what I was brought here for.'

'I know it too. Now we both need is porridge and sleep.'

'What of the morning meditation?' asked Elise.

'What need have I of the shadow when the reality has come?' said Soṇā.

Pesach

It would soon be Elise's 50ᵗʰ birthday and as if to celebrate, her periods had decided to declare their innings closed. There was a woman doctor at the surgery and Elise made an appointment to see her to discuss HRT.

Pieter was planning a special birthday party which she knew Elise would hate, so kept the numbers limited to only those close, and handed over to Fiene all the preparations to be carried out in secret, and of course, stored in the freezer! The day itself would in this year fall on Saturday, but this would not hold back Leah and Ursula from coming to join the celebration, together with Ruth and Sarah who were coming from London.

On the Monday, the Reverend Anthony Reynolds pleaded guilty to both perverting the course of justice by initially lying to the police, and contributory negligence manslaughter. He received a suspended prison sentence. Elise had not attended the trial.

It was on the Wednesday of that week, however, that as she sat in her study reading, the doorbell rang, answered by Grace.

'Mummy,' she said, coming into the study, 'there's a bald lady at the door who is asking to speak with you.'

Elise shot out of her chair and into the hall. Whether forbidden or not she rushed forwards and put her arms around Soṇā and held her tightly.

'How wonderful that you are here, Soṇā, and just in time for my surprise birthday party on Saturday that I know nothing about. Fiene!' she called out. 'Someone so very special is here.'

Fiene came out from the kitchen.

'Soṇā, I assume. We've been expecting you,' she said, utterly bewildering the new arrival. 'Come and have some tea and Dutch cake, even better than your own Dundee cake. You are more than welcome.'

Soṇā was feeling totally overwhelmed by her reception. Hearing the noise, Julia and Gale had also come, though primarily to see a lady who was bald!

Once the hurly-burly of her arrival was complete, Elise led Soṇā into the study, where she immediately paused to look at the burning candle.

'*Shekinah*', she said.

Elise smiled and they both sat.

'What did your mother-in-law mean when she said you were expecting me? We've communicated only once in the month since you were at Samye Ling, and I said nothing about coming.'

'Of course you did. It was present in every line of your letter, and I've been waiting.'

'Elise Westernberg, you are impossible!'

'You'll meet my husband later and he will agree.'

'But how could you know?'

'You told me on the morning of Tomas's death as we drove back in the Land Rover in all that snow. It was clear to me, and I knew it was also clear to you, and then I knew that this is where you would come – to be with your sister!'

'You're not easy to get to. The 8.02 bus from Eskdalemuir to Lockerbie, train to Carlisle and then to Newcastle and then to Northallerton and then the most unlikely bus journey which took me to most places in lower Wensleydale.'

'That's quite a journey in more senses than one and you must be very tired. Your room is ready and waiting, where you can have a shower and a rest. One rucksack suggests you might not have much in the way of a change of clothes, but I'll root out something of mine you can endure until we can go shopping tomorrow.

'Elise, I'm utterly bewildered.'

'I would imagine you are, so let's leave conversation until we're both up to it. I can imagine the last few days have taken their toll.'

She nodded and followed Elise meekly up the stairs.

When Elise returned from milking on the Thursday morning, she found Soṇā in the kitchen helping Fiene bake some bread.

'I must have coffee and porridge before anything,' said Elise, 'so I fear you may have to put up with my smelly attire.'

'I have survived so far,' said Fiene, 'and your husband usually smells even worse.'

After her breakfast, a shower and change of clothes Elise invited Soṇā to join her in the study.

'H'm,' said Elise, 'Your slim figure does greater justice to my old clothes than ever they did to me.'

'Although the Buddha is always portrayed as well built, shall we say, it would never do for a member of the Sangha to look as if they over-partook.'

'And are you still a member of the Sangha?'

'I'm glad you're beginning with an easy question,' she replied with a laugh, 'though I knew our conversation this morning would be tough, just as my conversation was on the day before yesterday with Rinpoche.'

'Tell me.'

'I told him I was in need of some time out and he reluctantly agreed to a two-week break at home with my parents in North Berwick, so here I am with you and your family in Wensleydale. Obedient – that's me! I think he knew he had no choice and that I was going to be on 8:02 bus whatever. But you said you were waiting for me.'

'I knew after Tomas died.'

'Oh, it was before then, Elise. It was the moment when you simply said without hesitation that you would come and baptise him. That was the moment when I knew I would have to leave.'

'I knew at that moment that the circle was now complete. Yes, it was *Karuna*, but for me necessity was laid upon me, and to have refused would have been the negation of all that had gone before. There were no voices, no lights in the sky, but I knew, in exactly the same way you have come to realise what you have had to do, however painful.

'But Soṇā, what matters now is today. Just think. As I awoke very early this morning, I thought of all the potential riches you have brought with you. Nothing need be repudiated or regretted because you carry great treasures with you wherever and whatever you will do, from which I am eager to benefit.'

'But what am I to do now?'

'Years ago, my spiritual guide, Jean-Pierre, gave me the perfect spiritual instruction. He said that my life should consist of nothing special, that I should just be ordinary. He knew, though, that the ordinary is the special, and that it was in the ordinary that I would come to know how to live. Not that five years in silence was what most people would consider ordinary.'

'No, they wouldn't.'

'But in a very real sense it was. I had to shed all the theories and ambitions that had characterised my life, my good and bad opinions. It took me five years and a lot of reflecting upon the deaths in which I had been given a part, to enable me to learn his simple lesson.'

'Meditation on our death is an important Buddhist practice, though you experienced these things not as ideas but in terms of flesh and blood literally in your hands, even on the telephone.'

'You are free to return to Samye Ling after your break,' said Elise, 'and they will welcome you back, but I hope you will remain here in Wensleydale living with us, not least because my friend Aishe will be glad to have on tap guidance and support for her own meditation practice she began with Martha Murray. She will be here on Saturday for the birthday party as will Leah, who also knew you would be coming. Pieter said to me last night how much he liked you and was glad you are going to be here to keep me out of mischief in a sisterly sort of way.

'But Soṇā, in different ways you and I have that which needs to be passed on. I have not felt remotely able to conceive how this could be done until I met you. If we look down the valley from our sitting room window, we can see the River Ure flowing onwards towards the city of York, by which time it becomes part of the River Ouse, but upstream it has many sources which by the time they are here are part of the one flow. I want to share the flow with you, and then allow it to go on for others to bathe in.'

Soṇā was unable to hold back the flow of tears.

'Elise, I know nothing.'

'Then you have just said the magic words which might just make it possible. But my darling, you do need a holiday first, so do nothing for a week or two other than get used to the Yorkshire air and accents, and perhaps we can go for walks up the dale together. You're safe, Soṇā. Oh, and I was forgetting you can make sure you don't spoil my surprise birthday party of which I know nothing, by telling me about it!'

'I wouldn't dare.'

'In the Jewish calendar it is the year 5769, though mostly it's still 2009, soon will come the great Jewish celebration of Pesach, Passover, commemorating the Exodus. It is highly unlikely that anything recorded in the accounts that have been handed down bear the slightest relation to reality, but at some time, somewhere, a group of people, perhaps quite small, achieved a moving onwards from what in the story is described as slavery to a new freedom. In critical-historical terms the story has no foundation in actual historical events, but the part of the story I most like is how they set out knowing nothing about what lay before them.

'You and I know that story from within. If, by any chance, you feel compelled to walk down to the Ure and walk through it in symbolic imitation, if you don't mind I'll wait for you on the other side and throw a lifeline.'

'You have already done that, and I am already safe on the other side. I know I'm happy being here with you and knowing nothing other than Shekinah.'

'Gosh in a moment I shall burst into a chorus of Doris Day singing "Que sera",' laughed Elise. 'I am slowly learning that the waiting room can take different forms, but I do know that when the doorbell rang yesterday afternoon, it was time once again for me, and for you to move on.

'When I met and married my beloved Pieter, I also acquired a mother and then three daughters. Now I have a sister and that fills me with such joy. "What will be, will be" but it will become clear, Soṇā, trust me, but of times and seasons we cannot know and that's how it must be.

Rod Hacking

ACKNOWLEDGMENTS

With the exception of the bomb in Tel Aviv (at which I was not present) and the death of the murder victim in Canada, all the other encounters with death happened more or less exactly as described. I thank the many 'teachers' who have taught me about death and the Reality, of which any and every attempt to speak is futile, but can be known in silence and beauty.

I was a frequent visitor to Bracebridge in the period covered by this book. I owe a great deal to my mother's husband, the late Norm Rosewarne.

In the early 1980s I served as confessor and director of a solitary Anglican nun and wrote the biography of Fr Gilbert Shaw who ministered to solitaries and enclosed communities of men and women.

As always, I am grateful to my friend Paul Mellor who reads my earliest efforts and corrects many mistakes of syntax and spelling – the remaining faults are my own.
I thank Robert Gussman for so very much in the way of wisdom and insight, and above all my dearest Maggie.

Printed in Great Britain
by Amazon